"I could take you a lot of places."

Holy hell, but what was she doing?

Heath seemed to have stopped breathing, though he took a step closer, his scent enveloping Joss. Instantly her mouth went dry and a steady throb built in her belly. She squirmed, but she was backed against the desk and had nowhere to go. Sanity was rapidly disintegrating around her, crumbling beneath an overwhelming ache to touch this man. To have him touch her.

"Of course I don't have my own ships, so I'd have to hitch a ride on one of yours." She barely recognized herself. There were reasons why she shouldn't do this, she knew. She just couldn't think of one right now.

Heath's expression shifted suddenly, as if something within him had given way. He took another half step closer, close enough that he was pressed against her skirts now, the hard steel of his legs nudging hers apart so he dominated her space and trapped her against him.

"Would you take me?" she whispered, and neither of them could pretend she was still talking about ships.

"Yes," Heath rasped.

And then he kissed her.

ACCLAIM FOR

*I've Got My Duke to
Keep Me Warm*

"Kelly Bowen is a fresh new voice with a shining future!"
—Teresa Medeiros, *New York Times*
bestselling author

"With this unforgettable debut, Bowen proves she is a
writer to watch as she spins a multilayered plot skillfully
seasoned with danger and deception and involving wonder-
fully complex protagonists and a memorable cast of sup-
porting characters...a truly remarkable romance well
worth savoring." —*Booklist* (starred review)

"4 stars! In this delightful, poignant debut that sets Bowen
on the path to become a beloved author, the innovative
plotline and ending are only superseded by the likable,
multidimensional characters: a strong-willed heroine and
a heart-stealing hero. Get set to relish Bowen's foray into
the genre." —*RT Book Reviews*

"Fans of romance with a touch of suspense will enjoy the
work of this new author." —*Publishers Weekly*

You're the Earl That I Want

KELLY BOWEN

You're the Earl That I Want

FOREVER

NEW YORK BOSTON

Copyright © 2015 by Kelly Bowen
Excerpt from *I've Got My Duke to Keep Me Warm* © 2014 by Kelly Bowen

Forever
Hachette Book Group
1290 Avenue of the Americas
New York, NY 10104

HachetteBookGroup.com

Printed in the United States of America

First Edition: August 2015
10 9 8 7 6 5 4 3 2 1

OPM

Forever is an imprint of Grand Central Publishing.
The Forever name and logo are trademarks of Hachette Book Group, Inc.

The Hachette Speakers Bureau provides a wide range of authors for speaking events. To find out more, go to www.hachettespeakersbureau.com or call (866) 376-6591.

The publisher is not responsible for websites (or their content) that are not owned by the publisher.

For Jaimie—my sister, my dearest friend,
and my unequivocal partner in crime.
I could always count on you to remember
to hide the pistols under the
carriage seat.

Acknowledgments ——————

A heartfelt thank-you to my agent Stefanie Lieberman. I can't say how happy I am to have you in my corner. Sincere gratitude to my editor, Alex Logan, whose keen insight and encouragement make every story better. And above all, thank you to my wonderful family for their patience and support.

Chapter 1 ————————

London, December, 1818

I need a wife."

Beside him the Duke of Worth choked on his drink.

"And I need you to help find me one. As soon as possible," Heath continued, ignoring his best friend's reaction.

"I must be drunker than I thought," the duke said, dabbing his chin. "For I could have sworn the Earl of Boden just asked me to find him a wife. And if that wasn't strange enough, the aforementioned earl is supposed to be in Liverpool turning everything he touches into gold. He couldn't possibly be in a London ballroom, certainly not without letting me know he was back in town first." Worth sounded affronted, though he was grinning as he said the last.

"Don't be an ass." Heath felt his own mouth twitch with laughter, but managed to tamp down any feelings of levity before they could interfere with his sense of purpose.

"Well, I've missed you too." The duke thumped Heath on the back and signaled to a footman to bring another drink. "Did you just get back?"

"This afternoon." Heath sighed.

"How were the roads?"

"Cold. Miserable." Heath leaned on the balcony railing, the din of a ball in full swing filtering up to where they stood. "But passable."

"And after days of being confined in a coach, you chose to come *here*? To the Baustenburys' ball?" Worth said with some disbelief, eyeing the crush of people below them.

"You're here."

"I have an excuse. My mother wanted to come."

Heath kept his face carefully neutral. "Yes, I saw her earlier. You know she's carrying, ah, a live chicken around under her arm again?"

"Is she? I thought she was going to leave the poultry in the carriage tonight." Worth shrugged, and then his eyes lit up. "Did you know Josephine is back in town? She's here somewhere tonight too."

Heath frowned. Since his recent marriage, the duke had grown rather comfortable with the dowager's bizarre behavior. Which was odd, given how much his mother's eccentricities used to bother him. Yet for the moment, Heath decided to put that strange development aside in order to focus on an even stranger event: the return of Lady Josephine to London. "Your long-lost sister finally came home?"

"Yes." Worth laughed. "And Joss will be thrilled to see you. You'll have to find her and make yourselves reacquainted."

Heath had a sudden vision of the curly-haired hoyden who used to scramble after them every summer of his boyhood. A whip-smart girl utterly resolute in her intention to drive anyone around her to madness with near-constant lectures on a confusing array of topics. Heath would be very surprised if she had changed significantly over the years.

Which was not to say that he wouldn't be dutiful and welcome the duke's sister back to London. On the contrary, he planned to do so with every proper gesture of respect. But at the same time, Heath very much doubted Josephine Somerhall had given him a moment's thought since he'd last seen her, especially since he hadn't been overly gracious to her in his youth. In fact, Heath might describe the bulk of his past actions toward Worth's little sister as abysmal. With some discomfiture he shoved those recollections aside. He'd certainly grown up since then, and whatever idiocy he'd suffered as a boy had little bearing on the matters at hand.

As if reading his mind, Worth peered at him over the rim of his glass. "So what's your excuse tonight, Boden, really? You're not usually one for balls of any sort."

The footman reappeared, and Heath accepted a glass of whiskey. He took a healthy swallow before he spoke. "Like I said, I need a wife."

"Holy God, you're actually serious." Worth's forehead creased, and the smile slid from his face. "When did you decide this?"

"When I got home from Liverpool and discovered my housekeeper had quit and my valet had eloped with my only upstairs maid."

"I'm not following."

"I've managed my family's business for more years than I care to remember. I dug the damn earldom out of a financial hole so deep I'm not sure I ever did find the bottom. My mother is still hiding in Bath, unwilling and unable to face society after the fiasco otherwise known as my sister's short-lived engagement to a madman. I did what I could to mitigate that indignity—"

"Very admirably," the duke interjected.

"—only to find myself with another sister so determined to elevate her social standing through marriage that I am constantly extracting her from compromising situations. And so are you, if I may be so gauche as to remind you."

Worth winced. "Ah yes, the unfortunate Ascot incident. Please let's forget it."

Heath ran a hand through his hair in suppressed frustration. "Since becoming earl, I've had crumbling buildings repaired, leaky roofs replaced, fences mended, workers hired, and outstanding taxes paid. All while still maintaining my business. I simply have no energy left to deal with the domestic aspect of my life, Worth. I need a partner. A pleasant, even-tempered soul who will accept my protection and the comforts I can provide her, and in exchange will expertly manage my household." He glanced down at the crowds of people.

"You're surveying the prospects."

"You make it sound so mercenary. But yes, I am exploring my options."

The duke snorted. "Well, what you've described to me is a well-trained broodmare," he said. "And I have a stable full of them. I shall ask my wife to select one for you, and you can have it, no strings attached. There's no need to do anything rash."

"That's not funny."

"I wasn't trying to be funny. I was trying to convey that you're selling yourself short."

Heath let his eyes rove over the masses of pretty,

pastel-clad women. "I don't think I am." He sighed. "I just want to be happy."

"You won't be happy with a match of convenience. You're too clever and too"—Worth struggled for a word—"passionate about life. You'll be bored to death."

"I like boring," Heath snapped. "For once, boring would be a nice change. What's wrong with wanting a wife who will not go looking to stir up trouble? One who can manage my household, bear my children, and provide pleasing companionship? Is that too much to ask?"

"The difficulties you've encountered in the past were not your fault," the duke protested.

"Not my fault, but my problem. And I'm bone-tired of solving problems." Heath sighed. Four years of ceaseless family scandal had exhausted his every mental and emotional resource.

"But that doesn't mean—"

"Not all of us are as immune to infamy as you," Heath said. "It just seems to roll right off your back."

"That is because I finally discovered what truly matters to me."

"It's also because you're a duke," Heath muttered.

Worth gave a self-deprecating snort. "Doesn't hurt."

Heath gave his friend a weary smile. He wished it were that easy. But Heath had a business to run, and his future success was linked to his reputation. He relied on his elevated social status and his good relations with suppliers and buyers and customers. He simply couldn't afford to ignore how the ton judged his family.

Heath drew another deep breath. "Boring," he repeated firmly. "I want boring. I want you to help me find the most boring woman here." Heath scanned the dancers.

"What about that one?" He gestured to an attractive brunette standing near the edge of the floor with a woman who could only be her mother.

"Ah, Miss Alice Edget. Daughter of Viscount Edget. Impeccable breeding along with a spotless reputation. A lovely girl, but not known for her, ah, wit." Worth made a face. "Conversation, I fear, would be rather limited."

"She sounds perfect."

"You can't be serious, Boden."

Heath crossed his arms. "These days, I am always serious."

"I've noticed. You were far more fun when you were merely the son of a soapmaker. Inheriting a fancy title has been the ruin of you, you know."

"Are you going to insult me or help me?"

Worth sighed. "Of course I'll help you. But at least wait for another month. There will be more eligible ladies in town by then."

"Introduce me to Miss Edget."

"No."

"No?" Heath repeated more harshly than he'd intended.

"I have been your friend since we were three years old. I cannot in good conscience allow you to consign yourself to a lifetime of mediocrity."

"If you won't do it, I'll find someone who will."

"You'll be asleep before you're halfway through a waltz." Worth stared at him, but Heath refused to look away. "Fine," the duke relented. "But don't say I didn't warn you."

⁓

Miss Edget was flawlessly polite upon Heath's introduction to her, even if her mother seemed less enthusiastic than he would have liked. Though that was nothing he hadn't experienced before. Not every ton member believed his fortune could adequately compensate for the fact that his title had been completely accidental or that he depended on the vulgar practice of industry and trade to keep his coffers filled. But Miss Edget placed her hand on his arm with no hesitation when he'd made his bow and Heath was encouraged that he was well on his way to proving Worth wrong.

"Are you having a nice time tonight, Miss Edget?" Heath asked as she executed the steps with perfect precision.

"I'm having a lovely time, my lord," she replied, even as the music stuttered and shrieked.

"What do you think of the orchestra?" he inquired with a small chuckle, hoping to put her at ease. The musicians were spectacularly inept.

"It's lovely, my lord." She smiled up at him.

Lovely? A herd of tortured donkeys would sound better. Though perhaps she was simply too polite to remark upon it.

"Did you enjoy the supper?" he tried.

"It was lovely, my lord." Her smile flashed again.

Heath hid a frown. "Tell me something about yourself," he prompted.

"Like what?"

Heath flailed for a suggestion. "Do you enjoy travel?"

Miss Edget shuddered, though she recovered with a brave face and another bright smile. "Not overly, my lord. I find it very upsetting to my constitution."

Heath struggled to keep a pleasant smile on his face. Well, that was no good. His potential wife might need to travel from time to time with him. Especially if he expanded his business in America the way he was planning.

"That is too bad. I believe you would like Boston very much."

"Is that in Scotland?" she asked, blinking prettily.

"Er, no," he managed.

"Is that where Lady Josephine was?"

"I beg your pardon?"

"My mother told me you are very close with the Duke of Worth."

"Yes. We've been friends for many, many years."

Miss Edget nodded, pleased with his answer. "That's lovely. It must be very advantageous to be friends with a duke."

Although Heath wasn't in the habit of viewing his closest friendship in quite such self-serving terms, he supposed it was the truth. But why were they talking about Worth at all? Or his sister?

"Er…"

"I heard my mother talking about Lady Josephine. She said she lived with savages. Is it true?"

"I'm sorry?" The question was so unexpected that Heath wasn't sure he'd heard properly.

"I heard she lived in strange places." Miss Edget was watching him with round eyes. "With *savages*."

"I can assure you, Lady Josephine did not live with savages. I believe she has resided in Italy for a good number of years." But even as he finished speaking, he realized he had no idea where Joss had really been for the last decade.

"Oh." She nodded. "Are there savages in Italy?"

Heath sighed. "No, Miss Edget, there are no savages in Italy."

In hindsight, Worth had indeed warned him, though Heath would never give him the satisfaction of knowing he'd been right. Alice Edget might not be exactly what he was looking for, but there were plenty of choices. He was an earl now, and an obscenely wealthy one at that. How hard could it be?

Heath had retreated back to the sanctity of the balcony overlooking the ballroom, nursing another glass of whiskey. He brooded darkly, examining the results of his efforts during the three hours since he had returned Miss Edget to the care of her mother.

He'd danced with at least a half dozen ladies, some seeming impossibly young, others impossibly jaded. The conversations had ranged from stilted to sycophantic, and Heath had been at a loss as to how to improve upon any of it. Worse, the topic of the Duke of Worth's sister had been introduced several times, veiled as a casual inquiry, but currents of speculation ran swiftly below each offhand remark. Heath most certainly hadn't come to this ball to be pummeled for information on the return of the prodigal Lady Josephine. He'd come as the Earl of Boden, to interview potential wives.

And he'd failed miserably.

Was there not a woman in London who possessed a modicum of intelligence paired with a pleasant demeanor? He wasn't looking for brilliance, though the ability to express an informed opinion about at least one worldly thing would be nice. He didn't require beauty, though a woman with a bit of backbone and confidence held a certain charm. And he wasn't so naïve as to think that his wealth wasn't the most important part of his appeal as a prospective spouse, but the poorly disguised hints about annual allowances were already starting to wear.

A subtle disturbance altered the pitch of the crowd in the corner of the ballroom below him, just enough to distract him from his musings. Something interesting was happening downstairs, and the revelers were chattering about it in voices that rose above the terrible clamor of the talentless orchestra. Idly Heath scanned the mob, looking for the cause, relieved to be a good distance from the disruption. It was comforting to know that at least one person here tonight had bigger problems than he did. A scandalous waltz danced between lovers, perhaps. The arrival of a man's mistress in the presence of his lady wife. Or maybe— His speculation died an abrupt death as he followed the craning necks and darting eyes of the guests closest to the refreshment table. Heath had finally found Josephine Somerhall.

Chapter 2

When Heath was nine, he'd put a frog down the front of Josephine's dress.

He'd been skipping stones at the edge of a pond with Worth, and Joss had simply refused to leave them alone. She'd been like a gnat, dogging the two boys, unrelenting with her questions and her presence.

At first Heath had tried to evade the persistent five-year-old, but she had stuck to his side like an unwanted burr. When he'd grumbled to her brother, Worth had only shrugged, seemingly disinclined to order his younger sibling back to the house, where she was undoubtedly avoiding lessons in music or dancing or deportment. So Heath had been forced to take matters into his own hands.

Heath had frogged his own sisters before, with spectacular results. Shrieking and hysterics, but most important, the immediate and rapid departure of the both of them. His father, of course, had tanned his hide for it later, but the peaceful interval had been worth it. So when Heath had spotted the creature half hidden under a log and scooped it up, along with a goodly portion of pond scum and muddy slime, his expectations had been high.

Looking back, he might have wondered why Worth

hadn't intervened. Why his friend had only raised a brow and gone back to skipping stones as Heath advanced on the imp who hadn't stopped to take a breath in her one-sided conversation in nearly fifteen minutes. And when he'd lunged at her and dumped his fetid handful of horror down the front of her dress, she'd only gone very still, her eyes slitting into turquoise shards of disbelief.

She'd shrieked all right, but for all the wrong reasons.

Amphibians, she'd snapped in her tiny, indignant voice, had very sensitive skin and should never be manhandled in such a fashion. She'd dug the struggling creature out from the front of her sodden bodice and had cupped it in her hands with great care. Heath had stammered something about its being just a dumb frog. Her sharp eyes had narrowed even further, and she'd informed him that it wasn't a frog at all, but quite obviously a common toad. The common frog, she informed him, had *round* pupils.

As if he should have known that.

He'd watched as she'd returned the toad to a safe crevice and then marched past him, her skirts bunched up in her hand as she used them to wipe the remaining muck from her throat and chest. She'd plunked herself down at the edge of the pond near her brother and picked up where she'd left off, only now her one-sided conversation was a lecture revolving around the biology of England's amphibian species. And for all of Heath's efforts, he had mud-splattered breeches, a filthy shirt, flaming cheeks, and the uncomfortable realization that he would never understand Josephine Somerhall.

Everything and nothing had changed.

The girl he remembered from carefree summers a lifetime ago had vanished, and in her place appeared a striking woman. She was dressed beautifully in amber silk, the simple style and color effortless on her body. Her face was sharper, more angular than he remembered, her generous mouth pursed in thought, the curve of her neck and shoulders graceful and efficient in their movement. Her blue-green eyes, always so expressive, still shone with the intense intelligence he remembered vividly. And her rich mahogany hair was cut short in defiance of the style of every other unwed woman in the room. Instead of waist-length, virginal hair bound tightly against her scalp, she had a riot of soft, careless curls falling over her forehead and brushing the lobes of her ears.

But the striking woman acted exactly like the young girl he remembered. He would have recognized her anywhere, even had she not just turned a priceless Chinese vase upside down and clamped it between her legs while she examined the bottom with a fierce concentration.

"Dear God," Heath mumbled under his breath. Lord Baustenbury had bought the Ming vase a month ago for a staggering sum. Joss was manhandling it like it was a cheap chamber pot, and if she were to drop it…

Around her, guests were casting looks of incredulity and disapproval in her direction. Lord Baustenbury, alerted by a footman to the potential peril of his new treasure, was rushing forward, a horrified look on his face. He reached Joss and, with exaggerated care, took the exquisite vase from her hands. She said something to him, and the rotund man almost dropped his treasure, righting it at the last second. His face went quite red.

A crowd was starting to gather, and Joss was gesturing now at the vase and speaking earnestly as he replaced it on its stand. Baustenbury was spluttering, and his complexion was now a shocking shade of purple. The man looked as if he were going to have an apoplexy.

Frantically Heath looked for Worth, but the duke had long ago disappeared somewhere with his wife, and Heath knew very well that he wouldn't be coming back anytime soon. He searched instead for the dowager duchess and found her settled in a chair on the opposite side of the ballroom, a multicolored hen roosting in her lap, deep in conversation with another matron and unaware of the disturbance in the ballroom. Not that she and her damn chicken would be able to help matters anyway.

Josephine Somerhall had always been somewhat oblivious to society's rules of decorum, and it would seem nothing had changed. Someone was going to need to intervene. And soon.

With a horrible feeling in the pit of his stomach, Heath understood that the someone in question was going to be him.

⁓

Everything and nothing had changed.

When Joss had decided to return to London, she hadn't given a great deal of thought to what to expect when she got here. She hadn't stepped foot on English soil for over ten years and hadn't been to London in twice that. Currently she was fighting a growing sense of disappointment, wondering if perhaps, in the years she'd spent abroad, something fundamental within her had changed. For she was already finding the ton's rigid expectations almost intolerable.

She'd spent the first part of the week with her family, rejoicing in the company of her mother and her brother and his new wife. There had been trips to the museums, explorations of dusty bookstores, and fierce debates that had lasted long into the night. But there had been very little interaction with outsiders, and so she'd been somewhat insulated from the opinions and judgments of others since her return.

This was the first ball she had attended since she'd been back, and she rather suspected it would be her last. Her attempts at conversation tonight had been met with patronizing chuckles from the men, all of whom suggested she not concern herself with matters that were clearly beyond her understanding. The women had simply edged away, snapping a barrier of prettily painted vellum in front of their faces as if their fans could protect them from whatever affliction had damaged the Lady Josephine.

A part of her knew she should make more of an effort to find common ground with the ladies and gentlemen here. Say what was expected of a duke's sister, which, as far as Joss had been able to determine thus far, was conversation restricted to gowns, shoes, and the weather. It was making for an incredibly long, dull evening, and she was trying hard not to give in to outright boredom.

Which was why, when Joss had spotted the beautiful vase set upon its pedestal near the tall terrace windows, her interest had been immediately piqued, if only for the beacon of familiarity it represented. Yet as she drew nearer to the piece, her heart had sunk. Examination of the bottom of the vase had confirmed her fears. She knew she was obligated to seek out Lord Baustenbury so that she might have a private conversation regarding the vase, as unpleasant as the prospect was.

No one liked to be told their treasures were fakes.

But the rotund earl had found her first and demanded that she remove her hands from his property, without giving her a chance to explain what she had been doing. Further attempts to clarify her actions had left the earl enraged and barely coherent. At the moment Joss was quite afraid that the man might suffer some sort of spell if he didn't take a deep breath soon. His complexion certainly suggested an elevated—

"Lady Josephine."

The address came from behind her, and she froze.

It was a voice from the past, deepened by age, but still wrapped with memories of hot summer days and crystal-cold ponds. It was the smell of fresh-cut hay and cowslips as she traipsed through the pastures, keeping up as best she could. It was the warmth of an indulgent smile, echoes of laughter and teasing, and as the years slipped by, it was the exquisite torture of a casual comradeship she had both treasured and despised for its inadequacy.

Very slowly she turned around.

The years had honed Heath Hextall in ways that were equally beautiful and disappointing. He was impeccably groomed, his gold-blond hair cut fashionably, his dress understated but more striking for its simplicity. But the mischief that had once lit up his beautiful blue eyes had been thoroughly extinguished, and Joss wondered if the charm and roguish good humor she remembered in the boy made up any part of the man Heath had become. She searched his face for hints of the ever-present grin she remembered, but his features remained severe and remote. Yet all of that did nothing to stop the flood of pleasure that rushed through her the second she met his gaze.

"I was hoping to run into you tonight," he was saying smoothly, as though he had just seen her last week. "Your brother said you were here." He turned to the enraged earl. "Lord Baustenbury, the duke and I were just discussing what a splendid evening you've arranged. His Grace asked me to pass along his compliments. *A rousing success* were his exact words, I believe."

Joss continued to drink in the sight of Heath while wondering two things: First, since when had an orchestra badly out of tune and watered-down rum punch become hallmarks of an evening's success? And second, when had Heath Hextall become such an accomplished liar? Her brother had said no such thing. And what's more, he'd left the ball hours ago.

Lord Baustenbury had stopped his spluttering, if not appeased by Heath's praise, then certainly soothed by the purported compliments of a duke. He smoothed a hand over the front of his evening coat and gave Joss one last glare before making the appropriate responses. The crowd, sensing that the potential drama had been diffused, started to dissipate, trading heated whispers. Joss resisted the urge to roll her eyes as Baustenbury lurched away under a full sail of righteous superiority.

"Lady Josephine," Heath said, "perhaps I might offer you a refreshment at this juncture?"

"I've never been Lady anything to you, Hextall, so don't think to stand on formality on my account." Joss was aware she was grinning stupidly as she took his proffered arm, but she couldn't bring herself to care. Her unabashed joy at seeing Heath after all this time was too great. "Unless you'd prefer I address you now as Lord Boden."

Heath winced at the mention of his title. "Your brother told you then."

"Of course he did. Both Worth and my mother kept me updated on the happenings in London via post," Joss said easily. "Imagine my surprise when I learned you had become an earl. My *lord*." She gave him a saucy smile.

"No need for formality," he said after a moment's hesitation.

"Thank heavens. I've called you Hextall for so long, I don't think I'd remember to do otherwise," she teased. "It's so very good to see you again." God, but that sounded blindingly inadequate. It felt more as if she had just found a piece of home that she hadn't realized she'd been missing.

"And you." His whole being was stiff. "I must ask what you said to Baustenbury." Heath steered her away from the vase and in the direction of the refreshment table. "And what exactly were you doing with his antique?"

"I told him he'd been swindled," Joss explained. "That vase he maintains is from the Ming dynasty is no more from the Orient than I am." She paused. "Well, that might not be entirely true. I suppose it could have been made in China. But certainly not four hundred and fifty to one hundred and seventy-five years ago. It's a very good fake, but a fake nonetheless." She sighed. "Lord Baustenbury didn't seem very receptive to my concern. Perhaps you should speak to him later. He might listen to you."

Heath made a strange noise in the back of his throat. "Do you think that perhaps this was neither the time nor the place to share such insights? That perhaps they might never need be shared at all?"

"I was trying to be discreet," she protested.

"Discreet?" His voice rose in obvious disbelief. "You had a Chinese vase between your legs!"

"It wasn't between my legs," Joss said crossly. "It was balanced on the tops of my knees. I didn't want to drop it. Not that it would have mattered."

"I don't understand why you had to touch it at all."

Joss sniffed. "I had to be sure it was a fake. I'd want to know, wouldn't you? Lord Baustenbury deserved the truth. And I will not apologize for it."

Heath muttered something under his breath. "May I ask how you came to this conclusion? About the authenticity of his vase?" he finally asked.

"The markings on the bottom of the vase are all wrong," she told him, still weaving through the crowd. "When one reads the characters, the central ones clearly suggest that one fornicate with oneself."

Heath stopped abruptly. "I beg your pardon?"

"I said, they instruct the reader to fornicate w—"

"I heard you the first time." He looked heavenward and resumed his journey to the far side of the ballroom.

"Whoever sold that vase to Lord Baustenbury is a crook. On an authentic piece, the characters should denote the dynasty and the reigning emperor. Those most certainly do not." She felt obligated to clarify.

"How do you know?" Heath turned, frowning fiercely.

Joss blinked at him. "I read them."

"You read them?"

Joss pushed a curl behind her ear. "Yes. I read a lot."

"Indeed."

"One must conclude that the craftsman who made that piece was either unskilled in the subtle nuances of the characters or has a curious sense of humor," Joss commented in his wake.

"Tell me you didn't inform Baustenbury of the last bit."

"That the characters are inconsistent with a Ming piece?"

"I was more referring to the specifics of the inconsistency."

"Oh." Joss grinned wickedly as they came to a stop. "You mean that the earl's prized possession clearly, in no uncertain terms, instructs him to f—"

"When did you get back to London?" Heath interrupted her with what sounded like an almost frantic desperation. He turned to signal a waiting footman.

"Last week. Though Worth told me you were out of town. Otherwise I would have insisted on a rematch at the chessboard. Perhaps you've learned a few tricks over the years. You never could abide getting beaten by a girl."

Heath straightened.

Joss waited for him to respond with a barb of his own.

"Mmm." He made another vague sound. "It's been a long time since you were home," he offered instead.

Joss felt her grin begin to slip as she watched him. "It has," she agreed. "Ten years." And in that time, she realized with some mystification, someone had kidnapped Heath and left this rigid imposter in his place.

The footman appeared suddenly and presented Heath with two glasses. Heath nodded his thanks and cleared his throat. "Something to drink?"

Joss selected one of the glasses, the rich color of its contents suggesting a welcome respite from the anemic punch. She took a deep, appreciative swallow of the whiskey. "The Irish do know their way around a distillery. My thanks."

Heath didn't answer, and another silence fell. Heavens, but who was this man? The old Heath would have been in stitches at the idea of stodgy old Baustenbury's fake antiquity emblazoned with graphic graffiti.

Joss took another sip of her fiery liquor, stalling. Her eye fell on the punch glass Heath was still holding, its watery contents untouched.

"Are you really drinking that?" she asked, wrinkling her nose.

"No. The punch is terrible. But you're drinking my drink," Heath told her. "This was supposed to be for you. I was not aware you had developed a taste for anything stronger."

Joss paused, the whiskey halfway to her lips. "Oh. I'm sorry."

"So am I. I had to bribe that footman to find me something that didn't put me in mind of grog." He placed the unwanted and offending beverage on the table.

Joss snorted. "Grog? That's not called grog. That's called a mutiny."

Heath grinned at her.

Instantly her stomach turned inside out, and an unholy thrill shot straight up her spine and lodged in her chest. Her heart skipped a beat. Maybe two.

Heath as a boy, with a roguish smile and a gleam in his eye, had been appealing. Heath as a man, with that same expression directed at her, was devastating. Enough to drive the breath from her lungs and make her knuckles whiten around her glass.

Joss would have thought that twenty years spent

traveling to places most people couldn't name, delving into cultures and experiences beyond the scope of the ton's imaginations, would have given her a modicum of sophistication. Enough, at least, to maintain her composure the first time an old friend offered her a damn smile, no matter how attractive he might be.

Joss squared her chin in self-disgust. "So tell me, how have you been?" she inquired, both hating and embracing the superficial distance of the query.

His grin vanished, and the stone-faced earl reappeared. She couldn't bring herself to be relieved, even if it allowed her heart to slow somewhat.

"I've been well, thank you," he replied. "And yourself?"

"Quite well, thank you." Good God, but now they sounded like a couple of bungling actors reading from a poorly written script. Joss took another healthy swallow of whiskey, giving herself a mental shake.

"What brought you back to London?" he asked politely.

She eyed Heath in speculation, wondering just how much he might be privy to regarding her rather unconventional family. Worth might have confided some aspects, but she very much doubted Heath knew everything. "I've been away too long. My mother isn't growing any younger, and my brother up and got married on me while I was an ocean away. I missed them," she answered, revealing nothing but maintaining the truth.

"Ah." Heath nodded. "Will you be staying for a while then?"

"I'm not sure yet."

"I see. Well, you look lovely tonight."

"Thank you. You look very handsome yourself."

"Thank you."

Bloody hell, but this was *excruciating*. Forget her own flustered reaction to this man. What the hell had happened to the boy who was more likely to steal her shoes and fill them with manure than address her with wooden compliments?

The orchestra struck up a waltz. "Let's dance," Joss said impulsively.

Heath looked startled. "I beg your pardon?"

"Let's dance." She gestured at the dance floor.

"Um."

"Oh, for God's sake, Hextall," Joss said, draining her whiskey and leaving her glass next to the others on the table. "Are you afraid I'll step on your toes?"

"No." He glanced about him anxiously.

A thought struck Joss, and her lungs compressed. "Are you married? Or engaged?" It was entirely possible he'd found a woman who—

"No." He looked uncomfortable. He hesitated. "Are you?"

An absurd sense of relief at his answer made her laugh. "I'd rather be drawn and quartered than be married. Hanging being optional."

"Oh." Heath looked nonplussed. "That seems somewhat melodramatic."

"No, I can assure you, it's not. I'd see my limbs posted on the four corners of the city before I used any of them to walk down an aisle. Marriage would be the end of me."

"You're saying that you've never once been tempted?" Heath asked dubiously.

"Never."

"Not a single man who you would consider?"

Joss tipped her head, pretending great consideration.

"Sir Francis Drake, perhaps. I think we would get along famously. Though I'm not entirely sure he doesn't have a tendre for a redhead. There is, of course, Sir Henry Morgan. However, I fear he is a little too temperamental for my tastes. Perhaps Captain James Cook would be a better choice."

"Pirates?" Heath looked exasperated now.

"I prefer the word *explorers*. And Cook most certainly was not a pirate."

"The Hawaiians might argue with you. And regardless, they're all dead."

"Dead? All of them? You don't say. Most disappointing." Joss pressed a theatrical hand to her bosom before brightening. "Oh well. I do suppose that solves my dilemma." She gave him a winning smile.

"You're impossible," Heath muttered under his breath.

"You asked."

"To my eternal regret."

"I see. Well, I am happy to stand here and eternally engage you in any number of random topics while you continue to procrastinate." Joss made a show of looking in the direction of the dance floor.

Heath looked pained. "I beg your pardon. Would you care to dance?"

She fluttered her lashes in an exaggerated fashion. "Why, I'd be delighted." She dropped her voice. "And here I thought you were going to make a lady ask twice."

"A lady doesn't ask once."

"And a gentleman would never have pointed that out in the first place."

Heath's lips thinned before he thrust his arm in her direction.

"Good heavens, such gallantry. It's a wonder you don't carry a walking stick to protect yourself from the adoring hordes."

"Don't make me reconsider."

"Never." She was enjoying this far too much.

Heath led her out on the dance floor as the music limped through the opening bars. "Wrong key," he muttered.

"They're getting worse by the set," Joss agreed. Though in truth, she could not have cared one whit if the entire orchestra had dressed like faeries and played tin pipes. Her only objective at the moment was to jostle the Heath she knew existed out of this reserved, unbending gentleman. She would aim to keep her tone light, her conversation witty, and her demeanor casual and relaxed.

He faced her and took her hand in his, waiting until she brought her other up to his shoulder. His exceedingly broad shoulder, Joss thought with a jolt of admiration. She concentrated on keeping her fingers balanced lightly on the fabric of his evening coat and resisted the urge to run them over his shoulder and down his bicep. As a youth he'd always been strong for his age—a decade later *powerful* was the only appropriate adjective. And the feel of that power under her touch was scattering her thoughts in a disconcerting manner. Her other hand remained trapped gently in his, keeping her captive and allowing his considerable heat to bleed through the two gloves against her palm. She drew a deep breath, but that only filled her nostrils with the scent of him, and it was exactly as she remembered—a faint hint of sandalwood underscored with something darker.

"I beg your pardon?" She jerked back slightly, realizing he had asked her something.

Heath was peering at her strangely. "I simply asked if you were ready." He tilted his head at the other dancers, who had already flowed into the steps.

"Of course." Joss cursed silently at herself. Good God, but she used to mock silly women who insisted that they lost their wits and their ability to speak at the mere sight of a suitor. This...sudden urge she had to simply gaze at the physical beauty of this man was embarrassing.

Joss cleared her throat purposefully and offered him a wry grin. "So how does it feel to be an earl?"

The lines around Heath's mouth tightened. "It's acceptable, thank you."

Acceptable? What kind of answer was that? "I had no idea your family stood to inherit the title."

"Neither did we. But a series of unfortunate deaths and suddenly 'distant cousin' becomes 'heir apparent.' "

She squeezed his hand lightly. "Ironic, isn't it? All those summers you spent in the country visiting the old earl. I remember you and my brother would climb up into the giant oak near the house and onto the roof, high enough to see our place. And you would talk about how much you loved it there and how you wished you were really neighbors. And now you are. Now Hazeldell belongs to you."

"Yes, I suppose it is ironic. Someone once told me I should be careful what I wished for."

Joss deliberately ignored his last comment. "Tell me, what was the first thing you did when you went back to Hazeldell as the Earl of Boden? Did you go fishing? Riding? Swim in the pool near the caves where we were never supposed to go because the water was too deep?"

"I replaced the roof."

"The roof?" Joss repeated in confusion.

"The roof on the manor house was rotten and in poor repair. Like every other building in the holdings." His answer was abrupt.

Well then. Perhaps she should try another topic. "How are your sisters?"

"They are doing well, thank you. Julia and her husband had a child this fall. A son."

"Ah, so you are an uncle now. Congratulations. Julia must be very happy. Please pass along my regards."

"I will."

"And Viola?"

"Traveling with an army of chaperones in New York."

"New York? That's a long way from home."

"Precisely."

Precisely? She waited for him to continue. Heath remained silent.

Joss scowled. This was ridiculous. Since he seemed disinclined to talk about the recent acquisition of the earldom or about his family, she tried the only other option remaining.

"How is your business?"

Heath looked down at her. "It's doing adequately, thank you."

Adequately, my ass, she sneered to herself. One need only read the London papers to know that Heath had taken the modestly successful business his father had started and almost single-handedly crafted an empire.

"How are you coming along with the hard?"

He almost dropped her hand. "I'm sorry?"

"Hard soap. Your father was always putting most of his resources into the production of soft, with only a small output of hard, and I remember that frustrating you."

Heath was looking at her strangely. "Er, soap. Yes, of course," he said after a moment. "I can't believe you remember that. But yes, I now produce a half dozen specialty hard soaps."

"I think that's wise," Joss said, sidestepping the skirts of another dancer.

"You do?" His surprise was almost comical. "I must confess you would be one of the few."

"Please don't misunderstand me. Your soft soap maintains a reputation of superb quality, and it is what your business and your fortune have been built upon. It's a staple in every household in England. But it's only a matter of time before the soap tax is repealed. And specialty hard soaps will become an affordable luxury for many, many more."

"That would be nice. Because right now I am producing them in my Boston factory."

"Because of the restricted production tonnage in England, I assume."

Heath nearly missed a step. "Yes. Though I import a percentage of what I produce in Boston back to England."

"You aren't limited to import then."

"Of course not. A ship must have full holds in both directions if it is to be profitable. I just purchased my fifth ship in Liverpool this past week." There was pride in that statement and Heath was more animated than he'd been all night. Joss was happy to let him keep talking.

"I export anything that I can sell easily in America for a profit," he continued. "Linen. Sail canvas, felt hats, rum, coal, spices, china, beer. It varies, depending on the demand and availability of product at the time. All of my ships, with the exception of one, sail from Liverpool."

Joss nodded. "Indeed. Deepwater harbor and lots of Irish immigrants willing to work."

"Yes," Heath agreed slowly before narrowing his eyes. "How, exactly, is it you are so well versed in tax laws and the export business?"

"I read. I believe I already mentioned that."

"It's a wonder you haven't gone completely cross-eyed with the amount of reading you claim to enjoy."

There it was again: the barest hint of the old Heath.

"My eyes are quite fine, as you can see. It is, however, according to popular opinion here tonight, one of my most grievous faults. Reading, that is." She looked up at Heath. "You used to tease me about it when we were both young. I suppose I shouldn't be surprised that you continue to do so now."

Heath grimaced. "I teased you about a great deal of things when we were young. Among other insults you didn't deserve. My apologies, for whatever they're worth now."

Joss shook her head. How could she possibly explain to Heath that his attention, however much it had been based in mischief, had made her feel visible? Visible and valuable at a time in her life when invisibility had been necessary to her survival as the daughter of the late Duke of Worth?

"Apology accepted," she replied lightly. "Yet you were one of the very few who tolerated, and even challenged, my admittedly ambitious ideas." She smiled. "And it would seem you haven't lost your touch. Did you know, this is the first interesting conversation I've had since I arrived tonight? Unless you count the one I had with Lord Baustenbury."

"I'm glad I could oblige you." Heath looked amused despite his best efforts.

"Well, I have something for you in return."

"You do?" He eyed her warily. "Tell me it's not a Ming vase."

"No." Joss chuckled. "I have an essence for you."

"An essence?"

"Yes."

"For what?"

"For your soap. What else would it be for? Keep up, Hextall. My brother used to insist you were the more clever of the two of you."

Heath closed his eyes briefly. "Has anyone ever mentioned how exhausting conversation is with you?"

"Repeatedly. Now do you want to know what I brought back with me or not?"

Heath opened his eyes. "Please. Do tell."

"It's an oil extracted from the ylang-ylang flower."

"The yee-ang-yee what?"

"You sound like a monkey. People are staring." Joss was biting her lip to contain her giggles. "Ylang-ylang. It's a flower that grows on a tree in the Far East. It's absolutely divine."

"I'm sorry. Why do you have this yee—this essence?"

"I used a soap in my travels that was made with the flower and coconut oil combined. It was the most heavenly thing I've ever put against my bare skin. I immediately thought of you."

Heath stopped abruptly in the middle of the dance floor, and the dancers around them grumbled at the obstruction.

Joss flushed. Oh God. That was not what she'd meant

to say. A vision of Heath, strong and warm and pressed against her own body, arose unwanted in her mind. Skin, heated and damp, flushed with passion and desire and— she stamped on her imagination before it went any further and pressed a hand to her flaming cheek. "That came out wrong. That's not what I meant. What I meant was that the fragrance was so unique I thought you could use it in your own...that is..."

The orchestra was laboring to an unsteady finish.

"I have an oil you might want to consider for scenting your hard soap," Joss said evenly. "If you would like to evaluate it for yourself, please feel free to call at my mother's house."

Heath's face might well have been carved from marble, so blank was his expression. "Of course. Thank you for your thoughtfulness. It was most kind."

Heath fled directly to Baustenbury's study, not caring if it was impolite or improper to be crashing into rooms clearly not intended for the use of guests. Which was telling because he usually cared a great deal about what other people thought. He went directly to the crystal decanter that sat on a small library table and, with a shaking hand, poured himself a full glass of whatever was in it. Pacing the richly carpeted room, he tried to regain his equilibrium.

Josephine was as capricious as he remembered— possibly even more so. Within the space of minutes, she had denounced a priceless antiquity, guzzled a glass of brandy like a sailor, asked an earl to dance, and then offered opinions on English tax law. It made his head spin, and he'd yet to find his balance since the moment she had turned around and smiled up at him.

He'd told her she looked lovely, but he'd been a coward. She wasn't lovely; she was mesmerizing. It had taken every ounce of self-control to keep her at a polite distance while her eyes danced with life and vitality and her smile threatened to infect his own disciplined composure. The feel of her body as they danced and the steady, sure pressure of her hand in his own had left him a little dazed. And when she had spoken out of turn, inciting images of her smooth, fragrant skin beneath his touch, his wits had scattered completely. Before tonight he'd never thought about Josephine as anything other than...Josephine. Worth's little sister. A cheeky girl with a crooked nose, a quick mind, and a smart mouth.

Except she wasn't a girl anymore. She was a woman, and one who threatened to make him forget why he had come to this damn ball in the first place. Though if he needed a reason to refocus on his objectives, he had only to heed the swath of whispers and stares Joss had left behind her while she remained unconcerned and unapologetic. In that regard she was like her mother, the dowager duchess, who to all appearances gleefully courted scandal as though it were a blood sport. But scandal was something Heath simply could not afford. In the last few years, his primary objective had been avoiding or covering up social debacles that were not of his own making. He wanted no more of them, no matter how attractive and clever and intriguing Josephine Somerhall might be.

All he desired was to return to a normal life, one in which the gossip sheets would desist from printing his family name with such alarming regularity. One in which

Heath might get the first decent night's sleep since the moment of his second cousin's untimely and heirless demise, when he'd left the title of Earl of Boden to come crashing down on Heath's branch of the family tree.

Heath's drinking had subsided to measured sips from his initial gasping gulps. The liquor had steadied his nerves, and Heath felt far more collected now than he had when he'd first stumbled into the study.

Joss had simply caught him off guard, that was all. A completely normal reaction when presented with an unexpected encounter with a childhood friend all grown up. She might now possess curves and allure she hadn't had ten years ago, but at her core, she was still just Joss. As wildly unconventional as she had always been. Something else to be managed and contained.

A clock chimed somewhere in the study.

Good Lord, but it was late. The long days of travel suddenly pressed down around him, and exhaustion settled like a mantle squarely on his shoulders. At the moment he wanted nothing more than to find his bed. The thought of having to forge on with more introductions and to construct witty and clever conversation was vastly unappealing. There would be other chances to meet and evaluate prospective wives over the next weeks, when the season would be in full swing. He would consult with Worth about which functions would offer him his best chance to find what he sought. In the meantime he would retreat to the blessed silence of his townhome and get a good night's sleep.

And forget about Josephine Somerhall.

Chapter 3

Before he'd become earl of anything, when he'd simply been Mr. Hextall, Heath had been perfectly capable of saddling his own horse. He saw no reason why a title should suddenly render him unable to perform such simple tasks, or deprive him of all the pleasures of riding. Heath's father had insisted they maintain a carriage and team and the staff to go with it to travel about London. But now with his father dead, his mother in Bath, and his sisters married and traveling respectively, Heath couldn't justify the expense for the sake of appearances. Instead he kept a gelding, a quiet, reliable beast that was perfectly adequate to see him wherever he needed to go. Should he require a covered equipage, there were plenty of hacks that could be hired at a fraction of what it would have cost to maintain his own. One didn't make a fortune by spending unnecessarily.

And on this night, he was glad of the freedom of a horse. The feel of the cold air against his skin was a welcome respite from the overheated, claustrophobic confines of the ballroom. The gelding plodded sedately back in the direction of St James's, and Heath made no effort to hurry the horse. He blew out a breath, a small cloud of fog that hung suspended before curling toward the sky and the stars that shone steadily against their inky canvas. It had tried to snow earlier, but the flakes had surrendered to a sleety rain, and puddles glittered across the streets. He closed his eyes and breathed deeply, the muffled silence of the night offering a much-needed respite.

He didn't see the body that crashed into his horse until it was too late.

The gelding shied and sidestepped nervously, but didn't bolt, even as Heath clutched the horse's neck to regain his balance. He gathered the reins, ready to kick the animal into a gallop should he find himself the victim of a robbery attempt, but the man who had careened into his horse lay in a crumpled pile on the side of the street and all Heath saw was blood. In the weak illumination of the nearest streetlamp, it was an ominous, rusty black, splattered in an evil pattern against the pavement, slowly spreading beneath the inert form.

Heath slid down from the gelding, his heart pounding. He glanced around for help, but the street was deserted. Quickly he crouched next to the body, hearing the wretched, racking sound of a man struggling for breath, and pushed the stranger to his back.

Wide, terrified eyes looked up at him, lips moving in a beseeching, silent plea, and it took a long moment before Heath realized he knew this man. "Mr. Smythe!" he exclaimed in horror. Heath opened his mouth to shout for help, but the man clawed at the front of his coat and pulled Heath down closer to his face.

"Lord Boden. Thank God. Don't make a sound," Smythe rasped. "They're looking for me. If they find us, they'll kill us both."

Heath stared at the man he knew as Gavin Smythe, officer of the Bow Street Runners. He had aged twenty years since Heath had seen him six months ago, when Smythe had been instrumental in helping him with a problematic thief who had repeatedly infiltrated his London warehouses. Now, in the sickly light, the officer's face was gray, lines of panic and pain carving deep grooves across his features.

"You have to listen to me," the man wheezed. He coughed, an ominous wet, choking sound.

"Sir, I must summon help," Heath said urgently. "Let me fetch a watchman. Or—"

"No!" Smythe was struggling to reach into his own coat, which gaped open. Heath saw a tufted hole in the breast of his coat and waistcoat, blood seeping from within. Bloody hell, someone had stabbed him.

With shaking hands Smythe drew out a heavy leather folder, tied tightly with string. "They're everywhere. Take this," he gasped. "Take it and keep it safe."

Heath accepted the folder, the surface slick and sticky. "What is this?" He was trying to think clearly, but there was so much blood.

The man was gasping desperately now. "You have to leave me. Don't let them find it."

"Who?"

"Get it to my... brother." He was struggling to talk. "Save him."

"Who?" he asked again.

"Brother. Set... up. For... retribution."

Nothing in that broken sentence made any sense. "Retribution from whom?"

"Save him. Promise me!"

"I promise," Heath blurted, shocked at the vehemence of the man's demand. Smythe, clearly spent from his efforts, subsided into a stupor.

Heath shoved the folder into his own coat and looked around frantically, but nothing moved. His first thought was to get Smythe to his town house, but that was still a fair distance, and it would be damned difficult to carry an unconscious man the entire way. Hoisting the senseless man up on his horse would be almost impossible by himself without risking further injury. For the first time, Heath cursed his lack of a carriage.

As if on cue, a vehicle turned the corner at the top of the deserted street, the team driven smartly by a bundled coachman perched up front. Heath nearly staggered with relief. Thank God. He had to get this man out of the street and to a surgeon.

Heath jumped into the path of the oncoming carriage, making the horses jerk their heads and snort their displeasure. The coachman hauled on the reins, and the carriage came to a sloppy stop. From the rear of the carriage appeared a footman, lithe and silent, a pistol drawn.

"Put that damn thing away," Heath ordered, eyeing the weapon, though he could only imagine how this looked, with his coat covered in blood and a body lying behind him. "This man is hurt badly, and I need help."

"Lord Boden?" It was the coachman who spoke. "Is that you?"

"Yes," he said, startled. There were no markings on the carriage to offer any clue as to its owner, and both servants were indistinguishable in their warm winter clothing.

The door snapped open. "Hextall?"

Heath jerked at the sound of Joss's voice. Bloody hell. Just what he needed. "What are you doing here?"

"I was going home."

"Where's Worth?"

"He left long ago. In his own carriage. This is my mother's."

"Is she with you?" He did not need to add the dowager duchess and her chicken to the chaos.

"No. She's still at the ball."

"Well, stay in the carriage." No lady needed to see this. He hurried back to Smythe and knelt beside him, struggling to lift him from the wet pavement.

"Don't be asinine."

Heath nearly dropped the semiconscious man, startled by the sound of her voice next to his ear. She was crouched beside him now, peering at the officer.

"Good Lord, this man has been stabbed. Probably missed the heart, though from the sound of his breathing his lungs weren't so lucky. Might have clipped a vessel from the amount of blood I see."

"What, are you a surgeon now?" Heath grumbled at her.

"Hardly," she replied. "Though I've had the opportunity to read some excellent anatomy books."

"Of course you have."

Joss seemed oblivious to his sarcasm. "Luke, help get him up."

The coachman was suddenly beside him, lifting the senseless man with ease. The movement seemed to jar Smythe from his haze, though his eyes remained unfocused.

"Go," he croaked. "Leave me. They'll kill you too."

"I'm not running like a scared rabbit and leaving you

here to bleed to death," Heath told him. "Tell me who stabbed you. Who tried to kill you?"

Smythe was trying to speak, fear clearing his eyes through the pain. "Three," he rasped. "Mounted. Swords... lanterns. One... left eye. They're not far behind."

"There will be a blood trail," the footman warned, "if someone is out looking for this man."

The words had barely passed from his lips when a faint shout reached their ears.

"Go." Smythe was pleading now. "They're coming. You hold England's fate—" Another spate of coughing stopped him. "Don't trust anyone."

"I don't understand what you're saying," Heath hissed.

"Perhaps I should fetch someone? Maybe a Runner?" Joss urged.

"No! Someone... they... betrayed me." Smythe started coughing again, trying to draw enough air, until his eyes rolled back in his head and he slumped in Heath's arms.

Heath swore.

"You know this man?" Joss asked urgently.

"Yes. Gavin Smythe. He's a Bow Street officer."

"Do you trust him?"

"Absolutely. He's a good man. A friend." Heath shivered, and it had nothing to do with the cold.

"Whoever those men are, I fear they are looking to finish what they started." Joss glanced down at the blood smeared across the pavement and then back in the direction from which her carriage had come. "We don't have much time."

"Put him on my gelding," Heath ordered, urgency making his voice hoarse. He needed to get Smythe out of here as quickly as possible, though he did not want to leave Joss alone.

They dragged Smythe's limp body over to the animal that was still standing patiently in the street.

"Can you ride?" he asked the young footman as he and Luke carefully hoisted him up on the horse's back.

"Yes, Joseph can ride," Joss said curtly before the footman could answer. "Better than the lot of us here put together."

Heath doubted that, but as long as he could keep Smythe upright, he'd do. "Then take him to my town house. Do you know where—"

"No," Joss interrupted. "Take him to my mother's. It's closer. And fetch a surgeon."

Heath shook his head. "I don't want you—"

"Stop arguing, Hextall. This entire exercise becomes pointless if the man dies."

Joseph swung himself up behind Smythe with impossible ease and held him steady. The man might simply appear drunk to a casual passerby who did not look too closely at the blood staining the dark wool.

"Give me your coat," she ordered Heath.

"What?"

"It's covered in blood." She was already yanking on the buttons on the front of it. "One less thing to explain if we have to."

Freezing air assaulted him as his coat was pulled from his shoulders. Heath caught the leather folder just as it tumbled from the inside. Joss tossed the coat to the footman, who stuffed it between himself and the unconscious man. "Go, Joseph. Hurry, and don't stop for anything."

Joseph turned the horse's head expertly, and the gelding moved off, disappearing into the dark. Through the gaps between the buildings, lanterns became visible near the top of the street and a horse whinnied.

Joss was already heading back in the direction of the carriage, and the coachman was climbing back up on the seat. "Get in," she said to Heath, and though she sounded calm, her face was set in tense lines.

"We can't outrun them," Luke warned from his perch.

"I don't want you to outrun them," she said to her coachman. "I want you to stall them."

"Understood," Luke replied.

Heath climbed into the small interior, Joss on his heels, the door clicking shut behind her. In the darkened interior, he couldn't see her expression, only hear the sound of her rapid breathing. The carriage lurched into motion, though one would have thought the coachman was incompetent or drunk or both given the manner in which it slowly wove from side to side.

Another shout came from outside, muffled through the walls of the carriage, and with it the sound of approaching horses.

Heath felt his jaw clench. "I've put you in danger."

"Would you have preferred me to have ignored you in the middle of the street?"

"Maybe. If those men stabbed Gavin Smythe—"

"Would you have driven past me if our roles had been reversed?"

"Of course not."

"Well then." She sniffed.

Heath wasn't at all reassured. "They are going to see all that blood. Even a blind man couldn't miss it. Hell, how much blood can possibly be in a body?"

"Ten pints," Joss said from somewhere across from him.

"Ten pints?" Heath repeated faintly.

"For an average-sized man. You can measure it as a percentage of body weight, so children or someone smaller will have a good deal less, of course, but..." She trailed off. "Not that that is important at the moment," she muttered.

"Oh, dear God." Heath realized he was clutching the leather folder in his hands so tightly that his knuckles were stiff. Distracted, he held it up, trying to get a better look at it in the weak streetlight filtering through the carriage window.

"What is that?"

"A folder or a ledger of some sort. It was Smythe's."

"I thought it was yours."

"No. He gave it to me before he lost consciousness. Said I needed to keep it safe."

Joss muttered something rude under her breath. "And you mention this *now*?"

"I beg your pardon. I was too busy trying to save a man's life earlier."

Her fingers bumped his in the shadows, and she pulled the bound leather from his hands.

"What are you doing?"

"Hiding it," Joss hissed. "Odds are this is what got your man stabbed in the first place."

Joss's backside was suddenly in his face as she half crouched and turned in the compact space. He leaned back as far as he was able as he heard a latch click in the darkness, followed by the sound of a squeaky hinge and an odd scraping noise.

The carriage lurched sideways, and Heath's hands immediately went up to steady her before he snatched them away. He shouldn't have his hands anywhere near Worth's sister's backside. He shouldn't have his hands anywhere near Josephine, period. He liked the feel of her far too much.

There was the sound of more latches being released, then the scrape of metal on metal. What the hell was she doing?

"Unbutton your shirt," Joss said as she yanked the curtains closed, plunging the interior into complete darkness. "And get rid of your cravat."

"I beg your pardon?" He heard her thump back down onto the squabs.

The riders were almost upon them now, shod hooves creating a loud clatter that rang sharply in the still night.

"There is a trail of blood that leads into the middle of this street. There the trail becomes a puddle and then abruptly disappears. This is the only carriage in sight. You tell me what they're going to conclude."

"That we picked him up."

"Yes. I suspect that they will stop us. In fact, I'm counting on it. It will give Joseph more time to get your Mr. Smythe to safety."

As if on cue, the carriage groaned to a shuddering halt as the ominous sound of approaching riders drawing even filtered through the walls. But within seconds a sinister silence fell all around them, broken only by the snort of a horse drawn up too tight and the sound of boots hitting stone as men dismounted.

Heath became aware Joss was shucking her own cloak, the sound of fabric slipping over fabric audible in the quiet.

"What are you doing?" he whispered.

"I can think of only one thing we could have been doing that would have made us oblivious to anything and everything beyond these curtains. Only one thing that might explain why you are not dressed in a coat."

She could not possibly be suggesting what he thought she was suggesting.

A faint rip signaled the loss of a seam somewhere in the darkness.

"Your cravat, Hextall, and be quick about it. Then the top buttons of your shirt."

Holy hell, but she meant to do the unthinkable. "You... me...that's...that's...that's absurd! You can't possibly be serious."

"You don't have to be so emphatic."

"That's not what I meant," he ground out. "Your brother will kill me."

"Not if these bastards do it first. Besides, it's hardly the first time I've seen you wearing less than more. You hardly ever bothered with shoes."

"It was summer. And we were *children*," he spluttered.

"All that familiarity should make this easy then."

"Your reputation will be ruined!"

"For God's sake, Hextall, you think those men care about me or my reputation? They stabbed and likely killed an officer of the law tonight to get whatever it is they want, and I rather suspect what they want is now hidden—"

A vicious pounding on the door made him jump.

"Open up!" a coarse voice yelled.

Christ, but this was really happening. Heath yanked at the linen at his throat.

"Come here," he said roughly, reaching for Joss in the dimness. He found her upper arm and pulled her onto his lap, positioning her so that his back was to the carriage door and she was hidden by his body. At the very least he could protect her from whoever was outside that door.

Her legs were straddling his waist, and he shoved her skirts up over her knees, allowing her to settle herself on his thighs. Joss slipped her arms under his evening coat and around his ribs as she wriggled against him. His body reacted instantly, lust spiraling, and he cursed. Not the time or the place.

Or the woman.

"What about your coachman?" Heath whispered frantically, tossing his cravat to the floor.

"Luke can handle himself."

"Fine." Heath would have to take her word. His concern was for Joss. And himself. "You and me—we saw and heard nothing. There was no Gavin Smythe, there was no blood, there was no mystery folder. Understood?"

"Yes."

"Nothing but me," he whispered, his hands delving under her skirts and coming to rest on the magnificent backside he had just sworn he would never touch.

"Nothing but you," she repeated.

The carriage door was wrenched open.

Even though he knew it was coming, Heath jerked in surprise as a gust of cold air and light flooded the interior of the carriage. Joss uttered a convincing shriek.

"Someone better be dying, Luke," Heath snarled, making absolutely no effort to move. "I told you I didn't want to be disturbed for any reason."

"So verra sorry, milord," Luke was babbling from the darkness beyond the door, slurring in a heavy Scottish burr as though he were inebriated. "But these men, they have—"

"Step aside." There was an electric silence as whoever held the lantern got his first look at the occupants of the carriage.

"Is he there?" someone demanded from behind him.

Joss shifted on his lap, and Heath knew she had a perfect view of the intruder. He tightened his hands on her hips, keeping her snug against him and shielded from whoever was behind them.

Very slowly Heath turned his head. There was a man leaning into the carriage, a hood drawn over his dark hair but not far enough to conceal the eye patch over his left eye or the angry scar that ran down the cheek below. He held a lantern in one hand and a wicked-looking rapier in the other.

"Who the hell are you?" Heath chose insolence and entitlement, knowing nothing smothered the suggestion of intelligence as effectively as arrogance.

The intruder didn't answer, only let his one good eye rove over Joss.

Heath's jaw clenched. "Take whatever you want. We were at a ball, not a bank, so try not to be too disappointed," he sneered.

"You think I come for coins?" The man finally spoke, his French origins clear in his speech.

"What the hell else would you be wanting?" Heath snapped. "I'm fresh out of diamond tiaras."

"Where is he?"

"Who?"

"We know he was here in the street. Where is he?" The one-eyed man jerked the blade at them.

Heath didn't even flinch. "I have no idea what you're talking about, but I would suggest it's obvious that whoever you're looking for is not in here."

"I am not so sure you don't know something. Perhaps saw something," the man said. The hilt of the rapier tapped against the carriage door. "A man. Perhaps he was... unwell."

"Does it look like I care about your sick friend?" Heath growled. "Now if you're not going to rob us, get the hell out. It's freezing."

"Where's your winter coat?" the stranger demanded.

"Jesus." Heath barked out a laugh that was devoid of humor. "I don't know how you charm a woman, but what I was doing until I was so rudely interrupted doesn't require clothes."

"You travel without your coat on this cold night?" He didn't sound like he believed a word Heath was telling him.

"I was plenty warm until a minute ago. Now I'm going to ask you one more time. Get the hell out of my carriage."

"Or what? Tell me, what is a man like you going to do to a man like me? You and your little dove? Hmmm?" He slid the tip of the rapier along Joss's exposed leg. "It would seem I have you at a... what is the word? Ah yes, a disadvantage."

Joss shifted against him again, and at first Heath thought it was to evade the cold blade against her skin. It was a second before he realized she was pressing her hands to his sides and Heath suddenly became aware of the feel of smooth metal against either side of his rib cage.

Holy hell, but Joss had had two pistols concealed under his evening coat this entire time.

He almost stopped breathing, out of disbelief or terror she might accidentally shoot him, he wasn't entirely sure which. What he had thought was the sound of latches being released when Joss had hidden the folder had actually been the sound of her loading and cocking the pistols. His gaze darted to hers, and she met his eyes evenly in the lantern light before she buried her face in his neck, feigning fright.

"Whatever happens, don't move too fast," she whispered against his ear. "Understand?"

Heath nodded against her. Jesus, if it came to that—

"What of your coachman?" the man continued.

"What of him?"

"Perhaps he saw something."

Heath pretended to heave an infuriated sigh. "Luke!" he snapped.

"Milord?" The coachman's voice came from outside the carriage.

"Tell these men if you saw a sick man wandering outside in the streets just now."

"Ne'er saw no sick man, milord. Jus' a dead one. An' he wasna wandering." Luke snorted drunkenly at his own apparent humor.

"Where?" the man asked. "And when?"

"O'er yonder." Heath could envision Luke gesturing in the direction of the bloody pavement. "But I didna stop. None o' my business, that. An' milord said no inn-erupsions. 'Cept you. But that's 'cause you got pointy swords."

"You're lying. I don't see a body."

"Them's body snatchers were already there when I saw it. They done taked it away. Saw their cart. Dead man worth good money now'days, you know."

Another silence fell.

"There. My coachman has told you what you want to know. Now leave." Heath didn't like the feel of this at all. These men were too calm, too unwavering in their actions and their questions, as if they'd already come to a predetermined conclusion. He shifted his body slightly and drew his hand from Joss's hip.

The stranger was staring at Heath's arm. "You've blood on your cuff."

Heath glanced down and swore inwardly. There was indeed a smear of dark red along the edge of the snowy white linen peeking out from the sleeve of his evening coat. "So?"

"I think you are not telling me what you need to. I think you are lying. You know where this man is. Perhaps you even know where the gold is."

The last flummoxed Heath. *Gold?* What gold? "I have no idea what you're talking about," Heath growled.

"Then how did blood get on such a fine shirt?"

Heath sneered. "I took exception to the last man who called me a liar."

The scarred man's lips pulled back into what Heath imagined was supposed to be a smile. "You are very amusing. Or brave. Or stupid." He paused, glancing back at his unseen cronies beyond the carriage door. "What do you want to do with them?" he asked in French.

There was another long pause before a different man spoke, replying in the same language. "Kill the man. Bring the woman with us—she might know something yet. Make it look like a robbery gone bad," came the terse order from the dark. "Then search the carriage. But be quick about it."

Every muscle in Heath's body tensed as the one-eyed man turned back to them. "It seems you are not so brave this night. Only stupid. Just like the others who refused to tell the truth." An evil smile split his scarred face. "*Vive l'Empereur!*" he shouted, and lunged at Heath's back.

A deafening explosion rocked the confines of the carriage. Their attacker jerked back, a look of confusion on his face, the rapier dropping from his fingers to clatter on the floor of the carriage. The acrid stench of gunpowder burned the inside of Heath's nose, and Joss threw herself from his lap to the opposite side of the carriage. In a single motion, Heath twisted and snatched up the sword.

The one-eyed man had crumpled to the pavement in front of the carriage door, facedown in a puddle, the lantern lying broken beside him. Heath shoved past him and leaped clear of the equipage, his blood roaring in his ears. A movement at his side had him wheeling, raising his blade just in time to block a savage swing from a second killer. Someone was shouting, and the coach horses were shifting nervously now. Heath's attacker kept coming, and Heath backed up, drawing the man away from the carriage and away from Joss.

His opponent was burly and already breathing hard from exertion. He carried a heavier sword than the rapier Heath had claimed, and he was using it like a battle-ax to chop at the finer blade. Heath was forced to dodge and weave, though at least this was something he knew how to do. Something he had spent hours perfecting, and instinct took over where fear might have impeded him. The man let out a roar of frustration and rage and took another run at Heath. Heath feinted to his left and lashed out with his foot, catching the killer at the knee. The man howled in pain and lurched sideways, before bringing his blade whistling down toward Heath's head. Heath ducked, and the force of the killer's swing, coupled with his wounded knee, threw the man off-balance. Heath simply allowed his blade to drop, bracing himself as the killer impaled himself on the blade with his own momentum.

Heath yanked the rapier from the dying man's chest and spun, looking for the next threat. But the one-eyed killer hadn't moved from where he'd fallen and Luke was standing over the body of the third villain.

Heath straightened, gasping, adrenaline surging through his veins. They'd stopped in a narrow street, the blank walls of the buildings on either side the only witnesses to what had just happened. He gazed numbly at the three bodies on the ground.

"What the hell was that?" Heath managed.

The coachman shrugged, bending to rifle through the coat pockets of the man at his feet. The scent of blood was everywhere, heavy and metallic, and with some disbelief, Heath realized their third attacker had had his throat slit.

"You killed him?" Heath blurted.

Luke winced. "Regrettably, yes. He gave me little choice."

The coachman had discarded his hat and scarf, and Heath realized that the man was younger than he'd originally thought. He wasn't any older than Heath, with gold-blond hair and a face that Renaissance artists would have begged to immortalize. Probably on a church ceiling somewhere, complete with a toga and a set of wings.

But at the moment, the angelic-looking man was kicking a sword away from the body lying at his booted feet, watching as it spun away into the shadows. "Whatever your friend did or didn't do, someone wanted him quite dead for it. Along with anyone with whom he might have crossed paths." Luke glanced up at Heath briefly. "Though my compliments on your skill, my lord. You fight well."

"A skill required when one attends Eton as a soapmaker's son and the charity case of an aging cousin," Heath replied grimly. "What are you doing?"

"This was the bastard who ordered you killed. I'm looking for a reason why." Luke came up empty and moved on to the man who had come at Heath with the heavy sword.

Good God. How could the man be so matter-of-fact about all this? And Joss...his eyes flew to the carriage and he stumbled forward, stepping over the body lying near the door.

"Joss? Are you hurt?"

"No." She was sitting on the squabs, the pair of pistols resting in her lap.

He wanted to touch her, hold her, make sure she was in one piece. Instead he curled his fingers around the doorway.

"Is he dead?" she asked. Her voice was steady, but her face was pale in the dim light.

"Yes."

"He was going to run you through."

Heath flinched. "Yes."

She jerked her chin at the pistols. "I reloaded. Just in case."

"I see that." Jesus, but how had this happened? How had he managed to leave an ordinary ball on an ordinary horse on an ordinary evening and suddenly find himself here? In a narrow lane in London in the blackness of night with three men who had tried to kill him now dead at his feet? With a coachman who was just a little too casual about killing and a woman who had nearly eviscerated him with a set of officer's pistols in the process of saving his life? He'd never needed a drink as badly as he did at that moment, and that was saying something. He'd had a lot of moments in the last years.

"I suggest that we leave, my lord. And quickly. I have no desire to wait and find out if there are more of them." Heath jumped, not having heard Luke come up behind him. The man moved like a damn cat.

"Right." Heath took a deep breath, the icy air filling his lungs. "Where are their horses?"

"Bolted when the guns went off."

"Just as well. Should we fetch someone?"

"Like who?" The coachman was wiping the blade of a lethal-looking knife on the sleeve of one of the fallen men, his strokes leaving dark smears. "And tell them what, exactly? Your Mr. Smythe said not to trust anyone. I might be inclined to agree with him."

Heath rubbed his temples. "He's not *my* Mr. Smythe!"

"He is now." Luke's knife disappeared somewhere in the folds of his winter clothing.

"What do we do with them?" Heath eyed the bodies.

"Leave them," Luke said, heaving himself back up and balancing on the footboard. "I'll send someone to collect them later."

Good God. He chose to ignore that for the moment. "Were they carrying anything? Any information that might tell us who they were?"

Luke shook his head. "Nothing at all." He sat and gathered the reins. "You better hope your Mr. Smythe has some better answers."

⁓

Joss had finally stopped shivering, the fear and the adrenaline slowly draining from her limbs, leaving her not a little shaky. She had been in sticky situations before but never had she come this close to watching someone she cared for die before her eyes. Heath had come within inches of a horrible death trying to protect her. And given the chance, Joss knew she would pull the trigger again with no hesitation.

She watched him covertly in the shadows as they hastened back to the safety of home, and considered his actions. Heath hadn't known that she'd had the pistols hidden under his evening coat—the shock of realization in his eyes when he'd finally understood had been unmistakable. But by then he'd already placed himself in the path of danger, keeping her shielded without a second thought. And while a pitiable part of her would have liked to believe he'd put himself in such peril just for her sake, Joss knew very well he would have done the same no matter who had been in the carriage with him.

Joss sighed and straightened her shoulders beneath her cloak. The fact remained that they had escaped relatively unscathed. And now her mind would be better applied to the predicament that lay before them. Like it or not, they were now embroiled in whatever plot Gavin Smythe had found himself in, and it seemed far more grave than she had initially imagined. The men who had stabbed the Bow Street officer had been prepared to kill a lord, his lady, and a servant with an indifferent coldness that had shocked her.

And yet...

"They weren't professional assassins," she mumbled.

"I beg your pardon?" Heath started from the seat to which he had retreated, silent and brooding as the carriage rumbled through the night. Every once in a while he would peer through the rear window, though Joss was fairly certain they weren't being followed.

"Those men. They weren't trained killers."

"What?" He finally turned to look at her.

"Professionals would never have let Gavin Smythe live, much less escape. And even if he had escaped, if the killers suspected us of harboring or assisting their fugitive, they would have killed you the first chance they got. And probably Luke. Neutralize the greatest threats immediately, while acquiring the weakest to extract information. That would be me. And they certainly wouldn't have dismounted. At least not all of them. A horse is a great advantage."

"*What?*" Heath was staring at her.

"They were sloppy. And arrogant." She paused thoughtfully. "Soldiers from the dissolved Grand Armée, I suspect. Though I thought their reference to gold was somewhat curious. What do you think they meant?"

Heath leaned forward, his face hard and intense. "We could have been killed tonight, and *this* is what you are thinking about?"

Joss frowned. Going through the facts in a calm, rational manner had settled her. She would have thought Heath would be of the same mind. "What should I be thinking about?"

"How about the fact that you almost shot me? Since when do you travel to and from balls with pistols hidden in the carriage?"

Joss ignored his question. "I wouldn't have shot you. I'm very competent. One must practice a great deal to be able to effectively handle the recoil. Besides, the business ends of the barrels were well beyond your rib cage."

"They were *against* my damn rib cage," Heath snapped. "I hate pistols. They're unreliable, notoriously inaccurate, and if you don't make your shot count, you're dead before you can reload. What if they had blown up? Or misfired?"

She felt a prick of impatience. "Then, assuming you didn't already have a rapier blade buried through your spine and lodged in your heart, you'd still be alive enough to pick out shrapnel from your skin." Joss picked up one of the pistols that still lay next to her on the seat, considering it in the shadows. "It is unlikely these would have failed to the extent you fear. They are exceedingly well crafted and impeccably maintained. Made by Joseph Griffin and John Tow when they had their shop on Bond Street. I'll admit they're a little long for my taste. I'd prefer something less bulky, but then you start sacrificing effectiveness when you go to a smaller caliber."

Heath dropped his head into his hands and swore.

"My apologies about your evening coat. And your waistcoat. And your shirt," Joss said.

Heath raised his head, incomprehension stamped across his features.

"I'm afraid they're quite ruined."

He glanced down at the two identical holes, one on either side of his evening coat, and at his waistcoat and shirt, which were marked with black scorch marks from the discharge of the guns, clearly visible even in the shadows.

"You charred my clothes," he blurted.

Joss winced. "I'll have them replaced."

"Did you have to fire both guns?"

"As well made as they are, they're still flintlock. As you pointed out earlier, I couldn't take a chance one might fail to fire."

Heath ran his hands through his hair, his frustration evident. "Where the hell did you get them?"

"My mother gave them to me."

Heath closed his eyes briefly. "I meant, where were they in the carriage?"

"The same place I hid your folder." Joss knelt to the side and flipped open her seat to reveal a hidden compartment. Nestled with the leather folder were two other pistols, a short sword, and a hunting knife.

"What the hell is all that?"

"Precaution."

"Against what?" Heath's voice was starting to rise.

Joss bit her lip, unsure of how to answer. "Against people who might take exception to the occupants or the location of the carriage." She handed the folder to Heath, closed the compartment, and resumed her seat.

"That makes no sense. I thought you said this was your mother's carriage."

"It is."

Heath uttered a rude laugh. "And she uses it for what? To conceal spies? To transport contraband in and out of London?" He thumped back on his seat.

"Not exactly." Joss squirmed.

"Explain what that means."

"I—" The carriage turned sharply and suddenly, and Joss glanced out the window. They had entered the narrow passage that led to the mews in the back of her mother's town house. "We're back," she said, relieved beyond measure. "Bring that damn folder with you when you come. Let's see what's so important it was worth killing for."

The horses came to a stop, and Joss reached for the door.

"Wait." Heath suddenly leaned forward and caught her arm. "I'm sorry," he said.

Joss froze. "For what?" The feel of his hand against her chilled skin sent heat flooding through her.

"You saved my life. And I didn't thank you for it. I offer no excuse other than that the events of the last hour have been ghastly and have left me not myself."

"Oh." Joss remained motionless, afraid to move. Afraid that if she did, she would find herself up against him, remembering how he had felt beneath her when he had drawn her to him. Afraid that she would want to confuse his gallantry and sense of duty with something far more dangerous.

"You killed a man tonight," he said.

Joss's insides lurched despite her best efforts. She'd been trying not to think about that part. "Yes."

He released her arm to brush a piece of hair away from her face. "I'm sorry you had to do that because of me."

Joss focused on keeping her breathing steady. "It wasn't your fault any more than it was mine," she said. "Those men made their own choices."

"That doesn't necessarily make it easier."

"No. What makes it easier is the knowledge that I

will always choose your life." She raised her eyes to his. "While I regret what happened tonight, I will never regret my choice. Ever."

In the shadows, she heard his breath catch, and he drew his hand away. "Joss, I . . ." He trailed off before clearing his throat. "Then thank you, Lady Josephine, for saving my life. I am in your debt."

The air between them crackled with unspoken emotion. Without thinking about what she was doing, she slipped her arms around Heath and laid her head against his chest. She closed her eyes and listened to his strong, steady heartbeat and breathed in the scent of him.

Snow. Sweat. Sandalwood.

After a second of hesitation, his arms went around her as well, his chin resting on the top of her head. Joss pressed herself farther into his heat, unable to help herself. She could feel the solid ridges of muscle along his back beneath her fingers, the unyielding strength of his arms where they encircled her shoulders. It would seem that, years later, Heath Hextall still had the ability to make her feel safe and valuable and visible, just as he had done as a boy. He was, at this moment, and as he had always been, an anchor in the storms she'd never seen coming. Her hands curled into the silk backing of his waistcoat.

Heath stiffened immediately. "Next time, please tell me when you have two loaded pistols hidden under my coat," he said. He'd probably meant it to come out as a jest, but instead it was more of a strangled plea.

She pulled away from him then, afraid that if she remained a moment more, she might do something stupid. Like kiss him.

"Of course," she murmured, pushing the carriage door open and climbing out into the freezing air. Joss took a deep, bracing breath, the frigid temperature doing an admirable job of jarring her back into sense and sanity. Good God, but after everything that had happened, she was acting like a silly, dewy-eyed debutante. It was almost embarrassing. She needed her wits clear and sharp, not clouded by impossible yearnings.

Joss heard Heath clambering out of the carriage behind her. "We should hurry then, Hextall," she said briskly, pleased with the firm resolution of her tone. "I only hope we're not too late."

Chapter 4 ─────────

You're too late."

Joss felt the hope drain from her chest. "He's dead?" She glanced at the body of Gavin Smythe, which lay on the cold marble of the dowager's hall, wrapped carefully in a sheet.

"Very." The verdict came from a veritable Goliath of a woman, disheveled and sleep-rumpled and dressed in what looked like a field tent from one of Wellington's campaigns. She put a massive fist on her ample hips and raised the lantern she was carrying. "You all right?" Her eyes raked Joss from head to foot before they transferred and acknowledged Heath. "Lord Boden."

"We're fine, thank you. Heath, this is Margaret. My mother's cook."

Heath gave Margaret a faint nod.

"Was this man a friend o' yours, milord?"

"Yes. He was." He was staring at the dead lawman. "He had cause to assist me on numerous occasions with recovering stolen goods from my warehouses." He paused, frowning. "Why in God's name is he out here?"

"Reckoned it was best to put 'im where there wasn't carpets. On account of the fact he was bleedin' all over the place. Hard to get blood out of them rugs. 'Specially if they're wool."

Joss saw Heath's jaw slacken. "Where's Joseph?" she asked Margaret hastily.

"Went to fetch the Darling brothers."

Joss nodded. "Good. When they get here, tell them there are three more off Berwick Street that they can pick up."

Margaret's eyes slitted. "What happened?"

"The men who murdered Mr. Smythe took exception to the existence of witnesses."

"Unfortunate."

"Indeed. They left us little choice."

"Did you recognize any o' them?"

"No." Joss paused thoughtfully. "Perhaps the Darlings might?"

"Who are the Darling brothers?" Heath demanded beside her.

Joss pressed her lips together. At this point there was little value in lying.

"The Darling brothers provide invaluable resources so that learned men of medicine can further their knowledge," she said carefully.

Heath looked at her blankly.

"They collect bodies, Heath." Joss sighed. "They are very good at what they do."

Margaret snorted. "What she means is that they are discreet and have a reliable rig. And excellent contacts." She pursed her lips. "Yer right, though. If the Darlings don't recognize them, they might know someone who does. Worth askin'."

Joss was aware Heath was staring at her.

"Why are you on familiar terms with resurrection men, Lady Josephine?" His voice sounded strained.

"They've helped my mother in the past."

"Your mother?"

"That part isn't important right now." Joss waved her hand, unwilling to get into awkward explanations at this particular time. "What is important is that we discover not only who killed your Mr. Smythe, but why."

"*We* shouldn't discover anything," Heath hissed beside her. "We should call someone who can deal with this mess in a lawful, procedural manner."

Joss met his gaze. "Like a Bow Street Runner?"

"Exactly."

"The ones your Mr. Smythe told you not to trust? The ones to whom you would need to explain how you came to be in possession of the remains of their colleague who has very obviously been murdered? I have no desire to see you arrested."

Heath threw up a hand in helpless frustration.

"Can we at least look at whatever it was that he gave to you to keep safe?" Joss tried for a reasonable tone. "Perhaps there is information in there that will help us best decide how to proceed. If there is nothing of value in that folder, then we will devise a believable story about the events of tonight and turn the murder of Smythe over to the authorities. Would that be acceptable to you?"

Heath looked down at his other hand, which still held the forgotten folder. "I suppose."

"Good." Joss pushed her hair out of her eyes. "We'll use the study. There's better light in there. Margaret, can you send one of the Darlings in when they arrive? I'd like to speak to them."

" 'Course." The cook nodded. "Her Grace know what's goin' on?"

"Luke went back to the ball to fetch her."

Margaret blew out a forceful breath. "Well, I can't see that there's much point in goin' back to bed now," she said. "You two still look chilled to the bone. I'll bring you somethin' to warm up yer insides and get one o' my girls to get the fire goin' for you."

"Might we have some warm milk, please?" Joss asked. "With cinnamon." She glanced at Heath, who looked startled. "Unless you'd like something stronger?"

"No," he replied after a second's hesitation. "Milk would be fine."

"Thank you, Margaret," Joss said, and the cook lumbered off with renewed purpose. "Come," she said, pulling gently on Heath's arm. He followed her without argument as she led him across the marble floor and pushed open a door near the rear of the house.

The space was chilled and dark, and it took them a few minutes to get the candelabra and lanterns lit. A young maid came and went, giving Joss and Heath a curious glance, but leaving a fire in the hearth, its warmth and light slowly penetrating the small room.

Joss took off her damp cloak and tossed it over a chair before picking up the largest candelabrum, setting it firmly on the polished desk. She straightened and realized Heath was still standing near the door, staring at the walls of the room with what looked like a mixture of fascination and revulsion. Joss glanced around, trying to imagine what it must look like through Heath's eyes.

There were chickens everywhere.

Images of poultry had been painted on the walls, farmyard scenes illustrated in vivid blues, greens, reds, and yellows. Still more were embroidered onto the couch pillows and sewn into the long drapes that covered the windows. Little porcelain and crystal and wooden birds lined the tops of the expansive bookshelves, and a large set of carved marble hens nested in a place of honor upon a long library table in the center of the room. But it was the heavy mantel above the fireplace on which Heath's attention was fixed. A half dozen mounted roosters in full plumage perched along its length, firelight reflected in their beady glass eyes.

"You haven't been in my mother's study before tonight, have you?" Joss sighed.

"No." He took a slow step into the room. "Worth described it once, but..."

"The drawing room and the dining room are decorated in much the same fashion. Just ignore it."

Heath came to a stop in front of the hearth, his mouth twisted peculiarly as he gazed the mounted birds. "Ignore it? How? They're leering at me."

"Roosters don't leer, Hextall. They do not possess the intelligence to leer."

"They're leering at me right now." He turned to look at Joss. "Why does your mother have dead roosters in her library?"

Joss crossed to where Heath stood. "They have their uses."

"What use could dead roosters possibly be?" He sounded incredulous.

Infallible distraction, for one, she thought, but tonight that distraction was proving unwelcome.

"Come," Joss said, urging Heath away from the hearth and toward the study desk. "Let's focus on what's important." She gestured at the folder Heath was still holding in his hands.

Heath allowed her to guide him away from the fire, glancing back only once at the ever-vigilant roosters. He came to a stop beside the desk, placing the folder gently on its surface, as though he half expected it to explode. He made no move to open it. "He told me to get this folder to his brother. Just before you got there."

"Mr. Smythe?"

"Yes."

"I see." Joss put her hands on the surface of the desk. "Do you know his brother?"

"I didn't even know he had one. He never once mentioned family of any sort."

"Did he say if his brother was in London?"

"No," Heath said, frustration bleeding into his words. "But before he died, Gavin Smythe begged me to save his brother from some sort of retribution." Heath sighed unhappily. "And I promised him I would. Yet I don't even know where he's at, or what he needs saving from—"

"Let's deal with one thing at a time," Joss interrupted softly. "All of the answers to those questions might be in this folder. We need to know what's inside."

"You're right, of course." Heath pulled at the strings, struggling with the knotted leather tie that bound the folder.

"Here, let me." Joss took it from his hands and he offered no argument. "Let's see what your Mr. Smythe died trying to protect."

Heath watched as Joss opened the stiff folder, a strange mixture of dread and anticipation swirling through him.

His tired mind was trying to guess what manner of documents it might contain. A passel of military secrets that were a holdover from the recent war? Incriminating evidence that might implicate lawmen in a plot of some sort? Plans of increasingly disgruntled men hoping to incite more revolutionary unrest, such as France had suffered through not so long ago?

Joss was bent over the desk now, her hair falling along her jaw and concealing her expression, but she had gone quite still. Concerned, Heath moved closer beside her, peering over her shoulder.

The document lying on top was old and written on what appeared to be fine vellum, discolored and slightly curled at the edges. It was illuminated in a way Heath had occasionally seen before, but only in centuries-old religious tomes kept in dusty libraries. Those examples, like the document in front of him, had been written in Latin. Most of the Latin he'd learned as a boy had fallen into disuse, but what he could decipher on these pages made absolutely no sense. A jumble of random words and phrases.

"What is that?" he breathed.

Joss only shook her head mutely and carefully laid a page aside. There were several pieces of vellum, the same muddled writing inscribed across all of them, the ink faded in some places, but overall well preserved. At the bottom of each, a seal had been affixed—not pressed into wax as he might do with his own correspondence, but stamped in rust-colored ink so that it could never be removed.

"Do you recognize that seal?" she asked, her voice sounding odd.

Heath bent closer to the documents, examining the illustration. It depicted a horse ridden by two knights, crosses clearly visible on the shields they held. What looked like Latin lettering circled the figures, though it was uneven and illegible in some places.

"I've never seen it before."

"You're sure?"

"Yes, I'm sure. Though it looks positively medieval." He frowned. "Why? Have you?"

"Yes." He waited for her to elaborate, but she remained uncharacteristically silent. "There are more letters," she said instead, setting the last piece of vellum aside.

The paper she now held in her hand was modern, the writing cramped but identifiable as French. Joss passed them to Heath, who riffled through them, noting the dates at the tops of the letters. There were a flurry from 1798, a few from the interim leading up until 1800, and the rest were more recent—1814 and later. Heath scanned the latest letters, his French more than adequate, but the missives seemed unremarkable. They were all unsigned and lacking an addressee, and their contents, as far as he could tell, were nothing but a dull dissertation on the daily events of a farm. They were something Heath never would have given a second glance had they not all borne the same strange seal at the bottom as the anti-quated vellum.

"What is all of this?" Heath asked.

"I have no idea." Joss said it slowly and without con-viction.

He'd heard that tone from her before. "I don't believe you. You do have an idea, though you just don't want to share it."

"You're going to think it ridiculous." Joss straightened and looked up at him. Heath thought her eyes looked rather feverish in the candlelight.

Heath doubted there was much that would surprise him anymore this night. "Try me."

"This," she said, gesturing at the pair of knights captured forever in ink, "is a Templar seal."

He stared at her before snorting in derision. "You're right. It is ridiculous. Laughably absurd, even. I would have thought you might have invented something more original if you thought to test my intelligence."

"I'm not inventing it." It was hard to read her expression.

He ran his fingers through his hair in exasperation. "And just where do you think you've seen this seal before?"

"Rome. On a handful of documents. And in Scotland. In stone."

"Stamped on a piece of pavement?" He was being difficult, and he knew it.

"Not exactly."

Heath watched as a small muscle worked along her jawline, and he forced himself to take a deep breath. He was tired, filthy, and still unnerved from the events of the last hour, but none of that justified his rudeness to a woman who was doing her best to help. Even if her help was wildly misguided.

Heath gestured at the stack of nonsensical documents. "A Templar seal," he repeated, with an effort to keep his tone from sliding back into impudence. "You are, I must assume, referring to the knights."

"Yes."

"The order that was disbanded and tortured and

executed five hundred years ago and has since been reduced to nothing but a collection of wild legends to entertain fortune hunters and religious lunatics?" He lost his battle with sarcasm.

Joss's eyes narrowed in a way he knew all too well. "You didn't pay enough attention in your history classes," she accused. "In 1307, at the time of the arrests, the order numbered in the thousands. Relatively few were actually arrested and executed. In fact—"

"Stop." Heath rubbed his face with his hands, his eyes feeling gritty and burning with exhaustion. "I can't do this."

"Do what?"

"Go along with this blarney."

Joss crossed her arms over her chest and pinned him with her gaze. "You think I'm making this up?"

"No." Heath sighed wearily. "I think you would very much like this to be some long-lost mystery that you can puzzle over. And while I don't deny that some of those documents are very old, I highly doubt that they contain anything as enticingly nefarious as whatever is swirling around that brain of yours. Joss, this is nothing more than a collection of indecipherable mumble-jumble along with a few dozen letters that describe crop rotations, for God's sake."

Joss's lips thinned. "Worth killing over."

A knock on the door interrupted them, and Joss crossed the room. He could hear her speaking quietly to someone.

Heath turned and stumbled over to a long library sofa and sat down heavily. He stared into the fire, avoiding eye contact with the leering roosters. His aching head felt as if it weighed a hundred stone.

"When I was in Ireland, I saw a number of works like the illuminated pages that are in that folder," Joss said from behind him, making him start. He hadn't heard her return, his mind preoccupied with the conundrum that was the late Gavin Smythe.

He turned slightly. "You were in Ireland? I thought you were in Rome. Or Scotland?"

"I was a lot of places," Joss replied, skirting the sofa. She sat down beside him and held out a steaming mug. "Here. Margaret brought this."

Distracted, he took it from her. The aroma of cinnamon rose, unleashing happy memories of cold, rainy days and a warm, fragrant kitchen. "I don't think I've had warmed milk with cinnamon since I was twelve." He wrapped his fingers around the welcome heat. "It was my favorite."

Joss smiled faintly and sipped from her own mug. "I know."

Heath watched her from over the rim as he brought his own drink to his lips. She had drawn her legs up to her chest, her arms wrapped around her knees. The amber silk of her gown puddled around her, golden in the muted light and making her skin glow. She was lost in thought, her fingers playing absently with the edges of the mug she cradled in them.

Heath had, until this moment, never really stopped to consider where Josephine had been all these years. All he knew was that, when Joss was six, she'd gone to live somewhere else. She'd returned home only during the short summer months, and after she turned fifteen, the summertime sabbaticals had ceased as well. Worth had mentioned something about cousins in Italy, but Heath had never asked further or stopped to wonder why

Joss would have been sent so far away when she was so young.

"Why were you in Ireland?" he asked now.

"To study Irish Gaelic." She didn't look up.

"You speak the language?"

"Yes."

"When were you there?"

"When I was sixteen."

"How many languages do you speak?" he asked suddenly, suspicion brewing.

"A few," she deflected.

"Define *a few*."

"Enough to get around." She hadn't yet looked at him. "Anyway, the reason I brought up Ireland," she said, before he could ask anything else, "was because those writings look very similar. It might help me determine how old they actually are when we examine them further." She jerked her chin in the direction of the desk.

I don't want to talk about the damn papers. I want to talk about you, Heath thought, and it caught him by surprise. "They're written in Gaelic?" he forced himself to ask.

"No." She worried her bottom lip with her teeth. "They're written in code."

"Code?"

"Yes."

"How can you be sure?"

"Because I can't read it." She frowned. "Yet."

Heath pinched the bridge of his nose with his fingers. This was well beyond what his tired mind could manage. He had always taken a great deal of pride in being able to sort through a problem with practical efficiency, but tonight his thoughts kept tumbling together, blurred by fatigue.

There was another knock on the door. Joss unfolded herself from the settee, and Heath regretted the loss of her company instantly. After everything, her presence seemed to steady him somehow.

Or maybe it was just the warm milk.

He watched as she opened the door wider, admitting a man Heath hadn't seen before. The stranger was no older than Heath and was of average height, with dark hair and a cheerful face that was unremarkable and easily forgotten. As he drew closer, Heath noticed bits of coal dust clinging to his warm but simple clothes. A collier then, Heath assumed, though he wondered why he was here. Perhaps he had seen something that could provide some answers.

Heath stood as the man drew near, Joss on his heels.

"Tobias, this is the Earl of Boden." Joss was looking expectantly at Heath, as if he should know this man.

"Good evening," Heath offered by rote.

"Good evening, my lord. And a true pleasure to meet you. Though I would have preferred our introduction could have been made under less unpleasant circumstances." Tobias's voice and inflection in no way matched his appearance. Had he not been dressed as he was, Heath might have pegged him as a barrister.

"I'm sorry. Who are you, exactly?"

"Tobias Darling at your service, my lord."

Heath started. He wasn't sure what he'd been expecting. Some cadaverous creature perhaps, pale and stinking from his nocturnal hunts. A man more comfortable with the dead than the living. Not the confident, articulate man standing before him, who, given the right costume, could just as easily have blended into the House of Commons as the dark alleys of Whitechapel.

Heath made some sort of appropriate noise in response to the man's greeting.

"I understand there are three bodies to collect?"

Joss nodded at Darling. "They're in the narrow lane that connects Berwick to Broad."

"I know it. Just as well we brought the coal cart tonight then, as filthy as it is," Toby muttered, brushing at his clothes in distaste. "They'd never all fit in anything else. We'll head there straightaway."

"The coal cart?" Heath was struggling to follow the conversation.

"A man needs a good excuse to be in the streets in the wee hours driving a cart with a hollow bottom." Tobias smiled faintly before a shadow passed over his face as he turned back to Joss. "I am appalled to think you were in such danger, my lady."

"I had Lord Boden with me. And Luke."

"Indeed." Toby gave Heath a speculative look out of the corner of his eye. "Well, if I can't identify your attackers, I'm confident I can find someone who can."

"At least two of them were French."

"You don't say." Toby tapped his chin. "More challenging, but not impossible. I'll need a day or two to ask around."

"Of course."

"I'll send word as soon as I hear something. You go through their pockets?"

"Luke did. They had nothing on them other than what they were wearing."

"Well, I imagine they'll not even have that by the time

we get there. It's bloody cold outside, and warm clothes are a popular commodity at the moment." The resurrection man grinned and stepped closer to the fire, as if to prove his point. His eye fell on the papers spread on the desk, and he froze.

"Where did you get this?" he asked.

Heath shot Joss a warning look but she was ignoring him. "The unfortunate Gavin Smythe had them on his person when we found him."

Heath frowned. The folder and its contents were not something he had intended to share with anyone.

"I've seen this before," Tobias said, picking up one of the vellum pieces.

Heath edged over to the desk, resisting the urge to gather all the documents up and hide them. It was a foolish reaction, he knew, given no one could read them anyway. "You've seen what?" he asked, probably a bit too sharply.

Darling didn't seem to notice. "This seal, or whatever it is," he said, pointing to the pair of knights at the bottom of the page.

"Where?" Heath demanded. "On another letter? Or a document?"

"On a body."

"A body?" Heath repeated.

"Two, actually. Not even a month ago. Both were tattooed with this same image." He raised his hand and put it at the base of his skull just above the hairline. "Here. We didn't find it until we'd shaved the corpses' heads."

"Good God." Heath was rather suspecting this night would have been easier had he never relinquished his hold on his whiskey.

Darling sniffed at Heath's tone. "Some of our clients pay extra to have their specimens shaved and washed before they are delivered. Not unreasonable considering where we procure them from."

Heath chose to focus on the latter. "Where did the bodies come from? The ones with this marking?"

"From one of the prison hulks anchored at Woolwich. My brother and I have a mutually rewarding relationship with an officer charged with disposing of the dead."

"Prisoners?" Heath asked, his brows drawing together.

"Yes."

"Victims of gaol fever?"

"No. Victims of other prisoners. Murdered."

"Do you know who they were? Or where they came from?"

"No. But there will be records. Those two most likely went through Newgate first if they were at Woolwich. If I can get you the names of those two prisoners, you'll be able to check."

"Please do." There was a possible connection there, Heath knew. A likely connection, even, between a Bow Street Runner and two men incarcerated on a stinking hulk on the Thames, though he was damned if he could begin to imagine at the moment how that knot might ever begin to be unraveled.

The resurrection man glanced at the clock on the desk. "Begging your pardons, I must excuse myself. There's work to be done and dawn is no longer too far off. My brother will be getting impatient."

"Of course." Joss finally spoke as she followed Tobias to the door.

"The man in the hall—Mr. Smythe—was he a good

friend of yours, Lord Boden?" Darling asked suddenly, pausing in the doorway.

Heath looked up, unsure.

"I was just wondering, my lord, if you might wish us to bury him. It wouldn't be in a churchyard, you understand, but we could find somewhere just as peaceful. Probably more so."

Heath blinked, bewildered at the offer from such a man. "Yes."

"I'll see it done," Tobias said, and strangely, Heath believed him.

Joss closed the door behind Darling and came back to the desk, gathering the papers back into the folder.

"You have peculiar friends," Heath muttered.

"Good friends," she corrected. "We are very lucky."

We? Heath thought, rubbing his eyes, too weary to argue that choice of words. "I'm going home now," he said, afraid that if he didn't leave now, he was going to collapse on the rug in front of the fireplace and sleep for a day. He should find a coat, find his horse, and find his own bed, yet somehow those three small tasks seemed like a monumental challenge at the moment.

"I think not," Joss replied pleasantly as she retied the bundle. Flakes of dried blood drifted onto the surface of the desk. "You will sleep here."

"I can't." Heath stared in dismay. "That isn't done. People will invariably find out that I spent the night here, and rumors will start. Servants talk. There is no escaping it."

"You will discover that our staff do not talk. And if the need ever arises, my mother will come up with a suitable excuse as to why you required her hospitality. You're not going anywhere tonight."

Heath was still shaking his head, even though the idea of not having to go back out into the freezing cold was distressingly appealing.

Joss rolled her eyes. "For pity's sake, Hextall, you'll be sleeping in a guest room. Not in my bed."

A vision of Joss, wrapped in soft sheets and nothing else, slammed into him, obliterating whatever lethargy had gripped him. Sleep with this woman would be time wasted in the most criminal manner, he thought with a sudden, shocking conviction. Heath knew exactly what he would do to that lush body of hers and the pleasure he would give her. Pleasure that would accomplish the impossible and render her smart mouth mute. Or maybe not mute. The idea of his name on her lips, whispering and begging, sent a tempest of desire unlike anything he'd experienced ripping through his gut. He actually had to put out a hand on the desk to steady himself.

Bloody hell, but exhaustion was making him delirious.

Though it had been no different in the damn carriage when they had arrived. The feel of her hands sliding over his back under his evening coat had sent the same jolt of lust through him, though at that time, he'd attributed it to the residual effects of their narrow escape. She'd had her head against his chest, thank God, for had she looked up at him in that moment, he might have kissed her senseless and regretted it later. Because this was Joss, for pity's sake. His best friend's little sister. She'd been a child to be tolerated out of loyalty to Worth, and now, as a woman, she was to be respected and kept at an appropriate distance for the exact same reason. Not fantasized about as if she were some sort of courtesan ripe for conquest.

"I can't." He wasn't sure what he was referring to anymore.

Joss made a rude noise. "Who knows how many more are out there, looking for this. Looking for you. There's no need to take foolish risks. Tomorrow will be soon enough to examine these further and make appropriate inquiries based on the conclusions we draw."

Heath tried to find an argument but came up with nothing.

"The guest room is always ready for unexpected visitors," Joss continued brusquely, eroding his resistance. She came to stand directly in front of him, as though she could physically restrain him from leaving.

He wondered what he would do if she did.

Heath took a deep breath. God, but she smelled good. Verbena, laced with a hint of coconut. And perhaps a spice, though that would have been from the warmed milk. His eyes were drawn to her mouth. There was a faint residue of cinnamon along the edge of her top lip and Heath fought the overwhelming urge to lick it from her mouth. He wanted—needed—to know what she would feel like beneath his touch.

Joss was gazing up at him, a faintly puzzled look on her face, those aqua eyes of hers like deep pools, filled with brilliant luminosity. Her hair had fallen over her forehead again in all of its unapologetic beauty, the soft curls inviting a man to thread his fingers through them so that he might tip her head and better control his access to those tantalizing lips. He reached up to brush a curl back again, just as he had done in the carriage.

Only this time he was going to kiss her. He would claim her lips and not stop there. From there he would stake a claim to the rest of her body and discover just how adventurous and bold that mind of hers really was.

His intent must have been written across his face for, in an instant, he saw her expression change and heard her breath hiss in her throat.

He staggered back. What the hell was he doing? What the hell was he thinking?

"I'm sorry. Where is the guest room?" he croaked, needing to get as far away from this woman as possible. Worth would never forgive Heath if he were ever to discover the lewd and lascivious manner in which Heath had been imagining Joss. No amount of alcohol or exhaustion could excuse his complete lack of control.

"Second floor. End of the hall," she said, and he hated himself for the unsteadiness he heard in her voice.

Dammit, but he was an ass. No better than the lecherous bucks skulking around every London ballroom, mentally undressing women with their eyes.

"Thank you and good night, Lady Josephine," he replied, and for the second time that night, he fled from her presence.

❧

Gavin Smythe had disappeared off the face of the earth. Again.

And worse, the documents had vanished with him. It had taken almost five months to track the wily Runner into his foxhole, and he'd finally been flushed, only to vanish without a trace. The Frenchman swore violently, and it echoed off the walls around him.

He had felt confident in his decision to use his own soldiers for the task, certain that the men he had personally selected were loyal, ruthless, and resourceful enough to capture Smythe. And, more important, recover the documents the Runner had disappeared with so many months ago. Yet something had gone terribly wrong.

His soldiers had yet to report, and this morning he'd sent out more men to scour the streets of London for any trace of them, but they, like Smythe, had vanished. Only their rented horses had surfaced, blood smeared on two of the animals' fetlocks. There was no doubt in the Frenchman's mind that those soldiers had met their demise somewhere in the darkness. It was just as well. Failure was unforgivable.

Yet their failure now left him with a bigger problem.

Before his men had left in pursuit of Gavin Smythe, they'd sent word that they'd mortally wounded the man. In fact, the Frenchman was quite certain Smythe was probably dead of his wounds by now. Which meant someone had come to the Runner's aid. Someone had killed his men, concealed the evidence, and helped the Runner and the documents he carried disappear.

Gavin Smythe had not had many friends left in London, on either side of the law. The Frenchman had made sure of that. Yet someone, somewhere, had helped him.

He would find that person, the same way he had found Gavin Smythe and the others. And when he found that person, he would extract the information he needed to achieve the glory his Emperor deserved.

And then he would kill him.

Chapter 5

Since she was a little girl, Joss had known she was different. Dolls had held little interest. Needlework, while it had its practical applications, stifled her with its repetitive monotony. Music had been a satisfying challenge, but Joss had found that she simply didn't possess the passion for it to do true justice to the brilliance of the composers. Mathematics were a delight, though she lacked the creativity to truly excel in the manner some did with their complex abstract theorems and hypotheses.

Languages, on the other hand, had captured her imagination and held it. They were like giant puzzles to be solved and mastered, and she reveled in learning each. There were groups of them that had clearly sprouted from a common base, and those were the easiest to learn. Others seemed creatures unto themselves, with no common denominator, and these were the ones Joss enjoyed the most. The feel of the different sounds on her tongue and the different rhythms and cadences of each. The shapes of the individual characters in alphabets and scripts, like tiny pieces of artwork, which could be linked together to divulge tales and secrets and knowledge.

Like the secrets in the bloodstained folder that was currently hidden, locked away in the spice pantry.

Joss had put it there last night and given Margaret the keys to guard. Not only did she think it was likely the safest hiding place, for she doubted anyone would look in the pantry for important documents, but Joss knew that if they hadn't been inaccessibly locked away she wouldn't have been able to sleep that night. She would have barricaded herself in the study, lit more candles, spread the missives out across the study floor, and pored over them until she had identified the pattern that would unlock their secrets.

And it would serve no one's interests if she was too tired to think clearly. From what Joss had seen thus far, this particular puzzle would likely take her days to solve, not hours. No obvious pattern or code in the illuminated text had immediately jumped out at her, and she did not believe for a second that the letters included in the folder were actually about a farm. There was a message hidden in both sets of documents somewhere, and she would discover what it was. This was not a simple riddle to be enjoyed. A man had died last night protecting whatever mystery it held, and she needed her wits to be sharp. Though sleep had still been a long time coming, and she knew very well it had less to do with the mystery and more to do with the knowledge that the Earl of Boden slept two doors down.

Perhaps it was just the events of the evening that had set emotions running higher and hotter than normal, but in her mother's study last night, Heath had looked at her with undisguised desire. He had wanted her. No, Joss corrected herself, he'd wanted a woman. For the instant he remembered who she was, he'd been horrified.

Try as she might to rationalize it, it still rankled.

"Thank God you're awake," came a voice from the doorway of the dining room.

"And a good morning to you, Mother," Joss replied as she entered the room, grateful to be released from her unwanted preoccupation with the conundrum that was Heath Hextall.

Eleanor, Dowager Duchess of Worth, was already seated at the table, dressed and coiffed impeccably, a cup of tea set next to a London newspaper, but she rose and came around the table to embrace Joss in a fierce hug. "I suppose it is, given the fact that you're still alive." She said it lightly enough, though there was an edge to her tone and worry creased her forehead.

Joss drew back. "I can't say I ever wish to experience that again."

"Good Lord, child, but the account I received from Luke nearly stopped my heart. I couldn't get home fast enough to see for myself that you were all right." All pretense of humor was gone as she resumed her seat.

"I should have waited up for you. I'm sorry." Joss slid into a chair opposite her mother.

The duchess shook her head in dismissal. "Don't be. You were obviously exhausted, and I certainly understand why. I was satisfied looking in on you." She paused. "How are you feeling this morning?"

"Fine," Joss replied, realizing that she was. "And starving." The aroma of bacon and toasted bread was making her mouth water. Joss stood, striding over to the sideboard and filling a plate, aware her mother was watching her closely. "I am also anxious to take another look at the documents that Smythe was carrying," she added as she helped herself to a healthy portion of eggs.

"Yes, Margaret showed them to me. What manner of documents are they?"

"I have no idea. Yet."

"I see. And you don't think that this is something that should be handled by the authorities? Perhaps brought to the attention of a constable or a magistrate?"

"No." Joss returned to her chair and picked up a fork.

The duchess sat back. "Very well, my dear. I trust your judgment."

"Thank you. Though the fact that we fetched the Darling brothers to assist us makes that point rather moot, wouldn't you say? Something about cows and barn doors?"

"Quite true." Her mother paused. "I understand you spent a great deal of time with Lord Boden last night. Not trivializing the tragedy that brought him to our door in the first place, but I must assume he saw and heard far more than was probably ideal once he was here."

Joss winced. "Yes."

"What would you suggest we do about that?"

"I'm not sure we have a choice. I believe we can trust him."

Eleanor patted her white hair. "I think your brother might say the same—" She stopped, and her eyes flickered over Joss's shoulder to the doorway.

Without turning around, Joss knew Heath was standing directly behind her.

"Good morning, Your Grace," he said, sounding every inch the stiff, unyielding earl who had first found her with a Ming vase.

"Good morning. Please have a seat, Lord Boden," the duchess requested. "I believe we do have a fair bit to discuss."

Heath cleared his throat, sounding grim. "Of course, Your Grace. But first I must apologize for any danger I might have inadvertently put your daughter in—"

Eleanor waved her hand impatiently. "From what I was told, Josephine was lucky you were there. Without your bravery, things might have ended much more tragically than they did. There is no need for an apology."

Heath had moved to take the chair beside Joss, and she saw him glance at her sharply. He'd shaved and dressed, the scorched remnants of his evening attire nowhere in sight, though his clothing was clearly on loan from whatever items her brother had left behind over the years. Worth was longer and leaner than Heath, and the linen shirt Heath had donned stretched taut over the breadth of his chest and shoulders. A coat had clearly been out of the question.

"I must ask what your intentions are," Eleanor said.

"I'm not sure of your meaning, Your Grace." He jerked slightly in his seat, and his eyes veered away from Joss.

"Your intentions regarding the situation that resulted in a dead Bow Street Runner in my hall and a pile of mysterious documents locked away in my spice pantry." The duchess was fingering the edge of her spoon. "Do you intend to have any further involvement with the matter? Or would you prefer to let us handle it?"

Heath stared at Eleanor. "I have no intention of placing this burden on you or your daughter. I fully intend to discover what it was that cost Mr. Smythe his life and, if at all possible, see that justice may be served. I made a friend a promise before he died, and I will endeavor to keep my word." There was no uncertainty in his speech.

The duchess considered Heath for a long moment

before her eyes slid over to Joss in silent question. Joss nodded slightly, a mixture of relief and apprehension pricking. Given the circumstances, Heath would need to be made privy to the secrets of the Duchess of Worth's household. Or at least some of them.

"Very good then, Lord Boden. Would you care for a cup of tea? It's already made." The duchess motioned to the pot in front of her. "Though if you would prefer coffee or chocolate, just say the word." Her blue eyes were shrewd and sharp.

"Tea is fine, Your Grace," Heath said slowly, and Joss could only imagine what he might be thinking. The duchess's usual absent expression was missing, and for anyone expecting the vague ramblings that Eleanor had perfected for social settings, the ensuing conversation might be a shock.

Carefully Joss reached over and poured a measure of tea into a waiting cup, setting it down by Heath's elbow.

"I understand you met a number of my staff last night," the duchess began. "As well as certain individuals who have had cause to assist me in matters in the past."

"Yes," Heath replied slowly.

"I am not entirely sure how much information was divulged. However, I know very well that you are an exceedingly clever man, Lord Boden. I have little doubt that you have drawn many, and likely reasonably accurate, conclusions about those individuals."

Heath was frowning fiercely. "You are referring to the fact that your cook, your footman, and your coachman—"

"Butler," Eleanor corrected.

"I beg your pardon?"

"If you are referring to Luke, he is my butler. He's good

with doors. And locks. His brother Joseph is my regular coachman, but Luke insists on driving from time to time. Joseph doesn't usually mind provided he gets the pistols."

Heath blinked.

The duchess took a sip of tea. "I'm sorry, I did not mean to interrupt. You were saying?"

"Only that it is apparent that the members of your staff," Heath forged on, "were not hired by an agency, nor were the positions filled by placing ads in the *Times*."

"No, they were not." Eleanor smiled faintly at Heath before the lines of her mouth hardened. "They are, however, extremely skilled at their duties. I will take exception to anyone who may suggest otherwise. Do you understand, Lord Boden?"

"I believe I am beginning to."

"Excellent." The duchess sat back and gazed at Heath. "How long have you been friends with my son, Lord Boden?" she asked pleasantly.

Heath shifted in his chair beside Joss. "Over twenty-five years, Your Grace."

"And what is the biggest complaint that my son has had about me during that time?"

"I beg your pardon?"

Eleanor smiled, her eyes flashing with amusement. She cocked her head. "My chickens? My absent mind? My obliviousness to the world around me? Or just my general eccentricity?"

"You are mistaken. Your son has had nothing but kind things to say, Your Grace." Heath said it with such smooth conviction that Joss turned to stare at him. Bloody hell, but if she didn't know better, she would have believed him.

Eleanor's white brows arched fractionally. "Now that

is a skill not many men have." She narrowed her eyes at Heath. "The ability to spare another's feelings and make it wholly convincing." She leaned forward again. "Thank you for the effort. But it's the chickens, Lord Boden. Worth has told me more times than I can count how much he hates chickens."

Heath stilled before picking up his cup of tea and taking a slow sip, watching the duchess. Very deliberately he replaced the cup on the table. "As do you. Hate chickens, that is."

Eleanor nodded in approval. "You do not disappoint, Lord Boden."

Joss hid a smile.

"Though you are not entirely correct," her mother continued. "In a wine sauce, with fennel and carrots, chickens are quite delightful."

"Worth has had cause to discover this for himself in the last year," Heath murmured. "That is why he has ceased to complain about the birds altogether."

Eleanor smiled. "Indeed he has. In the last year, my son has had cause to discover a great deal about me and this household that he was previously unaware of. There are many, many people who depend on us and the help we provide when they have nowhere else to turn. Unfortunately, the manner in which we perform this important work is entirely unacceptable to society and, more often than not, against the law. The ridiculous front I maintain is a necessary cover for our endeavors. The more bizarre my behavior, the easier it is to explain away truly peculiar situations."

"Who?" Heath had steepled his fingers before him. "Who comes to you for help?"

"Women," Eleanor said after a pause, giving Heath a hard, direct look. "Those who find themselves trapped in impossible marriages or betrothals where their safety and that of any children they might have is at risk. No matter if they might be the daughter of a tanner... or the sister of an earl."

Joss saw Heath's fingers curl involuntarily as the duchess's words sank in. "Julia?" he asked in a voice so low it was barely audible.

Eleanor held his gaze. "The man your sister was first engaged to was a very dangerous individual, as you suspected. I did what I could, but Julia had a true heroine protecting her. Perhaps one day you will meet the woman who saved your sister's life."

Heath swallowed convulsively. "I didn't know."

Eleanor's eyes softened. "You weren't supposed to know. We don't do this so that we can be recognized and have shiny medals pinned to our chests. The happiness your sister has found in her life now is why we do it."

He folded his hands back on the table in front of him. "Who else?" His voice was rough. "Who else do you help?"

The duchess gave him a crooked smile. "Now that is Worth's story to share. Do believe me when I tell you it was not his choice to keep this from you, for it is I who demand complete secrecy."

"You seem to have a great deal of secrets, Your Grace." Heath seemed to have recovered his composure, and his voice was once again even, his words precise. "Yet I must ask what this has to do with me. Or the matter of Gavin Smythe."

"Ever the businessman." Eleanor tipped her head. "I

am leaving tomorrow—hopefully for no longer than a sennight. There is a...friend with whom a visit is long overdue, and while I am somewhat loath to leave at this juncture, I am afraid it is of a somewhat urgent nature and cannot be avoided. While I am away, my staff is at your disposal, Lord Boden. You will find that they have many useful skills you may need in your search for answers and justice. Josephine will be able to assist you in the matter of the documents."

Heath looked over at Joss, his eyes utterly unreadable. "As I said, I do not wish to involve Lady Josephine in—"

"You may be clever, Lord Boden, but even you cannot do what my daughter can. I would advise you to accept her help if you want to achieve any manner of success."

Heath opened his mouth and then closed it.

"I am already involved," Joss said. "In case you might have forgotten."

"Well, I'm glad that's settled then." The duchess stood. "I'll leave you two to breakfast. I have to see a man about the sale of a diamond, and preferably before the rest of the ton manages to rise from their beds. It's best to avoid any awkward questions. Please let me know if there is anything else you might need before I depart." She patted Joss on the shoulder.

A silence fell as the duchess exited. Joss waited for Heath to say something. However, he remained quiet, drumming his fingers maddeningly on the snowy tablecloth.

Joss sighed and picked up her fork. She didn't pretend to assume he would be satisfied with the answers her mother had provided. But perhaps she could at least address her grumbling stomach before she would be required to address a grumbling earl. She took a large bite of her eggs.

"Did you not think it prudent to mention any of this to me last night?" he asked.

Joss chewed slowly. "Which part?"

"All of it." His words were flat.

"I have been very much absent for the things you wish to know about," she evaded deftly.

"But you did know about them."

"Yes."

His breath whooshed in annoyance. "Then you should have told me."

"You know now. Why dwell on the little details?" She shoved a square of buttered toast in her mouth.

"What else is your mother involved in? What else are you involved in?"

Joss pointed to her mouth and shrugged. Heath scowled and yanked her plate away.

"That's not fair," Joss protested through crumbs.

"Give me answers, and I'll give you your food back."

"That seems rather boorish."

"I prefer *expedient*."

"Fine." Joss sighed, resigned and bemused. "Ask away."

"What the hell are you wearing? Is that a nightgown?"

Joss glanced down at the brilliantly patterned red silk. "Of all the questions, Hextall, this is what you ask me first?"

"It's distracting talking to a woman in a nightgown."

"It's not a nightgown. It's a Chinese robe. And it's comfortable."

"You look ridiculous."

Joss snorted and stared pointedly at his shirt, which was stretched so far across his shoulders that the buttons at the top couldn't be done up. "Glass houses, Hextall."

A muscle jumped in his jaw.

"A piece of preserved peach, please," Joss said pleasantly.

"I'm not giving you anything until you answer my questions, remember?"

"Chinese robe, followed by ridiculous. My answer to your question, followed by your unnecessary comment." She motioned to her plate. "Look alive. Peach."

Heath picked up a fork, speared a small piece of fruit, and held it toward her. Joss reached for it, and he yanked it away.

"Don't be difficult, Hextall."

"I've forgotten how much I enjoyed this."

"What? Tormenting me?"

"Yes."

"You apologized last night for it."

"Perhaps I was hasty. I might be reconsidering."

His mouth was twitching, and Joss would have happily gone without breakfast to keep that wicked glint in his eye for a moment longer.

"If I starve to death, there will be no more answers, you know."

Heath sighed dramatically and held out the piece of peach, still impaled on the tines of the fork, bringing it to her lips. Joss grinned and leaned forward, closing her mouth around the fruit. She met his eyes, intending to make some sort of pithy comment, but whatever words she might have said died unuttered. He was watching her, his eyes hot, the same expression of desire shadowing his features as last night in the study. She became acutely aware of the intimacy of what he was doing, though a team of wild horses couldn't have convinced her to move away. If anything, she wanted to be closer. Wanted more.

"What the hell is going on in here?" thundered a voice from the door.

Joss jerked back at the same time Heath did, the fork clattering to the table and both of them spinning in their chairs toward the doorway. The Duke of Worth stood framed in the entrance, still dressed in his overcoat, his cheeks flushed from the cold. He wore a look of comical disbelief and horror on his face as his eyes went from Joss to Heath and then back again.

"Are you feeding my sister her breakfast, Boden?" Worth demanded incredulously. "In my mother's house?"

"No," Heath objected. "Well, yes. But—"

The duke's eyes bulged as he noticed Heath's attire. "Are you wearing my shirt? What happened to yours?"

Heath frowned. "It got ruined last night—"

"What?"

"It was my fault." Joss tried to insert an explanation. "I had my hands too close under his evening coat when—"

"You had your hands where?" Worth's eyes skidded to her, his mouth gaping slightly.

Joss flushed. Leave it to her brother to jump to the most debauched conclusion. "Oh, for God's sake, it's not like—"

"Are you wearing a nightgown, Josephine?" The duke's fists were clenched at his sides, and he was very carefully avoiding looking at Heath.

"It's not a nightgown," Joss nearly shouted.

"This would be easier if you'd let anyone say more than four words at a time, Worth." Heath's words were clipped and whatever laughter had been evident was long gone.

The duke crossed his arms over his chest, finally turning toward his friend, glowering. "Fine. Explain."

Heath did, though he glossed over the more distressing details with a coolness that Joss envied. He finished and sat back, his face stony.

"And you are both all right?" Worth's dismay was no longer directed at their attire.

"Aside from suffering an ill-fitting shirt along with the rather poor opinion of a duke," Heath growled, "we're fine."

Worth shifted, looking a little embarrassed. "I'm very sorry about that. I lost my head there for a moment. I was seeing things."

Joss forced a chuckle from her throat. "Most certainly. Hextall was only doing what Hextall does best. Torturing me." She glanced at Heath, but he had picked up the fork and was now studying it with intense concentration.

"You're right, of course." The duke cleared his throat, clearly wanting to move on from the topic. "Is there anything I can do about this situation with Smythe? Perhaps I can ask around—"

Heath shook his head. "Thank you, but no. Whatever sinister matter is afoot, I think it would be best if inquiries were made through more subtle channels. The Duke of Worth asking questions is bound to attract attention, and it may not be of the beneficial sort. I would not wish to see your family put in any further danger."

Joss watched as her brother frowned. "Perhaps you're right," he agreed reluctantly after a moment's reflection.

"We have the staff here to help," Joss told him. "Mother insists."

"The staff?" Worth repeated carefully.

"I know your mother prefers her chickens roasted," Heath said without looking up. "She made that quite clear earlier at breakfast."

The duke slumped against the doorframe. "Thank God," he said vehemently. "Keeping the truth from you for the last year nearly killed me. I hope you can forgive me."

Heath looked up at his friend with mild surprise stamped across his features. "Of course. Your first loyalty lies with your family. God knows you've been nothing but discreet when it's come to mine. I must assume whatever confidences your mother asked you to keep are no less important than the ones you've kept on behalf of my own family."

Joss sent both men puzzled looks, but they ignored her.

"A conversation best saved for another time," Heath suggested.

"Indeed." The duke nodded in agreement. "I will tell you my story then, though it's probably best if my wife is with me when I do."

"Why are you here, Worth?" Joss asked, when it was clear neither man would say any more.

"I was escorting my mother to the jeweler," her brother said easily. "We've found that we get a better price in London for rare diamonds when the Duke of Worth hovers in the background." He glanced behind him into the hall and, apparently finding that he wasn't immediately needed, slid into the chair at the end of the table, leaning forward toward Heath. He smiled in satisfied triumph. "Lady Rebecca Dalton."

Joss raised her brows in confusion. "What does she have to do with selling diamonds?"

Worth cast an impatient look in her direction. "Nothing." He focused again on Heath. "That's who Boden will marry."

Joss felt the blood crystallize in her veins. "What are you talking about?"

Her brother ignored her, speaking directly to Heath. "I spent a great deal of time thinking about your dilemma last night. Now, I've had the chance to speak with Lady Rebecca on a few occasions, and I've found her to be intelligent, capable, and courteous. Perhaps not a diamond of the first water, but a handsome woman, nonetheless. And she is available for the taking, this being her third season. I would imagine most men are intimidated by her mind." He sat back in satisfaction. "She's perfect. Exactly what you asked for."

"What you asked for?" It escaped before Joss could stop it, though the slip was nothing compared to the way her stomach had crashed into her toes. She was staring at Heath, though his expression hadn't changed.

The duke turned to her with a chuckle. "What, Boden didn't tell you? He wants a wife, and as soon as possible. A boring one, he says, who will serve as his domestic partner without turning his neatly ordered world upside down." Worth scoffed at the last. "As practical as that may be, it is my duty as his best friend to see that the woman he chooses will bring him at least a soupçon of happiness. That was the whole reason he was at the ball last night—to meet suitably boring and respectable young ladies. Kind of like the opposite of you, Joss." He gave her a good-natured grin.

"No, he didn't mention that." Joss made a heroic effort to keep her voice light. Why should she be so surprised? It made perfect sense. He was already thirty, with an established business and home. It was perfectly reasonable that he should wish to start a family. Why should she be feeling such a crushing disappointment at the idea that Heath would belong to another woman?

Because she wanted him for herself.

And there it was. She'd been clinging to a secret, selfish notion for years, harboring it in the very back of her consciousness, hoping Heath Hextall would one day decide that the annoying little girl who had trailed after him every summer had somehow become the only woman he couldn't live without. But he was looking for a wife.

And Joss would never be anyone's wife. The idea that she might play the role of—what had her brother referred to it as? A *domestic partner*—was enough to make her feet itch to run to the nearest port and sail far, far away. She would rather die than be ensconced as the mistress of a manor, expected to putter away her days applying her mind to rose gardens and menus. But if she truly cared about Heath, the way she told herself she did, she would wish him to be happy. She would be the friend he deserved and, like her brother, do whatever she could to make his wish a reality.

"And do you discount finding love as part of this undertaking?" Joss asked, striving to affect an air of mild interest.

Heath cleared his throat. He replaced the fork that had been in his hand on the table, lining it up with a butter knife. He turned his teacup in its saucer so that the handle pointed toward him, and then changed his mind and set it back the way it had been. "I certainly hope, though I do not expect, that love may grow from a mutual respect and kinship," he said slowly. "I only wish to find common ground from stable, established routines and congenial companionship." He was now studying the embroidery on the edge of the tablecloth.

Congenial companionship? Bloody hell, but that sounded

like the way Joss might describe her relationship with her maid. Or a favored hound.

Worth met her eyes and shrugged in helpless exasperation. "You don't have to do this, you know," he said quietly. "If this is something you no longer want."

"No," Heath said, his voice brusque and all business once again. "I would very much like to pursue a courtship of Lady Rebecca, if she is agreeable."

"You're sure?"

"Absolutely. When will I have the opportunity to meet the lady in question?"

"In that case, I will invite Lady Rebecca and her parents to attend our theater box tonight. You of course will be there, Boden. I am very confident you will like her." The duke sounded immensely pleased with himself.

Joss wanted to bolt. Away from the room, away from clever plans to place the man she wanted into the intelligent, capable, and courteous hands of another woman. Instead she pasted an approving smile on her face. "What a wonderful idea."

Heath didn't even glance at her. "I look forward to meeting her then. Thank you, Worth," he said, though his words were somewhat subdued.

"You're welcome." The duke tipped his head at the sound of his name being called from somewhere out in the hall. He stood, pushing his chair back. "That would be my cue. You must excuse me." He thumped Heath on the back. "Try not to tease my sister overmuch, Boden. She's much more diabolical now than when she was twelve." The duke strode out of the room, whistling.

Joss nearly toppled her chair in an effort to scramble after her brother. "I'll get started on the documents," she mumbled. "Hopefully by the time I have something to show you, one of the Darling brothers will have some more information about the men who killed Smythe. Don't do anything stupid until then."

"Like what?"

Like get married. Joss jammed her chair back under the table. "Like stir up trouble by asking ill-advised questions about French killers or ancient documents. You were absolutely right on that score—we certainly don't want to draw unwanted attention. You need to go to work. Or do whatever it is you would normally do on a normal day. Normal is critical right now."

"Joss—"

"And for God's sake, Hextall, see if Luke can lend you a shirt that fits."

Chapter 6————————

Normalcy had become like a mythical creature to Heath. There were legends of it, a distant memory of what it looked like, and everyone except him seemed to know where one might find it. His only effective method for luring this fantastical beast into the open was his work.

And work, Heath decided as he reached his townhome, was indeed what he would concentrate on today. Work was steady and predictable. Ledgers filled with tallies for coal and tallow and oils and wages. Orders for barrels and new sail canvas. Charts and maps and bills and numbers. All things that could be assembled into nice, neat, orderly arrangements.

The fact that he'd spent the entire ride home checking over his shoulder caused him no little dismay. Heath wasn't sure if he expected to be arrested for the murder of Gavin Smythe or if he expected another band of armed bandits to jump out from behind a building and assault him, demanding to know what he had done with a pile of documents no one could read. It made him irritable either way, for Heath knew very well paranoia was a sentiment that provoked smart men into making stupid decisions.

Equally aggravating was the knowledge that there

was something on the very edge of his consciousness, something that had been niggling at him all morning. He couldn't quite bring it into focus, but he knew it had something to do with Smythe. Something important he should remember, but try as he might, he couldn't force it to the forefront of his mind.

Heath sighed as he strode through his hall and climbed the stairs up to his bedroom. His butler had been nowhere in sight when he'd arrived home so he'd kept his coat on and now he was glad of it. The temperature in his house was positively frigid. Had no one bothered to light a fire since he'd left last night? He passed a small table at the top of the stairs that boasted a flower arrangement, though the blooms had long since wilted in their vase, abandoning their petals onto the dusty surface. He wondered if they'd simply frozen, and in the next instant, he wondered why he needed flowers in his house in December in the first place.

It wasn't as if he appreciated them. Though if he had a wife, she might.

Lady Rebecca Dalton.

Heath cautiously turned the idea that she might be a suitable wife over in his mind. Worth's pronouncement that morning had come as a bit of a shock, mostly because Heath had somehow managed to forget that he had gone to that ball in an attempt to find a wife in the first place. Instead he'd been distracted, quite legitimately, by the disturbing events that had occurred after he'd left the ball, and then, less legitimately, by Josephine Somerhall.

Joss was like a vortex, a whirlwind of energy and wit and magnetism that drew him in despite his best efforts to remain distant. She incited him beyond reason with her flashing eyes and quick smile and smart tongue. He'd stolen her food this morning, for God's sake. As if he were a boy of ten all over again and not an adult who had spent these last years perfecting restraint and respectability. And then, if that wasn't bad enough, he'd made the mistake of feeding her, an act of the most sensual nature that had set his pulse pounding and his groin tightening. Bloody hell, but Worth would have been justified calling him out for that.

Already furious with himself for his lack of control, Heath rummaged in his dressing room, cursing his newly absent valet. He had no idea why he'd ever hired one in the first place, since he'd been capable of dressing himself since he was two. And now the man had secreted his cravats somewhere that defied any sort of logic. He gave up and stalked through his bedroom and down the stairs to the small room he used as a study.

Lady Rebecca Dalton. He tested her name again as though saying it multiple times might make it seem more real. More attainable.

He'd never met her, but he knew Lady Rebecca was the eldest of five daughters belonging to the Earl and Countess of Dalton. The Dalton title was an old one, steeped in a rich history of service to militia and monarchs, and it was something the current earl took an immense amount of pride in. Not that Heath cared overmuch which of their ancestors had backed the right king at the right time, but the entire family, daughters included, were flawless representatives of the decorum and politesse expected from the aristocracy.

At the very least, she wouldn't be caught at a ball with a Ming vase between her legs.

Perhaps Worth did know what he was talking about. Perhaps she might consider his suit. If the match was facilitated by a duke, her father would be pleased. The fact that Heath was uninterested in a dowry of any sort would be just as pleasing for a couple with five daughters. And if Lady Rebecca was as intelligent and as capable as Worth had said, then Heath would be pleased too. A satisfactory situation all around.

Heath made a face. Why, then, did he feel so dissatisfied?

With weary movements he gathered up a collection of newspapers and letters he needed to review that had accumulated while he'd been in Liverpool. He desperately needed a respite from the entire debacle that had resulted from his ill-advised decision to attend the Baustenburys' ball. To think that yesterday morning he'd woken up blissfully ignorant of villains and plots and secrets and women, and he hadn't truly appreciated just how fortunate he'd been.

⁓

Heath kept an office in the warehouse space he owned near the London Docks and was there at least twice a week, whenever he wasn't traveling on business. It was small and cramped but had the benefit of being perched on the Thames, still the avenue by which a great deal of raw materials were imported, and large amounts of his soft soap were still shipped up- and downriver. The factories themselves sat just outside London, operating under the careful eye of a handful of reliable foremen selected by Heath to manage the day-to-day operations of production during his frequent absences.

As Heath climbed the narrow stairs to his office, the

familiar and expected smells of industry went a long way to help settle his nerves. There was, of course, the rather foul stench from the Thames that permeated everything, though the wind was blowing in a favorable direction today and carrying the worst of it away. Layered on top of that was the aroma of decaying wood, turpentine, and coal dust. There was a decided and welcome absence of gunpowder, blood, and verbena. And thus far, a lack of evidence anyone had followed him here.

Perhaps the day was looking up after all.

Heath strode into his small office space, expecting to find his chief overseer in his usual chair. The office was empty. Hmmph. He was not off to a good start.

Heath wandered over to his own desk, eyeing the stack of correspondence awaiting his attention. He didn't want to delve too deep into anything until he had had a chance to speak with his— The sound of booted feet hurrying up the stairs interrupted his thought.

A second later the door burst open, and a windblown man entered.

"Mr. Bennett," Heath said, "I can't tell you how happy I am to see you." The first normal, expected occurrence in twenty-four hours.

"It's good to see you back as well, Lord Boden." Bennett look startled to see him.

"Were you just returning from the docks?"

The man blinked and ran a hand through his dark hair. "Er, yes. The docks. Coming back."

Heath frowned. "Are you quite all right, Mr. Bennett? You seem a little on edge."

His overseer cleared his throat. "Never better, my lord. How were things in Liverpool?"

Heath let it slide.

"Busy. And very promising. The paperwork was completed for the purchase of the *Julliard* before I returned to London."

"She's in good condition then?"

Heath yanked at the scarf around his neck. "Much better than the price led us to believe. More the victim of an owner with an unfortunate penchant for dice and gin than anything the sea might throw at her. The repairs required are of a cosmetic nature and have very little impact on her seaworthiness."

"And the owner was unaware of this?"

Heath held out his hands. "If he was aware, he didn't seem to care. But he was in a deuced hurry to get his hands on my money. Any money, and as soon as possible."

Bennett grinned. "Well, then let's make sure the man gets his money. I'll see to the bank details today. That tub you have listing here on the Thames doesn't have another voyage in her."

"That tub was my very first ship," Heath said. "And she's served me well. I'll be sad to see the *Amelia Rose* broken up."

"I'd be sadder to see her go to the bottom of the Atlantic in a rough sea filled with cargo," Bennett said pointedly.

"Very true," Heath agreed. His overseer was nothing if not pragmatic.

He'd come to rely on Bennett heavily in the last years, so much so that he fully intended to appoint the man overseer of his entire American operation in Boston by the beginning of next year. Bennett had started working for Heath's father as an eleven-year-old and had learned the business from the ground up. Long before Heath had assumed control of the family business, he'd been aware of Bennett's shrewd attention to detail and his ability to root out inefficiencies. As much as he would be loath to lose him and his expertise in London, there was no one he trusted more.

Heath hesitated, feeling foolish, but asked anyway. "I don't suppose anything unusual has happened around here this morning?"

"Unusual?" Bennett gave Heath a wary look. "Not that I am aware of. Is there something—"

"Never mind," Heath said quickly. "Tell me what I should know about things that happened while I was away."

"You didn't miss much," Bennett said, ticking off items on the fingers of one ham-size hand. Years of demanding physical labor had turned him into a veritable monster of muscle. "One of the vats in the south building started leaking, and we had to shut it down for two days while it was repaired. I hired the additional cooper you requested. We got a new price for coconut oil, which you'll find on your desk. The supplier brought three barrels of it for you to inspect. I put them in the warehouse." Bennett shrugged. "Nothing else of note. Boring stuff, my lord."

"God, but I like boring," Heath said vehemently.

"Just so," Bennett agreed. "You want to take a look at that oil now, or later?"

"No time like the present." Heath paused. "May I ask you a question, Bennett?"

"Of course, my lord."

"Why aren't you married?" He had no idea what had

possessed him to ask that, or what he hoped to gain from the man's answer.

Bennett's dark eyes widened before they darted furtively away from Heath's. "You're asking some very strange questions today, my lord. Did something happen in Liverpool?"

"Not at all. I'm merely curious." Heath forced a smile but it felt more like a grimace. "You're about the same age as me. You have an excellent vocation. I certainly pay you well, though God knows it's probably not enough on some days. You're not missing any limbs, and you're quite intelligent. Why aren't you married?"

Bennett looked as though he wished the floor would swallow him whole. Which was odd, because Heath had seen the normally even-tempered man flustered at only one other time. And that had been when one of their largest storage sheds had caught fire.

"Not for lack of trying, my lord," Bennett mumbled.

"Ah. So you're courting a lass. One that you would take as a wife. But she hasn't yet agreed."

A muscle worked along the giant's jaw. "It's complicated."

Heath snorted sympathetically. "Isn't it always?" He considered Bennett. "Would it help if I put in a kind word on your behalf with your intended? You could introduce me to—"

"No!"

Heath blinked.

"What I mean to say, my lord, is that I appreciate your kindness and your offer. But I'm afraid it won't make any difference."

Heath studied his overseer. Bloody hell, but the man was sweating. If he'd thought to find reassurance and encouragement somewhere in this conversation on the matter of matrimony, he had erred very badly. "Well, let me know if you change your mind."

"Yes, my lord. Thank you, my lord."

An uncomfortable silence fell. Heath bent to pick up a newspaper that had slid from the pile on his desk onto the floor. His eye fell on the headline that shouted out the discovery of a corrupt city marshal. Heath froze, the subconscious memory that had been nagging at him all morning suddenly finding purchase.

"I need to leave," Heath blurted. He threw the paper back in the direction of the desk and missed it completely. The pages scattered haphazardly across the floor.

"But you just got here."

Bennett was giving him a look that rested somewhere between concern and bafflement, but Heath was already striding toward the door. If he hurried, he would be there before noon.

~

Heath was an exceptional card player. He didn't gamble often, but when he did, he almost always won. He was a student of body language, paying as much attention to the subtle nuances and expressions of his opponent as to the cards in his hand. People gave away their secrets unawares, and Heath had capitalized on that both in leisure and in business many times.

And at least one of the two Runners standing opposite him in the Bow Street offices had secrets. It had become obvious the moment Heath had strode in, introduced himself, and asked to speak with Gavin Smythe.

"Is there a reason you need to speak with Mr. Smythe?"

the older officer asked, and Heath watched as the man's eyes shuttered even as he removed the antique pipe from his mouth with a deliberate casualness. The scent of tobacco in the small room was overpowering.

The other officer was younger, a pair of spectacles balanced on the bridge of his nose and a battered hat pulled down over his forehead. He'd been reading a page from a thick stack of reports on the desk in front of him, but he'd abandoned his task the moment Smythe's name was mentioned and was now watching the earl with interest.

"I need him to work for me again." Heath put a good amount of pomposity into his response, even as he studied the older man. He would have to tread carefully here. Smythe's warning that someone among his Bow Street colleagues had betrayed him in some manner was still very fresh in his memory.

"Indeed? Mr. Smythe has had cause to work for you previously?"

"Yes." There was no point in trying to hide what would be a matter of public record, but the fact that this officer was asking about it was interesting. "Is he available or not? I don't have all day." He scowled in a show of impatience.

"Mr. Smythe no longer works for this office," the younger officer with the spectacles piped up.

"Since when?" Heath demanded.

"Since he was arrested in June." The bespectacled man seemed delighted to impart such delicious gossip. His colleague shot him a look of irritation.

"Arrested?" Heath had suspected, but his surprise wasn't entirely feigned. "For what?"

"For thievery."

"Bloody hell." Heath made a noise of disgust.

"It is never commendable to be forced to arrest one of our own." The older man sounded distinctly uncomfortable.

"And to think I paid a criminal good coin."

"It is indeed an unfortunate stain on the good name of these offices."

"Well, I hope he's rotting in a prison somewhere then. Or did they just hang him?"

Spectacles leaned forward. "Neither. He es—"

"Was released," the older officer interrupted loudly, and his partner stared at him, clearly perplexed.

"Released? Why? He was innocent?" Heath deliberately ignored the gaffe.

"There was not enough evidence to support the charge and he, ah, went free. But he is no longer fit to work in these offices."

"I see."

The officer's expression became one of calculation. "I don't suppose you've heard from him recently? Or seen him?"

Heath frowned. "Would I be here if I had?" He slapped his gloves on the side of his leg in irritation. "He would find no recourse with me. I have a business to run, and one that does not benefit from tolerance or lenience towards criminals. Believe me, you'll be the first to know if that bounder shows his face anywhere near me or my possessions."

"Indeed. That would be appreciated." It came with another assessing stare.

"His family must be ashamed," Heath suggested carefully. He had discovered nothing about Smythe's brother, though if anyone knew something, the men who used to work with him daily might.

"We have been unable to locate any family. You are familiar with these individuals?" The question was too quick and too sharp.

Alarms were sounding in Heath's brain. "Of course not," he scoffed carelessly. "I don't particularly care about Gavin Smythe. But I do have a problem with theft at one of my factories. I can assure you, I pay exceedingly well. Is there another officer who would be available for hire? Or am I wasting my time?"

Spectacles opened his mouth eagerly, but was once again cut off.

"I'm quite certain that there is another officer who would be available and willing to look into the matter," the officer intoned. "I would do it myself, but unfortunately, I am scheduled to be away from London for the next few days. If you care to wait, I shall have someone fetched for you, or perhaps you'd prefer to return this afternoon."

Heath pulled his timepiece out of his pocket with a sound of dissatisfaction. "I'll have my overseer stop by later today. I do not have time to wait." Heath slid his gloves back on, settled his hat on his head, and nodded at the two men. "Good day."

Heath exited the building and chose a direction in which the foot traffic was thin. He'd be easier to spot this way, he reasoned, walking slowly along the pavement. He hadn't made it to the first corner when Spectacles caught up with him. Heath smiled inwardly in grim satisfaction.

"My lord!" The man was hurrying after him, his unbuttoned coat flapping in the wind.

Heath turned and fixed the man with an expectant look.

"If you're still looking for an officer for hire, I would be available," the man puffed, coming to a stop.

"That was not the impression I was given," Heath replied coolly.

"Just ignore old Potter," he said, waving his hand in annoyance. "He hasn't been himself these last months. I think he's taken Gavin Smythe's arrest harder than the rest of us."

"Oh? Why is that?"

"He was the one who arrested him. A bad business, all of it."

"Because Mr. Smythe escaped?"

Spectacles looked startled. "How did you know that?"

"Your Mr. Potter was quite interested in if I had seen him recently. And if I had any knowledge of his family. I was left wondering why there was still such interest."

Spectacles gave him an assessing look, though not without approval, then lowered his voice as though he were preparing to impart Crown secrets. "I shouldn't be telling you any of this, but I must confess I still find it hard to believe Mr. Smythe was guilty."

Heath was inclined to agree. "Were you here the day Mr. Smythe was arrested?" he asked, not sure what he was after.

"No, Potter had sent me out to make an arrest that day. In fact, there were a number of us sent after three other dastardly thieves who had fled London." The officer's chest puffed out slightly. "But we prevailed. No matter how far they run, we always get our man."

Heath nodded with what he hoped was an expression of suitable regard.

"Perhaps you'll keep me in mind if you need assistance in the future?" the officer prompted. "I have an excellent record of success." He reached into his coat and pulled out a small card, similar to one a gentleman might leave while calling. *Edmund Banks*, it read, *Officer of the Bow Street Foot Patrol*.

"Absolutely," Heath said, tucking the card in his pocket. "I'll be in touch."

"Very good, my lord."

Heath spun on his heel and set off down the street, feeling the officer's eyes on his back as he went.

This was starting to get complicated.

⁓

Bloody hell, but this was complicated.

There weren't many codes that had stumped her in the past, but this one was certainly threatening to. Usually the pattern became obvious when mathematics were applied to the text. Numerically rank words or letters, group words with a common denominator and words with a specific arrangement or quantity of letters eventually revealed their secrets. Joss had focused on the oldest documents first, knowing they would most likely be the toughest, and so far that was the only thing she'd been correct about.

She groaned and stretched, realizing with a start that the day had slipped away. She vaguely recalled the shadows lengthening and someone coming in to silently light the candles, but she had been so engrossed in what she'd been doing she'd barely noticed. Her eyes were gritty, her head stuffy, her hair unattended to, and her fingers stained with ink. What she needed right now was—

"My lady, Lord Boden is here to see you."

Joss jumped, and she nearly upset the inkpot at her elbow. She grabbed it before it could tip and righted it with great care.

"Thank you, Luke." Did her heart have to skip every time the blasted man's name was mentioned? She'd gone the entire day with a normal pulse, but then again, she'd been well and truly distracted.

"I'll show him in—"

"No need." Heath was already pushing past the butler, his coat hanging open and what looked like a folded newspaper in his hands.

Luke shrugged and disappeared. Joss watched as Heath shrugged out of his heavy coat and dumped it over the back of an embroidered wing chair. His movements were hurried, as though he knew something of great import that was just waiting to burst forth.

"I woke up this morning trying to remember what I had forgotten," he said, coming over to stand near the desk.

"That makes absolutely no sense, Hextall." Joss was trying not to notice that Heath was impeccably dressed in evening wear again, his blond hair and blue eyes vivid against the dark relief of his clothes. She resisted the absurd urge to smooth her own hair and straighten her dress. As if anyone in this room besides her cared that she probably looked like a shipwreck survivor.

Heath paused long enough to eye the mess of documents and papers scattered across the desk's surface. "How did you fare today?"

"Not as well as you, obviously." She tried not to sound defensive. "It's complicated."

Heath might have smiled. "You don't say." He put an old issue of a newssheet in her hands. "I have something you might want to see." He was watching her expectantly.

Joss examined the paper. "A copy of the *Times*?"

"When I hired Smythe to look into the thefts from my

London warehouses, I had almost given up hope of ever getting any of my stolen goods back. Yet within a week, he'd recovered all of it. He was never anything but respectful and forthright with me, and I genuinely liked him. This summer, in some coffeehouse somewhere, I heard a rumor that a corrupt Bow Street officer had been arrested. It never occurred to me that it might be Gavin Smythe, and I dismissed the rumor out of hand, never giving that conversation another thought. Until now." He paused. "Read the article in the bottom left corner."

Joss glanced down, reading from the page. "It says that Gavin Smythe, formerly of the Bow Street Foot Patrol, was arrested this past June on a charge of thievery. Trial and sentencing are to follow."

"But he escaped sometime after his arrest."

Joss blinked. "How, exactly, did you determine this?"

"I went to the Bow Street offices and asked to speak to Gavin Smythe."

Joss looked at him in horror. "Was that wise?"

"Oh, for the love of God," Heath snapped. "Give me some credit. I went looking for a man to hire for some fictitious problem with one of my factories. Smythe worked for me before—that will be on record with the Runners. It isn't a stretch to think I would wish to do so again. If someone in those offices betrayed him, I want to know why. And how."

"Do you think Smythe was guilty?" she asked with interest.

"No, I don't." He snatched the paper back out of her hands.

"You think he was falsely accused?"

"That seems more likely. And maybe his brother has evidence to prove his innocence."

Joss digested that. "Regardless if he was innocent or guilty, the accusation would be damning. Perhaps I should take a look at the Newgate records tomorrow. There might be some more answers there. I could go first thing."

"Not by yourself you won't."

Joss made a face. "Why not?"

"Because it's not safe."

Joss laughed, something warm rising in her chest at his chivalry, however unnecessary it was. "The wharves of Bombay weren't safe either, yet here I stand."

"We're not in Bombay," Heath bit out. "We're in London, and I will accompany you anytime you feel the need to wander anywhere in the vicinity of Newgate." He stopped. "When were you in Bombay?"

"Two years ago," Joss replied, pushing out of her chair. She was getting a crick in her neck looking up at Heath.

"Doing what?"

"Translating, mostly." She leaned back against the edge of the desk and rolled her head from side to side, trying to loosen her muscles. "You would like it there, even though the heat can be something that defies description. It's a deepwater port, and the textiles they produce and export are like nothing you've ever seen. And then there are the spices, and the coffees, and the jewelry. You could sail your ships right in and load them up with all manner of exotic goods."

He studied her, as though he were seeing her for the first time. "Who were you translating for?"

"Initially the Marquess of Hastings. I was one of the many individuals who went with him to Calcutta when he became governor-general of India. Later on the East India Company became my full-time employer."

"Why?"

"Because I speak, read, and write a great number of languages. And because I'm a woman and I can often use that to my advantage, or to the advantage of my employers. There are a great number of men the world over who have left their tongues unguarded in my presence because they only see what they wish, an accessory brought to a ball or a card game or a dinner party with no other purpose than to smile prettily."

"You hire your linguistic talents out for money as a...spy?"

"A girl's got to eat." She gave him a wry smile. "And I don't spy, I simply listen."

"But surely your mother—"

"Uses her money for those who need it far more than I." Joss shrugged. "All this"—she gestured at the luxury around her—"is wonderful, and I am exceedingly grateful for the privileges it has afforded me. But material things can never replace the pleasure derived from knowing you need never be dependent on anyone for your survival. The knowledge that your freedom is a direct reflection of your own skill and aspirations. You of all people should be familiar with that, given what success you have built here in London."

Heath's face had inexplicably taken on that closed, remote countenance she despised so much. "Freedom is a casualty of success," he said. "It's cost me mine."

Joss stared at him in fascination. "Jesus, Hextall, but you sound like a bitter old man whose life is over before it's even begun."

His eyes met hers, a stormy, anguished blue. "Some days it feels that way."

The naked vulnerability in his words caught her off guard. "Why?"

"My father was a good father. But he suffered bouts of melancholy. Disinterest. Increasingly long periods of time when he would simply rattle about the house with no apparent purpose and unable to make even the simplest of decisions. By the time I was nineteen, I had assumed full control of the family business out of necessity. When the earldom fell into our laps, my father seemed to rally, adopting the title and the responsibility as his own. Except he never divulged to me, or anyone else for that matter, that the earldom was on the brink of dissolving under the weight of staggering debt. After he died, it was left to me to sort out the disorder." He paused. "As you pointed out, I have achieved remarkable success managing both the business and the earldom. But there was simply no other choice. My life was decided for me before I understood that."

"And if you'd had a choice? What would you have done differently?"

Heath shrugged helplessly. "I don't know." He stopped and took a deep breath. "I'm sorry," he said abruptly. "You're absolutely right. I sound like an ungrateful wretch. I have more than I could ever want or need. So much to be thankful for in my life."

Joss watched him, wanting to smooth the troubled lines from his forehead. "I once knew a boy who told me, when he was grown up, he would become a pirate king and sail his own ship to the four corners of the world in search of treasure," she said quietly.

His mouth twisted but his eyes remained hard. "That boy grew up. And discovered that there were no such things as pirate kings, and no time to search for treasure."

"Yet that boy now owns his own ships."

"He does."

"And what stops him from sailing them where he pleases? What stops him from doing and taking what he truly wants?"

His eyes caught hers and held them trapped within their brilliant blue heat. The remoteness was gone, replaced by a sudden predatory hunger that made Joss swallow convulsively. Her breath stuttered, anticipation and desire roaring to life and sending frissons of longing pulsing through her. The question she'd flung at Heath was swirling around in her brain now, demanding an honest answer from her own conscience.

What was stopping her from taking what she truly wanted? Because what she wanted was standing before her in perfectly tailored evening clothes, his hands clenched around a pile of newspapers, looking at her with such raw covetousness that it was making her nearly drunk with a reckless want.

"Perhaps one day I'll take you there," she said into the sudden silence.

Heath stilled. "To Bombay?"

"To start." She'd meant it to sound like a jest, but it came out as an invitation. "I could take you a lot of places." Holy hell, but what was she doing?

Heath seemed to have stopped breathing, though he took a step closer, his scent enveloping her. Instantly her mouth went dry, and a steady throb built in her belly. She squirmed, but she was backed against the desk and had nowhere to go. Sanity was rapidly disintegrating around her, crumbling beneath an overwhelming ache to touch this man. To have him touch her.

"Of course I don't have my own ships, so I'd have to

hitch a ride on one of yours." She barely recognized herself. There were reasons why she shouldn't do this, she knew. She just couldn't think of one right now.

Heath's expression shifted suddenly, as if something within him had given way. He took another half step closer, close enough that he was pressed against her skirts now, the hard steel of his legs nudging hers apart so that he dominated her space and trapped her against him. He dropped the newspaper carelessly and braced his hands on the edge of the desk on either side of her waist, bringing his lips a breath away from hers.

"Would you take me?" she whispered, and neither of them could pretend she was still talking about ships.

"Yes," Heath rasped.

And then he kissed her.

His mouth brushed hers, a lingering touch that sent needles of sensation darting through her body. His kiss spoke of restraint and the promise of something far more untamed, leashed only for the moment. Joss's eyes drifted closed, every nerve ending focused on the feel of his mouth. Heath stopped, pulling back slightly. She opened her eyes, finding his blue ones intent on her, hot with desire, waiting for her to choose what would happen next. She brought a hand up to his cheek, his skin newly shaven and smooth beneath her touch.

Joss slipped her hand around the nape of his neck and tilted her head up, finding the underside of his jaw with her lips, the uniquely male scent of soap and sandalwood and starch clouding whatever sense she might possess. She worked her way along the edge of his jaw, teasing and exploring, finally finding the hollow at the base of his throat. Heath's breath was now coming in a shallow, erratic rhythm, and his fingers left the desk and went to her hair, curling into her scalp.

She shuddered.

Heath made a low sound in his throat and pulled away, only to bring his mouth to hers in a kiss that no longer spoke of restraint. Now his lips were demanding and relentless, and he was taking what he wanted in a manner that left her little doubt as to his intentions. Her other hand slid around his neck and she pulled herself against him, feeling his arousal where he had her pinned against the desk. It was just as well she was wedged like this against him, because she wasn't entirely sure that her legs would have still supported her.

He was exploring her mouth now with more deliberation, his tongue teasing and challenging while his hands dropped to caress her back. His fingers trailed slowly down her spine before spanning her hips and traveling up her rib cage. He traced the edge of her bodice, brushing his thumbs over the fabric covering the peaks of her breasts, and she arched into his touch.

Heath made a noise of approval and dropped his mouth to her collarbone, leaving a trail of fiery kisses along the top of her chest. Her hands tangled in his hair, urging him lower, desperately wanting to feel his mouth where his fingers had just been.

Somewhere in the house a door slammed with a force that shook the walls.

Heath stumbled back, breathing hard. Joss grasped the edge of the desk for support, her lips swollen, her eyes heavy, and her body sluggish with unfulfilled desire. She was having trouble formulating a sentence. She was having trouble thinking at all.

"The theater," Heath breathed. "Bloody hell." He looked as disoriented as she felt.

"What?" she asked.

"I told Worth I'd meet him here so that I may share his carriage to the Drury Lane Theatre."

To meet Lady Rebecca Dalton and her parents. That hung between them, unsaid.

Joss felt an icy lump form in her chest and lodge somewhere in the back of her throat, choking and suffocating.

"Your brother has arrived, Lady Josephine," Luke said from the doorway.

Joss cleared her throat, forcing her brain to start working through the haze. "Is everything all right, Luke? We heard a commotion."

"Ah," the golden butler said placidly. "You are referring to the door. I'm afraid it got away on me." He looked pointedly between Heath and Joss. "My apologies if it disturbed you before His Grace did."

Joss could feel herself flush furiously. "Thank you, Luke," she managed, and the butler might have given her a sympathetic look as he left.

Heath blew out a breath. "I don't know what came over me. Joss, I'm so sorry—"

"Don't say it." She cut him off, unable to look at him and unwilling to hear an apology for something she'd never truly be sorry for. Even knowing how unwise it had been.

"It won't happen again."

"No," she agreed. "It won't."

Heath flinched.

"You want a wife, Hextall," Joss said, trying to keep the emotion out of her voice. She was saying this as much for Heath as for herself. "If you are committed to pursuing Lady Rebecca or any other woman, then it's not fair to anyone to be dallying with me on the side. I will certainly never be anyone's wife, and I don't like the idea of being a temporary diversion until a suitable bride can be found."

Heath ran his hands through his hair with jerky movements as though he were searching for a response. "You're not—"

"Ah, there you are, Boden." Worth strode into the room with brisk purpose, taking in Heath's attire with approval. "You look splendid. Even old Dalton won't be able to find fault. Though you might want to attend to your hair. It looks a little mussed."

Joss felt another wave of heat rush to her face.

Her brother turned to her, his expression changing to one of dismay. "Why aren't you dressed?"

Joss looked down at her gown in confusion. "I most certainly am dressed."

"For the theater," Worth said with exasperation. "Even you cannot get away with dressing like a scullery maid for an opening night."

Joss looked at him in horror. "Oh no. I'm not going to the theater." Beside the duke, Heath looked equally aghast.

"Yes, you are. These things work better if they're done as couples. The Earl and Countess of Dalton. Boden and Lady Rebecca." He tapped a long finger on her shoulder. "And you will be my other half tonight. As soon as you're dressed."

Joss would rather have pulled her fingernails out one by one than subject herself to an entire evening of watching Heath and Lady Rebecca together as a couple.

"Where's Jenna? She's your wife. Isn't this a wifely duty?" God, but she could barely say the word *wife* without feeling slightly ill.

"She left this morning with Mother." The duke pinned her with a stern gaze. "When I sent the invitation to the Daltons, I indicated you would be in attendance. Is there a problem now?"

Yes, she wanted to snipe. *And the problem just kissed me senseless.*

"Joss?"

She could plead a headache. Indigestion. A sudden flare-up of some debilitating tropical disease. The coward's way out.

"No," Joss mumbled. She wasn't a sulky, resentful child whose favorite treasure had just been snatched away. She was an adult whose duty was to maintain an open mind and a generous heart, and, above all, to support the people in her life for whom she cared the most. Even if it was at odds with her own selfish desires.

"I beg your pardon?" Her brother was tapping the toe of his boot impatiently.

"No," Joss repeated, lifting her chin. "There is no problem at all."

The duke nodded. "Good. You have ten minutes to get changed."

⌒

The Bow Street Runner ducked into the tiny tavern, his eyes scanning the smoky room. The French general was already there, sitting alone at a table and looking every bit as dangerous as the officer knew him to be. He didn't particularly like the Frenchman but believed in what he was doing. A unified Europe under the true Emperor was in the best interest of everyone, everywhere. No greedy kings and their minions living off the backs of hard-working men who had built their respective countries from the ground up. Things were changing, and one could either lead that change or be trampled by it. Revolutions were not borne on the backs of passive bystanders.

With that thought Potter straightened his shoulders and threaded his way through the crowd, sliding onto a bench across from the man.

"I had a visitor today," he said. The general did not like prevarication.

"Indeed?"

"The Earl of Boden. Asking about Gavin Smythe."

"Indeed?" The general was watching him under hooded lids. "And what did this earl want with Smythe?"

"Wanted to know if he was available for hire."

The Frenchman frowned. "For hire? Tell me why this is important."

"The timing is rather suspect, don't you agree?"

The general sneered. "If this earl is asking, then it would seem this aristocrat is ignorant of Smythe's arrest and disappearance, yes?" It was more of an accusation than a comment. "This is of no interest to me. You know I do not like to be bothered by things that do not interest me."

The officer felt a spurt of irritation at the man's arrogance. Potter wasn't one of his French lackeys, remnants of the dissolved Grand Armée that the Frenchman had brought with him when he'd arrived on the shores of England. True, the Frenchman might be their appointed leader, but this was England, not France. The French-man did not have access to the resources Potter did in the streets and in the courts. The Frenchman could not manipulate English law as deftly as a Bow Street officer. Potter had made things happen, and without him, their cause would have stalled long ago. And the Frenchman would be wise to remember that.

"The fact that your men let Gavin Smythe escape again should be of interest to you," he said testily. "You should have let me handle that."

The Frenchman's mouth drew into a hard line. "My men are loyal."

"Your men are idiots." Potter was tired of taking orders from a man who had no respect for him or the work he had done for him thus far. "Clearly they ignored my caution and underestimated the resources Smythe still had. And now both he and the documents are gone."

The general grunted, clearly displeased with the reminder.

The officer was on a roll. "Just like the other three prisoners. If you had let me handle that, we would have had answers, not corpses. Your soldiers are barbarians. Interrogation is a skill, not a back-alley skirmish."

The Frenchman leaned forward aggressively. "I do not like what you imply."

"I'm not implying anything. I'm simply telling you, if you had left it to me, I believe we would already have the documents or the gold in our possession."

"The same way you believe an aristocrat looking for Gavin Smythe so he can recover some stolen bauble is of any consequence." It was said with scorn. The general picked up his mug of ale in dismissal.

Potter tamped down his temper. The man was argumentative at the best of times, and he should have been used to dealing with it by now. "I looked into our records and discovered that Smythe has worked for the Earl of Boden before. Multiple times."

The Frenchman's ale paused halfway to his mouth. "Go on."

"The Earl of Boden is in the import and export business, amongst other things. He owns a warehouse on the London Docks. And ships. Enough ships to transport a heavy cargo."

"Now that," the French general said, "is interesting."

Chapter 7

Lord Dalton was silver-haired and portly, and carried himself with a severe, rigid posture that would have made any general proud. His wife was equally regal, her gown and her coiffure the very latest in French fashion. Upon introductions, the countess's eyes focused first on the duke as etiquette demanded, settled briefly on Joss, and then swept Heath from head to toe and back again, as if searching for flaws. Joss resisted the urge to whack the countess with her fan, if only to interrupt the imperious woman's evaluation of Heath, as if he were a bloody stud horse being led out into the ring at Tattersalls.

Their daughter, on the other hand, appeared to have missed inheriting the majestic bearing of her parents. Instead Lady Rebecca was unpretentious yet confident in her carriage. She possessed dark-blond hair, an open, honest face, and pretty gray eyes that met Joss's directly when they were introduced. She was courteous and polite, articulating a genuine desire to hear more about Joss's travels and inquiring after the health of the dowager duchess without a hint of a snicker.

The only time Lady Rebecca's expression slipped into displeasure was when she witnessed her mother's clinical examination of the Earl of Boden.

Joss liked her already. Dammit.

Refreshments were brought into the box as the theater filled, and Joss found herself seated next to her brother and directly behind the newly acquainted couple. She ignored Worth, who was busy making small talk with the Daltons, and pretended to be thoroughly absorbed in the playbill. A new play by a man she'd never heard of named Payne. The work was titled *Brutus*, which, Joss thought dourly, seemed suitably tragic given the circumstances.

She tried very hard not to eavesdrop on the conversation going on just in front of her, but it was nearly impossible without plugging her ears with her fingers and humming loudly. Lady Rebecca's dark-blond head tipped toward Heath in an attentive manner, and Joss realized they'd exhausted the social staples of the weather, the acting acumen of Edmund Kean, and the traffic congestion still lingering from the construction of Regent Street. Heath was now describing his soap factories. *Ha*, thought Joss with a shameful amount of satisfaction. That usually caused people's eyes to glaze over. It was unlikely Lady Rebecca would be any different—

"How do you think the development of mechanized rail transport systems will affect the way you ship your product?" Rebecca asked below her.

Joss's fingers crumpled the edge of the playbill.

Mercifully, the stage curtain swept up and actors tumbled out onto the stage. The crowd welcomed them with a great deal of enthusiastic noise before the din in the theater dulled to a volume that allowed the actors to be heard. Heath and Lady Rebecca abandoned their conversation, and Joss was able to stop grinding her teeth.

The play unfolded, and Joss tried her best to concentrate

on the story. Yet it was an impossible task. She already knew how the act on the stage would end, just as she already knew how the act directly in front of her in the theater box would end. Despite all good sense, the entire situation left her irritable and unsettled. Exactly what happened when one made the mistake of thinking with one's heart and not with one's head.

Her eyes drifted over the mass of people seated on the long benches in the center of the theater. A flash of something in the crowd caught her eye. A reflection off a quizzing glass? A silver snuffbox catching the light? It came again, and this time she found the source. A man, dressed in a plain dark suit with a striped waistcoat, his hat resting on his knee. He wasn't watching the play either.

He was watching her.

Heath was aware of Joss's every movement behind him. He could smell her exotic scent, hear the crackle of the playbill she held in her hand, and sense her restlessness. Though if he allowed himself to relive the feel of her in his arms, the taste of her on his lips, he'd be restless for the rest of the night too.

That kiss never should have happened. It didn't matter that it was the most incredible kiss of his life, that it had obliterated all sense and reality. Joss had been like a brush fire, igniting beneath his touch, burning white-hot and fast, and scorching everything in her path. In that moment, when he had let control slip, she'd had the power to reduce him to ashes. He'd known it, and still he had kissed her.

But Joss had been right. It would not happen again. She deserved better from him. Lady Rebecca deserved better from him. Starting now, Heath would regain control of his wits, try to forget his momentary lapse into weakness, and remember exactly why he was at this theater in the first place. Worth had gone to the trouble of arranging this evening especially for Heath. He'd asked for help, and the duke had given it freely. That was what true friends did.

They most certainly did not molest their friend's little sisters on study desks.

Heath set his jaw and straightened his spine, resolution soothing his conscience. One could not change past failings, but one could make amends with better decisions in the future. He turned slightly and focused his attention on the woman sitting beside him.

Lady Rebecca wasn't beautiful in the traditional sense, but she spoke and carried herself with a quiet confidence that was immensely more appealing than any number of pretty faces. He'd found her easy to talk to, and she'd not avoided the entire topic of his business, as many ladies had done in the past, but instead had put intelligent questions to him about a number of aspects. In fact, she seemed to be quite fluent in the logistics of the import and export industry, something that he found somewhat strange given her station, but admirable at the same time.

It was a little like talking with Joss, except without the uncontrollable lust that seemed to seize him every time he did so.

That should have pleased him. Heath had wished for boring, and as far as he could tell, Lady Rebecca was just that. He winced. That sounded rather caddish. Lady Rebecca was not boring, but certainly respectable. Genteel, demure, considerate, and well-spoken. Heath found it odd that she hadn't had a number of propositions of marriage in her previous seasons. Especially given that she was the daughter of an earl.

Heath slanted Lady Rebecca a look out of the corner of his eye. She sat perfectly still beside him, her hands folded in her lap, her expression unreadable as she gazed down at the stage. Perhaps she had had offers. Perhaps none had been to her liking. Perhaps her parents had discovered their eldest daughter was not as biddable as they had anticipated.

Perhaps Lady Rebecca was more like Joss than anyone might think. Heath frowned fiercely.

Perhaps he should stop comparing her to Joss, for God's sake.

Though it certainly was an avenue that begged to be investigated. It was one thing to choose a bride with whom he thought he would be compatible. But it was just as important for the woman in question to voluntarily choose him for the same reason. He would not, under any circumstances, take an unwilling bride to the altar.

Heath suddenly became aware that people were getting to their feet. An intermission then. Perfect timing. He would take this opportunity to have a private conversation with Lady Rebecca. The mill of the crowd as everyone set to visiting would allow them the shelter of a thousand chaperones.

He offered his arm to Lady Rebecca as they stood, and she took it without comment. The Earl and Countess of Dalton were exiting the box ahead of them, Worth leading the way, though Joss had already vanished. Lady Rebecca moved to follow, but Heath caught her arm at the door.

"May I speak freely with you for a moment?" he asked. "Before we join everyone else?"

Surprise flared briefly in her eyes before she nodded.

"I think it is apparent why we are all here tonight," he started carefully.

"You are looking for a wife." It was delivered with dispassion, though not unkindly.

Heath raised his brows. "Yes. The Duke of Worth spoke quite highly of you. He was under the impression that we might suit."

Rebecca shoulders rose. "We might. Though if I am to be frank, such things are difficult to determine after half an evening at the theater. Is there something specific you wish to know about me and my aptitudes?"

"Your aptitudes?"

"Indeed. Skills that you might find useful in a wife. For example, I am capable of organizing and hosting a dinner party for fifty, correctly seating everyone by rank, and making sure the correct courses are served at the correct times and that the correct utensils are available with which to consume them. I have been trained in music, and whatever my voice lacks, I have been told my competence at the pianoforte makes up for it. I am familiar with the day-to-day operations of a household requiring no less than forty servants and have little problem addressing deficiencies. I am a fair hand and would be capable of assisting you in your correspondence, should you decide to assign that duty to me."

Heath had been watching Rebecca's face carefully, and he wondered at the slight mocking lift to her mouth as she spoke.

"You are most accomplished, Lady Rebecca," he said carefully.

"Thank you, Lord Boden." She didn't sound overly

thankful, though perhaps he was imagining things. "Perhaps you might mention that to my mother. She often reminds me what a disappointment I am to the Dalton name because I have not yet achieved the single most important accomplishment for a lady—enticing a man to marry me."

Heath frowned. "I might suggest your mother has a very limited view of what accomplishment looks like."

Genuine interest sparked in Lady Rebecca's eyes, banishing the mocking cast.

Heath met her eyes directly. "Forgive my forwardness, but it is precisely that which I wished to speak to you about. To inquire if marriage is something you desire at all."

A faint shadow of what almost looked like unhappiness drifted across her wide face. "Isn't that what all women want? To find a man of suitable rank and wealth so that we may live out our lives without concern for our comfort?"

Heath couldn't help the half-strangled laugh that lurched up in his throat. "No. They most certainly do not."

Rebecca stilled. "No?" Now she wore a look of cynical disbelief.

"You might want to ask Lady Josephine about her feelings on marriage. I can assure you they are positively gruesome." Heath pretended that he found that amusing.

"Indeed? She does seem fiercely independent," Rebecca said with what might have been admiration and a reluctant smile. The smile faded, and she looked away. "I am not opposed to marriage, Lord Boden."

"Then what are you opposed to?"

Lady Rebecca was quiet for a long moment before

turning back to consider him. "My father wishes me to marry you because of your wealth. He is willing to overlook your industrial ambition because of it. Ironic, isn't it? Your wealth is a direct reflection of your ambition and your efforts, yet somehow, in our world, that is something to be *overlooked*."

"And what about you? Are you willing to overlook my ambition?" Heath was feeling his way gingerly through this conversation now.

Rebecca laughed, a deep, rich sound. "Ambition, Lord Boden, is the single most attractive quality that might be found in a man. Without it, one goes nowhere of worth. Accomplishes nothing of value." She was looking somewhere that only her mind could see. "Tell me about Boston," she demanded.

Heath tilted his head, somewhat thrown at the abrupt change in subject. "What do you wish to know?"

"Is it like London? Everyone trapped in rigid boxes, evaluated, measured, judged, and labeled based on an accident of birth?"

"Like any society, there are social striations to be sure," Heath said slowly. "But Boston, and America as a whole, is built on opportunity. Men who may take their ambition, pair it with luck and perseverance, and create for themselves whatever world they wish."

"Is it big?"

"Boston?"

"America."

"Bigger than you or I can possibly imagine."

"Then there are places where no one would ever know you. Where you could be who you want."

"Yes."

Rebecca smiled then, and it made her plain features glow with what looked like determined hope. She waved at someone over Heath's shoulder before replacing her arm on his sleeve. "Pretend we're having the time of our lives, Lord Boden," she said, "for my father and mother are watching us. In fact, half the ton is watching us. Probably to see what I'll do with so much ambition on my arm." She said it with a sardonic twist to her lips.

Heath offered her a strained smile. "If you married me, I would try my best to make you happy."

"I know." Her eyes softened before she looked away with what looked like guilt. "I believe you are a good man, Lord Boden."

Heath allowed himself to be drawn out of the entrance to the box and along the corridor. He wasn't sure if he was satisfied with the answers he had gotten, or even if he had asked the right questions. He liked Lady Rebecca's candor, though he felt as though he had missed something crucial. Something of import lurking behind proper words and poised assurances. At the very least, Rebecca had confirmed marriage was not a problem for her. Although the possibility of marriage to him was still a little fuzzy.

Rebecca dutifully moved off with her parents to make the rounds, no doubt to make sure their acquaintances were reminded that the Bodens were guests of a duke tonight. Heath caught sight of Worth leaning on the wall up ahead, talking animatedly with another gentleman. Joss was still nowhere in sight.

A flutter of alarm went through him, distracting him from marital musings. Normally he wouldn't think anything of Joss's absence, but then, normalcy had been in short supply recently.

"Where is your sister, Worth?" Heath asked, aware he was being rude and interrupting but not really caring.

"She went to visit with some of the ladies here. She'll be right back."

"She went alone?"

The duke frowned. "No, of course not. She said she was with Lady Roth."

"Of course." Heath made an apologetic noise and retreated. Good Lord, but he was starting to get paranoid. Seeing threats and treachery where there were none—and seeing Lady Roth enter a theater box up ahead, absorbed with the young man escorting her. There was no sign of Joss anywhere with her, and Heath doubted there ever had been.

He began moving through the crowd now with urgency, scanning the crush for a glimpse of a midnight-blue gown and a head of mahogany curls. Near the end of the curved hallway, he spotted Joss, mainly because she was the only one moving with purpose, threading between the large clumps of people that had gathered. A wave of relief swept through him, though it was short-lived. There was another figure behind her, moving with the same sort of purpose, dressed in a dark suit and a silver-striped waistcoat, his hat pulled low over his brow. Both Joss and the unknown man disappeared behind a large group of women who were talking loudly and laughing.

Heath cursed and craned his neck above the crowd, but he had lost sight of Joss. She was being followed, he was sure of it. Too much time spent around the docks of London had taught him never to ignore his gut. And right now his gut was telling him that something wasn't right. A flash of deep blue caught his eye. There, on the edge of the staircase leading to the lower floors. She was definitely in a hurry, and every once in a while, she would glance about as if making sure she wasn't being followed. The man Heath had thought he'd seen was nowhere in sight.

Heath fought his way through the press and took the stairs down as quickly as he dared without causing a noticeable disturbance. Yet when he got to the bottom, she was gone.

He quashed a rising bubble of panic. The crowd was thin down here, all the patrons either in the theater itself or visiting above on the upper floors. The distance from the stairs to the theater's main doors was too great for Joss to have traversed it without his seeing her, so she had to still be in the building somewhere. His eye fell on a small, unmarked door off to the side. There was nowhere else she could have gone.

He strode across the worn floorboards, relieved that he recognized no one. As if he knew exactly what he was doing, Heath opened the door with authority, slipping into the dimness of the space beyond and closing it quickly after him. He stood motionless for a moment, letting his eyes adjust and trying to determine just exactly where he was. A storage room, he thought immediately, judging by the faint mustiness of the air. A room not used regularly, but filled with strange shapes and shadows unidentifiable in the gloom. He took a step forward and froze, his heart seizing in his chest.

"Who are you and what do you want?" The voice behind him was rough but the blade at his throat was razor-sharp.

He took a deep breath, and under the mustiness, he

caught the scent of verbena. And coconut. He also became aware of the soft pressure of skirts against the backs of his legs.

"I must assume this is a rehearsal for your audition for the part of Lady Macbeth?" His heart stuttered back to life.

The knife dropped from his neck. "Jesus, Hextall, I could have killed you." Joss blew out a breath. "And for the record, Lady Macbeth got others to do her dirty work for her."

He turned, trying to make out her face in the darkness. "Most women do not carry knives on their person when attending the theater."

She might have smiled, but it was hard to tell. "What are you doing here?" she asked.

"I thought you might be in some danger."

"What sort of danger?"

God, he wished he could see her face. It was nearly impossible to tell if she was taking any of this seriously.

"I thought I saw a man following you."

"Mmm. Did he have blond hair and blue eyes and the inability to discern a frog from a common toad?"

She definitely wasn't taking this seriously. "What the hell are you doing in here, Joss?" he demanded with growing impatience.

"She's meeting me." A light flared briefly, then steadied as a small lantern was lit, revealing a familiar face.

"Mr. Darling." Belatedly Heath recognized the striped waistcoat of the gentleman he'd thought had been stalking Joss.

"Lovely evening for the theater, isn't it, my lord? Are you enjoying the performance?"

Heath stared at the resurrection man, the rough clothes of a collier replaced now by a dapper suit and hat, no different from the attire of hundreds of men milling just beyond the door. He had probably walked by the man outside and not recognized him. Performance indeed. "Why are you here, Mr. Darling?"

Tobias's face lost its expression of bland geniality, and his eyes sharpened. "I was informed that Lady Josephine was at the theater tonight with you, which was a delightful surprise because it saved me the risk of being seen twice in the same number of days at the same address. I do so love public places. Crowded, public places." He brushed at his sleeve. "I have some news regarding your, er, situation."

"You discovered the identity of the men who attacked us?"

Tobias shook his head. "Regrettably, no. I managed to find the livery where three riderless horses returned this morning. The horses had been rented, and the stable master confirmed that the men were, indeed, French. The men in question, however, did not give the keeper their names, only enough silver to stall any further questions."

Heath's lips tightened in disappointment.

Tobias was looking between Heath and Joss. "That's not all I was able to discover," he offered into the silence.

"By all means, don't keep us in suspense."

"The seal of the two knights on a single horse that was on those papers—your friend, Mr. Smythe, had the same tattoo on the back of his head."

Heath stared at him. "I never saw anything."

"No, you wouldn't have. The tattoo was above the hairline. You had to part the hair to even make out any sort of marking. It was my brother's idea to check before we buried him."

Beside him Joss had remained silent, listening. "The names," she finally said, "of the two bodies that came off the prison hulk that bore the same tattoo. Did you discover who they were?"

"Yes. That was the easiest thing I did all day." Tobias pulled a small square of paper from inside his coat. "Henry Villeneuve and Phillip Adam. The guard remembered them because of the circumstances surrounding their death. They had been sent ashore as part of a work gang, and at some point in time, they disappeared, only to be found later, dead in a storehouse near the riverbank. There was a third man who was killed in the same altercation, but he didn't have the tattoo. The official story, of course, makes no reference to disappearances or sheds and simply states that the prisoners died of undetermined causes while working. But the men had all been beaten. To be frank, I'd say they'd been tortured. The bodies were in rough shape."

"You're sure about the names?" Joss had gone quite still.

Tobias let out an aggravated sigh. "Quite certain."

"Sorry," Joss mumbled, but Heath could tell her mind was a million miles away already.

"What is significant about the names?" Heath asked the obvious question.

"Some of the most recent letters in that folder were addressed to Villeneuve and Adam, along with Smythe." She looked up at Toby. "Do you know what crime those two men had committed that resulted in them being sentenced for transportation?"

The resurrection man shook his head.

She chewed on her lip. "Doesn't matter. That's easy enough to determine for ourselves."

"If I hear anything else, I'll send word," Darling said. "Though I'm not hopeful."

"You've done plenty," Joss told him. "Thank you."

"Enjoy the rest of the performance, my lady, my lord." The man tipped his hat, extinguished his lantern, and slipped back out through the door.

Heath and Joss were left standing in the darkness again.

"Well, this changes matters somewhat," Joss said presently.

"How so?"

"We have three men. All with a tattoo that matches the seal on those coded documents. All arrested and all murdered."

"Joss, the men on the prison ship were probably killed by their fellow inmates, not by a band of murdering Frenchmen," Heath pointed out. "It's unlikely the two incidents are connected."

"Perhaps." Joss didn't sound convinced. "But the men are certainly connected."

"I'll allow you that," he said slowly.

"Perhaps they belonged to some sort of secret brotherhood."

Heath snorted. "Sacrificing virgins or bulls or whatever they do while dancing around bonfires under a full moon?"

"You're mixing your religious ceremonies, Hextall," Joss said, her words laced with annoyance. "Besides, that is irrelevant. What is relevant is that they're all dead now."

"What, you think someone is systematically killing off men with peculiar tattoos?"

"I think the records at Newgate will give us more

answers. And I think you should try being a little more receptive to possible theories."

"I'll be receptive to any theories that don't involve lost Templar knights and secret societies. I'll be receptive to something that is believable. Logical."

"Very well, Hextall. What's your theory?" Fabric rustled as Joss shifted in the darkness.

"Perhaps I'm wrong and Gavin Smythe was really a corrupt officer. Perhaps he had two partners, and somehow they stole documents from a French quarter they had no business taking. They are likely coded documents of a military nature, and there are still a large number of men in London who twitch when Napoleon's name is mentioned. The little Frenchman still has sympathizers everywhere on both sides of the Channel, and we all know what happened last time he was exiled."

"You think the letters are covert plans for another escape?"

"Maybe."

"Then explain the documents that are hundreds of years old."

Heath threw up his hands. "I don't know. Perhaps they are of historical value. Military strategy and whatnot."

"And the seal?"

"It's just a damn seal." Heath was running out of ideas in the face of Joss's persistence. "I have one that I stamp on all my soap barrels for identification purposes."

"And you tattoo all your employees on the back of their heads with this seal as well?"

Heath gritted his teeth, defeated. "Of course not."

"Then you admit that there might be more to it than an ill-advised theft of random documents."

"I don't believe this."

"Which part?" Now she sounded amused.

"Mainly the part where I find myself standing in a damn closet, in the dark, conjecturing conspiracy theories with a body snatcher and a duke's sister."

Joss poked him in the chest, the briefest of touches in the gloom. "You've lost your sense of adventure this last decade," she chided. "And your imagination hasn't fared too well either."

Heath swiped in the dimness and caught her hand with his own. "There is nothing wrong with my imagination," he growled. "I can imagine exactly what will happen if we're caught in this damned closet."

He felt her go motionless beneath his touch. "Of course," she said, and all the teasing had gone from her voice. "I've put you in a horribly awkward situation. Especially given that Lady Rebecca waits for you upstairs. You should go."

"Yes," he replied, making no effort to move. She was absolutely right. The Earl of Boden should not be found in a darkened storage room alone with the Duke of Worth's sister.

"You need to get back to Lady Rebecca," Joss said, a little more forcefully this time.

"Yes."

"She's quite lovely. I do think I would like her." Her tone was emotionless.

"Then perhaps you should marry her." The fractious words slipped out of their own accord. Why was he being so contrary?

"Now you're just being difficult on purpose."

"Yes," he agreed, but still, he couldn't move. Heath

closed his eyes, concentrating only on the scent of her, the warmth of her hand in his, the sound of her breathing.

"Go, Hextall. Now."

He opened his eyes. For just this moment, she was all his again, hidden away from eyes, cocooned in darkness and intimacy. He wanted to stay.

"Please."

Bloody hell, but he was doing it again. Putting himself in an untenable position where his resolution to maintain an appropriate distance from Joss was dissolving into a murky haze.

He dropped her hand. "Wait at least fifteen minutes before you follow me," he instructed, hating the cool reason of his words. "In case anyone sees me."

"This isn't the first time I've done this. I'll be quite fine." Some of her spirit had returned.

"Of course." He took a step away, only to stop again. "What do you mean, you've done this before?" When, exactly, had Joss been sneaking out of closets? And with whom?

"It means that you should stop dawdling."

"Joss—"

"For the love of God, Hextall, just go!"

Heath scowled and slipped out the door, the idea that Joss had had other clandestine meetings with men in darkened spaces making his mood sour further. But then she was a spectacularly good kisser, and one did not learn to kiss the way she did from sordid novels. One learned to kiss like that in private places. Like closets. Heath's hands clenched into fists at the very thought of—

"My lord!" The address finally broke through his ill-tempered fog as he was halfway across the foyer, and

Heath whirled in surprise. Benjamin Bennett was hurrying toward him, his coat askew, his face flushed and visibly disturbed. His rough work clothes were earning him a number of disapproving stares, but the man was oblivious to anything except reaching Heath.

"Mr. Bennett." His gut twisted unpleasantly. "What is wrong?"

"Your offices and the warehouse, my lord." Bennett reached him and stopped to catch his breath.

Heath's heart pitched into his throat. "Fire?" At least Bennett hadn't said *factories*.

Bennett shook his head, and Heath let out a breath he hadn't realized he was holding.

"Robbed, my lord. Everything ripped apart, furniture broken, barrels opened, files scattered everywhere. It's a horrible mess."

Heath felt an icy finger of dread slide down his back.

"Your offices haven't been robbed." Joss had materialized at his elbow, and he couldn't even bring himself to reprimand her for being there. Bennett was staring at her and then back at Heath.

"No," Heath agreed darkly. "They've been searched."

Chapter 8

Is anything missing?" Joss stood just inside the door of Heath's offices, the lantern light casting macabre shadows across every surface.

Heath had departed from the theater immediately after making his apologies and excuses, leaving the elder Daltons miffed, Lady Rebecca and Worth visibly concerned, and Joss nearly crawling out of her skin for the remainder of the theater performance. She'd sent a message to Luke via one of her brother's footmen, letting him know that someone, somehow, had linked the Earl of Boden with the late Gavin Smythe. And ripped apart his offices looking for what Joss could only assume were the missing documents.

Heath's head snapped up where he had been crouched, sorting through a pile of papers he'd apparently scavenged from the floor of his office. "Good Christ, but you startled me." He was still dressed in his evening wear, though he'd abandoned his coat and had rolled the sleeves of his shirt up to his elbows. Streaks of dust and dirt marred the once-snowy linen.

"I'm sorry." She bent and righted a small table that had been knocked over. "Where's Mr. Bennett?"

"Downstairs in the warehouse, trying to reassemble some sort of order." Heath scowled at her. "What the hell are you doing here? Do you have any idea what time it is?"

"I believe it is half of five."

Heath rubbed his temple with grimy fingers. "That wasn't what I meant."

"Ah. You thought that, after my brother took me home from the theater, I would cower in my mother's house? Perhaps wait for you to send me reassurances that this robbery that wasn't a robbery has been neatly resolved?"

Heath swore softly. "No, I didn't think that."

"I regret that I could not come sooner. Worth made me promise that I would not go haring off in the middle of the night."

"At least one Somerhall has some sense," he muttered. "Please tell me you didn't come alone."

"I didn't come alone."

Heath peered behind her pointedly at the empty space.

"Joseph is downstairs. Luke is on his way. I also brought two footmen who have, er, experience with providing personal security."

"Security? Do I want to know the specifics of that?"

"They used to work for Margaret."

Heath made a rude noise. "What, she paid them to guard pots? Keep the cheese safe?"

Joss sniffed. "Margaret owned a flash house before she became a cook. She paid them to keep her girls safe."

Heath blinked.

"You never wondered why our upstairs maids never blush?"

"No. I really didn't." He looked a little disturbed.

Joss ventured farther into the room. "My brother stopped by your town house after he dropped me off last night."

"I know. He sent me a message that my home had been searched as well." Heath said it wearily. "He was worried that something terrible had befallen my servants because no one was there when he arrived." He pushed himself to his feet and ran a hand through his hair in agitation. "But the only servant I had left was the butler, and he decamped for greener pastures sometime before yesterday."

"I see. Well, Worth has his staff cleaning up your town house now."

"And he has my heartfelt gratitude." He paused. "Does your brother know you're here right now?"

"I did tell him I would stop by this morning," she hedged.

Heath's eyes narrowed at her.

"Don't look at me like that, Hextall. It is morning, after all. Early morning, I grant you, but morning all the same."

He shook his head in defeat.

She lifted her chin. There were far more important things to discuss than the interpretation of the word *morning*. She repeated her initial question. "There isn't anything missing, is there?"

"Not that I can tell."

"So then we must assume that someone has made a connection between you and Gavin Smythe." She gathered two heavy ledgers that had been pulled from their shelves and placed them back in the bookcase along the wall. "Rather coincidental that your offices and home were searched right after you paid a visit to Bow Street," she remarked.

"There is no such thing as a coincidence," Heath told

her. "It would seem Smythe was right not to trust his old colleagues."

"I'm inclined to agree." Joss reached under her cloak and drew out the folder. "Thank God this wasn't here."

Heath blanched before staggering toward her. "Bloody hell, Joss, what were you thinking wandering around London with this?"

"It didn't seem prudent to leave it lying around."

"It wasn't lying around. It was in your spice pantry. Guarded by a cook whose image I'm sure Wellington used to threaten potential deserters. It would take the Huns and the Greeks and the Romans all working together to get past that sentinel."

"Margaret has other duties besides barring the door to the spice pantry. She can't loiter in the house forever. Besides, this seems like the safest place for them now. It's already been searched. Logic would suggest that it won't be searched again. At least not anytime soon." She smiled at him. "Where is your safe?"

"My safe?"

"You have a safe somewhere in this mess, Hextall."

"How do you know that?" he demanded.

"I know you. As a boy you were forever squirreling things away in tree hollows or in foxholes. Probably to keep them from me," she mulled thoughtfully, "and I can't imagine your habits have changed much."

Heath was gazing at her with an odd expression. Then, very slowly, he picked up a chair and set it by the far wall. Balancing on the seat, he reached up and tugged at the wide, rough trim that ran along the wall just under the ceiling. A board popped off, and a narrow door was exposed.

"The tree hollows were always the best hiding places," Joss said with no little satisfaction. "No one ever thinks to look up." She picked her way through the wreckage and handed the folder to Heath.

Heath made some sort of noise that Joss took to be one of agreement before sliding the folder into the box, closing the door, and replacing the board. He stepped down from the chair and came to stand near the edge of his desk. Joss retreated back toward the door, rescuing another brace of books on her way.

"When was the last time you saw Mr. Smythe?"

Heath toyed with the edge of a paper, frowning. "It would have been late spring. Before he was accused of any sort of crime."

"How often did you hire him to work for you?" Joss asked, sliding the volumes next to their mates on the shelf.

"At least a half dozen times."

"Would there have been a record of that?"

"I'm quite sure there is. Regardless, it was hardly a secret. The men around the docks here knew Smythe, his colleagues on Bow Street would have been aware he worked for me often, and anyone in the justice system would have been privy to his terms of employment here. He made several arrests on my behalf." Heath frowned. "But I was not the only one Smythe worked for. For anyone who looked, there would be a whole list of names on record at the Bow Street offices."

"But you are the only one with means of escape for someone on the run. Someone looking to flee London, or England, or Europe entirely."

"My ships."

"Yes. It would be logical to think that you might be in a

position to help a man who has, quite publicly, helped you in the past."

Heath leaned on the edge of his desk and ran his hands through his hair.

"The good news is that they didn't find anything," Joss said.

Heath looked up at her. "How is that good news? I'll be sleeping with one eye open from now on. Not," he grumbled, "that I'm getting much sleep anyway."

Joss chewed on her lip. "I think this was a fishing expedition," she said slowly. "Had they had solid proof that you were in possession of the documents or Smythe himself, they would have come for you, not your offices. Riskier to abduct a man, yet more expedient to search his mind in private instead of tossing his offices in public."

"Jesus, Joss. Is that supposed to make me feel better?"

"Well, yes. It is a confirmation that no one witnessed what happened the night Mr. Smythe was murdered. No one knows it was you who helped Smythe. Or that I did too, for that matter." She regretted the last words the moment she uttered them.

Heath stared at her, his eyes red-rimmed. "Oh God. You need to leave town. Stay at Breckenridge with your brother or—"

Joss cursed herself silently in her mind. "I am not leaving you." She stepped closer to Heath. "So please don't start an argument you won't win."

"But what if—"

"Kippers," Joss said, cutting him off. "And coffee, I think. It helps clear the cobwebs from one's head. Perhaps a ginger biscuit if there are any to be had."

Heath looked at her blankly.

"Breakfast, Hextall." She jerked her head toward the door. "We should get some. This"—she gestured at the mess around her—"will keep for a few hours while we get breakfast and then visit Newgate. We need to look at those records sooner rather than later."

Heath looked as if he wanted to argue further.

"I believe it was you who insisted that I couldn't go anywhere in the vicinity of Newgate alone." Joss closed the remaining distance between them, but didn't reach out to touch him. "I'll be safe with you."

Heath pushed himself away from the desk and stood. "Fine. But if there is even a hint of anything that's not quite right, I am tying you up, gagging you, and putting you on a coach to Liverpool. And I'll pin a note on your dress with explicit instructions to my captains that you are to be loaded into the hold of the next ship sailing for Boston."

"Of course." Joss fought to keep her face grave.

"I'm serious, Joss. I'll not have you mucking about in matters that have nothing to do with you yet might get you hurt. Or worse."

"I can take care of myself, Hextall."

"I know you can." He said it reluctantly. "But that doesn't mean it still doesn't terrify me. I am responsible for your safety."

Joss felt a well of emotion squeeze her chest. Impulsively she slipped her hands into his. "You cannot be held responsible for the well-being of everyone around you all of the time."

Heath made a cynical noise of disbelief. "No? What about the men and their families who depend on me to provide work and wages? Or the people whose livelihoods depend on me being able to drag the earldom out of debt and into this century? Or my sisters? Or my mother? The idea that I can't make them happy makes me miserable."

Joss tightened her fingers around his and weighed his words. "Can I say something?"

"Do I have a choice?"

"Not really."

Heath sighed in resignation. "Then by all means."

"You may have obligations and responsibilities to people in your life, that is true, but their happiness is not your domain. Happiness is something that one must choose. It cannot be provided or simply bought by another."

Heath scowled. "Easy for you to say, having been on your own for so many years. Traveling about and doing just as you pleased, based solely on your whims. Beholden to no one and responsible for only yourself."

Joss stepped back from Heath, her hands slipping from his.

"I'm sorry," he said after a moment. "That was unfair."

"No." It was a fair statement, given what he knew about her. Very suddenly she needed him to understand. Needed the boy who had teased her and the man he had become to understand. "Did you ever meet my father?"

Heath hesitated. "On very few occasions."

"Indeed." It had always been only the duchess in residence at Breckenridge when Worth would drag Heath into the cavernous house, Joss on their heels, all of them usually filthy and hungry from one of their adventures. Worth had told Heath that the duke did not care for the locale of the estate and preferred to spend his summers either in the city or with his peers at other country holdings. What Worth had never said was that it was just as well, for his father would certainly not have tolerated his only heir consorting with a soapmaker's son.

"He did seem like a rather, ah, forceful individual," Heath said.

Joss's eyes swiveled up to his. "Forceful? An interesting choice of words."

"What I mean is that he seemed like a very ambitious man. A man used to getting what he wanted, and I would imagine, based on Worth's rare comments about his demeanor, your father cared little for those who got in his way."

"Our father was brutal in his use and disposal of whoever and whatever was required to further his own ambitions. His desire for absolute power and prestige eclipsed any sense of right and wrong, and any hint of a conscience. Yet that wasn't what others saw. Society believed him to be strong, determined, and unyielding, traits always to be admired in a duke. It was my brother's greatest fear that, when he became older and the title passed to him, he would become the man our father was."

Heath nodded slightly, and Joss knew he wasn't surprised. Even with Worth's unwillingness to discuss the old duke, it would have been impossible for Heath to remain as close as he had with her brother for so many years without gleaning at least a few insights.

"I know they didn't get on well, especially as we got older," he said.

Joss almost sneered. "Save your diplomacy. My brother despised him with every fiber of his being."

A silence fell between them then, not wholly uncomfortable, just a pregnant pause marking a confession.

"Did you ever wonder, Hextall, why my mother sent me away when I was six years old?" Joss asked presently.

Heath gazed at her. The blue of his eyes seemed to have shifted to the color of the sea before a storm. "Yes. I've recently wondered."

"The summer that I turned six, my father spent one of his rare days at Breckenridge. He hosted a lavish picnic and invited only the most important men and their families. I suppose he needed to show everybody what a perfect family he had produced, despite that he had been cursed with an unnatural daughter."

Heath was frowning. "Unnatural?"

"I was considered an abomination in the rare times when I forgot to hide my intellectual abilities from him." Joss sighed. "To my father, a daughter should've been like a genuine Ming vase—silent, pretty, and having accrued value by the time one wishes to sell."

Joss stopped, resenting the suffocating emotion that was rising. In this she wished she could be like others, people who told her often that, in time, memories would be dulled and eventually fade from her consciousness. But they never did. Standing here, in the middle of a cool, damp, ruined office, she could still feel the warmth of the sun on her back and the scratch of the starched collar of her new white dress, hear the rise and fall of conversation interspersed with the clinking of china and crystal, smell the scent of cut grass and blooming roses on the breeze. She remembered the excitement of playmates and the promise of pilfered cakes and sweets.

"The day of the picnic, my governess was playing pall-mall with me and two other girls. My father was standing not far away, near the edge of the gardens, speaking with a group of men. My ball—it was red—rolled close to where my father was. When I ran to get it, I overheard them talking about the 1715 Jacobite rebellion and the riots that occurred in London. My father was loudly adamant that those riots had taken place in July. I picked up my ball and skipped back to my governess. But not before I said May twenty-eighth. The riots were on the Hanoverian king's birthday."

Heath was watching her, his eyes flinty and his jaw set into a rigid line, his posture suddenly stiff, as if he were bracing himself.

"I committed the unpardonable sin of pointing out that my father was wrong. In front of his peers." Joss fell silent, remembering now her immediate dismay that had quickly dissolved into terror.

"Tell me." It was not a question, really, nor was it a command. It fell somewhere in between the two, in the way it does when the speaker already knows the answer.

"My father took me inside the house. I knew what was going to happen, for it certainly wasn't the first time, yet somehow it still came as a surprise. Only this time, he broke my nose. The blood went down the front of my new white dress and splattered all over the red ball I still held in my hand, and I remember thinking that at least I won't ruin the ball too." She could feel the numbness in her face, taste the sharp, coppery blood that had streamed into her mouth and slid down the back of her throat. "My brother managed to find some salt pork, but it still took my mother over an hour to stop the bleeding. I never saw my governess again. Two weeks later Worth went back to school, and I went to live with my mother's cousin in Italy." She took a deep breath and touched the bridge of her nose with her finger. "It never did heal straight."

Heath had paled, his hands curling and uncurling by his sides in jerky movements. "I never knew."

"Of course you didn't. It wasn't something any of us spoke of, though for different reasons, I think. My mother because she was afraid of making it worse, for herself and for us. My brother because he was too young to stop it, yet no less ashamed of his helplessness. And me because..." She trailed off. "Because it was safer for me—safer for all of us—if I remained invisible to my father."

"I wish I'd known." The words were stark.

"To what end?" Joss asked. "There was nothing you could have done."

"I could have treated you better," he whispered. "I can only think now how awful I was to you all those summers," Heath mumbled, his eyes stricken. "How horrid I was at every opportunity—"

"No." Joss cut him off with more strength than she had intended. "You were my safe place. With you I was never afraid. A little muddier perhaps, from time to time, but always safe. With you I did not have to be someone or something else. I was free to speak and to be myself."

The cold had retreated from Heath's eyes, leaving a gentleness that was starting to shred Joss's veneer of steady poise. He recaptured her hands in his. "A boy's fourteen-year-old ego might be in danger of irreparable injury here," he teased her softly. "Please tell him there was at least a little fear. At least after the day you secretly cut every fourth stitch in the seat of my breeches when Worth and I left our clothes on the bank unattended to swim."

Joss smiled, knowing that was exactly what Heath had intended. "I thought they would have split long before you and my brother made it into the village proper."

"I was stuck halfway over the top of a fence with my bare ass glaring in the sun."

"There was a gate, Hextall, if you'd thought to use it, instead of showing off for the vicar's daughter."

Heath snorted. "Every boy over the age of twelve tried to show off for the vicar's daughter. She had the biggest, roundest—"

Joss raised a single brow.

"—eyes."

They were both grinning at each other, and now, instead of making Joss feel better, it was somehow making her throat close up.

The smile slipped from his face. "I'm so sorry, Joss."

Her own smile vanished just as quickly. "I don't want you to feel sorry for me. I want you to understand why I went away. It wasn't to picnic in France or buy pretty lace in Belgium or explore scenic palaces in Spain."

"Your mother was protecting you."

"Yes. Worth was safe at school, I was safe across the Channel, but my mother was never safe, not truly, not until the day my father died. This is why she does what she does now. Why I've been helping her all these years. To make sure other women will never suffer as she did."

"Or as you did."

"Perhaps," Joss said quietly. "Like yours, my life was chosen for me without my consent. Though I just never understood it until now." That unfamiliar pressure in the back of her throat was building and making the backs of her eyes burn. Joss felt a little shaken and a little raw and a little vulnerable, and if Heath said anything remotely kind at this juncture, she might just dissolve into a pathetic puddle of grief over so many things she had seen damaged and lost and so many wrongs that could never be righted. She had never been one for maudlin reflections, but baring her soul and her secrets to this man had somehow left her horribly fragile.

Joss forced her shoulders back and cleared her throat. "The point of this all, Hextall, is that there will always be unfair obstacles in life that make it easy to fall into a trap of self-pity. But each person has to decide for themselves if they will embrace or overcome those excuses. Happiness is something you must choose. Sometimes it is not always an easy choice."

Heath moved toward her and closed the distance she had established. He simply folded her into his arms, and just as on the night in the carriage, she found herself pressed up against the sheltering solidity of his chest, the weight of his arms secure around her back. She ignored her instant reflex to withdraw and resist his gesture, and instead let her churning emotions settle in the safety of his embrace.

"Joss," Heath said after a moment, the word rumbling through his chest and against her ear, and it was the way he said it that threatened to make her throat close up again.

Until now she'd kept those memories boxed up, the way one might an unwanted object. Shoved to the back of a shelf, not entirely forgotten, but noticed only sporadically and never examined in any great detail. Joss squeezed her eyes shut. She refused to cry. "Don't you dare say anything compassionate or sympathetic right now, Hextall.

Neither one of us will like the result. And I may never forgive you."

His breath escaped in a chuckle. "Would you prefer I pour ink into your tea again?"

Joss laughed, a sudden release from the constricting tightness that was suffocating her. Her fingers traced the seam at the back of his waistcoat, where they rested. "I had black lips for a week."

"After the village fence incident, you deserved it." He tightened his arms. "I was exceptionally proud of that one. You looked exactly the way I imagined a real witch might."

"Be careful. I have a long memory."

"Is that a threat?"

"More of a promise."

"Well, come then, Circe," he said, pulling back slightly. "I'll make it up to you if you promise not to turn me into a common toad."

Joss stepped out of his embrace, instantly bereft at the loss of contact. "How?" She desperately hoped it had come out as lightly as she had intended, because brewing in her head were all sorts of wicked ways in which Heath Hextall could make it up to her.

"Kippers," he said, "and coffee. And maybe some ginger biscuits, if there are any to be had." He grinned at her. "Let me take you to breakfast."

"A brave offer," Joss teased, ignoring the way her heart had begun hammering in her chest the moment he turned the full power of that damned smile on her. "Especially if you take your coffee black."

"I'll consider myself forewarned." His smile slipped as they moved to the door, and his gaze slid to the wreckage in his office.

"By the end of the day," Joss said, "it will be set to rights. I promise."

Heath glanced at her dubiously.

"You're not alone in this," she told him.

Heath stilled. "No, I'm not," he agreed quietly. He reached out to touch her arm before his hand dropped. "And neither are you."

Chapter 9

They ate at a small coffeehouse and by the time Joss and Heath arrived at Newgate, the sun was making a feeble attempt to penetrate the curtain of clouds. Already, despite the early hour and the freezing bite of the winter air, hordes of people were milling about. Some were laden with food or extra clothes for prisoners they were visiting. Others loitered against the walls, hunched against the wind, their expressions as bitter as the temperature. Still more hurried by, destined for the Old Bailey, their hands stuffed deep into the pockets of their coats, looking impatient or apprehensive, all waiting for the day's proceedings to start.

Joss and Heath joined the periphery of a group of warmly dressed women waiting near the Debtor's Door to deliver their offerings to family members inside. In between gnawing on what was left of a chicken leg, the guard at the door was doing a brisk business in granting admission, coins changing hands in a manner that told Heath this was a daily ritual for him. As Joss and Heath approached, the man stepped into their path, barring entry, the door behind him slamming shut. His eyes touched on Heath before making a more lengthy and lascivious perusal of Joss. Heath wondered what he saw.

Certainly not an earl and the sister of a duke, he knew. When Joss had arrived at his offices hours earlier, she had been wearing nondescript clothes, a warm and serviceable dress, and a borrowed cloak that had seen better days. Better to simply blend in with the masses, she'd told him when he'd asked, and he was reminded of the unmarked carriage she and her mother traveled in. And all the reasons they might have cause to do so.

Heath had likewise changed from his ruined evening wear into the only clothes he kept at the office—more suited for working in the warehouses and the docks than relaxing at a gentleman's club. The woolen scarf wrapped around the lower half of his face further obscured his identity, not that he was overly concerned anyone here might recognize him.

A factory worker and his wife, Heath guessed, still watching the guard's face as the man evaluated the two of them. Or perhaps a sailor recently off one of the ships creaking in the cold out on the Thames. Either way, Heath didn't much care what the guard thought, nor did he care for the insolent greed that was slowly creeping across the man's face. He'd seen that expression a hundred times at a hundred different customhouses and ports.

"State your business," the guard said, sounding bored and belligerent all at once. He wiped his grease-stained mouth with the back of his sleeve. "And I'll tell you what it'll cost."

Heath suppressed the annoyance that flared. It would be a colder day than this in hell before he gave this man the monetary satisfaction he sought.

Heath stared at the guard, keeping his expression completely neutral. "Nothing that would interest you," he said.

"Everything interests me." The man sneered and jabbed the chicken bone in Heath's direction.

Impulsively Heath turned to Joss. "You don't suppose he actually expects me to pay him, do you, dear?" he whined dully. He waited, suddenly unsure if she would understand.

But Joss's eyes widened and then crinkled at the corners.

"Dunno," she replied with a careless shrug, an accent he had never heard broadening her speech. "Never heard of payin' money to get into a prison. Only thought you had to pay to get out."

The guard was frowning. "Begone with the two of you if—"

"Oh, just pay him," Joss suggested.

"Listen to the little lady," the guard said.

"What the hell am I supposed to pay him with?" Heath demanded, ignoring the guard and moving so he blocked a little more of the doorway. He was aware of the queue that had formed behind him, shifting and stomping impatiently against the cold, barred from the entrance by their presence.

She glanced at the guard and the chicken leg clutched in his fist. "A leg of mutton?"

Someone nearby snickered.

Heath made a face. "I never brought any mutton."

"Oh, for pity's sake. Give him money."

"I never brought any money. Did you?"

Joss sighed loudly. "I got some," she said, fumbling in

her cloak and producing a small leather purse. "Why do I have to think of everything? God help our sons should they get their brains from their father."

"Better my brains than your tongue."

"You liked my tongue just fine last night."

Behind him, amid the escalating grumbling, someone guffawed, and Heath bit back a grin.

"Here," Joss said, yanking on the string that drew the bag closed. "Take some of this—" The bag tipped and a half dozen pennies scattered on the stone at their feet. "Nooooo," she wailed, bending to retrieve them.

"Jesus Christ," muttered the guard, starting to sound uneasy as he glanced at the crowd.

Heath dropped to his hands and knees beside her, hypothetically rescuing coins. He glanced over to find that Joss had her head wedged neatly between the knees of a hapless gentleman behind her in an apparent effort to rescue a penny that had rolled between his feet. The man was alternatively trying to disentangle himself and help her retrieve the penny, his expression a mask of bewildered horror.

"Get off your knees, dear," Heath said, pulling on her cloak.

"But it's gone," she sniffed, allowing herself to be helped to her feet. "All my money."

The gentlemen behind her had found the single penny and handed it back to her. Joss gave him a smile with sufficient radiance to make him blink and smile back.

Heath patted her shoulder. "Maybe we can take up a collection," he said on a note of inspiration. "Look at all these people, waiting to get in out of the cold. I think I even see a magistrate. They're plenty rich. Surely someone will pay this guard here to get this line moving again. It's bloody freezing out here." He turned around and raised his voice in the manner he saved for his cavernous factories. "If I may have your attention, good people, this guard here has requested—"

He was yanked off-balance as the guard grabbed at the sleeve of his coat. "Get on in with you then," he muttered, his face a mottled red.

"But—"

"Just go," snarled the man, yanking the door open. "You lot are more trouble than you're worth."

Joss was already striding through the door, and Heath hurried after her, not sparing the guard a backward glance.

"That was fun," she said, a decided note of glee in her voice.

Heath found himself grinning. "Wasn't it, though?" And he meant it, though the sensible part of his mind was threatening recriminations for taking so much delight in their ridiculous little performance. His smile slipped.

"Don't do it, Hextall," Joss said, linking her arm through his.

"What?"

"Lose your sense of humor on me now. It isn't just anyone who I'd put my head between a stranger's legs for."

Heath laughed out loud, a sound that startled him. "The poor soul may never recover from the experience. He was hopping around like you were breathing fire on the inside seams of his breeches."

Joss's smile widened. "He was, wasn't he? Though you could have just paid the guard," she observed.

"I have long since developed a policy of not paying

bribes to stupid men," he replied with relish. "In custom-houses or elsewhere."

"Only to clever ones?"

"Bribes and clever men make the world go round." He was aware that Joss was appraising him, still with a bemused expression on her face. "But you knew that."

She nodded with a chuckle.

"So how many sons do we have?" Heath asked, the eddies of his mirth making him feel a little drunk and a little reckless. Good God, when was the last time he had laughed?

"I beg your pardon?"

"You were worried that our sons might get their intellect from their father. How many boys did you think to have?"

"Oh, I should think at least five," she said happily. "And I'm certainly not worried about their intelligence."

"No daughters?"

"Maybe a few of those too, for good measure. Someone besides me will need to teach their brothers how to play chess properly."

Heath smirked. "Good God, but I've got my work cut out for me. I reckon we should get started right away. Do you have plans for lunch?"

Joss suddenly flushed furiously, and her eyes slid from his in the same manner they had after he'd made the mistake of kissing her. He cursed himself, wishing he could take that last rash comment back, but knowing it was too late. It was one thing to playact to set a grasping guard in his place, but it was another thing altogether to pretend that Josephine was really his. To imagine, even for a second, what it would be like to share a life and a future with this extraordinary woman who seemed to know him better than he did himself.

Joss started to pull her hand away from where it rested on his arm, but some perverse impulse made him catch it with his other hand and hold it steady. Perhaps he wasn't decent and strong enough to abandon the playacting just yet. But he at least owed her an apology.

"I'm sorry. That was crude."

Joss shrugged in dismissal, though her color was still unnaturally high. "There is nothing to apologize for."

"I've made you uncomfortable."

Joss shot him an arch look. "You've been trying your damndest to make me uncomfortable since I was three years old. I can't imagine why this would suddenly be a burden to your conscience."

"So you admit I made you uncomfortable." He couldn't help himself, nor could he help the grin that stretched itself across his face again. Joss indignant was a sight to behold.

Her eyes narrowed. "I admit no such thing. Least of all to you."

"You're blushing."

"I'm overly warm."

"Of course," Heath drawled. "In that case, I'd offer to help remove an article of your clothing to improve your comfort, but I fear your complexion might never recover."

Joss straightened, a grudging smile playing around her mouth. "And to think I was worried that you had lost your touch over the years."

"In tormenting you? Never. And I've a great deal of lost time to make up."

She laughed, and any lingering discomfort dissipated like a sun-scorched mist. "Duly noted," she said, with a wry shake of her head. "I'll be expecting nothing less than your best efforts from here on in, Hextall."

"Duly noted." Heath laughed again, and this time it came easily, as though the rust from years of disuse had given way.

Joss smiled up at him, her eyes dancing, and Heath's breath caught in his throat. How was it this easy? When had Josephine Somerhall's presence become something he required to find…happiness? Since when did he need to be in her company to find the burden of responsibility temporarily banished, the long-forgotten laughter and carefree joy of living reinstated with a single smile?

"You're woolgathering," Joss said, breaking through his thoughts.

Heath started, aware they had come to a stop and she was waiting for him. "I'm sorry."

Joss's elegant eyebrows shot up. "Good God, two apologies in as many minutes. You're not off to a good start in your crusade, Hextall."

Heath cleared his throat loudly. "I think we should take a look at those records now."

"Then by all means, lead the way, good sir." She was watching him expectantly. "And, Hextall?"

"Mmm?"

"Perhaps you might let me do the talking this time."

⌒

The criminal registers were stored in an airless brick room set well below street level. As it was, Joss did very little talking, simply stating to the turnkey who appeared to challenge their presence that they wished to look at the criminal register.

The middle-aged man let his eyes slide past Joss and travel the length of Heath's worn clothing before lingering on his boots. Boots that probably cost more than the clerk made in a year. "State the name and date and the information you require," he said agreeably. "And I will fetch whatever particulars you need."

"What we require," Heath interjected, "is to take a look at the criminal register kept from the month of June of this year. The information we seek is something of a sensitive and valuable nature that requires the utmost discretion."

"Of course," the turnkey said without a change in his expression before leading them down a maze of dark halls and unlocking a steel-strapped door. He lit a lantern hanging from an iron peg by the doorway and led them into the room, the air stuffy with the scent of bound leather and old paper. Shelves lined the room, filled from floor to ceiling with tomes, and a scarred table sat in the center.

The turnkey walked over to the shelves and withdrew a heavy bound book, not so different from an accounting ledger. He checked the date on the inside and then placed it on the table. "You'll find the records you requested in here."

"Perhaps you would be so kind as to leave the lantern," Heath suggested smoothly. "We would hate to keep you from your regular duties." He placed a guinea near the edge of the table. "We'll see ourselves out."

The man didn't hesitate before pocketing the coin and departing without a backward glance.

Joss pulled her hood down and unwrapped her scarf from her face. She moved quickly to the table, trying not to dwell on the fact that she'd managed to mortify the both of them by blushing like a schoolgirl the moment Heath teased her about procreation. God in heaven, but she'd attended numerous lectures on human anatomy, she'd observed two complete adult dissections, she could name every identifiable part of the male and female reproductive systems, yet she had *blushed*. It was humiliating.

And Heath had been joking, for God's sake. The first real laughter she had heard from him and she had morphed into some sort of frumpish prude and ruined it. The awkward moment had been mercifully smoothed over by Heath, but she needed to pull herself together. Especially if she was going to keep his company for any length of time.

With renewed determination Joss opened the cover, a cloud of dust rising and making her nose tickle. She sneezed and started turning the worn pages, bypassing hundreds and hundreds of lives, each reduced to a single row of handwriting. "If this was when Gavin Smythe was arrested and subsequently released, perhaps the two other men who were marked with the same tattoo were arrested near the same time."

"Sounds reasonable," Heath concurred, and nudged the lantern closer to the record book.

She slowed when she came to the entries for June, skimming the neat columns on the far left side, looking for "Smythe, Gavin." She flipped the page twice more before she found it.

"Here," she said, stopping abruptly.

Heath peered over her shoulder. "Where's the rest of it?"

Joss was chewing on her lip. Someone had written the date, his name, and a brief physical description, stating his profession as a Bow Street Runner. He had, according to the record, been accused of thievery and arrested on June 12, 1818. But the subsequent columns, details regarding the result of the allegation, were completely blank.

"I guess no one wanted to be the one to write the word *escaped* across the entry," Heath mused mildly. "Though his supposed innocence and release aren't noted either."

Joss shrugged. Her eyes dropped down to the next line and she froze. "Henry Villeneuve." Her finger slid farther. "And right below him is Phillip Adam. Hextall, look at the dates of their arrest."

She scanned the two entries. They had both been arrested on June 12, 1818, and had been accused of stealing unspecified valuables from the residence of an M. Leroux of Tower Street. Unlike Smythe, however, these men had been tried at the Old Bailey, sentenced to transport, and subsequently delivered to Woolwich. Someone, at a later date, judging from the deviation in ink color, had written, "died, Nov. 14" in the farthest right-hand column by each man's name. There were, however, no further clues as to their association. The physical descriptions differed radically, suggesting no familial connection, and Villeneuve was listed as a sawyer, while Adam was listed as a schoolmaster.

"The *Bellerophon* is at anchor at Woolwich," Joss mused. "They would have been imprisoned in that hulk together."

"Look at the entry below," Heath murmured in her ear.

She drew back slightly and tipped the lantern toward the page. "Williamson, Arthur. Arrested June 12, 1818."

She blew out a breath. "Good Lord. There's a letter in that damn folder addressed to Williamson. One of the more recent ones." Joss hunched back over the table, scouring the records before her.

Arthur Williamson, five feet four inches, of dark complexion pitted by pox scars. Brown eyes and hair. Missing third finger on left hand. A cobbler. Accused of theft from M. Leroux, tried at the Old Bailey, sentenced to transportation, held at Newgate until he was delivered to Woolwich, just like Henry Villeneuve and Phillip Adam.

And just as with the entries above it, someone had written, "died, Nov. 14" in the far-right column.

"A coincidence?" Heath asked from beside her.

Joss shook her head. "You told me there was no such thing as a coincidence. And statistically speaking, if one did the math in this case, such happenstance would never—" She caught the pained look on Heath's face and stopped. "I wonder if Arthur Williamson had a tattoo on the back of his head."

Heath shrugged. "No way to know now." He paused. "Unless...Do you suppose he was the third man killed with Villeneuve and Adam that Mr. Darling mentioned?"

"If he was, then he didn't have a tattoo. Toby was quite definite about that. No tattoo, but obviously a coconspirator." Joss made a dissatisfied noise. "This excursion has produced more questions than answers. We don't even know what it was they stole."

"Let's go ask."

"Ask who what?" Joss's brow creased.

"Let's go find this M. Leroux and ask what he had

stolen from him that wasn't important enough to be recorded but sent three men to rot in a prison hulk."

Joss stared at him in dismay. "Why didn't I think of that?"

"Because if you crammed one more idea into that brain of yours that I know is a seething pit of calculations and hypotheses, your head would likely explode." He threw his hands out from the sides of his head. "Boom. Like a barrel of gunpowder."

"You're hysterical, Hextall."

He leaned toward her, his lips curling. "Sometimes I come up with a few good ideas too."

Joss found herself smiling. "So you do."

⁓

Outside the door to the cramped records room, the turn-key fingered the coin he had just acquired in his pocket, turning the smooth, warm metal over and over. June of 1818 was proving to be a very lucrative month for him. The man who was currently snooping through the June registers was the second one in as many months, and both had paid exceedingly well for the privilege. But the first had left him with a promise of more. All the man had to do was send a message should anyone else come asking for the same information.

He wondered how much he might be able to get. The turnkey had heard the woman in the room behind him call the man Hextall, and that little tidbit had to be worth something extra. God knew his paltry pay here at New-gate was barely sufficient to keep enough food on the table and shoes on his children's feet. He strained to listen for anything else that might be of value, but they were speaking in hushed tones now and it was impossible to hear. No matter. He turned smartly and headed back in the direction of the stairs. Idly he wondered what was so important in those June records. In the next breath, he realized he didn't care.

He'd have his money by the end of the day.

Chapter 10 ─────────────────────

Tower Street was a miserable twist of road, short and stumpy and enclosed on both sides by leaning buildings that had seen better days a century earlier. Whatever watery sunshine had made its way through the clouds did not get past the hulking shadows of the tenements to the wet, sloppy stone beneath their feet.

The records hadn't given a specific address for Leroux, but Heath wasn't overly concerned. In the course of building his business, Heath had discovered that highly profitable information could be gleaned at the neighborhood tavern for the price of a pot of ale. He didn't imagine this case would prove any different, and it was as good a place as any to start.

The tavern on Tower Street was more of a cave, compressed on the ground floor under the weight of three stories of crammed humanity. They ducked under the low lintel and into the bowels of the building, the reek of gin enough to overpower the stench of the streets. Their feet still squelched unpleasantly, and the air was warm and suffocating. Heath gave himself a moment to allow his eyes to adjust to the dimness and then cast a look at Joss beside him.

She was glancing around casually, and if she found any of her surroundings distasteful, she was concealing it well. In fact, with her scarf wrapped over her head and tied under her chin and her hands shoved into the depths of her threadbare cloak, she simply blended in with her surroundings. She seemed unnaturally good at that, he reflected.

He led her over to a massive scarred table that had lost a leg and was propped up rather crookedly on a makeshift crate. At this hour of the morning, there were only a few drinkers hunched over their liquid breakfasts, and Heath rather suspected that they simply hadn't moved from the night before. A cadaverous man was looming in the corner, studying them suspiciously.

"What do you want?" he demanded.

"A drink of your finest," Heath said easily.

The man sneered, showing gaping holes where teeth once had existed. "My finest," he repeated, though at the sight of the coin in Heath's hands, two dented tin cups appeared and were dutifully filled. Heath raised his cup, the fumes making his eyes water slightly.

"Tell me about Leroux," he said suddenly. He always liked to watch a man's face when the unexpected was presented without warning. It invariably told him whether he was wasting his money or there was something valuable to be had.

In this case the man's eyes widened in their bony sockets, darting to the left and then the right before subsiding once again to a disdainful squint. "Never heard of the man," he lied.

"I didn't know he was a man," Heath said truthfully, placing his cup on the edge of the table. "That certainly helps." M. Leroux could just as well have been a woman.

Panic and alarm flitted across the hollowed features, and bony fingers raked through hair that might have been brown at some point. "Now, I never told you nothing."

"Of course you didn't. The French can be an unpredictable lot, no? All secretive and threatening to people asking questions."

The man released a tremulous breath. "Yes. But I never asked nothing. Though I say good riddance."

"Moved on about six months ago, did he?"

The question earned Heath a barely perceptible nod and a suspicious glare. "Why you asking questions you already know the answers to?"

"Where did he stay, when he was here?"

The man's eyes darted past Heath's left shoulder before coming back, obstinacy stamped across his face. "I'm not saying nothing more."

Heath nodded. There was little else he'd get out of this person that would be valuable. He gave the man a nod and turned, aware that Joss remained close to his side. He led her toward the door, suddenly anxious to get out of the foul miasma of the tiny room.

The cold air was a welcome respite after the claustrophobic feel of the tiny tavern, and he was glad to push the crooked door shut behind them. The satisfaction he felt with the answers he had gotten was tempered by the knowledge that Leroux was long gone.

"Well done, Hextall," Joss said. "I'm impressed."

He raised a brow. "If I'd really been trying to impress you, I would have drunk whatever was in that cup."

"Men drinking excessive quantities of unknown substances only impresses other men," Joss scoffed.

"You don't say."

"You got quite a bit out of a man who wasn't talking." Joss ticked off the facts on her gloved fingers. "Mr. Leroux was, in fact, a mister, French, and lived here until about six months ago." Joss turned and squinted down the street. "He lived in one of those two buildings."

"How do you know that?" Heath was testing her.

"Because a man's eyes always give him away."

"Now I'm impressed."

"Would you have been more impressed if I had drunk whatever was in my cup?"

He grinned at her. "Immeasurably."

Joss shook her head and laughed.

"He's not here anymore," Heath mused, sobering. "I'm not sure how much more information there is to be had. This might be a dead end."

"Well, Hextall, let's go ask."

He glanced at her sharply, only to find her eyes sparkling.

"Sometimes you have good ideas." She caught his hand and pulled him in the direction of the looming buildings. "Mr. Leroux left quite an impression on the tavern keeper. Surely he left an impression on someone else too."

The someone else they had hoped to find proved to be an elderly woman, diminutive in stature, her gray hair plaited in a long braid that reached her waist and her eyes sunken deep into lines of skin, yet no less sharp for their age. She had answered their knock suspiciously, and Heath had let Joss do the talking, rightfully assuming the woman would find another female less threatening. Yet the old woman had only shaken her head, muttering a few words of broken English, and had started to close the door when Joss suddenly began speaking rapidly in a language Heath couldn't begin to identify.

The transformation was rather remarkable, Heath reflected later. The woman had frozen before her face lost its pinched look and took on one of welcoming delight. Within minutes Heath and Joss had found themselves ushered into a cramped room and ensconced on the only two chairs while the woman rummaged through a cupboard backed into the far corner. The entire time the woman had not stopped talking, pausing only long enough to allow Joss to answer a query that she threw over her shoulder every so often.

"Her name is Alina, and she says she's very happy to be speaking the language of her home," Joss explained to Heath as the elderly woman filled up three chipped cups with a clear brew from a glass bottle. "Since her husband died, she does not often have someone to talk to."

"And where is home?" Heath asked.

"Moldavia," Joss answered. "Caught in the middle of messy political maneuverings between the Ottomans and the Russians."

"Ah."

The woman hustled back and pressed the teacups into their hands with enthusiasm, gesturing at Heath to drink. Cautiously Heath raised his cup to his nose, a pungent fruity aroma cutting through the air.

"It's not gin," Joss whispered with a smile. "And it's rude not to drink."

Heath took an experimental sip, and the alcohol scorched its way down his entire esophagus, leaving him blinking rapidly. He cleared his throat a number of times before taking another tentative sample. If one could get over the strength of the drink, it did leave a pleasant after-taste on one's tongue that reminded him faintly of plums.

Joss had resumed her conversation with Alina, who was now gesturing emphatically at the ceiling above her head, a torrent of words pouring forth.

"She says there was a man named Marcel Leroux who used to live above her," Joss translated. "A French soldier who had many friends who came and went. Walked across the floor at all hours of the night with their boots on." She was smiling at the indignation that had colored Alina's face, listening carefully. "And weapons, many, many of them, brought upstairs in the middle of the night and stacked in boxes above her head."

"How does she know this?"

"Some of the young men in the neighborhood thought to steal them. They were successful, to an extent, in that they managed to acquire a dozen rifles before the French soldier discovered them."

"And what happened then?"

"The men were found"—Joss frowned, casting about for the correct word—"gutted like hogs and strung up from the eaves of the building on the corner." She had paled slightly.

"How did she know he was a soldier?" Heath pressed.

Joss asked and waited. "She says she knows a soldier when she sees one. Her entire life has been dedicated to avoiding them."

"The men who came and went, were they French as well?"

"Most of them," Joss repeated Alina's answer. "But

some were English." She stopped, listening as Alina resumed her dissertation. "And the law came to this house more than once." She frowned. "A Bow Street Runner, I think, based on her description. She said he smoked a pipe and left ashes all over her step."

"He smoked a pipe?" That seemed rather too coincidental.

"That's what she said."

Heath stored that away for the moment. "Was he there to arrest him?"

Joss raised her hand. "No. To visit. Late at night. She doesn't know what they talked about for she says her English is not good enough, but they stayed for a long time and there was always a great deal of arguing. But she is certain Leroux was their leader. His voice was always the loudest and the last."

"Does she remember anything about the theft that Leroux claimed to have experienced?"

"No. Only that he suddenly disappeared one day. People were glad to see him go. They were scared of him."

"And she wasn't?"

Joss smiled faintly as she relayed Heath's question and listened to Alina's answer. "She says when I am as old as she is, and have survived as much as she has, I will find very little in the world left to fear." Joss fell silent as Alina continued, the woman's sharp eyes watching Heath now.

A little unnerved, Heath took another sip of his drink. He was distracted only when he saw the color creeping up into Joss's cheeks.

"What is she saying now?" Heath asked.

Joss shook her head. "Nothing of importance."

Alina raised knowing white eyebrows and gestured expectantly at Heath.

Joss sighed. "She says that she can tell my husband is a good man," she said stiffly. "Because he listens carefully to my answers." At the last, a little amusement broke into the stilted delivery of her words. "Apparently the ability to listen is well regarded in Moldavia. Perhaps you should search there for a bride."

"Did you tell her I am not your husband? That you would rather be drawn and quartered than find yourself shackled to me in holy matrimony?" He'd meant it as a joke, but there was an edge to his words that he regretted instantly.

Joss gave him a long, unreadable look.

"No, I didn't" was all she said.

⁓

Heath and Joss finally extricated themselves from the warmth of Alina's tiny home, finding themselves once again in the narrow streets. The clouds had thickened, threatening more snow or sleet, and the wind had picked up, whistling eerily. Joss hurried ahead of Heath, anxious in equal measure to be out of the wind and to be out of the lane.

And anxious to avoid any other questions that no longer seemed to have simple answers. When it came to matters of the heart, Heath had this horrible habit of making the careful logic she had constructed over the years utterly illogical.

"When did you live in Moldavia?" His inquiry came from behind her, muffled by the collar of his coat and more than a little resigned.

"I didn't," Joss told him, tucking her chin into her scarf, relieved to be able to provide an easy answer to an easy question. "But one of the Marquess of Hastings's servants was from there. I asked her to teach me her language. She was only too happy to comply. Like Alina, she missed home terribly, and being able to communicate easily with someone helped. She told me a great deal about her home and its customs and its people."

A gust of wind nearly tore the last words away and set a battered sign dancing on its chains above a doorway. Joss watched as it twisted in the wind, the words *Four Crows Apothecary* faded and barely legible. Someone had, more recently, painted four birds on the bottom of the sign, but they looked more like four chickens than four crows. Joss smiled inwardly. Her mother would have found that amusing. And Joss could only imagine what type of medicines might be found in the Four Crows Apothecary. She was quite certain each elixir would be comprised of four parts gin—

She stopped abruptly in the middle of the road. Heath, who had been hunched into his coat, walked squarely into the back of her, catching her at the last minute and managing to right the both of them.

"Bloody hell, Joss," he complained. "What are you doing?"

"Four," she whispered, her mind racing frantically.

"I beg your pardon?" Heath was looking at her with concern.

"There were four of them," she breathed. "*Four.*"

That was it. The missing piece. She'd missed it because, in the last set of letters, there had been only three. One each to Smythe, Villeneuve, and Adam. There hadn't been one addressed to Arthur Williamson.

Heath was watching her warily. "That look on your face scares the wits out of me. Four of what?"

"The letters were sent in groups of four. To four different men. Even the very early ones. That is the key. They can only be decoded if all four letters are present. I treated each document as an individual entity." She was aware she was talking too fast and pressed her hands to her cheeks as if that could slow the tumult of babble. "Four very different men who found themselves arrested, all on the same day, all under questionable circumstances. How did I miss it?"

She felt as if she might crawl out of her skin. God, but the answer had been in front of her the entire time. It was infuriating yet exhilarating all at once, the promise of an answer just out of reach. "Assuming there was one, the last letter to Williamson is missing. It wasn't in the folder." She paused, barely able to contain her mounting excitement. "Do you suppose the arrests were made on the same day deliberately?" she asked. "Just like how the Templars were arrested?"

Heath rolled his eyes at her last comment but dug around in his pocket and pulled out a small white card.

"Edmund Banks?" Joss asked. "Who is that?"

"A Bow Street Runner. On the day Mr. Smythe was arrested, he said he was making an arrest of his own. In fact, there were a number of officers involved. Arresting a gang of thieves."

"You think it was Villeneuve, Adam, and Williamson?"

"I hate coincidences."

"So you've said."

Heath shoved the card back in his pocket. "We've got one more stop to make."

Heath left Joss steaming impatiently in a small bakery nearby.

There was no chance he would risk bringing her into the Bow Street offices, making her a known and vulnerable entity before the keen eye of Potter. Or whoever else might have betrayed Gavin Smythe. Heath had a reasonable cause for visiting the offices. Josephine Somerhall did not. And even she couldn't argue with that.

Edmund Banks was sitting in exactly the same place he had been the last time Heath had visited. His eyes lit up when he spied Heath come through the door.

"Have you considered my offer, my lord?" he asked. "I promise you will not be disappointed."

Heath glanced around, noting that Potter was nowhere in sight. Good.

"Indeed. I have considered it carefully, though I have a question or two."

"Of course." The officer smiled confidently.

"It's regarding the arrests you made on the day Mr. Smythe was arrested. You mentioned them earlier."

Some of Banks's confidence slipped into what looked like confusion. "I'm afraid I don't understand."

"I'd like to understand the process," Heath said. "How you arrive at the decision to make an arrest."

"Didn't Mr. Smythe explain—"

"No, and to be truthful, I didn't really care. However, in light of the recent allegations, I want to make sure I better understand how it all happens. I'd hate to trust the wrong person again."

Banks's face cleared. "Of course." He smiled winningly.

"Well, in almost all cases, we catch the thief red-handed. Or we discover the stolen goods on his person or property."

"I see. And is that what happened in the case of the thieves you arrested the same day as Mr. Smythe?"

Banks frowned. "Not exactly."

"Then how did you know they were thieves?"

"The victim had had a number of personal documents stolen from him. He testified that he had seen the men in question take them from his residence. Our commanding officer, which is, of course, Mr. Potter, corroborated those claims and set us to tracking the villains. We were ordered to arrest the men on sight and bring them straightaway to London. The men were subsequently convicted based upon the strength of both the victim's and Mr. Potter's testimony."

"But you never actually recovered any of the stolen property?"

Edmund Banks shifted uncomfortably. "No, I'm afraid we did not. But I can assure you that in most cases—"

"So you never saw any stolen documents?"

"No, but—"

"What manner of documents were they?" Heath asked, knowing that it was a long shot.

Banks was frowning again. "I don't know." There was suspicion shining through his spectacles. "I fail to see why this is important."

Heath waved his hand. "Because I also have a number of documents pertaining to my business that are very valuable to me on a day-to-day basis. It would give me confidence to know that, if they were ever stolen, appropriate efforts would be made on your part to retrieve them."

Banks nodded. "Of course. We would take whatever measure necessary." He offered another toothy smile.

"Excellent." Heath paused, as if just remembering something. "The men you arrested—they were transported?"

Banks nodded smartly. "As far as I know, they are still rotting at Woolwich. Henry Villeneuve and his cronies will not bother anyone anytime soon."

Heath sighed. "Indeed they won't."

Chapter 11 _____

Heath filled Joss in on the way back to the warehouse, arriving to find the dowager's butler and coachman restacking a sea of empty barrels that had been knocked across the floor. As Heath looked across the vast space that had nearly been set to rights, he felt a twinge of guilt that he hadn't been here helping the men with the physical work, and worse, that it was the dowager's staff who had come to his rescue unasked.

The two men had discarded their jackets and coats and were working in their shirt-sleeves, flushed with exertion in the chill of the air, and Heath could hear them arguing happily as they labored with quick, untiring efficiency. They seemed unaware of Heath and Joss's presence.

"You're sure they're brothers?" Heath asked Joss as they picked their way across the warehouse. Where Luke was golden blond and muscularly compact, Joseph, stripped of his heavy coat, was lanky, his limbs seemingly sprouting from his torso at awkward angles. Even his dark hair stuck out from his head in a haphazard nest, making him look younger than he likely was.

"Quite sure. As they tell it, they had a very enterprising mother," Joss explained.

"Ah."

"They have an elder sibling as well," Joss told him. "His name is Paul, and he makes Margaret look positively dainty. He's up in Scotland for the winter, seeing to my mother's racehorses."

"They are all from Scotland then?" Heath asked, thinking of the burr that occasionally became evident in Luke's speech.

"More or less."

"What did they do before they came to work for your mother?"

"Lord Boden," Luke called, catching sight of them and preventing Joss from answering. "Almost done here," the butler said, wiping an arm across his perspiring forehead. He put his hands on his hips and looked around him with satisfaction.

"My thanks," Heath said sincerely. "You didn't have to do this. I could have pulled some of my men from the factories to help."

Luke made a sound of dismissal. "Your men have duties in their factories. We, on the other hand, have nothing but time since everyone is everywhere but at home." He glanced over at Joseph. "And my little brother here gets into trouble if he's not kept busy. But don't worry. I've been keeping an eye on him."

Behind him Joseph scoffed. "I have little use for warehouses and their contents," he said with a grunt as he heaved another empty barrel up against the wall. "Things that are bulky, cumbersome, and difficult to conceal, not to mention the complicated logistics required to move the goods." He shot his blond brother a pointed look. "Goods that can move themselves at a brisk gallop are much more attractive and lucrative."

Luke snorted. "You're biased."

"Come, now. No one in their right mind would keep anything as valuable as gold or silver or jewels in a warehouse," Joseph retorted, rolling another barrel upright and tipping it toward his brother. "When was the last time you found a cache of gold and pearl necklaces in a warehouse?"

"Never," Luke admitted, swinging the heavy barrel across his shoulders. "I suppose that is why I am so good at opening expensive doors."

"And windows," his brother added.

Listening to the cheerfully bickering brothers, Heath suddenly had a very good idea of what the dowager's butler had done before he had assumed his position. And for that matter, her coachman.

In another life Heath might have been appalled. Certainly incensed at the pair's cavalier comments. Yet at this moment, Heath found himself pleased, speculating that given the current circumstances, men with a skill set such as theirs might become very advantageous in the foreseeable future. He wondered how that had happened.

Beside him Joss had begun to shift restlessly.

"Those papers waiting upstairs are burning a hole right through your patience now, aren't they?" he murmured.

"As a matter of fact, they are," she replied unapologetically. "Now that I have the key." She pursed her lips. "Or at least I think I do."

"Then you found something useful in the records?"

Luke asked with interest, abandoning his work for the moment.

Joseph joined them, and Joss hurriedly related what they had found.

"Well, what did they steal?" the coachman asked with a puzzled frown.

"Personal documents of some sort, according to the Bow Street Runners who were dispatched to arrest them. Yet the arresting officers never actually saw any type of documents, nor recovered any proof that documents were ever stolen."

Joseph exchanged a look with his brother. "That doesn't sound right."

"Nothing about any of this sounds right. The arrests were made based almost entirely on the word of Mr. Potter. And a mysterious Frenchman of a military demeanor named Marcel Leroux."

"*Vive l'Empereur,*" muttered Luke.

"Do you think it was the folder that they stole? That those papers were the item of unspecified value?" Joseph wondered aloud.

Heath made a face. "We considered that. But the more I think about it, the less sense it makes. The letters were addressed to them. How could they be arrested for stealing their own post? I am quite convinced that those men were set up, in much the same way I am convinced Mr. Smythe was set up for a crime he never committed."

"As much as I am enjoying this exercise in conjecture," Joss interrupted pointedly, "if I were allowed to get started on these documents, we might actually accrue fact and not fanciful fiction."

The three men looked at Joss.

"Of course," Heath said. "I'll clear a spot on my desk upstairs."

"Wonderful." Joss was already edging toward the narrow stairway.

"We're almost done down here." Luke made a vague gesture. "Perhaps we'll nip out and see if any of my past colleagues might remember hearing of these particular thieves. It's an odd enough case that someone might recall something."

Joss had stopped at the bottom of the stairs at Luke's words, her hand resting on the railing. "Be careful then."

"Aye." Luke nodded, and he and Joseph returned to their work.

Heath strode over to the stairs leading up to his office and joined Joss, his hand going unconsciously to her lower back. "Come then," he said, guiding her up the narrow passage.

Joss's mind was clearly a million miles away already, her eyes slitted in the manner he knew so well. She barely acknowledged him as she ascended into the dimness. Her warning to Luke had made him remember the very real danger they were dabbling in. Men had died over whatever was in that folder.

He stopped suddenly and caught her elbow. "Joss." There was an urgency to his voice that he heard echo in the enclosed stairway.

She swung around on the stair above him, momentarily jolted out of her ruminations.

"Promise me you'll tell me what you find in those documents," he said.

A shadow of a frown crossed her face. "Of course. Why wouldn't I?"

"Because you're like as not to try and do everything on your own."

Joss's frown deepened. "I am not so foolish as to deliberately misunderstand the gravity of this situation."

"That's not what I meant." Heath ran a hand through his hair. "But you've been on your own and done everything on your own for so long now..."

"You say that like it's a bad thing."

"It's an admirable thing. So long as you accept help from time to time."

Her eyes softened. "You're standing here right now, aren't you, Hextall?"

He searched her face in the muted light. Her eyes were level with his own, standing as she was, and he found himself drawn in by their turquoise depths, ringed by a profusion of dark lashes. He became aware of her heat beneath his fingers where they still rested on her arm.

With his other hand, he reached up and traced the side of her face and the crooked bump of her nose. "I wish I had been standing here sooner," he whispered.

He heard her breath catch, though she didn't look away. A powerful surge of emotion caught him unawares, sending his pulse racing and every fiber in his body tightening. God, but he wanted to kiss her. Wanted to take her and make her his and keep her safe from ever suffering again.

Yet he might as well wish to capture a phoenix. Josephine Somerhall would never be captured and kept by any man, for she was a fierce, fiery spirit who had not only survived but thrived on her own. She'd built an inner strength and beauty and confidence that was dependent on no man.

He dropped his hand and felt the soft brush of her breath on his cheek as she exhaled.

With suppressed reluctance he gestured ahead of them. "After you, my lady," he said. "Your noble desk awaits."

Joss moved away, climbing the rest of the stairs silently, and Heath followed, wrestling with the feeling that somehow he was losing something. Or perhaps he had lost it long ago without ever realizing he had had it. Either way, it had opened up a hole somewhere in his soul that was becoming harder and harder to ignore.

Joss had paused on the small landing to wait for him, and he slid past her and opened the door to his office.

His first thought was that whoever had taken apart his offices had returned to finish the job. Two bodies whirled in surprise as the door bumped against a chair piled with books, sending everything crashing to the floor.

"Lord Boden!" The exclamation sounded a little strangled.

"Mr. Bennett?" Heath stared in surprise, not because of his presence, but because the man was cowering behind his desk with a decidedly hunted look stamped across his broad features. Heath's eyes snapped to the second person in the room, and he took an unintentional step back. "*Lady Rebecca?*" Only his ingrained manners prevented him from gaping like a landed trout.

"Lord Boden." Lady Rebecca recovered first, offering him an apologetic smile as she bent to pick up the books that had fallen. "You startled me. I didn't hear you on the stairs."

"Whatever are you doing here?" Heath blurted, unable to help himself. He was aware Joss had come to stand just behind him.

"I wanted to make sure you were all right," Rebecca said earnestly. "I was worried that your business may have suffered irrevocable damage or that you might have suffered property loss. I wished to offer my assistance in any manner I could."

Heath felt a wash of shame. Seconds ago he had been fantasizing about kissing Joss in a dusty stairwell, while the woman he was courting had been waiting for him in his office with her concern and good intentions. Jesus, he was a cad.

"Oh. Er. Of course. Well, thank you. But no real harm done, I assure you. Just a deuced mess, is all." Heath's eyes slid back to where Benjamin Bennett had straightened behind his desk. The man had relaxed somewhat, no doubt thankful to be relieved of the duty of sole entertainer of the Earl of Dalton's daughter while they waited for Heath to show up. The man was shy around women at the best of times.

"I take it you have met Mr. Benjamin Bennett," Heath said awkwardly. "My chief overseer."

"Indeed." Rebecca smoothed her skirts beneath her cloak and tucked tendrils of hair behind her ear. "He has been most kind. It was he who suggested I wait in your office for your return on account it is heated." She bestowed a small smile in the direction of the looming overseer. "I promise I have not been distracting him too much from his duties here."

"I'm glad your comfort has been seen to."

"Who on earth would do something like this?" she asked, looking around her at the disarray. "And what could they possibly have wanted?"

"I have no idea," he lied. "No doubt youngsters, out on

a lark, intent on causing mischief. As I said, nothing was stolen."

"Mmm." Lady Rebecca seemed to accept his explanation, and her calm gray eyes slid past him and touched on Joss. "Good morning, Lady Josephine," she said politely. "It's lovely to see you again. Did you also come to offer your assistance?"

"Indeed. Though I confess I had some early errands to attend to this morning that brought me in this direction," Joss responded easily. "I am just waiting now for my servants to finish the repairs they have undertaken downstairs."

Heath marveled for the briefest of seconds at the ease with which Joss somehow managed to manipulate the truth into something entirely different. In the next second, the reminder of Luke and Joseph jolted Heath out of his shock. "I do hope you did not travel here alone," he said to Rebecca with some alarm.

Beside him he caught Joss rolling her eyes and watched as Rebecca covered a cough that sounded suspiciously like a laugh.

"Of course not," she told him. "I have a groom with me. As far as I know, he is holding our horses outside."

Heath shook his head, troubled. "I did not see him or your horses when I came in."

"Yes, well, he was also holding some coins I gave him in case he got thirsty while he waited," Rebecca added with a sheepish twitch to her mouth.

Joss snickered, and Heath shot her a quelling look. Joss may have circumnavigated herself around the world, but the sheltered Lady Rebecca certainly had not. Lady Rebecca would not have a dirk concealed in the folds of her skirts. Lady Rebecca did not travel with a coachman and a butler with underworld connections and the deadly stealth of vipers. There was no need to encourage her.

"I thank you for your offer of assistance," he said to Rebecca. "But by the end of the day everything will have been restored to order, I assure you."

"Perhaps I can help you collect and organize some of the paperwork?" she inquired.

Heath didn't want Lady Rebecca anywhere near his office at the moment. She should be at home, safely secured in her drawing room, doing whatever it was normal women did daily. It was bad enough Joss was caught in the middle of this mystery. He would not be responsible for putting Lady Rebecca in danger as well.

"A generous offer, truly," he said, giving her his warmest smile. "And I thank you for it. But it is wholly unnecessary." He held out his arm to her. "Let me escort you home."

Lady Rebecca flushed slightly. "I think it would be better if my groom saw me home. I, ah, have a few items to pick up along the way."

"Surely you can get them at another time—"

"She needs to return with a shopping bag, Hextall," Joss hissed beside him. "Because she is currently supposed to be shopping."

Rebecca had the grace to redden further, though she looked somewhat relieved to be spared the pain of spelling it out herself. She shot Joss a grateful look.

"Oh." Heath cleared his throat. "Well, then, let me escort you to the nearest tavern, where we no doubt will find your willing groom eager to accompany you to your next stop."

Rebecca regarded him for a long moment, her thoughts hidden behind her impassive expression. "Thank you," she said presently. "Not many men would be so open-minded."

"You have no idea," Heath muttered to himself.

Lady Rebecca nodded at Joss as she took Heath's arm. She hesitated, almost wistfully. "Perhaps, Lady Josephine, you would be so kind as to call on me at my home one afternoon. I do believe I would very much enjoy hearing of your adventures."

Heath shifted uneasily, not at all sure he liked the idea of the woman he was supposed to be courting befriending the woman he couldn't keep his hands off.

"The years I spent living with savages, you mean?" Joss asked, a brittleness to her voice, and Heath's unease changed to surprise at Joss's sudden and challenging cynicism.

Rebecca smiled faintly and shrugged. "The only species of savages I have ever met have been lechers with wandering hands soaked in liquor and entitled expectations. If you have met a different breed in your travels, I'd be most curious."

Her comment elicited a startled chuckle from Joss. A slow, complicit smile spread across her face, though she refused to meet his eye. "I do believe I might have some very recent experience with that species. Perhaps I shall stop by and we can compare notes."

Holy hell, Heath thought a little wildly, feeling the blood drain from his face. The idea that Joss might be referring to the very memorable minutes he'd had her pressed up against a desk—and his hands everywhere they never should have been—had him in a cold sweat.

He cast a desperate look at Bennett, but the giant had morphed into a piece of furniture and was still resolutely silent, staring at the floor with single-minded determination.

"Shall we go?" Heath asked hastily. He got a better grip on Rebecca's arm and steered her away from Joss.

"Of course. Good day, Lady Josephine. Mr. Bennett."

Benjamin mumbled something under his breath, though Heath was far too preoccupied to be affronted by the man's appalling manners. His only goal was to get Lady Rebecca as far away from his office as possible.

And as far away from Joss.

⁓

It was nearly forty-five minutes before Joss heard Heath stomping back up the stairs. He pushed open the door, and she could feel the weight of his glare.

"You made that far too easy, Hextall," she said, not looking up. Mr. Bennett had cleared the surface of the massive desk and fetched her a comfortable chair, and she had just finished organizing the documents by date. "You should know a lady never kisses and tells. Though the expression on your face was priceless. You looked like you might be ill."

"That really wasn't funny."

"Oh, I can assure you it was." She finally looked up to find him leaning in the doorway, his arms crossed and his cheeks and nose reddened from the cold. "I just can't believe you rose to the bait with such magnificence."

He stalked over to the desk and braced his hands on either side, leaning down toward her.

Joss returned her attention to the papers, more to evade

his intense gaze than anything. His presence was suddenly making it hard to concentrate.

"Where did Mr. Bennett get to?" he asked.

Joss shrugged. "I'm not entirely sure. He disappeared after Lady Rebecca left."

"He's been disappearing a lot lately," Heath grumbled.

Joss didn't much care where Benjamin Bennett had gone. "Did you find Lady Rebecca's groom?" she asked, forcing her voice to remain casual.

"Yes." He paused. "You shouldn't encourage her, you know. She doesn't have your cunning or your awareness."

"I would imagine that is a point in her favor."

"Not when she is wandering around the London Docks in the company of a negligent groom it's not."

Joss shoved aside a small prick of self-reproach. "I think you could do far worse in a wife." Despite her best efforts, the more she spoke to the woman, the more she found herself genuinely liking Lady Rebecca. Beneath her perfectly polished exterior, Joss sensed something of a kindred spirit. "I really do like her."

"So you've said." Heath made some sort of noncommittal sound.

Joss looked up in speculation. "What? Have you changed your mind about pursuing a wife?" She refused to acknowledge the tiny beam of hope that soared.

"I can't just change my mind," he snapped. "I have already established certain expectations with the Daltons and Lady Rebecca. Not to mention whatever conclusions society has drawn regarding my intentions towards her."

Joss made a face. "That sounds...very upright and upstanding."

Heath scowled. "What do you suppose would happen

to Lady Rebecca's reputation if I suddenly were seen to cast her aside?"

"Is that what you want?" A morbid curiosity made her ask. "To be released from your commitments?"

Heath closed his eyes. "I don't know what I want," he mumbled. "I just want to do what is right."

"For whom?" Joss studied him, the tiny beam of hope growing into a steady light. She ignored all the reasons why such optimism was foolish.

He opened his eyes. "For my family. For my potential wife and her family. For the earldom."

"And do your wishes and your desires hold no weight in this equation?"

He impaled her with his gaze. "Not if they are something that I know to be unattainable." His eyes dropped to her mouth.

Do it, she wanted to demand. *Kiss me the way you kissed me before. The way that left me breathless and scattered and shaking. And wholly, completely yours.*

"How do you know they are unattainable?" It was a whisper.

He raised his eyes and stared at her long and hard. "Are you warm enough?" he asked abruptly, and once again Joss could feel him withdraw from her, in the same way that he had distanced himself in the stairway earlier when she had been sure he would kiss her again.

Joss glanced over at the coal brazier glowing in the corner. "Yes," she said unsteadily.

"Good. I'll leave you to it then?" He stood and gestured at the contents of the folder in front of her.

"Yes," she repeated.

"Will it bother you if I come and go?"

"Of course not. It's your office."

"Very good. I will tell Luke and Joseph to fetch you and see you home when they are done." He nodded at her once and then left the way he had come, the sound of his boots fading down the stairs. "You'll need to take that folder with you when you leave."

And Joss was left wondering if she had just lost something she hadn't known she'd had.

The damn earl had visited Newgate.

The clerk he had paid to advise him of such an occurrence had done just that, and if there had been a doubt in Potter's mind about the involvement of the Earl of Boden in the Gavin Smythe debacle, the man's perusal of the criminal records abolished it. It was obvious the earl knew something, certainly enough to be nosing around in the criminal registers. Looking for what, Potter wasn't sure, but if the earl was as intelligent as Potter feared he might be, he was going to be a problem.

And Potter would happily kill the man, except with Gavin Smythe gone and presumed dead and the documents missing, the Earl of Boden was their only existing link to the documents, the gold, or both. The French general would no doubt want to snatch Boden, tie him up, and deposit him in the nearest shed for questioning. He'd done just that with the three earlier captives Potter had worked so hard to track down. Or rather, his Bow Street officers had worked so hard to track down, all the while unaware that the prisoners had been innocent of the crime of which they'd been accused. Potter snorted, remembering the captives' protestations. But therein lay the beauty of the entire plan.

Every man they arrested was innocent.

Potter frowned again, coming back to the problem of Heath Hextall. Taking apart the earl's office and home had proven to be an exercise in futility and had undoubtedly spooked him. Though that sometimes worked to an advantage. Men often made hasty decisions when fear was a factor.

For now, Potter decided, he would simply watch and wait.

Chapter 12 ———————————

The story unfolded over the course of four days.

Four days in which Joss barely slept, ate only when prompted, and saw virtually no one. She'd started in Heath's offices, but finished in the privacy of her mother's study. Joseph drifted in from time to time to tell her he'd not yet found anyone who knew of Villeneuve, Adam, or Williamson, nor of anything they might have stolen that had been resold or recovered. Margaret barged in more forcefully, threatening to upend her tray of food on the reams of paper if Joss did not put down her quill and eat something. And Luke came in only occasionally, peering over her shoulder and leaving folded copies of the newspaper deliberately on the corner of the desk, which Joss ignored.

Combined, the letters revealed a tale of the likes Joss was still having a hard time absorbing. Even as she finished what she thought of as the last chapter and uncurled her cramped, ink-stained fingers, she still couldn't quite bring herself to believe. If she did, she might succumb to the icy fingers of dread that had mounted as each new set of letters revealed their secrets. Secrets that were indeed worth killing for. Secrets now etched forever within her memory.

Joss stood stiffly, dizzy with fatigue, and the room blurred a little at the edges. She needed a plan. She would have to send for Heath, she thought. Immediately. No, she amended, it would be better to go directly to him. Heath, better than anyone, would be able to lend some logical rationality and sanity to what was quite an irrational, insane account, even by her standards. It would all make better sense once he had read, scrutinized, and evaluated it. Hextall would know what to do. He always knew what to do.

That decision made, Joss returned the original documents to the folder, adding her own notes and decoded information, and tied the lot back up tightly with the leather strings. She stared at it for a moment in much the same way Heath had looked at it that first night. As if it might explode. And in the end, it had.

⁓

Joss wasted precious minutes searching for her gloves. She knew exactly where she had left them in the study, but they were gone now. No doubt a well-meaning maid had taken them to be cleaned. They'd been filthy when she'd returned from Heath's offices what seemed like a lifetime ago, but what did it matter? White gloves in winter were ridiculous. White gloves in London were idiotic in general. The entire city was heated with coal, for pity's sake, and the residue clung to everything. Black gloves would be more practical. Come to think of it, black gowns would also be more serviceable. With the added benefit of being less noticeable at night. A black bonnet, black cloak, black shoes—

"If I didn't know better, I would have said that you are planning on going out," Luke said from the door.

Joss jerked, banging her elbow painfully against the

edge of the library table where she had bent to search for the missing gloves. She shot an accusing look at Luke. "You need to wear bells. Or perhaps I'll get you a set of bagpipes you can play everywhere you go."

The butler winced, his handsome features wrinkled. "I'm not so fond of the pipes."

"I thought you were Scottish."

"When it suits."

Joss rubbed her arm. "What time is it?"

"Almost midnight. Much too late for you to be going out. By yourself." He said the last loudly and pointedly.

"Half of London is just leaving for their evening entertainments now."

"Not by themselves, they are not." Luke paused. "Where, exactly, do you think you're going?"

Joss experienced a peculiar surge of apprehension and excitement as the remnants of fatigue were swept from her mind. "I need to fetch Lord Boden. Immediately." She ran an experimental hand through her hair and grimaced as it snagged in the snarls.

"You're finished with the papers and such then?" he asked, his eyes drifting to the bound folder on the desk before returning to her.

"Yes." She yanked harder at her hair.

"Your hair looks like it feels," Luke verified dryly, before his face became serious again. "And you'll not be fetching the earl anytime soon."

"Why not?"

"He's at a musical soiree."

Joss gaped. "Hextall? A musical soiree?"

"Music by society's youth to welcome the impending festive season and all that," Luke confirmed.

Joss stared at him. "But he hates musical soirees. He can't abide by poorly played music. Is he drunk?"

"Not to my knowledge."

"Did my brother dare him?"

"No. The duke has gone to Windsor for a few days. Something about a thoroughbred mare he wished to purchase. A Christmas gift for his duchess, I believe."

"Then why..." She trailed off, regret squeezing her innards unpleasantly. "He is attending with the Daltons."

Luke was watching her, his face inscrutable. "You have not been reading the papers I have set out for you."

"Papers? No, I have not been reading the damn papers. I have not had time to read the papers." She sounded like a shrew, she acknowledged, but regret was starting to swell and sting.

Luke wandered over to the desk, where he picked up the neatly folded stack. "I thought you might be interested, since I know very well you haven't spoken with the earl in four days." He handed her the pile.

Joss scanned each, all opened to the social page. In each there was a mention of the Earl of Boden escorting or being seen with Lady Rebecca Dalton. More than a few made ill-concealed insinuations of a forthcoming wedding in the new year.

Once again the sense of loss she'd felt the last time she'd seen Heath assailed her, and the tea she had drunk soured in her stomach. If she were a good person, she'd be happy for him.

But she wasn't a good person. She was a jealous, envious, covetous person, and knowing Heath was with another woman left her aching and hurt and resentful. Joss stood and stalked to the hearth, flinging the papers on top of the burning coal. The fire flared hot and bright before subsiding, leaving only remnants of gray ash.

That very neatly summed up what existed between her and Heath. A steady warmth, punctuated by a brief blaze of passion that was reduced to nothing but a pile of dust that would be swept away by morning and forgotten. Yet what else had she expected?

Luke cleared his throat tactfully. "The last time I saw Lord Boden, he was leaving his office in a spectacularly foul mood. That was after he had returned to you after leaving Lady Rebecca with her errant groom. Do I dare ask the nature of your last conversation?"

Joss threw him a dark look. "I don't know. You seem to dare quite a bit."

"Yes, but scaling walls and roofs are nothing when compared to navigating matters of the heart."

"There are no matters of the heart at issue here," Joss muttered.

"This study desk might say otherwise."

Joss scowled even as the heat crept into her cheeks. "Forget the damn pipes. I'm getting you a military drummer to follow you around. Spying on people is going to get you killed one day."

"It wasn't intentional, I assure you. The door was wide open."

"That was a mistake."

"Indeed. You might even consider locking it next time."

Joss felt herself redden even further. "Not the door, the…" She cast about for a word that wasn't entirely mortifying to use with the butler.

"Kiss?"

"Yes!" She twisted the crumpled fabric of her skirts in her hand, as uncomfortable as she'd ever been. "I can't believe I am having this conversation with you."

"Would you prefer to have it with your brother?"

Joss looked at the butler in horror. "Hell, no. No, Worth won't ever hear of this." She strode forward until she was face-to-face with Luke, glad his height matched hers. "You. Will. Not. Tell. Him." She paused. "Please."

Luke held up his hands in defeat. "I won't say anything." He pushed himself off the wall. "But you should."

Joss goggled at Luke. "And say what? 'Don't mind if I dally with your best friend while you help him find a wife'?"

"You make it sound tawdry."

"Because it is!" Joss cried. "And I am not that woman. The woman who gets in the way of Hextall's happiness for her own selfish reasons. I'm supposed to be his friend."

Luke shook his head and put his hands on his hips. "Your brother is orchestrating this entire charade with Lady Rebecca because he believes it is what the earl wants."

"It is exactly what Hextall wants. He said it himself."

"Yet his actions say something completely different. The way he looks at you when he thinks no one is watching says something completely different."

Joss stared at the butler. "You have no idea what you're talking about."

Luke only returned her stare placidly. "Hmph. You never struck me as the cowardly sort."

Joss gaped at him. "Me? Cowardly? Hextall *apologized* after he kissed me." She pushed her hair off her forehead in frustration.

"Of course he did. Your earl has an overdeveloped sense of chivalry. It's a flaw, but one in which I'm sure correction is possible."

"He's not my earl," she ground out through clenched teeth.

"He would like to be."

"For the love of God, stop," Joss growled. She whirled and returned to the safety of the desk, furious with the futility of the entire topic.

"Would you like me to send word that you require Lord Boden's immediate presence?"

"Yes. No." She marshaled her composure. There was absolutely nothing to be gained by forcing Heath to choose between his evening with the Daltons and a summons from the Duke of Worth's sister. It was bad enough that he'd had to abandon the entire Dalton family at the theater when his warehouse had been ransacked. To publicly walk out on them a second time would be perceived as extraordinarily ill-mannered and tactless, and Heath was neither of those things. Though he'd do it in a heartbeat, she knew, if he thought she was in some sort of danger.

As much as she wanted Heath to see the contents of that folder now, logic prevailed. She wasn't in danger, or at least not any more than she had been yesterday or this morning. The information that lay innocently on the study desk had remained concealed for years, some of it for centuries. Another hour or two would make no difference.

"No," she repeated. "The end of the soiree will be soon enough. But I'm going to his house."

"To do what? Wait for the earl?"

Yes, Joss realized with a horrible twisting sensation in

her chest. *I'll wait. I've been waiting for the earl for my entire life.*

She just hadn't known it until it was too late.

~⌒

God, he hated musical soirees.

Even when it had been Heath's own sisters perching at the pianoforte or standing at its side to give their best oratory offering, they'd never ended fast enough. He had, however, become very accomplished at fixing his eyes in the distance, or in this case, at an unfortunate portrait of a long-dead ancestor complete with bulging eyes and bouncing ringlets, and letting his mind go where it was wont to go.

As a boy, his imagination had invariably gone to the adventures he and Worth might find every summer when Heath arrived at Hazeldell to stay with the old Earl of Boden. Heath's father had always insisted that maintaining a close relation with his elderly and titled cousin was good for business and good for appearances, and by association might even instill a little gentility into his rather reckless son.

Heath doubted the old earl had even been aware of his presence outside of the obligatory dinners, but the annual visits had gifted him with a loyal and lifelong friend.

Now that he was a man, Heath's mind once again strayed to the Somerhalls, but it was Josephine who now filled his thoughts constantly and completely. At the moment he was wondering what Joss was doing. Wondering if she'd managed to decipher whatever was in those damned documents, and if she'd succeeded, but hadn't told him.

Wondering if he should have just kissed her the last time he'd seen her and damn the consequences.

Four days and not a word from her. That was too long. He'd wanted to give her her space—hell, give himself some space—but he was second-guessing himself now. He had warned Joss not to try to do everything on her own. She was just too damned independent. Perhaps tomorrow, if there hadn't been word from her, he would go to the dowager's house and find out for himself exactly what was going on.

"I beg your pardon?" He was jolted out of his thoughts again by the realization that Lady Rebecca had just spoken to him.

"You're scowling," she murmured, tipping her head subtly in the direction of the young girl who was struggling through the overture from the *Marriage of Figaro* on her flute. "If she sees your expression, she'll likely burst into tears."

Immediately he rearranged his features into a look of bland interest. "Sorry," he whispered, shifting uncomfortably in his chair.

It was just like Lady Rebecca to be aware of a young girl's feelings. Bloody hell, Rebecca deserved better than this. She had been nothing but kind and congenial to him, though he'd had glimpses of a faint sadness that would sometimes touch her features when she thought herself alone. He liked this woman, dammit, and the fact that he couldn't seem to get Josephine Somerhall out of his mind to give Rebecca his full attention was leaving him racked with guilt.

"Is everything all right, Lord Boden?" she asked in a low voice. "You seem distracted tonight."

And every other night, she could have added, Heath thought, but was simply too gracious to say.

"I must confess I am not overly enamored of musical soirees," he replied, hating that he was hiding behind a half-truth. "I find them somewhat—"

The young girl with the flute hit a particularly discordant note.

"—jarring."

The corner of her mouth quirked as they exchanged a look of shared amusement.

Yes, Heath thought again, Lady Rebecca deserved better. And dammit, he would make sure she got it.

~

There was, blessedly, a break in the performances, during which their hostess ushered everyone back to the large dining room, where the long table had been pushed against the far wall. The surface was laden with a mouthwatering assortment of meats, cheeses, cakes, and large pitchers of lemonade. Heath lost track of Lady Rebecca somewhere in the crowd, though he'd not expected her to stay with him all evening. There were friends here he knew she'd wish to visit with.

"Setting yourself up to be wedded and bedded before Christmastide, eh, Boden?"

Heath forced a neutral expression onto his face before he turned to face Lord Braxton, the young heir to the duchy of Havockburn. The man was the very definition of arrogance and entitlement, and Heath harbored very little patience for him. "Braxton. Good evening."

"Are the rumors true?"

"Rumors?" Irritation pricked.

"I heard you were chasing the oldest Dalton chit all over London as of late." Braxton made a show of looking around Heath, pleased with his own hilarity. "But I don't see her chained to you tonight."

"I would imagine Lady Rebecca is enjoying herself with her friends. I am certainly not her keeper."

"Not yet, anyway." Braxton eyed Heath in speculation. "You should have chosen the second daughter."

"I beg your pardon?"

"The second daughter. Deborah? Dorothea? Something with a *D*, I think." He grinned conspiratorially at Heath and cupped his hands suggestively in front of his chest. "That one certainly received all the assets in that family."

Heath stared at Braxton, a slow anger beginning to burn.

The man, mistaking Heath's silence for uncertainty, elaborated on his wisdom. "You're rich enough old Dalton will likely give you any daughter you want. I'd reconsider if I were you. Plain is just plain, and the oldest one is like day-old porridge. She's practically a crone, and a blue-stocking to boot. She'll be a waste of good bed-sport and nothing but trouble, what with all that knowledge messing with her mind." He paused thoughtfully. "Although maybe that appeals to a man like you."

"A man like me?" Heath asked quietly.

Something in his tone must have alerted the duke's son that he had erred somewhere in his conversation. His face lost a little color. "A man involved in trade, and the like."

"And what, exactly, is it that you think appeals to me?" Heath's voice was dangerously low.

Braxton's eyes were darting nervously now. "Well, you

must like guarantees. Lady Rebecca can hardly be considered beautiful, certainly not enough to tempt another man. You'd be guaranteed that your sons are your own."

Heath curled his fingers into his palms to keep from breaking the idiot's nose. His eyes slid behind Braxton, colliding with a pair of utterly unreadable gray ones.

Bloody hell. He had no idea how long Rebecca had been standing there. Or how much she had heard.

"And, of course, there would be some land you would receive and—"

"Shut up," Heath snarled with barely leashed rage.

Braxton complied abruptly, the first smart thing he'd done.

"I would consider myself fortunate to have Lady Rebecca consent to be my wife. She possesses a beauty that does not rely on face paints or cleverly sewn bodices. And you are correct in that she is a woman of admirable intellect. I don't expect you to understand this, Braxton, but smart men like smart women because they make a man's life richer for the whole of it, long past the days when looks cease to matter. Because intelligent women become wives, not interchangeable accessories."

The duke's son was frowning as if trying to determine where the insult lay.

Heath might have laughed if he hadn't been so angry. "No one will ever remember what you wore, what you looked like, what you bought, or what you owned," he said. "The only thing they remember, Braxton, is how you made them feel."

Braxton had flushed a dull, indignant red, finally recognizing the slur on his own acumen. He raised a finger to point it at Heath. "You—"

"You," Heath cut him off, "can turn around and apologize to Lady Rebecca for your thoughtless, crude remarks."

Braxton paled again and swallowed, his hand dropping.

"And if Lady Rebecca is a better person than I, she might forgive you for your utter boorishness. And I won't feel the need to run you through at dawn."

Braxton visibly flinched, but it gave Heath only a small measure of satisfaction. He was aware that more than a few people had edged a little closer and had no doubt heard the entire exchange. He could only imagine the new set of whispers that would start. Yet there was no help for it.

Heath listened as Braxton stumbled through the obviously unfamiliar ritual of an apology, to which Rebecca granted him a civil and refined response that would have done any saint proud. As soon as he had finished speaking, the man fled without a backward glance, as if terrified that Heath might change his mind about a dawn meeting. Heath was left facing Rebecca, who hadn't moved.

"I thank you for your kind words, Lord Boden," she said, and though the words were benign, the tightness in her face was not.

"I only spoke the truth," he told her in perfect honesty. "Braxton is an idiot."

"I know." She was still studying him, and for the life of him, Heath couldn't begin to guess what she was thinking. "You did not need to call him out on my behalf."

"I didn't." Though the intimation had been clear that the Earl of Boden was prepared to defend Lady Rebecca's honor against any slur on her person. Heath heaved an inward sigh. He might as well have nailed the banns to the wall behind his head with his words.

"I'm relieved. The entire pretense of dueling is utterly asinine. Especially over words uttered by such a horse's ass."

A snort of laughter escaped before he could stop it.

"Will you?" she asked suddenly, her hands still against the green silk of her gown.

"Will I what?"

"Ask me to marry you."

Heath experienced the uncomfortable lurch in his stomach he felt every time he imagined doing just that. Her question was preposterous, he knew. One did not have frank discussions like this while standing at the far end of a refreshment table in a stuffy dining room, balancing corned beef and lemonade. Yet somehow it seemed like a conversation that should have been had long ago.

"I should," he said. "It is what everyone expects."

"And I should say yes." She paused. "It is what everyone expects."

They stood there, unmoving, regarding each other. Not happy. Not unhappy either.

"Don't do it before Christmas," she said, the shadows of sadness back in her eyes.

It was an odd request. Yet a reprieve at the same time.

"I won't."

"Thank you."

Heath offered her his arm, and they returned to the music room in silence.

Chapter 13 ———————————

The earl's house was silent. Like a damned tomb, Joss thought, chilled and dark and devoid of life. She passed a small table at the top of the stairs, a porcelain vase centered on its dusty surface. Naked stems sprouted from the mouth of the vase, their discarded petals lying forlorn and forgotten below.

What was the point of cut flowers in the middle of winter? she wondered idly, cupping a hand around the flame of her candle for warmth. So much effort for such a fleeting pleasure. Her mind drifted into memories of vivid sprays of color hanging everywhere, rich and fragrant amid heat and humidity, and she felt a sudden pang of sadness. Hextall would have been fascinated with the flora in India. He'd have taken one whiff of the rich, exotic scents that crowded the air and spent an exorbitant amount of time trying to figure out how to bottle them. It was too bad he'd never get to see it.

It was too bad she'd never have the chance to show it to him.

Her eyes wandered to the framed map hanging on the wall above the flowers, and she raised her candle. It was a map of Boston—a fascinating network of waterways and roads and land. Small notations marked current factories and planned building sites. She leaned closer for a better look.

"It's like a damn grave up here," Luke grumbled, suddenly appearing out of nowhere, an empty coal bucket dangling from his fingers. "No wonder everyone left."

Joss jumped. "What did I tell you about sneaking up on people? You're lucky I didn't faint away in fright and fall down the stairs." She set her candle on the table.

Luke gave her a long-suffering look. "You're not exactly the fainting sort."

"Keep this up and you're going to make me into one."

Luke made a rude noise. "What are you doing up here?"

"I got bored. And it's freezing downstairs."

"So you've come to poke about up here?"

"I wasn't poking. I was examining this map." She gestured to the wall and rubbed her eyes.

Luke peered at her. "You should go find somewhere to sleep," he told her. "You might not faint, but you look like you're going to drop where you stand. You've barely slept these last days."

Joss shook her head, which was admittedly fuzzy with exhaustion. "I'll wait up." The contents of the folder were too important.

"I just lit a fire in Lord Boden's rooms," he told her. "I'm sure he wouldn't mind if you—"

"I am not going to sleep in Lord Boden's bedroom, Luke, if that's what you were going to suggest. Don't be absurd."

"I was being practical. It's the only warm room with a bed in the entire house."

There was nothing practical about the way she was

imagining herself in Heath's bed. Her face heated, and she was glad for the low light. "No."

Luke shrugged. "Suit yourself. There is a large wing chair in the study you might find comfortable. I'm sure Joseph and the girls will have a fire going in there by now."

In the end Luke and Joseph and two of her mother's upstairs maids had accompanied her to Heath's townhome— the former pair because of a genuine concern for her safety and the latter simply because they were still awake and unashamedly curious about another expensive town-home. Whatever their motivations, Joss was grateful for the help and the company. Despite her bravado, it would have been miserable waiting for Heath in a cold, empty house.

"I'll wait up," Joss repeated. "There will be plenty of time to sleep later."

"Lord Boden won't be back for hours," Luke reminded her.

"I am aware," she retorted, less as a response than to counter another violent wave of jealousy stabbing into her gut at the reminder that Heath was still very much in the possession of Rebecca Dalton. It was like a fever, she thought, this morphing of a regular woman into a green-eyed ogre, intervals of subdued sanity punctuated by wild deluges of delirious, thrashing emotion that left her shaky and helpless to stop it from repeating.

Luke gave another one of his shrugs. "You coming down then?"

"In a minute." She needed to compose herself again. "I'd like to take a closer look at this map," she said by way of excuse.

"As you wish." Luke adjusted his grip on the bucket's handle and disappeared back down the stairs.

Left alone, Joss could hear the rattling and banging coming from downstairs as fires were lit in the hearths below. Every once in a while, a giggle would float up in response to something one of the men had said. It was likely more life than the house had seen in a year.

She should go back downstairs. The study lights would be lit by now, and she could spread out her notes and the contents of the folder there, so that all was in order when Heath returned. Yet she hesitated, unmoving, standing in the hallway outside his bedroom. An inviting glow beckoned from within, and Joss took an unconscious step forward. And then another, and another, until she was standing inside. She ignored the twinge of guilt that told her she had no right to invade his privacy in such a manner. There was no reason she should ever be in here. No reason that she cared to dwell on, anyway.

Her eyes slid to the bed in the corner. It, like the rest of the room, was Spartan in appearance, plain, square, and unadorned. It was unmade, the blankets pushed to the side in a jumbled heap as if Heath had just left, and she was assailed immediately by a mental image of him sprawled across its surface, his arm up over his head, as he used to sleep under the giant oak as a boy on hot summer afternoons. Her mouth went suddenly dry, a steady throb deep within her. She would not look at the bed and imagine. Imagine what it would be like to share it with him. Imagine what it would be like to wake up next to him every morning. There was no point in wishing for impossible things.

She forced her eyes away and scanned the rest of the

room. There was a narrow door on the far wall, dark in silent shadow, which Joss assumed was the entrance to his dressing room. On her right was a washstand, a number of towels draped over the side almost concealing it in much the same manner that a chair had been completely hidden by a pile of discarded clothes. She wandered toward the dressing room, pausing to examine another map that had been pinned to the wall. It depicted Europe and most of Asia and the vast stretch of water that collided with the eastern coast of the Americas. Heath had made tiny notes along the northern sections of the American coastline that were impossible to read in the low light. She'd never been that far west. She'd have to ask him what had interested him enough to document it on such an expensive map.

Joss left the map and entered the dressing room, skirting a deep hip bath placed in the center. Here the scent of sandalwood was stronger. There was a small stack of hard soap bars near the side of the tub, and Joss bent, setting the folder aside. She reached for the bar on the top of the stack, inhaling deeply.

Sandalwood, with the same darker undertone that she had always associated with Heath. She took another breath, concentrating. Cedar, perhaps. She set the bar aside and picked up another, with a faint smile, savoring the sharp tang of lemon. It smelled almost good enough to eat. She exchanged that for a third, breathing deeply and closing her eyes. Coconut. One of her favorites. Memories swirled of dark nights, steamy with heat, and days of brilliant sunshine reflecting off water of a surreal color. She wondered when Heath had started using the oil in his hard soaps. It certainly wasn't common in England at the moment.

But then Heath had never done anything common. He had always taken risks, acted on his instincts, trusted his gut. At least until he'd become earl of a failing earldom. And then he'd become…different. Contained. Restrained. Unreachable.

At least to her.

Joss backed out of the dressing room and paused by the bed, the loss she had felt earlier growing and expanding, a living, breathing thing writhing through her body. Without considering what she was doing, she sank onto the mattress, turning onto her side and pushing her face into the pillow. Just for a minute, she told herself, she would pretend. Allow herself the indulgence of imagining that she belonged. Here, in his bed. In his house. In his life.

She breathed deeply, the scent of Heath all around her. She reached down and pulled up the blankets, tucking them under her chin.

Just for a minute.

Potter was tired of the cold.

Tired of waiting outside houses and offices and shops and theaters while the Earl of Boden went about his life. A very dull, boring life, as far as he could tell, and the officer was beginning to doubt his earlier convictions that the earl had ever been involved in the disappearance of Gavin Smythe or the documents that the Frenchman so badly wanted. He wondered if the earl had simply gone to verify for himself that what Potter had told him was true.

He wanted to be doing something useful to help their cause—something more than following an earl around London like an obedient lapdog.

Because England was a diseased country, with its anti-quated class system, the poverty and crime that ran rampant, and the petty corruption and self-indulgent leadership of the monarchy. England was a country that was ripe for revolution and change. A country that would thrive under the vision of Napoleon Bonaparte. But time was running out for the exiled Emperor. Just today he'd heard rumors that Bonaparte's health was failing rapidly. If they were ever to succeed in restoring the Emperor to his true calling, they needed to find the documents that would lead them to the vast wealth concealed somewhere in this wretched country. Revolutions were not cheap.

The Runner shifted restlessly, stamping his feet in the cold. Every time the door of the expensive townhome opened, light and warmth and strains of music floated out into the street, and he was reminded again of how miserable he was, hunched against the cold. The earl was at a damn musical soiree, for God's sake, he thought, not a covert meeting of spies and assassins. A spurt of impatience and irritation heated his blood. He was a Bow Street officer, a man of resourcefulness and action. He was tired of waiting for something to happen. If the Earl of Boden knew anything about the secrets Gavin Smythe had concealed, or the documents, or the location of the hidden treasure, there were plenty of ways to extract information in a much more expedient manner. It was time to take a page out of the Frenchman's book. Messy, perhaps, but effective, and he would be well rewarded for his efforts.

And if the earl knew nothing—well, then the country certainly wouldn't miss another aristocrat.

Chapter 14 ⸻

There were lights on in his house.

Narrow bars of golden light spilled past his curtains onto the pavement in front of his townhome, the reflections shivering in damp puddles. That was the first thing Heath noticed when his gelding trudged past the house on its way to the mews in back. A momentary spurt of panic lanced through him, followed by embarrassment. Thieves or assassins would hardly stop to light the sconces and candelabra once they had broken into his house. He glanced up to see the faintest curl of smoke rising against the night sky. And they certainly wouldn't light fires in his hearths.

He hurriedly stabled his gelding, tense and listening for any intrusions, but the mews and courtyard remained dark and silent. He circled around the front of his house, trying to peer in the windows. Except whoever had lit the fires and the lights had drawn the drapes and all he could see was what he'd seen from the pavement—slivers of warm light escaping along the edges.

He wondered if his sister Julia and her husband were in town. Perhaps she had sent word ahead of their impending arrival and he had somehow not received her message or forgotten it altogether. He pressed a hand to his forehead, trying in vain to remember. It wasn't like him to forget something like that, though it would be like Julia to arrive and simply start setting things to rights.

Nevertheless, he would proceed with caution. Silently he slipped down the stairs to the servants' entrance. There was a faint dusting of coal at the bottom of the stairs, and more than one set of footprints had travailed from the coal vault through the door. Someone had been busy. The only fires Heath had lit in the last week had been in his bedroom and his study, and only when it got cold enough that he could almost see his breath in the air. It had simply been easier to spend his time elsewhere.

Silently he crept through his deserted kitchens. He couldn't remember the last time a meal had been prepared down here. Again, it had been far easier to eat elsewhere. He put a hand on the stair railing, staying light on the balls of his feet and trying to avoid the worst of the squeaks in the worn wooden planks.

The hall was empty and chilled, though the door to the room he used as a study had been closed, a warm glow beckoning from underneath. Yet all around him was silence. From the wall he pulled down an antique cavalry sword that someone two generations ago had thought made a nice addition to the wood panels. It was dull and heavy, but it was something if he had to defend himself.

He approached the door, the low murmur of voices indistinguishable. Ever so slowly he turned the knob and gave the door a mighty heave, charging into the room.

"We surrender," came a wry voice from the far side, and Heath came to an abrupt halt, the tip of the antique sword hitting the pile of his antique rug with a graceless thud.

The speaker was a redhead, with the kind of cynical eyes that betrayed the inability of life to surprise her any longer, nor to dim her amusement with it all. She had round cheeks and a round bosom, and if she stood up, Heath was quite sure the roundness would continue. All of which was of little consequence since she was seated at what had been his library table. Though at the moment it looked like a table more suited to a gaming hell than a St James's library. A deck of cards, a handful of dice, and his good crystal glasses filled with a liquor he didn't recall buying.

And a second, even more voluptuous woman was sitting across from her, a cheroot hanging from her mouth and a dueling pistol resting casually in her hand, aimed directly at his heart.

"Lord Boden, I presume," the second woman drawled, a cloud of blue smoke snaking languidly around her head and winding toward his ceiling, the barrel of the gun making a slight gesture in his direction.

"Indeed." The voice came at his shoulder, and Heath jumped, his heart lodged in his throat.

He cursed foully and spun to find the dowager's blond butler standing just behind him, a knife flashing once in the servant's hand before it disappeared into the folds of his clothes. Goddammit, but the man could have slit his throat and Heath wouldn't ever have seen it or heard it coming.

"Janie would have shot you first," Luke said, Heath's thoughts clearly stamped across his face. "I was just insurance."

"Insurance? What the hell?"

"Sorry for the scare, my lord. But we heard someone

come creeping through the servants' entrance and up the stairs and I had rather expected you to use the front door. Since you live here and all. We took appropriate precautions."

From the corner of Heath's eye, Joseph materialized from behind the study door that was still gaping open, the hall dark and empty beyond. As with Luke, a flash of steel caught the candlelight before it disappeared as well, buried in some unseen pocket or seam. The coachman hurriedly pushed the door shut.

"All the heat was getting out," Joseph explained some-what apologetically to Heath.

"What the hell are you doing in my house?"

"At the moment, playing vingt-et-un, my lord. I hope you don't mind we took liberties with your coal vault. It was damned cold in here. Lady Josephine said it was the least we could do." Joseph paused. "Did you wish to be dealt in?"

Heath blinked. Of course Joss was behind all of this. He should be furious, he knew. Only Josephine Somer-hall would have the audacity to show up uninvited and unannounced in the middle of the night with a handful of . . . servants and make herself at home without a thought to his peace of mind. She could have at least sent a note. She could have given him some warning that would have prevented him from sneaking into his own house like a common thief.

He loosened his grip on the hilt of the cavalry sword. He'd work up to anger. At the moment, however, his heart had resumed its rightful place within the confines of his rib cage, and the welcoming warmth of the room was a luxury he'd not experienced in a long time.

"No, I don't wish to be dealt in."

The redhead was pouring a generous amount of whiskey into a glass while openly admiring the cut of the crystal. Heath wondered if he'd be short a set of tumblers by tomorrow.

"Here, milord," she said, holding the glass out toward him. "Ye look as if ye could use it."

Heath shuffled forward and took the glass from her hand, taking a healthy swallow, and despite himself, closed his eyes in a moment of pleasure. Definitely not his whiskey. He didn't possess the necessary connections to smuggle in the smooth Scottish blends. The thought made his eyes pop back open.

He peered at the two women, who were shamelessly peering back at him. "And who are you?" It was rude, and he didn't care.

"Depends," answered the redhead, her lips curling, seemingly delighted by his question. She exchanged a suggestive glance with her friend and her smile widened. "Do you have any requests, my lord?"

Luke cleared his throat subtly. "Ladies," he admonished. "Behave."

The redhead pouted, though not without laughter dancing in her eyes. "Anne," she said by way of introduction, then gestured at her companion on the far side of the table. "And this is Janie. A pleasure, my lord."

"Her Grace's upstairs maids," Luke elaborated. "Though it was your downstairs they took care of tonight."

"Don't I wish," murmured Janie, her dark gaze dropping far south of Heath's face.

Oh, sweet Jesus. Heath resisted the urge to pull his coat tighter around him under Janie's appreciative, if amused, perusal. "Where is she?" Heath demanded. Whatever scheme Joss had up her sleeve this time, his patience was at an end.

"Upstairs," Luke answered, not pretending to misunderstand whom Heath was speaking of. "Lady Josephine finished with those papers. That's why we're here. She wanted to show them to you as soon as possible. But I certainly wasn't going to let her come here on her own. We were just passing time, waiting for you to get home."

Heath stared at the butler. "She finished with the folder?"

"That's what she said."

"Bloody hell, man, why didn't you say so? Why didn't *she* say so? Why didn't she send a message to that damned soiree? I could have been here hours ago." Heath set his glass back on the table with a thump and tossed the useless sword onto a couch.

"She didn't want to disrupt your evening, my lord," Luke said to his retreating back.

Heath made a low sound in the back of his throat as he yanked open the door. Joss had disrupted every evening he'd had since she'd shown up at that very first ball, whether she knew it or not.

"She's sl—" The door closed behind him on whatever it was the man had been about to say, and Heath rushed across his chilled hall and took the stairs two at a time.

It was the lure of answers that was beckoning him so acutely, he told himself. The possibility that they could finally discover whatever it was that had cost Gavin Smythe his life, and deal with it accordingly. Make sure the matter was placed in the appropriate hands so that they could wash their own of it. Move on with their lives and stop looking over their shoulders. If it was a military matter, as Heath suspected, he would—

He stopped abruptly at the top of the hallway, his hand on the wall. His bedroom door was cracked slightly, a diffused glow escaping and casting a long leg of light across the hallway. There were no other signs of life anywhere down the hall, the farthest bedroom doorways nearly invisible in the cold darkness. Silently he moved forward, his feet soundless on the long woven runner, and stopped before the door. He raised his hand to push it open but paused, his arm frozen in midair.

"Joss?" His voice seemed overly loud in the silent space, but he received no answer. He stood in front of his bedroom for a moment, feeling foolish. This was his house, for God's sake. His house, his hall, his bedroom. He had every right to go wherever he pleased. He pushed the door open and strode into the room.

Joss was sleeping. Curled up in the center of his bed, his blankets pulled up over her shoulders, her dark hair tumbling across his pillow. And in that instant, Heath was overcome with a feeling of such savage possessiveness that it robbed him of breath.

Mine, his brain whispered over and over, until it became a din that threatened his sanity. *Mine, mine, mine*.

Josephine Somerhall belonged to him. She was exactly where she should be. Where she should have been a long time ago.

He drank in the sight of her. Her slightly parted lips, the dark fan of her lashes, the disheveled riot of curls that lay against her cheek. She looked different, somehow, in sleep. Awake, Joss was a force, continually in motion, cloaked in a dazzling, impenetrable veil of confidence and independence and strength. But asleep, she seemed . . . exposed. Vulnerable. Her hands were folded into the blanket, tucked under her chin, and he could see the ghost of the little girl with the crooked nose who had been forced to grow up much too soon.

He lowered himself to the edge of the bed. The longing and desire that was ripping through his body was unbearable. Though Joss had rarely been far from his mind, he had thought he'd had this under control. Four days of not speaking to or seeing or touching Josephine Somerhall had furthered the illusion that he had conquered his irrational physical infatuation and need for her. Four seconds in her presence had shattered it.

He shrugged out of his coat, and then his evening coat and waistcoat, letting the garments fall to the floor. Careful not to wake her, he lay down beside her, his head resting on the pillow only inches from hers, as if he could somehow commit her face to memory. As if this might be the last chance he would ever get to be here, like this. With her.

They had lain together as children sometimes, under the shade of mighty oaks when the heat had left them listless and languid and unwilling or unable to look for mischief. Her brother would be with them, and the three of them would stare up into the canopy of the trees, watching squirrels squabble and sparrows flit from branch to branch. On the rare occasions when Heath had tolerated it, Joss would sometimes rest her head on his arm or shoulder and launch into one of her earnest lectures on something she had spotted in the flora or fauna surrounding them. He'd found it amusing then. Exasperating at times. And now he wished he could get each and every one of those moments back.

He reached out and brushed the hair back from her face.

Joss's lips curled slightly and she tilted her head, resting her cheek against his fingers. Her eyes opened.

And she shrieked.

It was more of a strangled gasp, really, though her arms and legs pinwheeled as she flailed backward in a tangle of twisted blankets and skirts. Heath lunged for her but his hands closed on empty space, and Joss promptly fell off the far side of the bed with a thump. There was silence for a moment, and then her arms appeared on the edge of the mattress, followed by her head as she pulled herself back up.

She looked at him, her simple gown creased, her hair standing at odd angles from her head, her cheeks flushed, and her eyes flashing.

"Did you stop to think, Hextall," she said through clenched teeth, "that given the events of the past week, I might react badly to finding a strange man on top of me upon waking?"

"I wasn't on top of you." He would have laughed at the picture she presented, but her words had left him harder than a rock and shifting in agony. He should have been on top of her, he thought. On top of her and in her. "And I'm not a strange man," he added in a valiant effort to distract himself.

"That's debatable." She ran her hands through her hair and hauled herself to her feet, her mantle of invincibility firmly back in place. She rubbed at her eyes before spinning and hurrying into his dressing room.

Making sure she was out of sight, he rolled over onto his back, adjusting the fall of his trousers before swinging his legs over the edge of the bed. By the time she re-appeared at the doorway, he thought he'd pulled himself together quite admirably.

"I finished," she said, and in her hands she held the folder that had started this entire mess. "But I would assume you already knew that."

"Indeed. Luke offered it as the reason he was gambling in my study at two o'clock in the morning with his brother and two—"

"Maids."

"—maids. What else would I have said?" he asked disingenuously.

Joss narrowed her eyes at him, but didn't answer. Instead she said, "You needed to see this. Right away."

Heath sobered. "Please, tell me what you found. Are they documents of a military nature? Political secrets?"

"Um. Sort of." Joss took a few hesitant steps toward him. "Promise you'll keep an open mind."

"Do they say anything about Gavin Smythe's brother? Or his whereabouts?"

"No." Joss closed the distance and sank down on the end of the bed, twisting so she was almost facing him. With careful deliberation, she placed the folder between them. She smoothed her hands over it, as if searching for a place to begin. Twice she looked up at him uncertainly. "Promise you'll keep an open mind," she repeated. "Some of it is a little fantastic."

"I promise," Heath told her, a faint sense of disquiet rising. What could she have possibly found that would be preventing her from simply telling him?

Joss blew out a breath. "The documents that Gavin Smythe carried were indeed all letters," she started. "The first set were written in 1307, and then sporadically through the centuries, ending with a final series written in this current year. The sender changes, of course, through time, though he or she is never identified, and the seal at the bottom of each letter remains consistent. On their own, the documents mean nothing. If a single letter had ever fallen into the wrong hands, there would be no harm done. Only by possessing all four letters can the single message in each group be deciphered. I missed the pattern at first because the dates are not all exactly the same within a given year. The last set of letters consists only of three." Her fingers played with the leather cord, tying and retying the knot that bound the folder.

"Well, what do they say?" he prompted gently.

"You're going to have a hard time accepting this," she said slowly, still struggling. "Believe me, I still do."

Heath cast about for something relatively benign. "Start with the seal. Were you able to determine if it was, indeed, a Templar seal?"

Joss laughed, a strangled sound. "It's not a Templar seal. I was wrong about that."

Heath gave her a sympathetic smile. "Don't feel too badly. It was very unlikely that—"

"It is the seal of the Templar and Hospitaller orders united."

He laced his fingers together, taking great care not to react. "I beg your pardon?"

Joss opened the folder and took the topmost document out. "This seal"—she pointed to the image of the two knights on a single horse—"is the seal that represents the two groups, united in a single purpose."

"That is not possible. History tells us they were very

separate. Rivals, even. Very different in their doctrine and their discipline. The Templars were a wealthy military order. The Hospitallers were of a much more humble, nurturing nature. Doesn't their motto read something like 'For the faith and in the service of humanity'? They couldn't be more different."

"True. But they had a common enemy at the beginning of the fourteenth century when the first letters were written."

"I must assume you are referring to the French king. Philip the Fifth?"

"Fourth. Who was disgracefully in debt to the Templars, coveted their wealth, viewed their presence in France as a very real threat to his authority, and decided to do something about all of it. He declared them all heretics, had them arrested, employed the Inquisition to torture confessions, and disbanded the entire organization. And, of course, moved to confiscate their lands and their fortunes."

"I still don't see how this has anything to do with the Hospitallers."

"That was the moment they had their eyes opened. If a king could single-handedly destroy one of the most powerful Christian orders in Europe, which was, supposedly, under the control and the protection of the pope, then what was preventing them from suffering the same fate the next time a greedy monarch eyed their own lands and holdings and decided to make them his?"

"But the Hospitallers weren't rich, nor were they military in their bearing."

"And that was their saving grace. They weren't a threat, even when the lands annexed from the Templars were ceded to them over the years following the arrests. They were the perfect custodians of the Templar fortune."

Heath stood and paced in front of the hearth. "How could a secret like this possibly have been preserved for five centuries? It's preposterous, really. Someone, sometime would have let something slip. It's human nature."

"No one knew."

Heath made a face. "The treasure did not just hide itself."

"The Templars who originally hid the treasure knew only that they were hiding their fortune from a greedy king and were sworn to secrecy. But the task of keeping it protected after that fell to four men, appointed by Jacques de Molay, the Templar grand master, and Fulk de Villaret, the Hospitaller grand master. Four men who took an oath to never allow that wealth to be made available to any monarch or leader to be used to do violence against other peoples."

"Four men." Heath's eyes slid to the letters.

"Yes. It is not clear whether they were originally Templars or Hospitallers, though I suppose now it is irrelevant. The names have changed over the centuries, new men who have replaced the old guard. But always only four."

"Smythe. Villeneuve. Adam. Williamson."

"Indeed. The last four guardians."

Heath stopped his pacing. "Let me make sure I'm understanding you correctly. The Templar treasure still exists, hidden somewhere for the last five hundred years, its secret location guarded by four men."

"That about sums it up, yes." She scowled at him as she caught the expression on his face.

He made an effort to relax. "I'm trying here, Joss, truly I am."

"Look," she said, spreading the first four letters out in front of her, along with what Heath could only assume was her decryption of the documents. "The first set of letters was written in the late summer of 1307, before the arrests, and before the Templar fleet carrying their treasure vanished from La Rochelle." She stopped. "The Templars knew from informants that the French king was planning to move against them and had taken precautions to keep their wealth from falling into Philip's hands. But they badly underestimated Philip's hunger for power and the fanaticism of the Inquisition."

Heath returned to the edge of the bed and thumped back down, sending two of the pages fluttering. "Where did they hide it then? Where did the ships go when they fled France?" he asked, having no idea if he was even asking in any seriousness.

Joss set down a second set of letters. "Malta."

"Malta? What the hell was in Malta?"

"Nothing, as far as I can tell, at least in the early fourteenth century. An isolated, half-forgotten island, traded and bartered amid a shifting political landscape like an afterthought."

"Surely someone might have noticed ships arriving and disgorging piles of gold upon their shores."

"Not necessarily. It's an island, after all. There are always ships coming and going. Unloading all manner of goods. And if the fleet had separated, arriving at different times, no one might have noticed anything out of the ordinary. And I am quite certain the treasure would have been well camouflaged."

Heath caught himself before he rolled his eyes. "Fine. Then assuming the treasure was successfully hidden on the island—"

"It was. And the Hospitallers finally took full control of the island in 1555, and set to building." She held up another set of letters. "The entire city of Valletta, surrounded by forts and bastions, was built in less than fifteen years. One of the most indomitable in the Mediterranean, containing churches, schools, and, most importantly, one of the biggest and finest hospitals in the world. Funded secretly by a portion of the treasure buried within the safety of its walls."

"So you're telling me the treasure is in Valletta."

"Not anymore." She shuffled through another set of letters and passed them to Heath. "Twenty years ago, when Napoleon invaded Malta, the French seized the fort, looted the churches, and destroyed the Hospitallers' strongholds. That set of letters suggests that a general under Napoleon Bonaparte's command discovered evidence that the treasure existed."

"But they didn't find it?"

"No. And as soon as the British had forced the French from the island, the treasure was moved. The guardians couldn't take the chance it would fall into the wrong hands now that its location had been exposed."

"And to where did they move it?"

Joss cleared her throat and placed the next-to-last set of letters in his hands with exquisite care. "Britain."

"Britain," Heath repeated flatly. "So they what? Dug it up in the middle of the night, loaded it onto ships that just happened to be waiting, and dumped it on our shores? Tell me you don't expect me to believe that."

Joss sighed. "It wasn't done in a night. It was done over many months, by a small number of knights selected by the guardians, so as not to arouse suspicion. In much the same way as it arrived, I would expect. Smuggled and disguised."

"Disguised as what?"

"I don't know." For the first time frustration bled into her words. "I can't decode the last group of missives without the fourth letter."

"Where is the treasure now? Besides the rather broad suggestion of Britain?"

"I don't know. The last letter to Williamson is—"

"Missing," Heath finished. "God's teeth." He heaved himself back to his feet and stalked to the map that hung on his wall. His fingers traced the lines of latitude, sliding inexorably west. "Why Britain?"

"I don't know, though I would guess it would be because Britain was one of the last strongholds against the advancing French army. Possibly because Britain would have been one of the few places that would be virtually inaccessible to the French."

"So somewhere in Britain sits a fortune that has, for the last five hundred years, remained concealed under an island fortress."

"The fortune that could buy an exiled Emperor his freedom and a new army. If his sympathizers and his agents could only find it."

Heath felt a cold trickle of sweat slide down his back. Her story was asinine. Something that wouldn't even be believable in a novel. Yet there were puzzle pieces falling from everywhere in the far reaches of his mind now, slotting into place with a brutal efficiency. Gavin Smythe's last desperate words about England's fate. The corpses bearing the same tattoo found on documents five hundred years old. The mysterious Marcel Leroux, and the men and the weapons that had filtered through the Tower Street rooms. And there was another thought, not fully formed, hovering beneath the obvious. Heath frowned, but he couldn't seem to catch it. He left it for the moment.

"What are you thinking?" Joss was watching him carefully. "You've got that look you get when you're deliberating something that isn't in a neat column of sums. I can't tell if you believe any of this or not."

He couldn't tell if he believed any of this or not. "Whether I believe it is irrelevant," he said, and then held up his hand when it looked as if she might protest. "What is important is that there are others who clearly believe it. Or at the very least they believe something of great value was concealed by Gavin Smythe and they are willing to kill to uncover it."

Joss fixed slitted eyes on him.

"Oh, don't look at me like that, Josephine Somerhall. I'm trying to be the voice of reason."

She gestured to the papers still spread around her on the end of the bed. "I have five hundred years' worth of reasonable voices right here."

Heath rubbed his forehead. "Fine. For the moment, let's assume that there is a fortune hidden in Britain that may have had its origins in Templar holdings and that is of extreme interest to agents of the former French emperor. What else would—" He stopped and frowned. "Is it only money that was hidden?"

"Ah." Joss seemed to understand immediately and she gave him an assessing look. "I thought you didn't believe."

"I said it doesn't matter what I believe."

"Mmm-hmm." Her brows lifted slightly. "The answer to your question then is yes. The messages only reference caches of currency, mostly in the form of gold. There is never mention of any religious artifacts or the like that the Templars were accused of hiding. Nothing that clever, manipulative leaders have used since the beginning of time to inspire people to a lunacy and madness no amount of money can ever achieve. No Holy Grail, no Ark of the Covenant, and no chamber pot an errant angel might have pissed in."

"Are you trying to be funny?"

Joss sighed. "Maybe a little? Because if this is all true, if there is really a lost treasure hidden somewhere being hunted by men willing to kill for it, then there isn't really anything left to laugh about."

"Yet they do not know where it is hidden either."

"No. They need these." Joss held up the most recent missives. "And the last letter."

"Or perhaps they need Smythe's brother. The brother I still can't locate." The last bothered Heath beyond measure. He'd had three of his clerks scouring local parish records these past days, looking for any mention of a Gavin Smythe, or a man who might be related, but they had come up empty-handed. He was out of ideas and it felt as though he had failed his friend. He ran a hand over his face. "Perhaps his brother has the last letter. Perhaps he stole it to keep it safe. Perhaps that is what Smythe feared he would suffer retribution for."

"Well, Mr. Smythe's brother is doing a damn good job of keeping himself invisible if he has it," Joss muttered. "Because there certainly isn't a clue to his location in here." She closed the folder and drew the leather strings tight, setting it on the mattress beside her.

"I think you should do the same. Become invisible, that is. There are killers out there, looking for the secrets Gavin Smythe died trying to protect," Heath reminded her, apprehension making him uneasy. "These people aren't fooling around, Joss. If there truly is a lost treasure, the trail to it is paved with death, no less so now than it was five hundred years ago." He crossed his arms. "You need to leave London. Surely the duchy has some far-flung lands in the direction of Wales. Or Scotland. Ireland would be even better. I hear Christmas is lovely in the country."

Joss shook her head. "I'm not going anywhere, nor am I arguing about this with you, Hextall."

"This is a potentially very dangerous situation." Irritation rose at her stubbornness.

"I understand that."

"Do you? Because for the last week, I've been looking over my shoulder at every corner. Tonight I sneaked into my own house with a sword in my hand. And I won't even mention your reaction when you woke up earlier." He looked pointedly at the far side of the bed, where she had landed in an inglorious heap. "Just as well you weren't armed or I might have found myself short an appendage."

To her credit she blushed furiously. "You startled me, is all. I certainly didn't mean to fall asleep."

It caught him unaware. "Then what the hell were you doing in my bed?"

She seemed to recognize her slip at the same time she realized she was still sitting on the very bed in question. Her eyes slid away from him. "That is . . ."

The desire that he'd thought he'd banked roared back to life. The idea of Joss lying in his bed, waiting for him, *wanting* him, set his pulse roaring in his ears and fired his blood.

He closed the distance between them in three steps. He reached down and tipped her chin up, forcing her eyes back to his. The dark desire he saw reflected in her gaze nearly undid him right there.

"I just..." She faltered.

"Just what?"

"I wanted..."

He dropped to a knee in front of her, his eyes level with her own. "What? You wanted what, Joss?"

"I wanted to feel what it would be like. To belong to you." The words came out in a rush, a confession stripped of everything but truth.

The world fell away then, everything that wasn't Josephine extraneous and inconsequential.

You've always belonged to me. He caught her face in his hands, and she closed her eyes, her breath soft and shallow against the insides of his wrists. *You'll always belong to me.*

He leaned in to her where he knelt, his mouth claiming hers, hearing her soft whimper as she surrendered to him. He wasn't gentle, nor did she seem to wish it, opening beneath his onslaught with abandon. His hands dropped to her knees, pushing her legs apart and shoving her skirts up to her waist. He pulled at the ties to her stockings, sliding them down her legs, and ran his palms over the smooth skin of her thighs and calves. Under his touch, her muscles flexed, shivering in tiny movements as his hands slid closer to the juncture of her thighs.

He pressed kisses at the base of her throat, tipping her head back even as his fingers found her slick entrance. He felt, rather than heard, her ragged intake of breath beneath his lips as he stroked her. She shifted, angling her hips closer to his explorations, and he indulged her, sliding a finger into her dampness. He was rewarded by another gasp against his mouth.

She was all heat, her reactions to his ministrations instant and honest and searing, and he had never been so aroused. He withdrew his finger, cupping her backside with his hands, and pushed himself to his feet, lifting her up off the edge of the mattress. Her hands caught his shoulders and twined around his neck, finding his mouth again with her own as he held her tight against him. Her legs were wrapped around his waist, the ridge of his erection surging up through his trousers against her core, and he gritted his teeth against the primitive need that crashed through his veins.

Holy hell, he wanted her. With a blinding desperation that defied anything he'd ever experienced before. Trying to regain some control, he set her in the center of the bed, coming to kneel over her. He kissed her again, more deliberately this time, a sultry invasion of her mouth. Promising, teasing, tempting. Joss made a sound of impatience, her fingers in his hair, at the back of his neck, then sliding over his back, urging him down on top of her.

And we will get to that, he thought through a fog of lust. *Just not quite yet.*

He nudged her leg outward with his knee and once again caressed the inside of her thighs, brushing the soft curls at their center. She whimpered this time, pressing herself up and into his hand as he slid his fingers back inside and applied pressure to the most sensitive spot of her folds. She writhed beneath him, and he let her, feeling her reach for the inevitable.

She was moaning softly, her eyes closed, and her pleasure at his hand was the most intoxicating, heady sensation he had experienced. The sounds she was making were wrung from her center, uncensored and unpracticed, captured in each of his kisses. His fingers pushed deeper and stroked harder, and he dragged his mouth from hers. He moved lower, withdrawing his fingers and setting his tongue in their place. With a cry she arched, convulsing and shuddering as she came hard against him.

Heath let her ride out the aftershocks and the eddies before he pushed himself forward, lowering himself to the bed beside her. His mouth found the sensitive hollow behind her ear before gently nipping and teasing her lips. He could feel her breath on his face, the rapid rise and fall of her chest as she caught her breath.

Joss's eyes opened slowly, finding his and holding them. He reached for her hand and laced his fingers through hers.

"That," he whispered hoarsely, "is what it would feel like to belong to me."

Her breath hitched slightly.

"I want you," he said. "So badly."

Joss reached out her free hand and touched his face. "You are an incredible man, Heath Hextall. And not just because you make me feel beautiful and desired."

Heath tightened his hand on hers. Her tone was all wrong. It was gentle and . . . desolate.

She was watching him strangely, and with horror, Heath recognized the faraway expression in her eyes. It was the same feeling he had experienced when he had lain beside her in sleep, trying to fix that moment in his memory, knowing it would be the last.

"Don't say it, Joss." She was slipping away from him, but he didn't know how to stop it.

"I can't give you what you really want, Hextall. I can never be what you want."

"You have no idea what I want." He wanted to shout, but it escaped as a whisper.

"I will never be happy trapped in a crumbling manor house, the sole purpose of my life reduced to planning parties and menus and making sure the staff polishes the family silver once a month. I can't pretend to enjoy supervising the garden design, decorating the drawing room, and making sure I am welcomed in the hallowed halls of Almack's."

Heath wanted to shake her. She was being impossible. "Not everyone wants that in a wife," he snapped.

"You do."

If she had struck him, it would have had no less effect.

"You said it yourself. You need a domestic partner, someone who will not upset your well-ordered life."

They were his words, he knew, yet he no longer recognized them. No longer recognized himself. A helpless, guilty anger rose in him then, a terrible self-loathing. How had it come to this? Promises, commitments, desires, half of the head and half of the heart, warring over what was left of his honor. Not that he had much honor left.

"I'll only leave again, Hextall," Joss said, as if that would help him come to any sort of accord with his demons.

"What if I asked you to stay?" He couldn't ever remember feeling this raw.

"Don't."

Heath let go of her hand and pushed himself from the bed. He snatched his coat from the floor and yanked it on.

"I can't stay," she repeated, her voice low and miserable.

Heath strode to the door. Neither could he.

Chapter 15 _____

There was only one place Heath could go where he might find a reprieve from the feeling that he had somehow been trapped within the confines of a sinking ship, with no way to escape. How had this happened to him?

He had been so sure he had known what he wanted. Not that long ago, he'd thought he'd finally arrived at a point where he could control the direction in which he would navigate his future. Against impossible odds he'd managed to steady his ship. Set a logical course. And then Josephine Somerhall had blown back into his life with the subtlety of a cyclone, and Heath had found himself standing on the bowsprit of that same ship, leaning into the wildness of the tempest and loving every second of it.

Joss, with her unpredictable, impulsive, independent nature. Joss, with her willingness to push her boundaries and her boldness in challenging his own.

No matter that he wanted her with an intensity that defied reason, he could not take her. He had already publicly committed himself to another woman—a woman who was kind and intelligent and would give him everything he had thought he wanted. Lady Rebecca didn't deserve the harsh repercussions that would come should he go back on his word. If he lost his honor and his self-respect in the futile pursuit of a woman he could never possess, what would he be left with?

The docks were desolate at this late hour, a perfect reflection of his mood. The rhythmic slap and suck of the murky river water was punctuated by an occasional creak or groan of fatigued timbers, and these were his only company as he made his way to his warehouse. Passing through weak pools of light cast by the lanterns mounted on poles. He'd almost reached the entrance when a figure lurched out of the darkness, staggering into his path. Heath recoiled, his hand going to the knife he had concealed in his pocket.

"Penny for th' poor?" The shadow morphed into the silhouette of a man hunched drunkenly against the cold.

Heath stepped back slightly, relaxing, his hand releasing the hilt of his knife. He could at least offer the man some warmth and something to eat. He tried, whenever he could, to help the souls who loitered about the docks, scrounging for money or discarded—

The man stumbled against him, pushing Heath backward, and suddenly Heath was presented with a pair of pistols leveled at his chest, the barrels glinting dully.

"Don't make this any harder than it has to be for yourself, Lord Boden." The voice was low and most certainly not inebriated.

Heath swore, fury at himself crashing through his veins. He had been distracted, and he had let his guard down, and now there was a man, his face hidden behind a scarf and a hat that had been pulled low, aiming a brace of pistols at his heart. "Goddammit, but I hate guns," he muttered. "What do you want?"

"I want Gavin Smythe."

Heath drew in a deep, calming breath, close enough to the man that he could smell the rank odor of sweat mingling with the earthy scent of pipe tobacco. "I would think, as his colleague, you would know the whereabouts of Gavin Smythe better than I, Mr. Potter," Heath said, and saw the man stiffen in surprise. "You had him set up and arrested, after all."

"You think you're clever, don't you?"

Heath shrugged, his mind racing. His own knife was in his pocket, yet a bullet was simply much faster than a blade. "I must confess, I am surprised to find a Bow Street officer running amok through the streets of London, waving a flag in support of a little French madman."

Potter sneered at him. "England is rotting from the inside out, and there are many of us who would see it saved. The time for revolution is now. The Emperor will return, and he will reward those who are loyal."

"Indeed." Heath felt a cold trickle of sweat down his back. With that admission, Heath knew there was no way Potter would allow him to live. His eyes traveled over the docks, still deserted. There would be no one to hear. No one to see. His body would be found in a few days, floating in the Thames, the victim of a mugging gone horribly wrong.

"We've been watching you, and you might have fooled some, but you haven't fooled me. The minute you went snooping through the Newgate records, I knew you were involved. My patience is at an end, and I'm tired of waiting for answers. Where is Gavin Smythe?"

"Tell me why you want him, and I'll tell you where he is." Heath glanced at the inky water lapping against the wooden pilings. If he could get closer to the river basin, he'd take his chances in the Thames.

"You're not in any position to negotiate."

Heath forced himself to remain calm. "Perhaps. But if you kill me now, you'll never find out where Smythe is. Or what he told me. It was a fantastic story—"

The pistols jerked. "You know where the treasure is."

"I might. But I'm having a hard time remembering now." He tried to shift.

"Bad things happen to men who can't remember," the officer hissed. "Painful things."

"So I understand." Heath decided to take a chance. "Yet I must assume the three prisoners you tortured to death at Woolwich weren't very forthcoming with their answers either. Otherwise we wouldn't be here."

The man's breath stilled behind him. "That was Leroux's doing. How do you know about that?"

"I know a lot of things. I know Marcel Leroux might have tortured those men but it was you who put them on that prison hulk to begin with. You who sent an army of unsuspecting officers to arrest men you knew to be innocent."

"I did what had to be done."

"And so you did. Gavin Smythe was more of a problem, though, wasn't he? He took all his secrets with him when he escaped."

"Smythe no longer matters. Tell me what I want to know, and I'll make sure you die cleanly and quickly. Where is the gold?"

"You'll never find it," Heath told him, hoping to unbalance Potter. Perhaps if he could—

"Where is it?" Potter shouted.

"Oh, for the love of God, just tell the man," came a

bored voice behind him, and the blood froze in Heath's veins. "If you two were on stage at Drury, they'd be throwing rotten tomatoes by now. The audience despises when the actors ask the same question over and over. It's horribly redundant, really."

Potter's eyes swung to the space over Heath's right shoulder, and Heath turned his head slightly to see Joss standing under a pool of lantern light, a voluminous cloak wrapped around her body and some sort of woolen cap jammed on her head.

"Get out of here," Heath growled through clenched teeth, not turning around. "You shouldn't be here."

"I got tired of waiting." She sounded drunk or dull or both.

"Who the hell are you?" Potter demanded, impatient and angry, his eyes swinging back and forth between Heath and Joss.

"No one," Heath snapped. "She's no one."

He heard her huff behind him. "Now that's just plain mean."

"Oh God." Heath was going to kill her. Provided they remained alive long enough for him to do it.

"Stand over by him," Potter ordered Joss, waving his pistols.

"Bloody hell, but you don't need to wave those damn things at me," she said indignantly.

Heath felt her at his back then, peeping around his shoulder as though she had only now seen the danger aimed in their direction.

Potter's eyes had focused on Joss. "Where is the gold?"

"There's that damn question again," she grumbled. "It's in the bank, of course."

"The bank?" The expression on Potter's face would have been comical had he not still been holding pistols.

"Where else would you keep gold?" Joss giggled, then hiccupped. "Ugh," she groaned, "I think I might be ill. Can we go home now?" She leaned against Heath's back, as if needing him to support her. Her arms were braced under her cloak against the sides of his ribs. He frowned slightly. Something felt wrong. Her arms seemed too narrow—

Every muscle in Heath's body clenched. Holy hell. This wasn't happening. Not again.

"I feel dizzy," Joss complained. "I need you to stay still, Hextall. Very, very . . . still."

Potter smiled, an awful, empty expression, and turned to Heath. "I'm going to shoot her first, and hopefully that will jog your memory, Lord Boden. If that doesn't work, then I will take you somewhere a little more . . . secluded, and you and I will be able to come to a better understanding then."

Potter took a single step in their direction.

At least one of Joss's bullets caught the man in the shoulder, spinning him in a half circle before he tumbled to the ground. In a flash Heath was on him, kicking the man's pistols away from where he had fallen. He knelt beside the officer and seized him by his shoulders. "Where is Marcel Leroux?" he demanded.

Potter was gasping for breath, his face slack with shock. "She shot me," he wheezed.

"You'll live." It didn't appear that anything vital had been hit, though the man was bleeding heavily.

Joss reached him and crouched low. "Did he say where Leroux is?"

Heath resisted the urge to pick her up and shake her for the idiotic risk she had taken. "No," he said instead.

The officer groaned and shifted. "He'll find you, don't worry. The man has eyes everywhere. He knows you have it. And he'll come for it."

There was the sound of running feet, and Joss turned slightly. In that second Potter lunged forward, a blade flashing toward Joss's neck. Without thought Heath threw his weight into the man, deflecting the knife and sending Potter's head snapping backward. It hit the pavement with a horrible wet thud, and the man went instantly limp.

Luke reached them just as Joss was scrambling backward, and Heath was struggling to disentangle himself from the body lying beneath him. He stood, his attire once again marred by blood and scorch marks. He remained still for a long moment, trying to collect his composure.

"Just what the hell did you think you were doing?" he asked Joss.

"Saving you."

"I didn't need to be saved."

"I disagree. You were followed. I saw this man from your window when you stormed out of your house, and I couldn't imagine that would lead to anything good."

"I didn't storm—" Heath blew out a breath between his teeth. "I had it under control," he lied. He was shaking a little and he thought the fib might soothe him.

"I heard every word. He would have shot you. Well, me first and then you."

"Where the hell were you?" He directed his ire at Luke. "Why was she by herself?"

"We thought that Joss would have the better chance of getting close without arousing suspicions." Luke said it as though it should have been obvious. "If you had advised us of your intentions to leave your town house, my lord, one of us could have accompanied you here to prevent this sort of thing from happening." The butler's tone was faintly critical now.

Heath rubbed his face with his hands. What was happening to his life? When had he lost so much control? Not so long ago, his evening excitement had been limited to a good stewed beef, a friendly card game, and perhaps a quiet brandy before he retired. He barely recognized his life anymore.

"Take her home," he said to Luke. He glanced at the lifeless form of the traitorous Runner. "And fetch Mr. Darling."

Heath transferred his gaze to the water, unable to look at Joss without seeing that damn blade flashing in the sickly lantern light. The idea that someone would wish to harm even a hair on her head sent a rage so black and so vicious crashing through him that he could barely breathe. She was his. His to protect, his to love.

Except she wasn't.

In the end Joss had gone back with Luke, though she had insisted on waiting for him at his place. Heath hadn't bothered to argue. Did it matter, really? Luke had expressed his objections to leaving Heath alone given the events of the last half hour, but eventually he too had capitulated when Heath had accepted one of Joss's pistols and promised not to leave his office until daylight, or until one of the dowager's footmen arrived to watch his back.

He flinched. He'd never thought a soapmaker turned earl would ever require a bodyguard.

Heath trudged into his warehouse, drained, heading for his office. Without bothering to light a candle, he made his way to the stairs, the path as familiar to him as the back of his hand. He needed some space. Some space to think and to figure out what he was going to do. He didn't trust himself around Joss right now. Or anyone else, for that matter.

He climbed the stairs in silence and turned the knob, pushing open the door.

A scream echoed around him, and a flash of green silk swirled across Heath's vision before a monstrous shadow, moving at a deceptive speed, obscured the impression. The shadow snarled, feeble candlelight flickered wildly, and Heath ducked at the last second as something went whistling by his head to shatter against the wall behind him.

"Whoever you are, you take one more step and I'll tear your head clean off your shoulders," the monster threatened.

"*Bennett?*" Heath gasped. "What in God's name are you doing?"

"My lord?" The address was full of shock.

"Did you just throw something at my head, Bennett?"

"I thought you were a thief."

"Dear God." Heath put his hand on his chest, feeling the wild pounding of his heart. Bloody hell, but at this rate, he was going to be dead of a heart condition before his next birthday.

His overseer was backed into the far corner, and as the candlelight steadied, Heath's eyes were drawn to the glow of green silk behind Bennett's booted calves. In dawning comprehension, Heath's gaze snapped up to Benjamin's chest, seeing his rough shirt rumpled, the tails hanging out from his breeches.

An intense relief rocked through him. Bennett was here for reasons that had nothing to do with stolen documents and men who wanted him dead. "What the hell is going on here, Bennett?" he asked, though the answer seemed rather obvious.

"My lord," Bennett was babbling, "I'm so sorry. I can't— I don't— Oh, dear God. I meant to say something before but..."

Heath put his hands on his hips. He couldn't decide if he should laugh or be furious. The events of the last half hour had left him feeling a little unhinged. "Do you think I might at least have the pleasure of an introduction?"

Bennett's face went waxen.

Heath felt the first stirrings of unease. "Mr. Bennett—"

"He should have told you long ago." The woman stepped out from behind the giant with a sigh. "As should I."

The ground shifted slightly beneath Heath's feet for the briefest of moments, before righting itself.

"Lady Rebecca."

"I should have told you," she said a little sadly, "that first night at the theater. But I didn't know you then. Didn't know what kind of man you were."

"What kind of man I was?" Heath repeated blankly. He was having a hard time assimilating everything.

"If you would have Ben dismissed. Or worse. Because of our relationship." She sighed again. "And then, after that, when I knew you to be a fair and decent man, I could never seem to find the right time. I'm sorry I've deceived you."

Heath was trying to find something intelligent to say, but fragments of thoughts kept slipping away from him like darting minnows. He watched as she smoothed her disheveled hair, righted her slightly crooked bodice, and slipped her hand into Bennett's before raising her steady gray eyes to his.

"We love each other," she said simply.

"How long?" he managed.

"A year." It was Bennett who answered. The man straightened, his jaw set and his face stony. "I mean to marry her, Lord Boden. I've always meant to marry her from the day I first saw her standing on the London Docks."

"I'd come to see for myself the ships that had sailed from the Americas. And China and India."

"She was by herself," Bennett clarified.

"I was so tired of being told to simply enjoy my tea and not worry my pretty little head about where it came from. I was tired of being told that a woman simply does not have the capacity to understand such matters." Rebecca looked over at Bennett, her gray eyes expressive and soft. "Ben didn't tell me I wouldn't understand."

"No. I told her she must be lost," the overseer said dryly.

"And I told him I knew exactly where I was. What I really wanted to know was how tea was packed for import." She smiled at Bennett.

"I thought she was crazy. Said as much."

"I said he was probably right." Rebecca was looking up at the dark giant with adoration. "To which he replied, 'In that case, it would be easier if I just showed you.' And I fell in love right then and there."

Heath had been listening, a little dazed, his head swiveling back and forth between the two as if he were watching a tennis match. There was a bubble of something expanding in his chest, pressing upward. He cleared his throat. "But your parents—"

"Think I have done a lot of shopping in the last year." Rebecca misinterpreted his question. "My groom is quite a bit richer for his silence."

"Your groom should be shot." His reproach lacked any sort of conviction.

Rebecca shrugged unapologetically.

"I see. And what were you going to do about me? Leave me at the altar?"

She had the grace to flush furiously. "I would never have let it get that far. I should never have let it get as far as it did. Yet being with you stopped the constant criticism from everyone in my life, including my parents, who are under the assumption that I am nothing without a titled, wealthy husband. I used you, Lord Boden, and for that, I am truly sorry."

The sensation building within him was starting to crystallize now, sending peculiar frissons into the back of his throat, his brain, the backs of his eyes. Like tiny champagne bubbles released and bursting by the thousands at the surface.

Bennett's face hardened, though he spoke evenly, drawing Rebecca to his side. "What do you mean to do, Lord Boden?"

"Do?" Heath still hadn't marshaled his wits.

"I accept the consequences of my actions. But I will

not tolerate any slur on Rebecca's good name, nor will I turn my back on her." Bennett's dark eyes were unforgiving and hard as flint. "Her honor is mine to defend and I'll do whatever it takes."

Suddenly Heath found himself laughing. Not a dignified chuckle, or a subtle snicker, but an uncontrollable, hysterical, gasping laughter that sent his hands to his knees, his vision blurred by the tears of mirth pouring down his cheeks. He wasn't sure how long it went on before he wiped his face with the sleeve of his coat.

"My lord? Are you quite all right?" It was a wary question from Bennett.

"No, I'm not all right," he said when he was able. "Not so long ago, I attended a ball thinking I could find a wife and settle down to a life of pleasant predictability. Since then someone has tried to kill me twice. I've become the custodian of a conspiracy that defies all reason, discovered that the chickens were all for show all along, and now count a man who collects bodies for a living as a friend. And the worst of it all is that somehow, in my efforts to do the right thing, I've lost the love of my life."

Bennett and Rebecca were watching him carefully.

"You haven't lost her." It was Rebecca who spoke.

Bennett swallowed audibly. "Becca—"

"He's not talking about me, you great oaf," she said without looking away from Heath. "I have no idea what anything else you said before that means, but I know you haven't lost her."

Heath blew out a shaky breath.

"The choice between being happy and being right isn't much of a choice, is it, Lord Boden? Especially when being right leaves you bereft of everything that ever mattered in the first place." Rebecca looked up at Bennett, adoration clear across her features.

"No," he said hoarsely. "It isn't." And it had taken him much too long to learn that. "I have to go now."

Rebecca smiled at him. "I rather suspect you do."

Chapter 16 _____

Joss was kneeling in front of the bedroom window, the curtains parted slightly, staring out into the darkness, frost creating a perfect frame around the edges of each pane. Her elbows were resting on the sill, her chin propped up in one hand, while the fingers of her other hand traced patterns through the moisture that had condensed on the glass. She'd discarded her damp and gunpowder-stained dress, and he saw it lying on top of the pile of his clothes still draped over the disregarded chair. Instead she had unearthed one of his old dressing robes against the chill. It was belted at her waist, the sleeves turned up at her wrists, and the sight of her in his clothes stirred a primitive possessiveness that left him a little dizzy. As if the robe were physical proof that Joss already belonged to him and only him.

She'd pulled her hair off her neck and twisted it at the back of her head, secured with what looked like two little ivory sticks buried in the mass of mahogany curls. She had a beautiful neck, long and elegant, displayed to perfection. He watched her lean forward as she peered at something outside, letting his eyes travel the length of her spine as it curved beneath the fabric. Without considering what he was doing, he moved closer, his feet soundless on the heavy rug. He wanted to touch her. Run his hands along the column of her neck and down the arch of her back, and trap her hips against his own body. His mouth was dry, his heart was pounding, and he was as hard as a rock. He had no control around this woman.

"You promised you weren't going to leave that office until the sun was up." Her voice was subdued, and she didn't turn around.

Heath started. "How did you know I was here?"

"I can see your reflection in the glass. And I can hear you breathing. You must have sprinted up both sets of stairs." She lifted her elbows from the sill, and the curtains fell closed.

Heath took another step closer and dropped to his knees behind her. Joss froze.

"It's not the stairs that's left me breathless." He leaned closer, inhaling the intoxicating scent of her. Then he reached up and pulled the ivory pins from her hair, releasing soft, tumbled curls.

She made a small noise in the back of her throat, but didn't move.

Heath pushed his fingers into her hair, letting the silky-smooth strands wind around his fingers. Gently he tipped her head to the side, exposing the soft skin of her neck just behind her ear. He bent and pressed his lips there, allowing his tongue to graze the hollow. Joss shuddered violently, and Heath stilled. He suddenly became aware that her breathing was as ragged as his.

"I should never have left you in the first place," he murmured. "I've been spending too much time looking for other things I thought I wanted. Things I thought were the right things and would make me happy. But they didn't. They never could."

"Oh." Her voice was barely audible. "But Lady Rebecca—"

"Has found her own happiness. I want you, Josephine Somerhall. On whatever terms you wish. It's only ever been you."

She shuddered again. "Yes," she whispered, and the shaft of lust that pierced through him at that one tiny syllable left him gasping.

He brought his mouth back to the side of her neck again, only this time his hands slid from her hair. His mouth tasted and teased, while he slid his fingers over her shoulders, down her upper arms and then alongside the swell of her breasts. He rose on his knees and pressed himself closer to her back, letting her feel his arousal. She sucked in her breath, and Heath moved his hands so that they were cupping her breasts. His thumbs grazed over her nipples, already hard and peaked, and he groaned, grinding his hips into the softness of her backside, unable to help himself. She twisted, trying to turn to him, but he held her steady, knowing that if he were to kiss her, claim her mouth and allow her the freedom to pleasure him, he would be lost, and all of this would be over before it even began.

"Wait," he murmured against her ear.

Joss made a small sound of frustration, and he grinned, before he reapplied his fingers to her breasts and her sound of frustration turned into something far more dangerous. Her own hands reached up behind her head, and her fingers tangled into his hair, pulling him closer and causing her breasts to strain against the fabric of her robe. Heath dropped his hands to the belt at her waist, tugging at the knot and pulling it free. The robe fell open, and Heath forced his hands inside the folds, yanking the fabric over her shoulders and down her sides, feeling her heated skin beneath his palms. He let them roam hungrily over her ribs, covering her abdomen and exploring the soft triangle at the juncture of her thighs.

Joss's fingers clenched in his hair even as she rocked back against him. Heath was sweating now, trying to pace himself, but the pressure building within him was becoming difficult to control. He reached up and pulled her hands away, pushing her forward on her hands and knees so that he could strip the robe from her body completely. His hands grasped her hips and held them, even as he strained against her. God, but he if stayed here like this, he would succumb to his desire and take her right here, right like this with Joss braced beneath him. And he would, he knew, but not this time. This first time he wanted to see her eyes as she came apart.

He stood, pulling her to her feet in front of him, her robe pooling at her feet, her back still pressed against his chest. He ran a hand down the length of her spine, then over the lush roundness of her backside. Her skin was flushed and damp, and he could feel her pulse pounding beneath his touch. With the other hand, he yanked his shirt off over his head, tossing it to the side, wanting to feel that heat pressed against his own skin.

His mouth returned to her neck, and his hands covered her heavy breasts, and she arched with a sigh of pleasure. And then suddenly she was sliding back down the length of him and twisting so she was once again on her knees before him. Her hands slid down the small of his back, then traced the twin ridges of muscle that ran over his hips. They stopped when they reached the waistband of his trousers, and then her fingers were working on the buttons and his trousers joined her discarded robe.

"Better," he thought he heard her mutter before pleasure nearly blinded him as she took him in her palm. Her fingers ran the length of his erection, caressing the tip. He could feel himself jerk in her hand and with some alarm, he reached down and hauled her up against him, knowing he was teetering on the edge.

He stood before her, breathing hard, searching her eyes. Everything he had ever done in his life he had done with careful consideration and evaluation of the consequences. This, this thing that was Joss, was unlike anything he had ever encountered. He only knew it was right. And inevitable and inexplicable and he didn't give a damn about anything other than his utter need for this woman.

Heath caught her chin in his hand, ran the pad of his thumb over her mouth. Her eyes were glazed with desire. He bent his head and touched her mouth with his, a fleeting touch, barely there. He pulled back, reaching for restraint, hearing the blood pounding in his ears. It was Joss who kissed him next, her hand snaking around his neck and pulling his mouth to hers. She caught his bottom lip with her teeth, nipping, teasing, torturing. Her tongue played with his, expertly invading and retreating and leaving Heath desperate. Her breasts were crushed against his chest, his erection pressed into her belly, and every time she moved, she created a tormenting friction.

It wasn't until she slid her mouth to the underside of his jaw that whatever control Heath had left snapped.

He bent and shoved his hands under her buttocks, pulling her off the floor and hard up against him so that he could feel his cock pressed against the slick entrance of her folds. In two steps he was at the bed, falling into the center of it, Joss beneath him. Her legs wrapped around the backs of his own, and Heath claimed her mouth with a feral need. He shifted so that he was poised at her entrance. Her hands were stroking his ass and urging him farther, and with a savage groan of pleasure he drove into her.

Beneath him Joss stiffened, and Heath froze. After the longest five seconds of his life, she relaxed.

"Tell me you're not a virgin."

"I'm not a virgin." Joss paused, a wicked smile creeping across her face. "Anymore."

His breath hissed as she moved experimentally beneath him. She was going to kill him yet.

"Is that a problem?" she asked.

"Good Christ, Joss." He withdrew and pushed back into her ever so slowly. She tightened her legs around him.

"That would be a no then?" She sounded a little breathless now.

"I want this to be perfect for you."

"It is perfect. I'm with you." She reached up and ran her fingers along his jaw and to his lips. "Can we stop talking now, Hextall?"

Heath bent and kissed her again, feeling her hands slide to the back of his neck. "Heath," he murmured in her ear. "I want to you to call me Heath."

Joss's hands paused in their journey. "Heath," she whispered softly, and the sound of his name on her lips nearly sent him over the edge.

He rocked into her again, his hands braced on either side of her as she learned the rhythm. Her fingers were digging into the muscles of his back now with each thrust. He bent his head, kissing her mercilessly.

Joss moaned softly. "Heath," she whispered again, and it came out like a plea. He pushed hard against her once and then twice, and in a heartbeat, she stiffened again beneath him, but this time her eyes were closed and her head tipped back as her orgasm ripped through her. Her arms were wrapped around his waist like a steel band, as if she could somehow pull him even closer. He watched her beautiful face as she rode the waves of pleasure, gritting his teeth against his own release, which was roaring down on him. He pressed his mouth to the column of her throat, feeling her pulse pounding against his lips and tasting the salt on her skin. With a growl of desire, Heath thrust into her heat with a need so desperate the very edges of his vision blurred. A harsh gasp of pleasure was wrenched from his lungs as he withdrew completely, collapsing against her and spilling himself against the softness of her abdomen.

Presently Heath came back to himself to find his head buried in the hollow of her neck, his sweat mingling with hers. With an effort he levered himself onto his elbows, still feeling her chest rising and falling against his as her breathing slowed. Very gently he pushed aside a mahogany curl that was clinging damply to her forehead.

Joss's legs had slid from around him, and with exquisite care, he disentangled their limbs and extricated himself, rolling off the bed. He went to the washstand and returned with a damp cloth, gently wiping her skin. She lay quietly beneath his ministrations, and he could feel her watching him.

Heath returned the cloth to the basin and came back to the bed, sinking down slowly beside her.

"Not that I have anything to compare it to," Joss said after a moment, "but that was extraordinary." Heath could almost see her memorizing and cataloging each tiny nuance of their lovemaking.

"Yes," Heath agreed, thinking that the word *extraordinary* was so insufficient. He was still trembling, for God's sake.

"Is it always like that?"

"No," Heath said with perfect honesty. Before Joss he'd had control. Before Joss his emotions had never become entangled with sex. "It's not always like that."

Joss propped her elbow up on the pillow and rested her head in her hand, considering him.

Heath tried not to notice how the movement displayed her beautiful breasts so perfectly. Breasts she made no effort to cover. "You should have told me earlier. That you were a virgin."

"Why? Would you have done something different? Would it have made you want me less?"

Heath let out a strangled laugh. "No. God, no." He swung his legs back up on the bed and rolled toward her, feeling her skin meet his, the warmth of their bodies trapped against the cool air of the room. He stuffed a pillow under his arm and met her eyes.

"I want you all the time, Josephine Somerhall," he growled. "I want you from the second I wake up until the moment I work myself into an exhausted stupor that allows me to find sleep. I want you like this, naked and hot and sweaty, every time you're near me. Every time you touch me. Every time you look at me."

Her eyes had widened, and her breathing had become shallow. He reached out and stroked her jaw and the hollow of her throat, letting his fingers slide down the slope of one exquisite breast. "I've had fantasies about your body while having tea with your mother. I've pictured you beneath me when I've been eating dinner with your damn brother. I've imagined what you can do with your tongue when you're not talking." He was whispering now, his mouth inches from hers. "If I didn't have you, I would have lost my mind. I still might." He kissed her, slowly, deliberately. "But you could have told me you'd never made love before."

Joss's eyes had drifted closed. "I would have thought my inexperience would have been obvious."

"I've never kissed a virgin who kisses the way you do." God, but that hadn't come out right. It sounded like an accusation.

"You've kissed a lot of virgins then?" Her eyes were open again, and her lips curled lazily.

He deserved that. "That's not what I meant—"

"I was a virgin, not a twenty-five-year resident of a convent. I've been kissed before."

Heath made a muffled noise. "That was singularly apparent."

"Are you jealous?" Joss asked with ill-concealed amusement.

He was, he realized, very jealous at the thought of other men touching her. Of other men teaching her. "Maybe," he replied gruffly.

Joss grinned. "Don't be. You are clearly a very skilled lover. The women I've discussed this with all assured me that it is a rare thing to achieve the pleasure I experienced the first time one has sex."

Heath blanched. "The women you've discussed this with? What women?"

Joss cocked a head in the direction of the floors beneath them. "When one wishes to learn about something, one should speak to an expert, do you not agree?"

"Please direct any further questions to my person." Or he might never be able to look an upstairs maid in the eye ever again.

"Oh? You consider yourself an expert then?"

He gave her an arch look before kissing her deeply. "You tell me," he said when he'd finished.

"Yes." She was breathless again. "I can agree to that."

"It will only get better, I promise you that."

Joss licked her lips. "You sound very sure of yourself."

"I am. Next time I'll have you screaming." Heath rolled over farther, pressing her back against the pillows and nipping at her mouth.

"Oh," breathed Joss. "Now?"

"No, not now," Heath said with real regret. He searched her eyes, feeling suddenly awkward. "You're probably sore."

"A little," Joss admitted.

"I'm sorry."

Joss caught his hand with her own and brought it to her lips. "I'm not. I wanted this. I wanted you."

She released his hand, and he trailed it over her shoulder and down to the curve of her hip. "You have a beautiful body," he told her, wondering at the complete ease with which she reclined against him.

"You make me feel beautiful." She ran a hand across his chest, her fingers lingering at the base of his sternum. "Especially like this."

Desire flooded him anew, and he could feel himself growing hard again. Dear God, but Joss was going to snap every tiny shred of restraint he had managed to recover in the last five minutes.

"It's late," he said, "and we should get some sleep."

"Mmm." She was smiling at him, and her hand was starting to travel down toward his groin. "Are you sure?"

"Yes," he managed through gritted teeth, rolling over just enough to pull the blankets out from beneath them and covering them. If she started something now, he would be just as powerless as he had been earlier to stop it. But she wasn't ready for him. Not just yet.

Joss sighed, even as she snuggled against him.

He drew her into his arms, feeling fiercely protective and deliriously happy all at once. "Don't sound too disappointed, Lady Josephine. There are a lot of hours before dawn. And after that, there are even more daylight hours. I am of a mind to try all of them. Repeatedly."

He felt her smile against his chest. "I'm glad it's you," she murmured.

Heath pressed a kiss to the top of her head and waited until he felt her body relax and her breathing become slow and steady. "It will always be me," he whispered.

⁓

Marcel Leroux watched the body snatcher load up the corpse of the Bow Street Runner.

The man had been useful, but he couldn't say that he regretted his demise. Potter had become too quarrelsome and secretive, and Leroux hadn't been wholly convinced the Runner hadn't had his own plans for the missing gold. He'd been furious that Potter had decided to take matters into his own hands without consulting him. An army without discipline was doomed to fail, and such disloyalty could not be trusted nor tolerated. Which was why Leroux had become suspicious and followed him tonight.

Ironically, it was the man's impatience that had gotten him killed. Well, that, and underestimating his quarry. Two things he had continuously accused Leroux's own men of. It was rather poetic, if one stopped to consider it.

Potter had been right about one thing, however. The Earl of Boden was involved in this up to his neck. He had no idea who the tart was who had shot Potter—a servant by the looks of it—but it mattered not, really. In fact, she had done him a favor. And the events of tonight would undoubtedly spur the earl to action, if they had not already done so. He hadn't heard all of the conversation that had transpired between the earl and the Runner, but he had certainly heard the important part.

You'll never find it, the Earl of Boden had nearly shouted at Potter.

Mais oui, Potter wouldn't find it. But General Leroux would.

Chapter 17 ————————————————

Joss woke to a gray sliver of light escaping the edges of the curtains and a fire that had nearly died. Beside her the bed was empty, the sheets cold to the touch. Heath had been gone for a while then. She sat up, reaching for her clothes, pausing as she remembered that the sleeves of her dress were stained with gunpowder and the hem was a mucky mess. She'd donned Heath's robe last night because it had seemed practical and she'd seen no reason to suffer in a damp dress. As it turned out, she hadn't worn it long. And she most certainly hadn't been cold.

She smiled to herself at the thought. Never had she felt more beautiful, more cherished, more *perfect* than she had last night with Heath. He knew her strengths, he knew her weaknesses and her quirks, and he accepted them all. Wanted them all. Wanted her, just as she was.

Her gown had dried, and she brushed off the worst of the stains before dressing and heading downstairs. Here the fires had been fed and a welcoming warmth met her. The sound of voices from the dining room drew her from the stairs and across the hall. She entered the room to find Heath seated on the far side of the table, Tobias Darling across from him. Both men had cups of steaming tea in front of them, their plates were scattered with the crumbly remnants of some sort of pastry, and papers were spread between them. To all appearances they might have been two merchants discussing business over breakfast.

Both men stood as she came in, and the searing possessiveness in Heath's eyes sent such an intense thrill of pleasure through her that her knees went a little wobbly.

"Good morning, Lady Josephine," he said in a measured voice. "I trust you slept well?"

"Indeed, thank you." She willed herself not to blush as she turned to the resurrection man. "Toby. What a pleasant surprise."

"I thought the least I could do was to offer the man breakfast. The London Docks were a bit out of his way last night," Heath said.

Toby held up a hand. "Yet no less profitable," he replied mildly. "I have a Scottish surgeon who is very fond of bullet wounds. And winter is always conducive to shipments north."

Joss frowned. "At the rate we're going, you and your brother will be able to retire by January."

Toby laughed.

"That wasn't supposed to be funny."

Heath was still standing, waiting for her to be seated. He moved to help her into her chair and then seemed to think better of it. Instead he caught her face in his hands and kissed her thoroughly, his mouth warm and sure. He pulled back, looking inordinately pleased with himself, and pulled out her chair.

Joss sank onto it, a little breathless, aware Toby was watching her with bemusement.

Heath resumed his own seat and touched the leather

folder that lay on the table at his elbow. "I was also hoping Mr. Darling would be able to provide us with a few more answers."

"You believe me." Joss finally understood.

Heath met her eyes. "Yes. If I had any lingering doubts, the Bow Street officer with sympathies to the exiled Emperor was very convincing."

"Very well. What do we know?"

"We know that a cache of wealth has been hidden somewhere in Britain. We know that four men were appointed to guard it, each bearing a specific tattoo, yet somehow their identities were discovered, and they, along with the missing treasure, were tracked here by men loyal to Napoleon Bonaparte. And we know that each of these men was falsely accused of a crime, so that they might be captured before they could vanish. Only Gavin Smythe managed to escape, and with him, he took the documents that might lead to the location of the hidden treasure."

"Yet now they are all dead."

Tobias was looking curiously at them. "This all sounds quite intriguing, but what, exactly, is it that you believe I can help you with? I would suggest that my area of expertise has since passed, no pun intended."

Heath turned and spoke to Darling. "This has been something that has been bothering me for a while, yet I couldn't put my finger on it until now. You said there was a third man who was killed with Villeneuve and Adam."

Toby nodded. "My brother and I collected his body as well. But that one didn't have a tattoo."

"Yes. And that is what has been bothering me. Do you remember his name?"

Toby's forehead furrowed in concentration. "William. Or Williams?"

"Williamson?"

Toby's face cleared. "Yes. That was it. Williamson. Smaller man, brown eyes, brown hair, pox scars across his complexion."

Joss felt her stomach sink in disappointment. That sounded like the exact description of Arthur Williamson that had been in the Newgate records. "Missing a finger on his left hand as well, I suppose," she said dispiritedly.

"No."

"No?" Heath asked. "How can you be so sure? A moment ago you couldn't remember his name."

The resurrection man tossed Heath a look of mild irritation. "I might not remember a name—in almost all cases it's better if there isn't one—but I never forget a corpse. Especially one that wasn't whole. No one pays full price for a damaged corpse. Those bodies were in bad enough shape as it was, and a missing finger would have reduced its value even more. Now, if the corpse had extra fingers, *that* would be worth something."

"You're sure the third corpse you took off the *Bellerophon* wasn't missing a finger?"

"I'm sure." Toby continued to look affronted. "And it wasn't the *Belle*."

Heath's brows drew together in confusion. "But isn't the *Bellerophon* the prison hulk at anchor at Woolwich?"

"She is," replied Toby. "But the *Retribution* is anchored there as well. The three corpses you're so interested in came off the *Retribution*."

Joss was afraid to breathe, so infinite was the silence that fell across the table. Her gaze collided with Heath's.

"*Retribution* is a ship, not a noun," she whispered finally.

"A brother in brotherhood, not blood," Heath rasped.

"Arthur Williamson is still on that prison hulk."

"Yes."

"He's still alive. That was what Gavin Smythe was trying to tell you. The only reason the real Arthur Williamson is still alive is because everyone believes him to be dead," Joss said. "The third man that Potter and Leroux had tortured wasn't Williamson."

"How long before Leroux and his men figure that out?"

"I don't know. But the second that they do . . ." Joss trailed off, not needing to finish.

"And before he died, I promised Smythe I would save him. Not from retribution, but from the *Retribution*. There is an innocent man still wrongly imprisoned." He stopped. "I can't petition for his release through the courts. I can't simply walk into the Old Bailey and demand the liberation of Arthur Williamson."

Joss winced. "No. Williamson needs to stay dead if he has any hope of surviving." She paused. "You will honor your promise to Gavin Smythe." It wasn't really a question. Everything she knew about Heath Hextall gave her her answer.

"Of course I will. Williamson is innocent. It's the right thing to do, promise or no promise." He looked at her helplessly. "But how? We just break him out of prison? Out of a prison hulk?"

"Sounds reasonable."

"Reasonable? Have you lost your mind? There are guards and officers whose only job is to keep the prisoners in prison. And then let's not forget about the band of ruthless, murdering madmen who are now, probably more than ever, watching my every move, convinced I am in possession of a lost Templar treasure."

"I said reasonable, Hextall, not easy."

Heath stared at her.

Joss bit her lip. "There is a way to get an innocent man off a prison hulk and, at the same time, convince those who are sure you have the Templar treasure that it is as lost as it has been for the last half millennia." She paused. "But we're going to need some help."

Chapter 18 _____

The tinker's cart had broken down again, this time at the top of a hill.

A wheel leaned against the side, broken and warped, for anyone who cared to look. Joseph lay on his back just under the canted cart, a hammer in his hand.

"Are you done yet?" he grumbled at his brother, who lay beside him under the cart, looking not at the broken wheel, but out at the activity of Woolwich Warren below them. "I'm freezing my damn ass off."

Luke's charcoal flew over the page as he sketched the *Retribution*, paying careful attention to the docks and the buildings and the distances between them all. "How many guards on the west side?" He ignored Joseph's question.

The horse thief turned his head slightly. "Six. And another dozen who are watching the convicts working on the mud flats."

Luke frowned. "Too many. You see any sign of Darling?"

"Not yet."

The sound of an approaching horse had Luke shoving the paper down the front of his coat as Joseph began hammering industriously at the axle. An officer mounted on a tall gelding stopped in front of them, and Luke crawled out from under the cart.

"You need to move along," the officer said, eyeing the cart with distaste.

"Aye, jus' as soon as we get a new wheel on." Luke bobbed his head.

"Hurry it up. You don't want to be here when I get back." The officer threw one last glance over his shoulder, and his gelding moved off.

Luke and Joseph both watched him go before Luke rolled back under the cart and retrieved his sketch. He added the riverbanks and the tide markers to it, letting his eyes slide downriver, estimating how fast the current was flowing. There was a sudden movement behind him, and another body rolled under the cart and Luke yelped.

"Jesus, Darling, you scared the life out of me."

"Good news." Toby ignored his complaint. "A man missing a finger on his left hand was carted out of the Warren yesterday morning. Apparently he lost the load of ballast he was bringing up from the river, and the guard got a little ambitious with his cudgel. I am made to understand that his arm was badly broken trying to defend himself."

Luke stared at the resurrection man in dismay. "How is this good news?"

"Because he was put in the *Retribution*'s surgery." Toby rolled farther on his side and reached into his own coat. He pulled a paper much the same as Luke's from inside. "He'll be easily accessible."

Accessible, Luke thought, *but probably weak and insensible*. Which would make things more complicated.

Joseph peered over his shoulder. "I say, that drawing is a lot better than yours," he remarked.

Luke studied the sketch, a perfect cross section of the *Retribution*, labeled crudely but completely. "Is this accurate?"

"I sure as hell hope so," Darling muttered. "It was expensive. Greedy bastard. Next time that damn officer has a body he needs to make disappear because one of his guards got carried away, it's going to cost him a whole lot more."

"I hope we can get to Williamson before you do then," Luke told the body snatcher.

~

The Dowager Duchess of Worth returned to London with a ghost.

Heath had arrived at the duchess's townhome the following morning, instantly captivated by the sound of someone playing the pianoforte. He'd followed the beautiful, flowing notes past the study and into a small morning room where the pianoforte sat bathed in pale winter sunshine.

The ghost was facing him, her eyes closed and her head tipped to the side. A blissful smile played across her face, her pale blond hair twisted neatly at the back of her head and matching the yellow wool of her sensible, simple dress. She was oblivious to his presence, immersed in the sonata that rose and receded beneath her fingers. The sight sent gooseflesh prickling across his skin.

"She's good, isn't she?"

He started slightly to find the duchess standing next to him.

"She's dead," he whispered hoarsely. "I saw her die myself years ago."

The dowager smiled. "No. You saw her blow up a boat." She moved farther into the room, and Heath followed.

"It was very convincing." He couldn't take his eyes from the supposedly dead marchioness.

"That was the idea."

Behind them the doorway darkened, and Heath turned, starting once again, but this time in recognition. The newcomer was tall, with dark-gold hair and an easy smile. His eyes slid over the occupants of the room, coming to rest on Heath with a welcoming grin of pleasure.

"Montcrief," Heath murmured, wondering what the ex–cavalry captain was doing back in London.

Jamie Montcrief lingered in the doorway as the final notes of the music crested and died away. He smiled and approached the pianoforte, helping the apparition to her feet. "Superb," he told the ghost, "as usual." Montcrief turned back to Heath with another easy grin. "Lord Boden. A pleasure to see you again. It's been much too long. Have you met my wife?"

The dowager stepped forward. "Lord Boden, let me introduce you to Gisele Montcrief. You may remember her as Gisele Whitby, or the former Marchioness of Valence."

"A pleasure," he said, and he was pleased with how normal his voice sounded.

"Likewise." Gisele inclined her head. "How is your sister? I hear Lady Julia is married now. And has recently had a son." Her words were gentle.

"Yes."

"Is she happy?"

"Very."

Gisele smiled, a genuine one that reached her eyes. "Good."

Heath stared at her, comprehension suddenly dawning. "You were the one. You saved my sister from the marquess."

"Yes. Though I had a little help." She glanced up at her husband, a thousand words passing between them in that single look.

"I don't know how to thank you adequately."

"Your sister's happiness already has. I don't do what I do for accolades." Heath had heard the dowager say the same thing.

"What are you doing here?" Of all the questions rattling around in his brain, it was the only one that seemed important at the moment. For a woman who had gone to great lengths to make herself disappear, it couldn't be in her best interest to linger in London. If Heath had recognized her even after all this time, so would a hundred others.

"For the last sennight, Her Grace has been kind enough to assist me with a situation that required a little more, ah…finesse than usual." Her words were light enough, but her face had hardened. "The family that we smuggled in and settled upstairs consists of three children and their mother. They will remain here, in confidence, until their mother heals enough for them to be able to travel north. Then they will start over. Like I once did."

Heath's eyes slid to the duchess. "You weren't visiting friends, were you?"

"Mr. Montcrief and his wife are most certainly friends," she replied guilelessly.

He turned back to Gisele. "Then why stay?"

"Because I owe Her Grace a favor," said the dead marchioness with a slow, indomitable grin. "And because I heard you need to blow up a boat."

Lady Rebecca Dalton sat across from her mother and her sisters in their drawing room, a study in feminine dedication to the art of the embroidered rose. She'd never really liked this room with its frills and knickknacks and lacy pillows. She'd never really liked the absence of books and newspapers and maps, all of which resided in her father's study and had, for as long as she could remember, required a great deal of subterfuge on her part to view. And she'd never liked the superficial, judgmental quality that conversation usually took in this room, led by her mother and followed by her sisters.

Rebecca had become extremely skilled at tuning it all out, but today she listened, even as her mind raced in a thousand different directions. She was trying to decide how to best control the conversation so that her delivery was not perceived as contrived. It would be important—

"Now, don't get excited, but I heard from a little bird that Lord Braxton was very complimentary regarding your beauty at Lady Roth's musical soiree the other night, Delilah, dear." Lady Dalton spoke without raising her head.

Rebecca's needle paused in mid-flight, even as she was overcome by a fit of coughing.

"Do you have something you wish to say, Rebecca?" The words were impatient.

"I was just wondering if he said exactly what it was that enamored him so much?" She couldn't help herself.

Her mother looked up sharply at her, her eyes narrowing, as if searching for a hidden criticism in her words. "Do not ruin your sister's pleasure at a compliment well earned," she snapped. "Delilah has worked hard to appeal to the most desirable of bachelors, unlike you. You seem to have done almost everything to chase them all away, what with your disinterest in everything ladylike. You should just be happy the Earl of Boden has such low standards."

"I would argue that the Earl of Boden has exceedingly high standards in all things," Rebecca said placidly. At least the things that mattered. Like love. And loyalty. And happiness.

"And that is the crux of it all right there," came the waspish reply. "The fact that you dare argue at all." Her mother was in fine form today.

Rebecca shrugged, which seemed to irk her mother even more. She ignored Delilah, who was looking at her in spiteful triumph. Her other sisters had their heads down, pretending to be absorbed in their work.

"Well, I think I would enjoy being a duchess," Delilah said smugly.

"You would make a splendid duchess," her mother agreed.

"Speaking of duchesses," Rebecca said, drawing the pink silk thread through the fabric stretched across her frame, "the Dowager Duchess of Worth has invited us to an evening of charitable giving. In the spirit of Christmas."

Five heads swiveled in her direction.

"The Dowager Duchess of Worth?" Rebecca couldn't tell if her mother was horrified or delighted.

"The Earl of Boden, even given his low standards, is best friends with the Duke of Worth. When I become his countess, I'll likely be spending a great deal of time with His Grace. Is it so surprising that his family wishes to include ours in social activities?"

Her mother spluttered, and Rebecca hid another smile.

A duke was a duke, and no matter how odd the dowager might appear to be, to snub her was to snub the duke.

"What sort of evening?" Delilah asked suspiciously.

"Bringing warm food and warm clothing and our voices of hope to those in need."

"Where?"

"Woolwich Warren."

"Woolwich Warren?" Her mother's frame fell to her lap. "But that's..."

"East," Rebecca supplied.

"I don't like to travel in the cold," Delilah whined.

"Hence Her Grace's suggestion for warm clothing."

Delilah pouted. "What is this Woolwich Warren? Is it an orphanage?"

Rebecca stared at her sister, wondering how she could possibly be related.

"It's a *prison*," her mother said, and she was definitely horrified this time.

"Actually, it's not a prison. The Warren and the dock-yards are only a staging area for the prisoners and the work they do. The ships anchored out on the river serve as the prisons. But the Warren itself consists of an artillery repository, a foundry, an academy for gentlemen entering the engineering or artillery service, barracks—"

Her mother curled her lips in distaste. "A lady has no business knowing such details. I can't even begin to imagine how you came by such information."

"I read."

"Much to your misfortune."

Rebecca shrugged. "I'll pass along your regrets then. I'm sure you won't even be missed, as I believe there is already quite an assembly who plan to go. The Countess of Jersey and the Duchess of Wellington have pledged their support. And I am told the Duchess of Havockburn has committed to providing over one hundred pairs of woolen mittens for the incarcerated children. And the Countess of Baustenbury has instructed her servants to bake or buy at least that many loaves of bread over the next two days. I suspect she does not wish to be outdone by a duchess, but it is to the benefit of the prisoners all the same. Shall I arrange to send along a pie on your behalf, Mother?"

Lady Dalton's eyes had gotten wider with each name Rebecca dropped. "Of course we will go," the countess said before any of her daughters could protest. "We cannot be seen to be shirking our Christian duty to those inferior to ourselves. Our actions might even bring about the reformation of some."

"They're convicts," Delilah said with disgust.

"All the same," her mother scolded, "their transgressions are not ours to judge. We must accept people as God made them and love them all the same."

"You are so wise, Mother," Rebecca said without a hint of irony.

"Of course I am." The countess preened. "Now someone fetch me Cook."

Benjamin Bennett stood on the dock, his hands on his hips, surveying the activity with satisfaction. Barrels were being rolled out from the warehouse with brisk efficiency, and men were loading them onto riverboats waiting to be rowed out to the *Amelia Rose*. The old packet ship had been the first one Lord Boden had purchased, more than a decade ago, and she was worn out. Her timbers were rotten and her masts weakened, and she would have been broken up long ago if not for the earl's sentimental attachment to her. The earl had confided one night, after one too many whiskeys, that he'd named the vessel after the daughter of a country vicar. Bennett rather suspected there was another first buried in that confession.

The *Amelia Rose* rocked gently at anchor as the first of the riverboats reached her. Bennett had hired an army of laborers and rivermen and paid them exorbitantly. In gold. He'd never seen an actual gold piece in his life, but the Duchess of Worth had far-reaching resources, and the small chest had been delivered to the warehouse by a pair of footmen who looked more like pugilists. From the disbelieving looks he'd received, none of the men Bennett had hired had seen a real gold piece either, but the money had disappeared fast enough into eager hands. Most important, rumors of gold and speculation about what the Earl of Boden had stored in his warehouse that he needed loaded so quickly were swirling on the docks and down the alleys. Bennett resisted the urge to glance around. He knew they would be watching.

Within minutes crews of men were aboard the *Amelia Rose*, and the sealed barrels were winched aboard. She'd be low in the water by sunset, Bennett knew, and probably leaking like a sieve. No captain in his right mind would turn her to the open ocean, but it didn't matter. She didn't have far to go.

⟡

A heavy bank of clouds had rolled in late in the afternoon and sulked stubbornly over the city as night fell. The sporadic lights from the banks and the wharves and the docks were the only sources of illumination out on the frigid water, thin shards of quicksilver, shifting and scattering across the mirrored surface. Dancing lanterns from watermen's boats moved back and forth across the stretch, and occasionally a shout or a song reached her ears on the breeze.

Joss studied the ship, tethered by heavy chains to the bottom of the river. She squinted at the uppermost decks, lantern light silhouetting the topmost lines of the prison. It looked unlike any ship she'd ever seen—a tiny village of ramshackle sheds and buildings having been nailed and propped along the entire length of the hulk. Most of the rigging had been removed and ladders had been nailed to the gunwales. Someone had used the appropriated rope and tied clotheslines from the bowsprit to the deck railings, and tethered laundry flapped like ghosts in the gloom. A single mark of domestication amid almost five hundred men who, justice deemed, could not be domesticated.

Here the stench was almost overwhelming. The rancid, rotting odor of the Thames and its mud flats mingled with the stench from too many human bodies crammed and chained into the bowels of a rotting prison. Joss had been on dozens and dozens of ships in her life, some for long months, and each had its own unique odor, though none had ever been what she would describe as pleasant. Stagnant bilge water, unwashed bodies, livestock excrement, tar, and oakum. Yet all of that was always offset by the tang of a salt wind as it screamed across the surface of the ocean and scoured the decks, seasoned with sunshine and the promise of hope and adventure. The husk of a ship that sat before her was an entity she had never before encountered. There was no hope to be found here. If one could bottle the scent of emotion, this was what despair and anger and regret would smell like.

The surgery was on the port side, crammed in the very far corner of the stern on the upper deck. Joss didn't even want to think about what they would do if Williamson wasn't there. If he'd been moved or returned to his stinking berth below. The task of finding a single prisoner, and one who, if he was as intelligent as Joss suspected, had no interest in being found, would be nearly impossible.

"You ready, love?" The question snapped her out of her musings, and she turned to find Anne watching her, the woman's eyes two dark pools against the fairness of her face.

"Yes." Joss pulled her cloak farther around her shoulders. "You sure you still want to do this?"

Anne laughed. "Don't ever think I'm not grateful for what your mama has done for us, but folding sheets and beating rugs can get a mite tedious." She patted her hair. "Nothin' amiss with a little excitement now and then."

"If it all goes wrong, you get the hell off that ship," Joss warned. "I have no interest in doing this all over again to break you two out of a prison somewhere else."

"Janie and me have done this afore, milady. Gotten out of worse places. You worry about you. Besides, Janie's brought her guns."

Joss sighed. "Try not to kill anyone."

Anne shrugged. "No one that don't deserve it, anyway."

Joss took a last look at the hulk looming in the darkness, a void in the light of civilization. She set her shoulders and accepted the proffered hand. "Thank you, Mr. Darling," she said, and stepped into the waiting rowboat.

There was a string of lights stretched out west of Woolwich, and from the water, it looked like a long, glowing, segmented snake winding its way down the darkened road. Eventually the snake stopped its slithering toward the Warren and more lights appeared from its innards, these like fireflies darting in the darkness and descending en masse.

"What the hell is all that?" asked the guard called Henry, peering over the rail of the *Retribution*, the discomfort of the cold momentarily forgotten.

His partner frowned and joined him at the railing. "Carriages," he said in disbelief. "There must be a hundred of them."

Henry pulled out an ancient telescope and fitted it to his eye. It had been his grandfather's, and the brass exterior had seen better days, but the glass inside was still good and surprisingly clear. It was easy to make out the color and shape of a mob of skirts advancing toward the docks under the lantern light that accompanied them. "Women," he said dumbly.

"What do you mean, women?" The telescope was yanked from Henry's hands.

Across the water the sounds of feminine voices rose together, and Henry swore he could feel the *Retribution* list as every convict whose chains allowed leaned toward the starboard portholes.

"Are they singing *hymns*?" The question was incredulous.

Henry retrieved his precious telescope and fitted it to his eye again. "They're all carrying things. Hell, they got servants carrying things."

"What sort of things?"

"Food," Henry said slowly. "Bread. Cheese, I think. And bundles of blankets. No, maybe they're clothes. Oh, sweet saints, I think there is a keg of ale." His telescope came to an abrupt halt, and he snorted. "There's an old lady with a chicken under her arm. She seems to be their leader."

"A live chicken?"

"Aye." He squinted through the glass and felt his mouth drop. "Bloody hell, but it's wearing a coat."

"The lady?"

"No, the chicken."

"Barking mad, every single one of them," his partner sneered.

Henry agreed. His experience with the aristocracy was limited but what he saw in front of him confirmed the theory. "As if any of the bastards here deserve any of what they've brought." He did, after all, spend night after freezing night up here on the deck of a rotting ship, with five hundred men beneath his feet who were as likely to kill him as they were to listen to anything he had to say.

Officers were emerging from their quarters on the shore now, trying to stem the tide of female philanthropy. But the mob simply swirled around them without a pause in the cadence of its song, and Henry could see a handful of ladies in animated conversation with some of the officers, making broad, sweeping hand gestures toward the ships. The glow from a hundred lanterns assembling lit up the shore and docks like a sunrise.

A little farther up, under the orders of their mistresses, dozens of servants were wrestling any available rowboat they could find into the water and loading baskets and crates. Officers were running back and forth now, trying to prevent the boats from leaving the shore with their illicit cargoes. There were only a handful of guards left on board the *Retribution* for the night watch, but each one of them had left his post and stood at the starboard railing, staring at the spectacle unfolding just beyond the edges of the banks.

"Do you suppose any of that might reach this ship? For us, I mean?" Henry said, rather forlornly. He could almost taste the biscuits and the bread that were no doubt wrapped in those baskets. He'd bet his life they'd even been made with white flour. A perfect, thin crust and no risk of losing whatever teeth he had remaining. There wasn't a chance in hell he would dole any of it out to the wretches belowdecks.

"Don't expect so." His partner sounded just as doubtful. "None of those fancy ladies in their fancy clothes are goin' to row themselves out here."

A thump below them startled Henry, and he dropped his precious telescope, his hand snatching at the empty air too late. He lunged over the railing, only to be brought up short by the vision on the water beneath him.

There were three of them, wrapped in dark cloaks, grinning up at him, and there was no doubt what sort of trade they peddled. One had his grandfather's telescope in her hand, and she held it up.

"Did ye think we'd forget about you fine gentlemen in amongst all this giving spirit?" she called out, her voice bawdy and full of laughter. "Happy Christmas."

Henry exchanged a glance with his partner before eyeing the women in the little riverboat. They'd been rowed out by a riverman, who looked bored, if not mildly amused, his oars resting over his thighs as he waited to discharge his passengers.

"It's not Christmas yet. Shove off," Henry demanded, though his command lacked any sort of conviction. He was the most senior guard on board the *Retribution*, and he had to at least pretend to be following protocol, even if the harlot below now held his most prized possession in her hand.

"You're no fun," the woman's voice floated up, full of promise and oblivious to his demand. "We bring good food, good wine"—she patted a mound of baskets and bottles behind her—"and good times." She made a rather suggestive gesture with her hand.

"We do not allow unauthorized guests on board. Our officers do not countenance it."

Laughter met his feeble declaration. "The officers who leave you out here every night while they go ashore and eat warm suppers and sleep in warm beds? They'll never allow anything to be brought out here, and you know it. But we took the liberty of, ah, appropriating some of their finer offerings, and we say what's good for the goose is good for the gander."

Henry hesitated.

His partner poked him in the ribs. "Just for a half hour," he hissed. "They'll never know." He jerked his chin in the direction of shore, where the hymns had gotten louder and the chaos more widespread. "We deserve it."

Henry looked at the half dozen faces around him, showing varying levels of agreement that ranged from satisfaction to outright excitement.

"You want this geegaw back or not?" The woman was

waving his telescope in her hand, and that was all it took to decide him.

"Yes." He turned to the waiting men. "Fetch me a ladder."

⁓

The port side of the hull was black as pitch, the light from the shore facing the starboard side creating deep shadows. Heath steadied the tiny skiff, listening for any sound above their heads that they'd been spotted, but all was silent. The rail above was deserted, the sentinels no doubt hanging over the starboard side, gaping at the spectacle on the riverbank. The skiff scraped gently against the hull, almost inaudible against the steady slap of river water.

Heath tipped his head back and looked up dubiously. "You're sure you can do this?"

Luke was already on his feet, his hands running over the hull. A rope with some sort of hook attached to the end was slung over his shoulder. "Child's play," he scoffed.

Heath made a disbelieving noise.

The butler flashed him a grin over his shoulder and patted the hull fondly. "It's wood. And poorly maintained wood at that. Full of crevices and irregularities. Not so much different from old brick and stone. Though slate is a different matter, especially in the rain." He flexed his fingers and wiggled toes encased in some sort of leather slipper. "Now don't go anywhere, my lord," Luke said, and suddenly he wasn't in the boat any longer.

Heath stared as the compact man ascended the side of the hull, swinging and clinging like a damn spider. The lower hull was scaled with deliberate care, his fingers and feet finding careful purchase, though once Luke reached the barred gunports, Heath had only a vague impression of swift movement over his head. Luke was dressed almost completely in black, and within minutes the man had simply vanished into thin air.

A rope suddenly slithered down the side and landed with a soft thud in the bottom of the skiff. Heath grabbed it and gave it a yank, feeling the pull in reply. He glanced at the far shore once more, certain that they would be seen at any minute, but the ship was angled just enough that the shadows probably concealed them. He seized the rope in both hands and pulled himself up. The skiff bumped the hull once and then caught the current, spinning away in the darkness, and Heath regretted its loss, yet there was no help for it. A strange skiff, tied to the hulk, would only serve as a beacon of their intentions should someone notice it.

Heath ascended the rope, hand over hand, his muscles complaining. By the time he had passed the orlop and had reached the upper deck, every muscle was screaming in fatigue. Luke had made it look so easy, dammit. And the man had been carrying the rope, not using it. Pride made him grit his teeth and swing himself higher. A blond head popped out from an opening beside him, nearly sending Heath's heart through his chest and the rope through his fingers.

"Thought you'd stopped somewhere for tea," came the whispered chuckle.

Heath accepted the proffered hand and was pulled into the *Retribution* through an open gunport, landing in a heap in the dark, his chest heaving from the exertion. Luke was pulling in the rope, leaving no visible trace they'd ever been there. The man wasn't even breathing hard. But he was grinning like a fool.

"You're enjoying this," Heath grumbled, shaking the fatigue from his fingers and arms.

"Immensely," Luke confirmed. He glanced around, peering into the darkness. "Have I mentioned how much I enjoy storerooms? Particularly deserted storerooms?"

"I thought you enjoyed dressing rooms. Particularly deserted dressing rooms filled with sparkly things."

"Yes, well, I have broadened my horizons as of late." He held up a bundle of newly acquired clothes.

Heath was already yanking at his shirt. "Then perhaps you can return to peruse the rest of the contents later. Time is not on our side."

Joss was pulled aboard the *Retribution*, landing in an awkward heap, though not before the guard had managed to squeeze her backside with glee. She kept her face serene, watching as Anne and Janie appeared over the railing in a flurry of gaudy skirts and much giggling. Two guards were hauling up the baskets and boxes of food and wine.

They'd rowed around to the port side near the bow, away from the eyes on shore, though the entire time they'd ascended, Joss had waited for a shout, letting her know that they'd been spotted. Yet none came, and Joss could only assume they'd experienced a small miracle or the duchess had outdone herself and the chaos on the shore was awe-inspiring. Either way, she didn't take the time to ponder it. Instead she moved into the shadows of a make-shift tool shed that was canting wildly toward the bow.

She eyed the men who were watching her and resisted the urge to yank up her bodice.

"Good heavens," trilled Joss nervously, making her eyes wide and round, which given the current circumstances was not difficult at all. She was fully prepared to throw herself overboard should it come to that, Janie's guns or not. "What happens if a murderer comes up here? There aren't very many of you." *Six*, she counted with no small measure of relief. "Is this all of you?"

"Men in chains at night don't need an army to keep them quiet." The guard who had dropped the telescope was looking at her, his expression an equal mix of anticipation and lust. "Us six are more than capable. So if you're worried about bein' interrupted, don't."

A round of guffaws met his declaration, and Joss exchanged a look with Anne and Janie. They had been worried about being interrupted, but for entirely different reasons.

"Let's get to it, sweetheart." The guard made a grab for Joss's arm.

"What's the rush, sailor?" Anne practically purred, stepping in front of Joss. "You'll get your turn, but eagerness is for boys, not a fine man like yourself."

The guard spluttered slightly, not sure if he was being insulted or complimented.

"Besides," Anne continued, waving her hand at the baskets of food and drink now lying on the deck. "There is plenty of everything to go around." Insinuation dripped from every word, and the men were absorbing every drop. She bent, retrieving a bottle of wine, and, without pause, yanked the cork from the mouth and tossed it overboard. "A party is always better when you're not thirsty, don't you think?"

This was met with a number of murmurs of approval.

"Ladies?" Anne turned toward Joss and Janie, and they wasted no time in snatching up their own bottles and passing them into enthusiastic hands. "Now, what shall we toast to?"

"Happy Christmas!" called out one.

"It's not Christmas yet, fool," someone protested.

"Tonight it sure as hell is."

"You can't use *hell* and *Christmas* in the same toast," piped up another.

"Gentlemen." Janie spoke for the first time. "Perhaps I might suggest a toast my ma used to give." She wriggled her shoulders, letting her cloak fall to the edges of her arms, and Joss watched as her generous breasts nearly fell out of her bodice. Joss was sure that, if the entire British Navy sailed past them at that moment, not a single man would lift his head to take note.

"In the journey of life, may you come more than you go," suggested Janie, and there were delighted laughter and snickering all around.

"Then let's drink, gentlemen!" Anne called, and Joss watched as the bottles were tipped and wine was poured with gusto down thirsty throats.

None of the guards seemed to notice that the women didn't drink.

⌒

The man might have climbed like a spider on the outside, but inside, Luke moved like a damn cat. Behind him Heath felt clunky and obvious, though the only sounds they could hear were the creaking of the ship's timbers and a hum that rose and fell at odd intervals, punctuated by the occasional *thunk*. The prisoners below, Heath realized, moving as they could, conversing with whom they might. He wondered if the stench, as pungent and cloying as anything he had ever had the misfortune to experience, muffled every noise the way fog did on the nights it rolled in thick and noxious.

"It should be that door," Luke whispered, jerking his chin in front of them.

According to Tobias Darling, the surgery was the cabin visible from the stern, aft of the deserted storerooms and the first mate's cabin. Heath glanced up, listening, but there was only silence. He desperately hoped that the mate's cabin was as deserted as the storeroom. And hoped that Joss and her mother's upstairs maids had made it on board and had the men well entertained. He could feel his jaw seize up at the thought. What the hell was he thinking, *hoped*? He didn't hope that another man was even looking at Joss, much less touching—

"Focus, my lord," Luke murmured in his ear. "Lady Josephine can take care of herself."

"I didn't—"

"Your thoughts are written across your face."

Heath forced himself to draw a steadying breath. Of course Joss could take of herself. That didn't mean he had to like it.

From his belt Heath drew his knife, the slide of steel in leather overloud in the silence. Both men froze, but nobody came running.

Heath crept forward, easing the door open.

The air in the surgery was chilled, though it smelled fresher because someone had left the tall stern window at the far end cracked. A lantern had been left lit, and it swayed ever so slightly from its hook on the overhead beams, the light flickering whenever a gust of winter air forced itself through the narrow opening at the edge of the window. A long counter ran the length of the room on the far side, though there was no evidence of any instruments or bottles. Heath surmised the surgeon must carry his own supplies. He couldn't imagine that anything that could be used as a weapon would be left lying around a prison ship.

Though the men in the surgery did not look as though they were in any shape to take on anybody. There were three of them lying on cots, formless lumps under ragged woolen blankets, and all of them appeared to be asleep. Each of them was chained by the ankle to a large iron ring bolted into the floor near the end of his cot, the heavy links snaking from under the blankets. Heath crept forward, trying to get a look at the men's faces without any of them waking and seeing him.

The first one was most certainly not Williamson. He had bright-red hair, and what looked like a blazing fever. His face was gray and bathed in sweat, and his head was rolling from side to side in delirium. Not sleeping, Heath thought with some sympathy, and not with long to live either. He left him and moved to the second cot. This man had brown hair and a scarred face, though whether it was from pox or simply the ravages of a hard life was difficult to tell. His eyes were closed, and whatever ailed him was concealed under the blanket. Heath grimaced and silently drifted to the last cot.

The last man in the surgery was resting on his back, his left arm lying across his chest, bandaged from his wrist to his shoulder. Spots of blood were leaking through the linen. His other arm was limp by his side, and Heath could see the marks where the surgeon had bled him near the crook in his elbow. He looked pale, though his waxen complexion clearly highlighted the rash of pox scars across his cheeks. His hair was more black than brown, though the low light might have been deceiving. Heath glanced back at Luke, who shrugged. When he turned around again, he found the man watching him.

"You've come to either kill me, torture me, or both, so get on with it," he said flatly.

Heath's eyes flew to the other prisoners.

"They'll not hear a thing. The one on the far side will be dead by dawn, and this one here had his left foot removed three hours ago. He's still insensible from the gin." The assessment was not without pity.

"Arthur Williamson, I presume," Heath said.

"I don't tell anyone to presume anything." The man coughed raggedly.

Luke was already on his knees next to the cot, tiny tools that looked like twisted hairpins working in deft fingers.

"You're looking well for a dead person," Heath observed.

"What are you doing?" Williamson was struggling to push himself up. He looked between Heath and Luke suspiciously. "Who are you?"

"Friends," Heath replied. "Your colleague, the man I knew as Gavin Smythe, sent me here to fetch you." *In a very convoluted way*, Heath thought, but this didn't seem the time or the place to wax eloquent.

Williamson's eyes narrowed even as hope flared. "Then he is still alive?"

Heath flinched. "Unfortunately, he is not."

The hope faded. "He was murdered." It wasn't a question.

"He was."

"By you?"

Heath scowled. "No, not by me."

Williamson regarded Heath for a long minute before his head fell back on his pillow. "Then what are you doing here?"

"Helping you escape."

"Why?" The sound of a lock releasing punctuated his question, and Luke made a sound of satisfaction.

"Because I made a promise to Gavin Smythe before he died and I intend to keep it," Heath snapped. He hadn't expected to have to defend his actions to the man he was helping.

"I suppose I'll have to trust you."

"I suppose you will."

Williamson sat up slowly, squeezing his eyes shut against an apparent wave of dizziness. Heath caught him before he could topple. Without any preamble Heath parted the hair at the back of the man's head, revealing dark lines of ink just visible.

"Satisfied?" Williamson said with a grimace.

"Yes." Heath didn't bother to apologize.

"How do you plan to get off this damned ship?" the man asked when he was able.

"A brisk swim," Heath answered.

"I'll never be able to manage," Williamson said weakly. "I've got one useless arm and the damn surgeon took whatever blood that was left."

Heath grunted. "I never said you had to swim." He

untied the bag he carried from around his waist and yanked it open, thrusting its contents toward the injured man. "Put this on."

~

Joss was pressed up against the inside of the ship's shed door, her eyes screwed shut as much against the sight of the guard trying to paw at the front of her dress as against the fetid reek of his breath. Her fingers were an inch away from her knife, strapped against her hip under her skirts, accessible through the slit in the fabric made especially for such a necessity, though she was praying desperately she would not have to draw it.

The man swiped at her breasts again and missed altogether this time, a curious, confused expression on his face. And then he had no expression at all, his features going slack as he simply deflated and collapsed at her feet. Joss exhaled, weak with relief. With wobbly arms she straightened the guard's head, maneuvering him next to his similarly unconscious comrade as best she could.

Dammit, she'd thought there had been enough laudanum in those wine bottles to render a rhinoceros senseless. She'd never drugged anyone before, but for some reason she had envisioned that the effects would be a little more...instantaneous. Instead she been forced to laugh and evade roving hands for minutes that had seemed like hours until the first two guards had started showing signs of drugged inebriation far beyond what would be expected from drinking a half bottle of wine. She'd led those two into the toolshed then under the guise of more carnal pursuits, to avoid the suspicion of the remaining guards, who were still drinking and tearing through the cooked pheasants and baked biscuits the women had provided. To their credit Anne and Janie kept the other men so distracted that Joss was sure they hadn't even noticed when they'd left the group.

Cautiously Joss cracked the door open and peered out onto the deck. It was unnaturally quiet, the ribald laughter and conversation gone. Only the faint noise of the ship coupled with the faint sounds of hymns still being sung on the shore reached her ears. She edged out onto the deck, careful to keep herself away from the pools of light emitted by the lanterns hanging overhead. She padded soundlessly forward, only to find a pile of sleeping men, some propped against barrels, others laid out flat on the deck. Anne was expertly twisting Janie's hair up even as her friend was polishing the barrel of her pistol with the edge of a pretty silk fichu.

Joss crouched and half crawled to the starboard side of the deck, spying on the crowd that had swelled on shore. So far it appeared her mother and her army of unapprised women were still keeping the officers busy with their altruistic madness, but Joss wasn't under any illusion that they had more than minutes before someone realized something was amiss.

Anne and Janie joined her, their bellies flat against the deck.

"Where are Hextall and Luke?" Joss hissed.

Anne's lips thinned. "I don't know. But they might think about hurrying." She put a brass telescope to her eye. "Because we're about to have company."

There was a boat on the water that Joss hadn't noticed, farther upriver, manned by guards and being rowed in their direction. She felt her blood go cold.

"The cavalry is on its way," murmured Janie. "No doubt coming to investigate why the *Retribution* has become so...sleepy."

Joss swore. There was no way they could get back to shore in their boat without being seen by the oncoming officers. They'd allowed for the possibility of discovery. But to have their allowances put to the test was enough to make her break out in a cold sweat.

She cast a nervous eye back out to the water, only to discover a second boat was on its way toward them.

"You two need to go," Joss said, crawling backward and out of sight of the approaching boat.

"Soon enough," said Anne, following. "But not before—"

"If you're caught on board, you'll be arrested. You'll end up on one of these damned hulks drifting off to some port on the other side of the world. And my mother will never forgive me." She'd never forgive herself. This wasn't their fight or their cause.

"Then let's get you the hell off this ship."

Joss spun to find Heath standing behind her, a man braced between him and Luke. She resisted the urge to fling herself into his arms and instead eyed the prisoner, pleased with what she saw. She nodded at him and then at Anne and Janie.

"Let's hurry then, ladies."

～

The three women tossed their worn cloaks overboard and went down the ladder first, Heath following to deposit his load in the bottom of the waiting boat. Tobias Darling flashed him a strained smile and Joss turned back to where Heath waited on the bottom rung of the ladder still hanging from the railing.

"Stall them as long as you can," he said. "But try and keep your distance."

"Haven't we had this conversation somewhere before?" she joked bravely, worry stamped across her features.

Heath grinned at her and leaned forward, kissing her hard.

"Don't do anything stupid, Hextall," she whispered, before turning and claiming her spot in the boat. She donned the new cloak and bonnet waiting for her.

"Good luck, my lord," Toby said, and with three quick strokes of the oars, he had distanced the little riverboat from the *Retribution*.

~

Joss sat primly in the little riverboat. They'd been seen, she knew, as they rowed away from the hulk. There'd been a shout, a flurry of conversation, and the oncoming boat had altered course, heading directly for them. Toby had pasted on a dull expression, and the rhythm of his oars didn't change. Within moments the larger vessel slid across their bow, and he reversed, keeping a careful distance between them.

An officer dressed in uniform was leaning over the bow of his own boat, a displeased look on his face. He opened his mouth to speak, but Joss beat him to it.

"Move your vessel at once," she demanded in a tone her father had perfected and she had always hated. "How dare you prevent us from returning to shore."

The officer's eyes darted to the occupants of the little boat before coming back to her, no doubt trying to ascertain exactly whom he was dealing with. Joss resisted the urge to check her appearance again. The women were all wearing ridiculously expensive cloaks, trimmed in fur, more suited for a ball than a boat. Their décolletage had gone from daring to demure with the addition of delicate lace fichus, and their hair had been properly hidden under fine bonnets and hats.

"If I may address you, Lady . . . ?"

"You may not," she snapped. "Did you not hear me? I demand that you remove yourselves."

The officer bristled, though he seemed unsure of what to say under such bizarre circumstances. He settled on a tentative admonishment. "It is not safe for ladies such as yourselves to be out here alone."

She sent him a scathing glare. "We would not have had to find our way out here by ourselves, if you men had assisted us in bringing our provisions to the prisoners in the first place."

"The prisoners' needs are well met, my lady," he protested. "They are not mistreated."

"Yet you deny us the satisfaction of Christian charity. What kind of man does that make you, I wonder?"

The officer drew back under her onslaught, his face tight, but didn't answer. Not that she'd expected him to. She was simply buying as much time with her performance as she could.

The man's eyes slid to the boat, where a gray-haired lady with a yellow bonnet sat slumped in between Anne and Janie. Janie was waving a vinaigrette under the woman's nose. "What's wrong with her?" the man demanded.

Joss stiffened and shifted slightly, blocking the officer's view. "Your guards on that ship were horrid," Joss said. "They would not let us come aboard, nor would they let us deliver our provisions. In fact, their language was so crude it sent my aunt into a fit of the vapors. Don't think my father won't hear of the ghastly treatment we received."

The officer considered her, seeming unimpressed by her threat. Joss stared right back. Dear God, but she didn't think she'd be able to do this much longer. If they came any closer and got a better look at the occupants of her little boat...

"Captain!" the shout came from one of his men.

The captain turned and then followed the man's finger. Along the rail of the *Retribution* two men dressed in the standard clothing allotted to the convicts could be seen running toward the stern.

"What the bloody hell?" the captain swore.

The men disappeared, and then the stunned silence was broken by the faint sound of a splash. Seconds later two swimmers were clearly visible, struggling and splashing for all they were worth downstream of the hulk toward a waiting ship.

Anne and Janie let out suitable shrieks of distress. "Escaping murderers!" one of them gasped.

"Guards!" the officer bellowed in the direction of the *Retribution*. "Guards!" he repeated, a little more desperately this time.

He got no reply.

"Is this a regular occurrence, Captain?" Joss demanded, letting a note of hysteria into her voice.

But the captain was roaring orders, and his boat turned clumsily in the direction of the escaping swimmers. It banged into their own boat twice before his men managed to reverse their vessel and maneuver around them. The guards manning the oars were in a panic, and it was a full minute before their boat straightened enough to pursue the fleeing convicts, who had, by this time, nearly reached a waiting packet boat.

Someone, somewhere, was ringing a bell, the sound jarring as it bounced over the water. Alerted by the disturbance, more officers on shore were struggling to get boats into the water, though most of them were half filled with provisions and disgruntled ladies.

Joss wanted to watch the scene unfold, wanted to make sure Heath would be all right. Instead she forced herself to remain seated, nodding at Toby.

The oars dipped powerfully once again, and their little boat slid silent and forgotten toward the chaos of the shore.

~

Heath had expected the cold, but he hadn't expected the way it cut through his skin and muscle and settled into his bones, making his limbs clumsy and his movements slow and painful. The ship was so close now. He glanced at Luke and then behind him, a flotilla of vessels coming hard in their wake. They were still a distance off, but the gap was quickly closing.

"I always wondered how Hawkins and Drake felt when they ran into the Spanish Armada," he said though clenched teeth.

Luke wheezed what might have been a laugh. "You have an odd sense of humor, milord."

"Do you think once a man voluntarily swims in the Thames in December with another, he might stop calling him *milord*?" Ten more yards. His arms felt as if they were made from lead, and it was only a healthy dose of fear that kept them moving.

"Sounds reasonable." Luke's words sounded stilted.

Heath's movements were becoming more and more labored. Icy water closed over his head before he found the surface again, gasping. Suddenly two strong hands were under his arms, pulling him up and out of the water.

"Bennett," he managed.

"Nice of you to arrive," his overseer said. "I thought you'd stopped for tea somewhere."

⁓

It had taken Heath longer than he would have liked to haul himself aboard the *Amelia Rose*, his limbs stiff and uncooperative, but he had no doubt that two convicts had been seen climbing aboard the packet ship by a hundred pairs of eyes. He could feel the *Amelia Rose* slipping steadily down the river, away from the lights of Woolwich Warren, the banks on either side of them becoming dark and empty.

He cast a glance over his shoulder in the direction of the closest riverboat approaching from the direction of the *Retribution*. There was an officer in the bow, pointing at the deck of the *Amelia Rose* in frenzied desperation, his rowers hauling at their oars in flustered inefficiency. Behind him more boats had been launched and were in pursuit. They'd eventually close the gap, Heath knew, but by then it would be too late. The destruction of the *Amelia Rose* would mark the death of the escaped convicts from the *Retribution*, preventing the massive manhunt that might otherwise ensue.

And perhaps, if they were lucky, mark the destruction of a vast treasure.

~~

The pandemonium on shore was absolute. Rumor of escaping convicts had spread throughout the crowd, and mayhem ensued, every gentlewoman scrambling to return to the safety of her carriage. More than one woman had swooned and was being helped along by acquaintances or servants. Horses snorted in fright, and grooms hung on to their bridles and cursed, trying to turn their equipages where there was simply no room to do so. Dogs ran through the crowd, snarling and fighting over food that had been dropped, and a dozen chickens flapped in distress, careening through the air. Officers were shouting and pushing through the tidal wave of women, trying to restore order, but it was a lost cause.

Joss paid little attention, concentrating only on the approaching shore downstream, toward the east side of the Warren and the Plumstead Marshes. The hull of their little boat ran aground, and Joss leaped out, assisting Anne and Janie, who were struggling to get their passenger safely on shore. She turned to see if their arrival had been noted, but they were ignored, an unwanted group of women assisting another who had clearly been overcome by the uproar.

By the time Joss turned back to the river, Toby and his boat had vanished back into the night.

The women made their way up the bank, the ground spongy beneath their feet and long grasses slapping against their skirts. A trail had been cut through the marsh grass, running south along the edge of the Warren, and they followed it, the din of the chaos retreating behind them.

Just ahead an unmarked carriage waited at the top of a moderate incline, in the exact spot where a tinker's cart had broken down earlier. A lantern suddenly flared to life, and Joseph was beside them, helping them up the last few yards.

In the light of the lantern, Joss got a good look at the prisoner's face. The exertion of their escape had taken its toll. Williamson was barely conscious, his complexion pale where it wasn't covered in bruises, and sweat covered his forehead under his bonnet and wig. He held his arm close to his body, and blood had seeped through the fabric of his dress and smeared along the edge of his cloak.

The dowager was holding the carriage door open, and she stared as they started to lift the man into the interior, his head lolling limply. "Good Lord," she puffed, before Joss could speak. "Is he dead?"

"Not yet," Joss replied grimly.

~

Bennett had lit a torch, and the flame snaked menacingly as he held it aloft. "Miz Montcrief says, once she's lit, we'll have only minutes before the fire burns through the oil-soaked straw that she's stacked on the upper and main decks," he said. "She's laid lengths of fuse down through the hatchways to the lower decks and directly into the powder. There'll be a lot of smoke at first, she says, enough to give us the cover we need to get to safety, but we want to be far, far away when the fire reaches the powder below."

Heath nodded and reached for the torch. "I'll do it. You get Luke into the boat." He jerked his chin in the direction of the rope lashed to the starboard side railing beneath which their escape waited, out of sight of the oncoming guards.

Luke was shivering, his hands jammed under his armpits in an effort to find some warmth. "I am a firm believer in hasty exits," he said, already moving to the rope. "And this seems like an excellent opportunity to make one." He disappeared over the side, making his way down to the waiting skiff.

"But, my lord—"

"I need you to be ready to row," Heath said through teeth clenched against the cold. "Because my damn arms are so frozen, they'll likely fall off if I try."

Bennett gave him an unhappy look. "Very well," he said. He reached inside his jacket and withdrew a leather-bound folder. "I brought this like you said. What had you wanted me to do with this, my lord?" he asked.

Heath took the folder from Bennett. "Leave it—"

The *Amelia Rose* suddenly listed hard, the deck beneath Heath's feet jarred out from under him with a deafening sound of splintering wood. He landed hard on his hip, the torch falling onto the deck and rolling away, instantly igniting a pile of straw stacked against the port-side railing. He could hear the sound of shouting, and through the smoke he could make out the outline of a smaller ship, caught against the port side of the *Amelia Rose*.

Beside him Bennett had gone to his knees. Heath scrambled to his feet, shoving the folder down the front of his jacket.

"Go," he shouted, shoving Bennett toward the rope. Around them the fire was spreading, racing greedily through the fuel layered across the deck. His overseer reached the railing and swung himself over, vanishing from sight amid scrabbling hands and a flurry of curses. The deck tilted violently again, and Heath pitched backward, nearly tumbling down the hatchway. He struggled to his feet, bracing himself against a trio of barrels that had been lashed to the upper deck. He took a single step forward and froze, the sound of a pistol being cocked by his ear surprisingly loud.

"Don't leave just yet, my lord."

Chapter 19 ——————————

The crack of splintering wood was followed by a muted thump that echoed through the darkness, and suddenly the river was lit up like a bonfire at Beltane. All eyes were now riveted on a packet ship drifting in the middle of the river. It had been rammed by a smaller vessel, the packet's hull visibly damaged in the ghoulish light cast from the flames now burning out of control. The fire leaped and roared and raced across the upper deck, and the escaping convicts who had been seen climbing onto the ship were swallowed by billowing clouds of smoke that rolled out across the river like an encroaching wall.

The riverboats that had been launched from the Warren instinctively checked their speed at the sight of the fire and the unknown ship still trapped up against the packet. In the glow from the flames, Joss watched in horror as men from the second ship swung themselves over the railings of the doomed *Amelia Rose*. "*Vive l'Empereur*" rang out over the water, dozens of voices screaming their battle cry as they too disappeared into the smoke.

From her vantage point up on the hill, she could see a small skiff spin away from the packet on the starboard side, moving northeast toward the far bank. The light from the fire silhouetted the shape of two men, one dark and broad, the other fair-haired and compact. Bennett and Luke. There was no sign of Heath. Where the hell was Heath?

Bile rose in her throat and her breathing became shallow as she tried not to panic. Yet a hysterical bubble of panic rose anyway. They had underestimated these Napoleonic patriots. In their attempt to destroy the legend of a treasure that was already soaked in blood and betrayal, they had underestimated the reckless, ruthless desperation that had been evident all along.

⁓

"Monsieur Leroux, I presume," Heath said, without turning around, hearing shouting as men tried vainly to douse the fire. He sent a silent plea for Bennett and Luke to get away from the *Amelia Rose*. The fuses would be burning even now, strings of flame creeping steadily down the hatchways, into the bowels of the ship, and ever closer to the barrels of black powder stacked beneath them.

The barrel of the pistol touched the side of his head. "I do not like it when people take what is mine."

Heath cleared his throat. "I heard." He weighed the chances he could make it to the water against the chances a bullet would lodge itself in his skull before he'd gone two steps. They were rather poor odds.

"This ship is mine. And all the gold on it."

"Gold? You are mistaken, *monsieur*. I am a soapmaker, not a king. There is no gold on this ship. A ship, I fear, that is about to go to the bottom of the Thames."

The Frenchman dug the barrel of the pistol into his skull. "My men will take care of the little fire," Leroux sneered. "Englishmen can never be counted on to do anything right."

The man was clearly insane, Heath realized. Whatever efforts the Frenchmen were making to smother the fire were no match for Gisele Montcrief's skill at setting one. The fire was taking on a life of its own, a living breathing thing that had the little packet ship groaning and dying beneath its onslaught. Heath coughed as the smoke swirled around them, the acrid fog stinging his throat.

"Captain," a man wheezed, appearing out of the smoke, his face blackened and his eyes red and watery, "I fear we are too late. The fire, it is unstoppable. We must flee."

The Frenchman snarled at the soldier, a sound of disgust. "Open that," he demanded, pointing at the barrels by Heath's hip. "And you will see for yourself what we fight to preserve. What belongs to your Emperor. Perhaps then you will not cower like a frightened child."

"But, Captain—"

"Open it!" Leroux roared, and the man flinched and obeyed, drawing a short sword from his side and levering it under the sealed lid of the nearest barrel.

Heath edged a little farther past the open hatchway. Beneath his jacket the leather folder pressed uncomfortably against his abdomen. The *Amelia Rose* listed harder, creaking and groaning as the flames ate away at her timbers. The heat was becoming almost intolerable. His life, Heath knew, could now be measured in seconds.

The soldier had pried the lid of the barrel off, and he pushed it aside, staring down at the contents. He stuck a finger in and sniffed. "Soap?"

Leroux leaned forward in disbelief, and Heath spun, staggering to the far side of the hatchway, yanking the folder from within his jacket. He was still too far away from the railing to make it before Leroux's bullet did.

Leroux leveled his pistol at Heath's chest. "Where is it?" he yelled, wild with rage. "Where is the gold?" His eyes fixed on the folder Heath clutched in his hand. "You know where it is. You've had that all along."

"Yes," agreed Heath. "Smythe gave it to me before he died. So that the location of the gold would remain hidden."

The fire had climbed into the rigging, devouring rope and canvas, and embers and ash were swirling down around their heads like a volcanic snowstorm.

"Captain," the soldier pleaded. "We have no time. We must—"

Near the bow the foremast toppled over the port-side railing in a firestorm of sparks, crashing over the deck of the French ship still alongside the packet. Without a second's hesitation, Heath tossed the folder down into the open hatchway and sprinted toward the bow railing, looking back only once. Leroux roared again in rage, but he had flung away the pistol and was clambering down to the main deck in a desperate attempt to save the Templar documents.

Heath threw himself from the upper deck of the *Amelia Rose*, the icy water rushing up to meet him. He surfaced, gasping, his arms and legs churning desperately toward the north shore, away from the inferno that rose above him.

And then the *Amelia Rose* detonated.

❧

The firestorm was a spectacle to behold.

In the blink of an eye, the packet ship and the slightly smaller vessel that had been unable to free itself simply disappeared. The explosion sent a sound like rolling thunder across the river and over the land, felt in the bones before it was heard. Bits of flaming debris were launched into the air to fall in the water, extinguished immediately. Within minutes all that was left was a morass of floating wooden pieces and a strange trail of suds foaming across the surface of the water.

The riverboats from Woolwich that had withdrawn from the conflagration now surged forward again, looking for survivors. Other rivermen set their boats and barges toward the wreckage, probably searching more for something to salvage and sell than for survivors.

Joss stood frozen by the carriage, silent and afraid that if she moved, she would lose whatever tenuous grip she still had on her composure. Everything around her seemed to be happening slowly, as if she were trapped underwater and watching from a distance. Beside her, Joseph made a sound of distress.

"They would have gotten off before that went up," the dowager said presently, her words tight. "In fact, they'll probably beat us back."

Joss wanted to believe that. Needed to believe that.

Along the barrack fields just west of them, the sound of pounding hooves could be heard, men in uniform racing toward the Warren.

"I suggest we not dawdle," the duchess said succinctly, clapping her hands. "There will be soldiers crawling all over the Warren and the surrounding areas shortly. I do not intend to be here when that occurs." She ushered her upstairs maids into the carriage.

Joss didn't budge. She didn't want to get into the carriage. What she wanted to do was run down to the river and throw herself into the water to search for Heath. Ridiculous, the rational part of her brain knew, for the weight of her skirts coupled with the cold would take her straight to the bottom of the Thames in a matter of minutes.

"Heath Hextall is a man of great resource," her mother said beside her, her voice full of understanding and sympathy. "You must trust that he survived."

Joss shook her head, loss and anger and regret shoving and crowding into her chest. "I love him." And the thought that she might never tell him that was ripping her heart into tiny little pieces.

Her mother patted her arm gently. "Of course you do, dear. You have since you were five years old and he put a frog down the front of your dress."

Joss turned to stare at the dowager. "It was a toad," she whispered.

Her mother smiled, but her words were firm. "He is a good man, Josephine. But you do him a disservice by standing here and believing the worst." She jerked her chin in the direction of the carriage. "We need to get Mr. Williamson to a surgeon immediately. If he dies, then everything that has happened here tonight is for naught. You must concentrate on what you can do now. Not what you wish you could do. Understand?"

Joss nodded. "Yes."

"Good. Now get in the damn carriage."

⁓

It felt as if he'd been kicked by a mule. Or more likely a team of them. The percussion of the explosion seemed to suck the air away from the space around his head before pummeling his entire body with a force that knocked the breath clean from his lungs. Water closed over him, a blinding blaze of light followed by blackness. For a moment he lost sense of where he was. Heath could see nothing, hear nothing. He drifted, dizzy and disoriented, until his lungs started to burn, but when he opened his mouth to drag in a labored breath, there was only water choking him.

He panicked then, thrashing against the numbing cold. Above him a light flared briefly, and he angled himself toward it. He had to find the surface. Yet the cold was like a heavy blanket, wrapping itself around his limbs and making movement cumbersome and sluggish. The surface seemed to be getting farther away, not closer. The edges of his vision dimmed, a creeping blackness that was starting to undermine his resolve.

An image of Joss popped into his head, her hands on her hips and her beautiful blue-green eyes narrowed in disapproval. She would be lecturing him at this juncture, about the amount of time it takes an earl to drown, measured in minutes, or perhaps the amount of water, measured in pints, that it takes to fill up an adult male's lungs. He frowned. He had no interest in drowning. He had no interest in being added to Josephine Somerhall's damn trivia collection.

Heath kicked hard, and suddenly his head broke the surface, and he sucked in a breath before he sank below the icy water again. He flailed his arms, his hand coming into contact with something hard. His fingers closed around it, and he dragged himself toward it, bringing his head back above the surface. He gasped, forcing his arm farther over the flotsam, and laid his head on his shoulder, his eyes closed and his chest heaving. He drifted like that for seconds or hours, a speck of debris amid a sea of it.

Presently he opened his eyes, only to be presented with a view of two enormous rounded breasts bobbing in the water, one on either side of his hand. He blinked, his mind as uncooperative as his muscles, until he realized that he was wrapped around the beautifully carved figure-head that had once graced the bowsprit of the *Amelia Rose*. From under his shoulder, her wooden face stared up at him in reproach.

He started to laugh then, a gasping, uncontrolled noise that he was helpless to stop.

He was still laughing when Benjamin Bennett reached him and hauled him out of the water, dumping him unceremoniously into the bottom of the little skiff.

Joss had helped bring the unconscious prisoner into the dowager's town house. There was water to heat, blankets to fetch, and candles and lanterns to be found and lit. All of which any of her mother's servants could have done, but Joss needed something to do. Anything to keep her mind off the fact that Heath, Luke, and Bennett had not yet returned. Jenna Somerhall, the Duchess of Worth, arrived with her surgeon's bag then and ordered everyone from the patient's crowded room.

Adrift, Joss paced in the study. She picked up a book and set it down. Picked up another and let it drop from her fingers. They'd drawn every curtain in the townhome, concealing the activity within to prying eyes, but every noise outside on the street had sent her flying to the window. And still they didn't return.

The sky was just beginning to lighten when Joss heard the door behind her open. She spun to find Joseph standing in the doorway, a piece of paper in his hand, a grim expression on his face.

"It's from my brother," he said, gesturing to the note. "It says Luke and Bennett took him to the earl's town house. It was closer. And not so crowded."

"Is he alive?" Joss croaked.

Joseph raised his hands helplessly. "It doesn't say that he's not."

"Is he hurt?"

He thrust the note in her direction. "It just says where they are."

She was already stumbling to the door. "Help me with a horse," she said.

"They're already waiting outside."

Chapter 20————————————

She crashed into Heath's home, knowing she looked disheveled and panicked and more than a little wild, and she didn't care. Bennett, alerted to the disturbance, met her in the hall, a look of startled confusion across his face.

"Where is he?"

"Didn't you get our note?" he asked. "Luke sent a note so that you wouldn't worry—"

"Where is he?" Joss demanded, trying but failing to curb the edge of hysteria she could hear in her voice.

"We took him upstairs," he replied, "but he's—"

Joss didn't hear the rest because she was already running up the stairs, her skirts in her hands and her heart in her throat.

We took him upstairs, Bennett had said. Not that he'd gone upstairs, or walked upstairs, or retired upstairs, but that he'd been taken upstairs. Unable to do so under his own power. A hundred different possibilities ran through her mind, each one worse than the last. He'd been shot. Stabbed. Caught in the explosion that could be heard for miles around. The very idea that he might be lost to her left her physically ill.

She reached the top of the stairs, knocking over

the vase filled with naked stems, and skidded into his room, expecting blood and chaos and who knew what else. But his room was deserted. His bed was empty, a fire glowed cheerfully in the hearth, and there was no sign of disaster. A soft light coming from the dressing room cast a golden rectangle across the floor, and Joss hurried to the door.

He was in the bath.

Her dread drained violently from her body, leaving her feeling almost drunk. Only Heath's shoulders and head were visible above the steaming water, though twin islands that were his kneecaps poked up in the center. His eyes were closed, his golden hair dark with damp and curling over his forehead and around his ears. He was breathing steadily, the breadth of his shoulders spanning the width of the tub. The soft light of the candelabrum fell across that smooth expanse of skin, carving out hollows and valleys created by bone and muscle.

He was safe. He was whole and safe. Her legs gave way, and she found herself sliding down the doorframe, coming to sit in an inelegant pile on his dressing room floor with a thump. For some absurd reason, she felt like crying.

"Joss?" His voice was rough, but full of concern.

"They told me you were taken upstairs," she mumbled.

"Joss, what are you doing here? Are you hurt? Why are you sitting on the floor?"

"No," she said, pushing herself back to her feet with unsteady movements. "I'm not hurt. I thought you were. I thought you had done something monumentally stupid."

He sat up in the bath. "I did. I went swimming in the Thames in the middle of December. Twice."

She couldn't bring herself to laugh.

"I'm fine, Joss. There is nothing wrong with me that a hot bath couldn't fix."

She still couldn't answer. The backs of her eyes were burning fiercely, and her throat was closing up.

"Joss?"

She waved her hand, swiping at the tear that had escaped down her cheek. Another followed in its wake and then another.

"Joss, come here."

She shuffled to the edge of the tub, squeezing her eyes shut against the tears that refused to stop.

"Are you crying?"

"No." She sniffed, refusing to open her eyes. "I'm not."

"You're crying. I've made you cry."

She took a shuddering breath. "It's only taken you twenty years, Hextall. You should probably mark the date in your calendar."

She heard him shift, the water slapping against the edges of the tub. His hands grasped hers, warm and wet and strong. "Look at me, Joss."

She shook her head and screwed her eyes shut tighter. This was mortifying—

She shrieked as she was suddenly yanked off-balance and pulled forward into the tub.

She crashed into his chest, her thighs banging against the edge of the tub, and came to rest on top of him, water sloshing everywhere.

"What the hell, Hextall?" she gasped, her cheek smashed against his collarbone just above the surface of the water.

"You're not crying anymore."

She hiccupped. "No, but I might be in danger of drowning."

Heath released her hands. "I don't ever want to make you cry, Joss."

Joss struggled to push herself off his chest, water dripping from her hair and her bodice, and looked down at him. "I love you, you idiot. And I was scared I'd lost you."

"You won't ever lose me." He reached up and pushed a damp curl from her forehead. "I belong to you."

She dipped her head and kissed him.

"God, I love you," he murmured against her lips.

She sighed and deepened her kiss. His hands went to her waist, caressing her back, and then tangling in her hair, pulling her closer. Except there was nowhere for her to go in a tub meant for one and he made a noise of annoyance.

"I'm sure in a novel this might be considered romantic, but I can't move right now," Joss said, chuckling.

"Well, now, that's no good." He leaned forward and wrapped his arms around her waist, hauling them both to their feet in the middle of the tub. "I need a bigger tub," he said before he caught her head in his hands again and kissed her, his tongue catching the drop of water on the edge of her lips. "And when I get one, I'm going to make love to you in it. A lot."

"I should be scandalized right now," Joss murmured.

"You should be naked right now." He was yanking at the laces of her dress.

"You're going to rip it."

"Good." His eyes were scorching.

"Gentlemen don't rip the gowns off their ladies."

"I have no interest in being a gentleman." The soaked

fabric gave way beneath his hands, and her dress slid into the tub, leaving her in only her chemise.

Joss swallowed, desire rising fast. She raised her hands to his shoulders, letting them slide over the crisp hair of his chest and along the hard edges of his ribs.

He put his hands at the neck of her chemise and it met the same fate as her dress. "Better," Heath growled before he claimed her mouth.

It was a clash of tongues and lips and teeth, and Joss groaned, pressing against the length of him. She could feel his arousal against her stomach, the slick heat of damp skin when their bodies met. The air around them was heavy with humidity, the warmth from the water around their legs rising. Abruptly Heath broke the kiss and climbed from the tub, holding his hand out for Joss to do the same. Her feet had no sooner hit the floor than he scooped her up in his arms and stalked into his bedroom, tossing her onto the center of his bed and coming down beside her.

"I can barely think, I want you so badly," he said.

Joss thought she might have made some sound of agreement, but she was no longer capable of speech. His hands were stroking her breasts and her abdomen, working their way lower until his fingers brushed the folds of her sex. She arched against him, shamelessly needy. He withdrew his hand and rolled onto his back, pulling her with him.

Joss found herself straddling his hips, his erection nudging her entrance. Her hands were braced on his shoulders, the muscles hard beneath her palms. He was watching her, his breath coming harshly.

"I want you to see," he said. His fingers trailed along

the lengths of her arms and then back up, and Joss shivered first at his words and then at his feather-light touch.

She bent her head and kissed him, soft kisses along his lips, her tongue teasing his. Her hands roamed over his chest, tracing the ridges of muscle and stopping to play with the pebbled peaks of his nipples. She bent farther, replacing her fingers with her mouth, tasting the heat of his skin. The movement pushed her back farther against his cock, the rigid length of him pulsing at the contact.

His breath hissed. "Please," he gasped.

Slowly Joss slid back, accommodating the tip of him. He jerked beneath her, his hands going to her hips, his fingers digging into her flesh.

"More," he groaned.

She complied, opening herself to him and letting him guide her so that he filled her fully. She rocked against him, watching as his head tipped back in pleasure. Another movement, a slight withdrawal, before she rocked back again and he groaned again, his hands sliding up her ribs to cup her breasts. It was exhilarating and erotic, this taste of intimate dominance that he'd given her. This admission of the power she possessed.

Yet for every movement that brought him pleasure, an answering heat built in her, a fire that had ignited in every fiber of her body, and she wasn't at all sure it was something she knew how to control. Instinct and impulse were guiding her now, and she lifted herself slightly, feeling him slide from her nearly entirely before she came back down to sheath him again.

Heath moaned, a low guttural sound. "Yes," he whispered. "Don't stop."

She couldn't have stopped if she had wanted to. Her

hips rolled faster now, every movement bringing her body closer to release. Her own breath was coming in gasps, her eyes locked with his. The first contractions of her orgasm started slowly, gathering strength and speed until her entire being became one of desperate, wild want. Heath's hands came back down on her hips like a steel vise, holding her prisoner as she whimpered helplessly, grinding against him.

"Heath," she said, though she wasn't sure if it was a plea or a command.

"Let go, Joss," he demanded, thrusting hard up into her.

Pleasure crashed violently through her, and her eyes closed, her head dropped, and her hands dug into the muscles of his shoulders as though she could anchor herself.

Beneath her his entire body was straining, his own hips bucking as he pulsed and throbbed deep within her. She remained motionless, savoring the aftershocks and tiny ripples of pleasure that coursed through her even when her limbs had been left liquid.

Joss collapsed on his chest, her cheek once again pressed against his shoulder. They had somehow ended up near the edge of the far side of the bed, the blankets and sheets a tangled mess beneath them.

"We don't need a bigger tub," she said presently when she had caught her breath. "I think we need a bigger bed."

Heath laughed, the beautiful sound rumbling through his chest against her ear. "I think we should get both." He paused and considered the bedposts with a wicked gleam in his eye. "And maybe some ropes."

"Ropes?"

"Every good pirate king needs ropes to tie up his captives."

"You've decided to become a pirate king?"

"Yes," he said without a second's hesitation. "Being a proper gentleman has become quite dull."

Joss smiled and propped herself up on her elbows. "It's about damn time you figured that out."

He watched her for a long moment, his eyes searching hers. "I'm going to need a translator who would be willing to travel with me, because as a pirate king, I fully intend to sail to all four corners of the earth. Do you know a good one?" His voice was still light, but his eyes had darkened to a deep blue.

Her breath caught. "I might."

He reached out and touched a finger to the side of her face. "I've also discovered I have no use for a domestic partner, but I am going to need a first mate. Someone who knows their way around the world. Now I am thinking that person is going to be harder to find. Any ideas?"

"One."

"I'm also going to need a best friend. And the woman I love more than life itself."

Joss bit her lip.

"Would you take me with you?" he whispered.

"Yes," she said.

He kissed her hard then, a searing kiss that branded her as his own. "Thank God," he breathed as he flipped her onto her back and moved on top of her. "I was worried my first act as a pirate king would be kidnapping."

Chapter 21 ——————————

Arthur Williamson regained consciousness the next afternoon.

Jenna Somerhall had hovered over her patient all night, and now her pale eyes were shadowed with fatigue, but she looked quite satisfied.

"He'll live," she pronounced from outside his door. "No thanks to the half-wit who nearly bled him out with a lancet." She hefted her surgeon's bag. "His arm is broken, though the break was clean and I was able to set it last night while he was unconscious. There were a number of lacerations I cleaned and stitched. I've seen worse. He'll heal."

"Can we go in?" Heath asked from behind her.

Jenna shrugged. "By all means. I would think you've earned the right to an honest conversation." She yawned. "I'm going to have a nap in my old rooms upstairs. Send someone to fetch me if anything changes for the worse."

Joss nodded and watched as she left, about to push open the door to the room. Heath put a restraining hand on her arm, and she looked down to see him holding out a pile of documents tied with string, the ancient illumination glinting in the light.

Her eyes widened. "Bennett told me that the folder was destroyed on the *Amelia Rose*."

Heath smiled faintly. "The folder was destroyed. Along with four months' worth of coal receipts from my soap factories." He paused. "I'm learning a few things from your family along the way."

"What do we do with these now?" Joss asked.

"Let's go ask," he said.

Williamson was awake, propped up among pillows in the dowager's green guest room, no longer looking as if he was on the brink of death. His face had regained some color, his wounds had been neatly bandaged, and he was sipping at a cup of broth.

"Good afternoon," he said, setting aside his cup.

"You're looking much better," Joss told him.

"I've been in good hands. Your surgeon is exceedingly competent."

"She is that," Joss agreed.

"Where was she trained?"

"The track."

"The track?"

"She's a track surgeon. Thoroughbreds and an occasional donkey. She tends to people when the need arises."

Williamson blinked at her. "I see."

Heath had drawn a chair close to the bed and motioned for Joss to sit. He remained standing, his hands clasped behind his back.

Williamson looked between them. "Thank you. For doing what you did last night. For risking as much as you did."

Joss saw Heath nod out of the corner of her eye. "It was the right thing to do," he said.

"Your surgeon told me you lost a ship in the process."

"Yes. Not only did it guarantee your theoretical demise, it was necessary in the theoretical destruction of a Templar treasure. Any individuals who sought it in the name of an exiled emperor are now dead or believe a fortune in gold now rests on the bottom of the Thames."

Williamson regarded them silently, his eyes betraying nothing.

Heath unclasped his hands and held the documents tied with string in front of him. "It was a little hard to believe at first, I admit," Heath said.

"And what is it that you think you believe?" Williamson's eyes touched briefly on the papers before returning to Heath's face.

"The sudden disappearance of an entire order and all of its substantial wealth. The assistance of the Hospitallers and the construction of a fortress on Malta. The invasion of the very same island by Napoleon Bonaparte and the subsequent removal of that fortune to the shores of Britain."

This time Williamson couldn't hide his startled surprise. "That is quite a story," he said carefully.

"Isn't it?" Heath tossed the papers on the edge of the bed.

"How exactly did you come to these conclusions?"

Heath jerked his head at Joss. "She reads."

Williamson's eyes swiveled in her direction with speculation before returning to Heath. "Indeed."

"The night Gavin Smythe died, he begged me to save you," Heath said. "To get these documents back to you. And so we have. What you do with them now is up to you."

With his good arm, the guardian pushed the blanket that covered his body to the side. He struggled to his feet, swaying slightly before finding his balance. He picked up the documents that lay on the corner of the bed and slowly walked over to the hearth.

"Gavin was right to trust you," he said. "And there are no words that can express my gratitude for keeping safe for a time what we couldn't. Though Gavin should have done this a long time ago."

Without a second's hesitation, he dropped the documents onto the coals.

The paper and vellum curled instantly, smoke snaking thick and white from underneath before the pile burst into flame, burning fast and hot.

Joss was aware she had come to her feet, unsure what she was feeling as she watched the documents reduced to nothing but ash. An acute resentment, perhaps, at the knowledge that what had nearly cost them their lives had been destroyed in a single heartbeat, with nothing more than a casual movement of a man's hand. Yet there was a lingering relief that they had.

Williamson leaned on the mantel, staring into the fire. "These letters were preserved over time, so that there would exist a record of what happens when men's greed surpasses grace. But now, in its discovery outside of our brotherhood, that record itself is dangerous and cannot be allowed to survive."

He was right, Joss knew. Others would come hunting, their motivations perhaps different from those of Marcel Leroux, but no less dangerous for it.

"How was it ever discovered in the first place?" she asked. "How were you ever identified?"

Williamson returned to the bed, sinking down on the mattress. "When the French invaded Malta, this set of documents was discovered and seized before it could be destroyed, though the guardian I replaced died under a French blade in the attempt. They also discovered a small cache of gold set aside for the expansion of the hospital, which prompted them to begin their search for the rest.

"And they might have found it too, had it not been for the English blockade. While the French were slowly starving to death, we were able to recover the folder and its contents, and made the decision to move the treasure. The risk of that sort of wealth falling into French hands—or any sort of military hands—was too great."

"So you moved it."

"Yes. As soon as the English took command of the island. Which was just as well. Even before Waterloo, we were advised that there were Frenchmen who had covertly returned to the island. Searching for buried gold."

"So someone under the command of Bonaparte had been able to read the documents."

"I believe so, yes."

"Is that how they followed you here?"

"Perhaps." He shrugged. "But moving such a cargo has risks in itself. However we tried to disguise our actions, there still existed the men who transported an unknown cargo from the bowels of the fort to the docks. There still existed the men who loaded and unloaded our ships and might have doubted the manifest, or wondered where such quantities of nails and coal and steel bars had come from and where they were going. For clever men asking clever questions, a careless comment in the wrong ear could have brought the French to these shores. As we have done for the past five hundred years, we tried to blend in with the society around us. Perhaps we were wrong to do that, for it left us vulnerable. And cost me three brothers."

Joss studied him. "What will you do now?"

"Return to my brethren and complete my service as a knight and a guardian." He smiled faintly. "For wealth such as that is only as good as the people who control it. I've decided I rather enjoy the climate of this island. I do believe I'd like to try my hand at farming. I never did like making shoes." He paused, his expression becoming serious as he studied them both. "Will you ask me where it is? The treasure?"

"No," Heath replied before Joss could say anything.

"Indeed? There are a great deal of things that a man could do with that kind of money."

"I have money. And however much it can buy comforts, it has never been able to buy me true happiness." He moved behind Joss and wrapped his arms around her, resting his cheek against the side of her hair.

"So you will keep our secrets."

"Of course."

Williamson smiled and leaned back against the pillow. "I suppose I'll have to trust you," he said.

Heath tightened his arms around Joss. "I suppose you will."

Chapter 22 _____

A fog had settled over Liverpool on Christmas Day.

It was soft and thick and left beads of moisture on everything it touched. It was a little like walking in a cloud, Joss thought, blinking away the drops of water that clung to her lashes. She waited on the dock as Heath relayed last instructions to Benjamin Bennett on board the *Julliard*, watching the smudged silhouettes of the two men as they stood on the deck.

The fog would delay Bennett's departure, no doubt, but Joss doubted the overseer would be unduly distraught. She was quite sure he and his new bride would find ways to pass the time before they could depart for Boston. She smirked, though a tug on her sleeve distracted her.

"Are you Lady Josephine?" A boy of no more than eight or nine was at her elbow, wrapped in a worn coat and woolen cap.

"Yes." She gave the boy a puzzled look. He didn't appear to be selling anything, nor stealing anything from her pockets. And how did he know her name?

The boy thrust a piece of heavy paper into her hand and vanished into the fog as quickly as he had appeared. She made to go after him, but recognized the futility. She could barely see Heath standing twenty feet away from her, much less a small boy intent on disappearing. She glanced down at the missive in her hand and her breath caught.

It was addressed to the Earl and Countess of Boden, the capital *E* drawn with a flourish and illuminated with red and blue ink, similar to documents she had held in her hands not so long ago. She stared at it, motionless.

"What's that?" Heath asked, coming up behind her. "Another list for Bennett? Or Rebecca?" he teased.

"I don't know."

Heath plucked it from her hand, his blond brows furrowing as he saw the address on the front. "Where did this come from?" The teasing had left his voice.

Joss shrugged. "A boy I've never seen in my life." She nudged him. "Open it."

Heath looked at her, his expression a mask of comical apprehension. "Have you forgotten what happened last time we opened something that looked like this?"

"This one has our names on it, Hextall."

"I think that makes it worse."

She snatched it from him with a huff of impatience and cracked the seal, opening the page. Her eyes skimmed the writing, tiny details and numbers and notes.

"What does it say?" Heath asked, leaning into her.

"It's ownership documents. For a clipper named the *Azalea Rae*." She looked up at him before returning her attention to the page. "Currently at anchor at the Manchester Docks, Liverpool."

"I don't understand. Who owns it?"

She cleared her throat. "You."

Heath was scowling now. "I don't own a ship called the *Azalea Rae*. I think I would remember that."

"Well, this says you do. And that it's here. Somewhere in front of us." She waved her hand at the ships moored at the docks, only the closest ships visible as ghostly silhouettes in the fog.

"That's ridiculous."

Joss pulled Heath's hand. "Let's look."

"I'm not looking for a ship that doesn't exist."

"Humor me."

Heath heaved a sigh. "Fine. I'll give you ten minutes. And then, when we don't find a ship that doesn't exist, we're going to return to our hotel, take all of our wet clothes off, and not put any more back on until tomorrow."

"Your sense of adventure is slipping again, Hextall."

He caught her arm and pulled her to him, kissing her long and leisurely. "Oh, I can assure you I have all sorts of adventurous ideas," he murmured against her mouth. "Just not ones that want an audience."

He stepped back, and Joss knew her color was high.

"Nine minutes," he said, and Joss laughed and took off running.

The massive docks were constructed almost in the shape of a full circle, the side that faced the river gaping open to provide access to the ships wishing to enter the basin. The *Julliard* had been moored almost at the river, so it was easy to circumnavigate the structure, and Joss paused as she passed each ship, carefully reading the names.

"Two minutes," Heath said from somewhere behind her. "And for the record, I have full intentions of saying I told you so— *Oof.*" He ran into her as she abruptly stopped.

She was standing at a sleek clipper, *Azalea Rae* clearly visible in gilded paint across the stern.

"If you don't want her, can I have her?" Joss asked, knowing the value of such a fast vessel.

Heath had been staring at the clipper, but now he strode forward. "I'm sure this is a misunderstanding. Perhaps her captain, if he's on board, will be able to clear this up. Wait here." He disappeared into the fog.

He returned a moment later, looking disturbed. "You need to see this."

He helped her on board the ship and led her across the deck, and then down to the captain's cabin. They saw not a soul. Propped on the small table bolted to the floor, on top of a stack of folded newspapers, there was another note, bearing Heath's name.

"Did you open it?"

"Yes."

"What does it say?"

"It says thank you." He looked dazed.

Joss reached for the first newspaper. It was a copy of the *Edinburgh Gazette*, dated four days ago. In an article near the bottom of the page ran a commentary on the intentions to expand the University of Edinburgh Medical School, the Royal Infirmary of Edinburgh, and the Surgeons' Hall. Funds from an anonymous source had been made available, and more than one person quoted vehemently declared that the Edinburgh medical and teaching facilities would become the best in all of Europe.

Speculation was rife, yet nobody could claim responsibility for the largesse.

She replaced it and picked up a copy of the *Edinburgh Advertiser*, a similar article within its pages. She eyed the stack of newspapers. "It would seem Mr. Williamson has been busy."

"Mmmm." Heath seemed not to have heard her, still looking around him like a wide-eyed child just given a pony. "How fast do you think this thing goes?"

Joss rolled her eyes. "Were you hoping to get to Bombay by nightfall?"

Heath laughed. "Maybe." His attention returned to her and the newspapers she held in her hand. "Do you ever wonder where it is? The treasure?"

Joss smiled and tossed the papers on the table, coming to stand in front of Heath, wrapping her arms around his neck. "I know where it is."

"You do not." He snorted, even as his own arms went around her waist, pulling her close.

"I do."

"Tell me."

"There is a pretty little chapel in a pretty little glen in Scotland," she said. "Not that far from Edinburgh, really. It has the most incredible carvings in it. They cover almost every surface. Quite overwhelming, to be frank. But if you walk down the south aisle and look at the bottom left-hand corner of the window there, you'll see a carving of two knights astride a single horse. The strength of the Templars and Hospitallers combined for the good of all."

"Mmm." Heath was watching her. "Perhaps you'll take me there someday." He kissed her gently.

Joss smiled and kissed him back.

"Perhaps I will."

To save an innocent girl, Gisele Whitby needs a daring man to help her with her cunning scheme. But when she meets Jamie Montcrief, the rogue in question may foil her plan—and ignite her deepest desires...

Please see the next page for an excerpt from

I've Got My Duke to Keep Me Warm.

Chapter 1 —————————

Somewhere south of Nottingham, England, May 1816

Being dead was not without its drawbacks.

The tavern was one of them. More hovel than hostelry, it was plunked capriciously in a tiny hamlet, somewhere near nowhere. Her mere presence in this dismal place proved time was running out and desperation was beginning to eclipse good sense.

Gisele shuffled along the filthy wall of the taproom, wrinkling her nose against the overripe scent of unwashed bodies and spilled ale. She sidestepped neatly, avoiding the leering gaze and groping fingers of more than one man, and slipped into the gathering darkness outside. She took a deep breath, trying to maintain a sense of purpose and hope. The carefully crafted demise of Gisele Whitby four years earlier had granted her the freedom and the safety to reclaim her life. True, it had also driven her to the fringes of society, but until very recently, forced anonymity had been a benediction. Now it was proving to be an unwanted complication.

"What are you doing out here?" The voice came from beside her, and she sighed, not turning toward her friend.

"This is impossible. We'll not find him here."

Sebastien gazed at the sparrows quarreling along the edge of the thatch in the evening air. "I agree. We need a male without feathers. And they are all inside."

Gisele rolled her eyes. "Have you been inside? There is not a single one in there who would stand a chance at passing for a gentleman."

Sebastien brushed nonexistent dust off his sleeve. "Perhaps we haven't seen everyone who—"

"Please," she grumbled. "Half of those drunkards have a dubious command of the English language. And the other half have no command over any type of language at all." She stalked toward the stables in agitation.

Sebastien hurried across the yard after her.

"The man we need has to be clever and witty and charming and courageous and...convincingly noble." She spit the last word as if it were refuse.

"He does not exactly need to replace—"

"Yes, he does," Gisele argued, suddenly feeling very tired. "He has to be all of those things. Or at least some of those and willing to learn the rest. Or very, very desperate and willing to learn them all." She stopped, defeated, eyeing a ragged heap of humanity leaning against the front of the stable, asleep or stewed or both. "And we will not find all that here, in the middle of God knows where."

"We'll find someone," Sebastien repeated stubbornly, his dark brows knit.

"And if we can't?"

"Then we'll find a way. We'll find another way. There will—"

Whatever the slight man was going to say next was drowned out by the sound of an approaching carriage.

Gisele sighed loudly and stepped back into the shadows of the stable wall out of habit.

The vehicle stopped, and the driver and groom jumped down. The driver immediately went to unharness the sweat-soaked horses, though the groom disappeared inside the tavern without a backward glance, earning a muttered curse from the driver. Inside the carriage Gisele could hear the muffled tones of an argument. Presently the carriage door snapped open and a rotund man disembarked, stepping just to the side and lighting a cheroot. A well-dressed woman leaned out of the carriage door behind him to continue their squabble, shouting to be heard over the driver, who was leading the first horse away and calling for a fresh team.

Gisele watched the scene with growing impatience. She was preoccupied with her own problems and annoyed to be trapped out by the stables where there was no chance of finding any solution. Still, the carriage was expensive and it bore a coat of arms, and she would take no chances of being recognized, no matter how remote this tavern might be.

She was still plotting when the driver returned to fetch the second horse from its traces. As he reached for the bridle, the door to the tavern exploded outward with enough force to knock the wood clear off its hinges and send a report echoing through the yard like a gunshot. The gelding spooked and bolted forward, and the carriage lurched precariously behind it. The man standing with his cheroot was knocked sideways, his expensive hat landing somewhere in the dust. From the open carriage doorway, the woman began screaming hysterically, spurring the frightened horse on.

"Good heavens," gasped Sebastien, observing the unfolding drama with interest.

Gisele stood frozen as the unidentifiable lump she had previously spied leaning against the stable morphed into the form of a man. In three quick strides, the man launched himself onto the back of the panicked horse. With long arms he reached down the length of the horse's neck and easily grabbed the side of the bridle, pulling the animal's head to its shoulder with firm authority. The horse and carriage immediately slowed and then stopped, though the lady's screaming continued.

Sliding down from the blowing horse, the man gave the animal a careful once-over that Gisele didn't miss and handed the reins back to the horrified driver. The ragged-looking man then approached the woman still shrieking in the carriage and stood before her, waiting patiently for her to stop the wailing that was beginning to sound forced. He reached up a hand to help her down, and she abandoned her howling only to recoil in disgust.

"My lady?" he queried politely. "Are you all right? May I offer you my assistance?"

"Don't touch me!" the woman screeched, her chins jiggling. "You filthy creature. You could have killed me!"

By this time a number of people had caught up to the carriage, and Gisele pressed a little farther back into the shadows of the stable wall. The woman's husband, out of breath and red-faced, elbowed past the stranger and demanded a step be brought for his wife. Her rescuer simply inclined his head and retreated in the direction of the tavern, shoving his hands into the pockets of what passed for a coat. He ducked around the broken door and disappeared inside. He didn't look back.

Gisele held up a hand in warning.

"He's perfect," Sebastien breathed anyway, ignoring her.

Gisele crossed her arms across her chest, unwilling to let the seed of hope blossom.

"You saw what just happened. He just saved that wretched woman's life. You said courageous, clever, and charming. That was the epitome of all three." Sebastien was looking at her earnestly.

"Or alternatively, stupid, lucky, and drunk."

It was Sebastien's turn to roll his eyes.

"Fine." Gisele gave in, allowing hope a tiny foothold. "Do what you do best. Find out who he is and why he is here."

"What are you going to do?"

Gisele grimaced. "I will return to yonder establishment and observe your newfound hero in his cups. If he doesn't rape and pillage anything in the next half hour and can demonstrate at least a tenth the intellect of an average hunting hound, we'll go from there."

Sebastien grinned in triumph. "I've got a good feeling about him, Gisele. I promise you won't regret this." Then he turned and disappeared.

~

I am already regretting it, Gisele thought dourly twenty minutes later, though the lack of a front door had improved the quality of the air in the taproom, if not the quality of its ale. She managed a convincing swallow and replaced her drink on the uneven tabletop with distaste. Fingering the hilt of the knife she was displaying as a warning on the surface before her, she idly considered what manner of filth kept the bottom of her shoes stuck so firmly to the tavern floor. Sebastien had yet to reappear, and Gisele wondered how much longer she would be forced to wait. Her eyes drifted back to the stranger she'd been studying, who was still hunched over his drink at the far end of the room.

She thought he might be quite handsome if one could see past the disheveled beard and the appalling tatters currently passing for clothes. Broad shoulders, thick arms—he was very likely a former soldier, one of many who had found themselves out of work and out of sorts with the surrender of the little French madman. She narrowed her eyes. Strength in a man was always an asset, so she supposed she must count that in his favor. And from the way his knees rammed the underside of the table, he must be decently tall. Also an advantage, as nothing caught a woman's attention in a crowded room like a tall, confident man. Beyond that, however, his brown hair, brown eyes, and penchant for ale were the only qualities easily determined from a distance.

It was the latter—the utter state of intoxication he was rapidly working toward—that most piqued Gisele's interest. It suggested hopelessness. Defeat. Dejection. Desperation. All of which might make him the ideal candidate.

Or they might just mark him as a common drunkard.

And she'd had plenty of unpleasant experience with those. Unfortunately, this man was by far the best prospect she and Sebastien had seen in weeks, and she was well aware of the time slipping past. She watched as the stranger dribbled ale down his beard as he tried to drain his pot. Her lip curled in disgust.

"What do you think?" Her thoughts were interrupted

by Sebastien as he slid next to her on the bench. He jerked his chin in the direction of their quarry.

She scowled. "The man's been sitting in a corner drinking himself into a stupor since I sat down. He hasn't passed out yet, so I guess that's promising." She caught sight of her friend's glare and sighed. "Please, tell me what I *should* think. What did you find out?"

Sebastien sniffed and adjusted his collar. "James Montcrief. Son of a duke—"

"What?" Gisele gasped in alarm. She involuntarily shrank against the table.

Sebastien gave her a long-suffering look. "Do you think we'd still be here if I thought you might be recognized?"

Gisele bit her lip guiltily and straightened. "No. Sorry."

"May I go on?"

"Please."

"The duchy is...Reddyck, I believe? I've never heard of it, but I am assured it is real, and the bulk of its lands lie somewhere near the northern border. Small, but supports itself adequately."

Gisele let her eyes slide down the disheveled stranger. "Tell me he isn't the heir apparent."

"Even better. A bastard, so no chance of ever turning into anything quite as odious."

Giselle frowned. "Acknowledged?"

"The late duke was happy to claim him. Unfortunately, the current duke—a brother of some fashion—is not nearly so benevolent. According to current family history, James Montcrief doesn't exist."

Giselle studied the man uncertainly, considering the benefits and risks of that information. Someone with knowledge of the peerage and its habits and idiosyncrasies could be helpful. *If* he could remain sober enough to keep his wits.

"He hasn't groped the serving wenches yet," Sebastien offered.

"Says who?"

"The serving wenches."

"*Hmphh.*" That might bode well. Or not. "Married? Children?"

"No and no. At least no children anyone is aware of."

"Good." They would have been a difficult complication. "Money?"

"Spent the morning cleaning stalls and repairing the roof to pay for his drink last night. Did the same the night before and the night before and—"

"In other words, none." Now that was promising. "Army?"

"Cavalry." Sebastien turned his attention from his sleeve to his carefully groomed moustache. "And supposedly quite the hero."

She snorted. "Aren't they all. Who says he's a hero?"

"The stableboys."

"They probably had him confused with his horse."

"His horse was shot out from under him at Waterloo."

"Exactly."

Her friend *tsk*ed. "The man survived, Gisele. He must know how to fight."

"Or run."

Sebastien's eyes rolled in exasperation. "That's what I love most about you. Your brimming optimism."

Giselle shrugged. "Heroes shouldn't drink themselves into oblivion. Multiple nights in a row."

Sebastien leaned close to her ear. "Listen carefully.

In the past twenty minutes, I have applied my abundant charm to the chambermaids and the barmaids and the milkmaids and one very enchanting footman, and thanks to my masterful skill and caution, we now possess a wealth of information about our new friend here. The very least *you* can do is spend half that amount of time discovering if this man is really as decent as I believe him to be." He paused for breath. "He's the best option we've got."

She pressed her lips together as she pushed herself up off the bench. "Very well. As we discussed?"

"Do you have a better idea?"

"No," she replied unhappily.

"Then let's not waste any more time. We need help from some quarter, and that man is the best chance we have of getting it." Without missing a beat, he reached over and deftly plucked at the laces to Gisele's simple bodice. The top fell open to reveal an alarming amount of cleavage. "Nice. Almost makes me wish I were so inclined."

"Do shut up." Gisele tried to pull the laces back together but had her hand swatted away. "I look like a whore," she protested.

Sebastien tipped his head, then leaned forward again and pulled the tattered ribbon from her braid. Her hair slithered out of its confines to tumble over her shoulders. "But a very pretty one. It's perfect." He stood up, straightening his own jacket. "Trust me. He's going to surprise you."

She heaved one last sigh. "How drunk do you suppose he is?"

"Slurring his *s*'s. But sentence structure is still good. I'll see you in ten minutes."

"Better make it twenty," Gisele said slowly. "It will reduce the chances of you ending up on the wrong end of a cavalryman's fists."

Sebastien's dark eyes slid back to the man in the corner in speculation. "You think?"

Giselle stood to join the shorter man. "You're the one who told me he's a hero. Let's find out."

Jamie Montcrief, known in another life as James Edward Anthony Montcrief, cavalry captain in the King's Dragoon Guards of the British army and bastard son to the ninth Duke of Reddyck, stared deeply into the bottom of his ale pot and wondered fuzzily how it had come to be empty so quickly. He was sure he had just ordered a fresh drink. Perhaps the girl had spilled it on the way over and he hadn't noticed. That happened a lot these days. Not noticing things. Which was fine. In fact, it was better than fine.

"You look thirsty." As if by magic, a full cup of liquid sloshed to the table in front of him.

Startled, he looked up, only to be presented with a view of stunning breasts. They were full and firm, straining against the fabric of a poorly laced bodice, and despite the fact that they were not entirely in focus, his body reacted with reprehensible speed. He reached out, intending to caress the luscious perfection before him, only to snatch his hand back a moment later when sluggish honor demanded retreat. Mortified, he dragged his eyes up from the woman's chest to her face, hoping against hope she might not have noticed.

He should have kept his eyes on her breasts.

For shimmering before him was a fantasy. His fantasy. The one he had carefully created in his imagination to chase away the reality of miserable marches, insufferable nights, unspeakable hunger, and bone-numbing dread. Everything he had hoped to possess in a woman was sliding onto the bench opposite him, a shy smile on her face. And it was a face that could start a war. High cheekbones, a full mouth, eyes almost exotic in their shape. Pale hair that fell in thick sheets carelessly around her head and over her shoulders.

He opened his mouth to say something clever, yet all his words seemed to have drowned themselves in the depths of his drink. He cursed inwardly, wishing for the first time in many months he weren't drunk. She seemed not to notice. Instead she cheerfully raised her own full pot of ale in a silent toast and proceeded to drain it. At a loss for anything better to do, he followed suit.

"Thank you," he finally managed, though he wasn't sure she heard, as she had somehow procured two more pots of ale and slid another in front of him.

"What shall we toast to now?" she asked him, her brilliant gray-green eyes probing his own.

Frantically Jamie searched his liquor-soaked brain for an intelligent answer. "To beauty," he croaked, cringing at such an amateurish and predictable reply.

She gave him a dazzling smile anyway, and he could feel his own mouth curling up in response. "To beauty then," she said. "And those who are wise enough to realize what it may cost." She drained her second pot.

Jamie allowed his mind to slog wearily through her cryptic words for a moment or two before he gave up trying to understand. Who cared, really? He had a magnificent woman sitting across the table from him, and another pot of ale had already replaced the second one he had drained. This was by far the best thing that had happened to him in a very long time.

"What's your name?" Her voice was gentle.

"James. James Montcrief." Thank the gods. At least he could remember that. Though maybe he should have made an effort at formality? Did one do that in such a setting?

"James." His name was like honey on her tongue, and her own dismissal of formality was encouraging. Something stirred inside him. "I like it." She gave him another blinding smile. "Why are you drinking all alone, James?" she asked.

He stared at her, unable, and more truthfully, unwilling to give her any sort of an answer. Instead he just shrugged.

"Never mind." She tipped her head back, and another pot of ale disappeared. Idly he wondered how she still remained sober while the room he was sitting in was beginning to spin. She tilted her head, and her beautiful blond hair swung away from her neck, dizzying in its movement. "You have kind eyes."

Her comment caught him off guard. He did not have kind eyes. He had eyes that had seen too much to ever allow any kindness in. "I am not kind." He wasn't sure if he mumbled it or just thought it. Inexplicably, a wave of sadness and loneliness washed over him.

"What brings you here?" she asked, waving a hand in the general direction of the tavern.

Jamie blinked, trying to remember where *here* was, then snorted at the futility of the question.

"Nowhere else to go," he mumbled. The accuracy of

his statement echoed in his mind. Nowhere to go, nowhere to be. No one who cared. Least of all him.

"Would you like to go somewhere else, James? With me?" Her words seemed to come from a distance, and with a frantic suddenness, he needed to get out. Out from the tavern walls that were pressing down on him, away from the smells of grease and bodies and smoke and alcohol that were suffocating.

"Yes." He shoved away from the table, swaying on his feet. In an instant she was there, at his side, her arm tucked into his elbow as though he really were a duke escorting her across the ballroom of a royal palace. He could feel the warmth of her body as it pressed against his and the cool silk of her hair as it slid across his bicep. Again he wished desperately he weren't so drunk. His body was dragging him in one direction while his mind flailed helplessly against the haze.

"Come," she whispered, guiding him out into the cool night breeze.

He went willingly with his beautiful vision into the darkness, dragging in huge lungfuls of air in an attempt to clear his head. He pressed a hand against his temple.

"Are you unwell?" She was still right beside him, and he was horrified to realize he was leaning on her as he might a crutch. He straightened abruptly.

"No." He concentrated hard on his next words. "I don't even know your name."

She stared at him a long moment as if debating something within her mind. "Gisele," she finally said.

He was regretting those last pots of ale. Thinking was becoming almost impossible. "And why were *you* drinkin' alone, Gisele?" he asked slowly.

The sparkle dimmed abruptly in her face, and she turned away. "Will you take me away from here, James?" she asked.

"I beg your pardon?" His mind was struggling to keep up with his ears.

She turned back. "Take me somewhere. Anywhere. Just not here."

"I don't understand." Blade-sharp instincts long suppressed fought to make themselves heard through the fog in his brain. Something was all wrong with this situation, though he was damned if he could determine what it might be. "I can't just—"

Jamie was suddenly knocked back, tripping over his feet and falling gracelessly, unable to overcome gravity and the last three pots of ale. Gisele was yanked from his side, and she gave a slight yelp as a man slammed her back up against the tavern wall.

"Where the hell have you been, whore?" the man snarled. "Like a damn bitch in heat, aren't you?"

Jamie struggled to his feet, fighting the dizziness that was making his surroundings swim. He reached for the weapon at his side before realizing he couldn't recall where he'd left it. He turned just in time to see the man pull back his arm to slug Gisele. With a roar of rage, Jamie launched himself at her attacker, hitting him square in the back. The man was barely half his size, and the force of Jamie's weight knocked both men into the mud. A fist caught the side of his head in a series of short, sharp jabs, only increasing the din resonating through his brain. Jamie tried to stagger to his feet again, but the ground shifted underneath him and he fell heavily on his side.

"Don't touch her," he managed, wrestling with the

darkness crowding the edge of his vision. Usually he welcomed this part of the night, when reality ceased to exist. But not now. This couldn't happen now. He had to fight it. Fight for her. Fight for something again. He pushed himself up on his hands and knees. He looked up at the figures looming over him. Strangely, Gisele and her attacker were standing side by side as if nothing had happened. The buzzing was getting louder as Gisele crouched down beside him, and he felt her cool hand on his forehead.

"So sorry," he mumbled, his arms collapsing beneath him. "I couldn't do—"

"You did just fine, James," she said. And then he heard no more.

Fall in Love with Forever Romance

A TASTE OF SUGAR
by Marina Adair

For fans of Rachel Gibson, Kristan Higgins, and Jill Shalvis
comes the newest book in Marina Adair's Sugar, Georgia series.
Can sexy Jace McGraw win back his ex, pediatrician Charlotte
Holden, with those three simple words: we're still married?

Fall in Love with Forever Romance

"Lovable men and lovable dogs make this series a winner."
—JILL SHALVIS, *New York Times* bestselling author

Even AFTER

Great Series! Great Price!

RACHEL LACEY

EVER AFTER
by Rachel Lacey

After being arrested for a spray-painting spree that (perhaps) involved one too many margaritas, Olivia Bennett becomes suspect number one in a string of vandalisms. Deputy Pete Sampson's torn between duty and desire for the vivacious waitress, but he may have to bend the rules because true love is more important than the letter of the law...

Fall in Love with Forever Romance

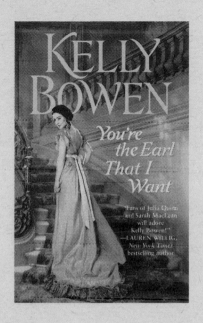

YOU'RE THE EARL THAT I WANT
by Kelly Bowen

For Heath Hextall, inheriting an earldom has been a damnable nuisance. What he needs is a well-bred, biddable woman to keep his life in order. Lady Josephine Somerhall is *not* suited for the job, but he's about to discover that what she lacks in convention, she makes up for in passion.

Fall in Love with Forever Romance

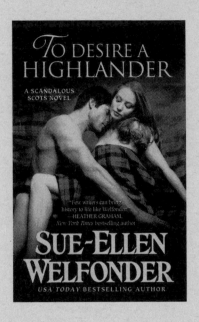

TO DESIRE A HIGHLANDER
by Sue-Ellen Welfonder

The second book in *USA Today* bestseller Sue-Ellen Welfonder's
sexy Scandalous Scots series. When a powerful warrior meets
Lady Gillian MacGuire—known as the Spitfire of the Isles—he's
shocked to learn that *he's* the one being seduced and captivated...